Paul Ford is an editor at *Harper's Magazine,* a regular commentator on *All Things Considered,* a writer for TheMorningNews.org, and sole proprietor of Ftrain.com.

GARY BENCHLEY,
ROCK STAR

A NOVEL BY

PAUL FORD

A PLUME BOOK

PLUME
Published by Penguin Group
Penguin Group (USA) Inc., 375 Hudson Street, New York, New York 10014, U.S.A.
Penguin Group (Canada), 90 Eglinton Avenue East, Suite 700, Toronto,
Ontario, Canada M4P 2Y3 (a division of Pearson Penguin Canada Inc.)
Penguin Books Ltd., 80 Strand, London WC2R 0RL, England
Penguin Ireland, 25 St. Stephen's Green, Dublin 2, Ireland (a division of Penguin Books Ltd.)
Penguin Group (Australia), 250 Camberwell Road, Camberwell, Victoria 3124, Australia
(a division of Pearson Australia Group Pty. Ltd.)
Penguin Books India Pvt. Ltd., 11 Community Centre, Panchsheel Park,
New Delhi – 110 017, India
Penguin Books (NZ), cnr Airborne and Rosedale Roads, Albany, Auckland, New Zealand
(a division of Pearson New Zealand Ltd.)
Penguin Books (South Africa) (Pty.) Ltd., 24 Sturdee Avenue, Rosebank,
Johannesburg 2196, South Africa

Penguin Books Ltd., Registered Offices: 80 Strand, London WC2R 0RL, England

First published by Plume, a member of Penguin Group (USA) Inc.

First Printing, October 2005
1   3   5   7   9   10   8   6   4   2

℗ REGISTERED TRADEMARK—MARCA REGISTRADA

LIBRARY OF CONGRESS CATALOGING-IN-PUBLICATION DATA

Ford, Paul, 1974–
Gary Benchley, rock star / Paul Ford.
p. cm.
ISBN 0-452-28663-8
1. Young men—Fiction. 2. Rock musicians—Fiction. 3. College graduates—Fiction.
4. Williamsburg (New York, N.Y.)—Fiction. I. Title.
PS3606.O743G37 2005
813'.6—dc22   2005011582

Printed in the United States of America
Set in Sabon
Designed by Leonard Telesca

For everyone who believed in Gary Benchley.

GARY BENCHLEY,
ROCK STAR

New York City

Before I moved to New York from Albany, I wrote out a careful, step-by-step plan:

1) Rock out.
2) No more data entry.

But now I'd lived in the East Village for a month, staying at my friend Carl's place, and New York was not giving up its fruits. Regarding step one, rocking out, I was only permitted to sing in the shower, because Carl's roommate, Keith, hated my voice, and Keith's dachshund, Harris Glenn Milstead, Jr., barked at me whenever I started to use my pipes. And, given that I was crashing in Carl and Keith's living room, sleeping next to Keith's aquarium, there was no way to bring out my acoustic guitar from its case, unless I wanted to play along with the always-on TV and deal with Keith's disappointed looks.

I'd come southeast expecting, reasonably, to get an apartment, and then see if the landlord would let me pay him the security deposit after I moved in. But the landlords weren't having it.

LANDLORD: I need from you proof of full-time employment.
GARY: Bro, I am going to be employed when I get an apartment, OK?
LANDLORD: You need proof of employment *before* you live here.

No matter how sensible I tried to be, the landlords only shook their heads. Within my first six weeks the three thousand dollars I'd brought from Albany, representing a full summer's worth of living with the moms while working data entry, was down to five hundred dollars. Partly, this was my fault. I'd gotten excited about moving to the city and bought two hundred dollars worth of CDs my first week. And I'd somehow spent six hundred dollars on drinks and dinners.

Carl was getting frustrated with me. "How's it going?" he asked one afternoon, coming in from work to find me sitting on the couch.

"Always good," I said.

"Any luck with the apartment?"

"Bro, I'm trying," I said. "But this city, you know?"

"You'll feel a lot better when you're not sleeping on my floor," he said.

"You know, if I could just meet some people, maybe get a band together . . ."

"Where are you looking? What about Queens?"

Queens—Queens is Albany east of the Hudson. I couldn't compromise like that. It was Williamsburg, in Brooklyn, or here in the East Village. These were the neighborhoods where things were happening, where artists were creating, where I would belong. But no matter how much I explained to potential roommates that, the minute I had a place, things would start happening, that the security deposit would *be there,* they just looked at me without any belief.

LOFT-LIVING HIPSTER: Dude, without a security deposit I really can't make it work.

GARY: Dude, I thought Craigslist was about community.

Carl wasn't happy about me lingering in his apartment floor, but we'd been roommates my junior year, and you can't play that much Gran Turismo with someone without developing a deep bond. He would let me slide for another month. But Keith was a problem. He clearly wanted me out. Also, he refused to let me use his stereo. Iron and Wine were banned. The Mountain Goats: *verboten*. So I lived in a musicless, cashless void, my few resources dwindling.

Keith would sniff when he saw me, and make little tongue-click noises when I spoke. I tried to reach out to him by becoming friends with Harris Glenn Milstead, Jr. I tried every bit of persuasion available on that dog, turned on the Benchley charm, snacked him up at every opportunity. He would accept my snacks in brotherhood, then turn on me. Once, in the shower, as I belted out the new Death Cab, he leaped in with me and began to tear at my ankles. I would lean over for a dropped fork and find his teeth tearing into the Benchley hand. It was a metaphor for my entire journey.

I began to have doubts that I could make it work. I had no idea how to crack either the apartment or job nuts. Finally, though, I got a call: Excelsior Temps.

GARY: What do you need me to do?
WOMAN: It's a data entry job. It says you can type?
GARY (*soul leaving*): Yes.

It turns out that this is a terrible time to rock, but a terrific time for data entry, because all of the companies that fired all their people and outsourced to India and Ghana still have work that needs to be supervised here. Yes, never working in data entry was my #2 goal. But my choice was: hypocrisy or Albany. I chose hypocrisy.

For a week I worked in the Empire State Building in Midtown. I'd always thought of the building as something like the Washington Monument, a big symbol without a practical use, but it's actually just a bunch of low-ceilinged offices. Each day, I'd take the train up to Midtown, take an elevator, and enter data for an insurance firm. None of the other temps spoke English, which made the work a little lonely. It was also disappointing working in the tallest building in NYC and only going up to eleven. Still, it was better than living with the moms in Albany. Much better.

Consider a representative Albany morning a few months back, in early July, not long after graduation: I'm downstairs having a Mom-made waffle. Mom's boyfriend, Jad, comes in, baseball cap already on, and kisses Mom. To me, he says, "Gary, your mother truly deserves the best things in the world. She's the most beautiful woman I've ever known."

Mom is smiling, and I'm pretty happy for her, right then. She's had to deal with a lot since my dad left, and has had bad luck with men. She deserves a guy who thinks she's beautiful.

Then Jad says to Mom, "Today, I think I'll go to the jewelry store and get you a real pearl necklace." Mom opens her mouth in shock, and hits him with a dish towel. They laugh. For some reason they think I don't know what a pearl necklace means in this context. So I shove the waffles into my mouth, but all I can think about is Jad smashing the pig all over and above my mom's (admittedly ample and still-firm) bosoms.

Some Albany summer nights, I would hear Bob Dylan coming from the CD player in my mother's room, *Time Out of Mind* turned up too loud. It was always the same album, and, hearing Bob's nasal voice, in the gloom of my room, I'd brace myself for what was coming next. By track four or five, the sound of Dylan would mix with the sounds of my mother reaching her peak. I'd hold a pillow over my head and hum to drown her out. My room was decorated with dinosaur wallpaper, put up when I was eleven, so I'd spend those minutes looking at the leaf-nibbling brontosaurus, and the axe-backed stegosaurus, until the cries of ecstasy died down. Jad's low groans would follow, and then some laughter and giggling. Someone would turn off the Dylan, and I could finally sleep.

Once, when it was too much to handle, I put on my stereo and began to play along to the Flaming Lips with my drums, hoping to drown out the noise from the other room, trying not to think about how my mom gets much, much more than I do, albeit from a man who manages a hardware store. And right at that part of the Flaming Lips's "What Is the Light" where the shit kicks in, my mom came to the door, all sweaty, and asked if I could just do something quiet for a little while because she and Jad were trying to have a conversation. Close up that nightgown, zip that zipper, a conversation.

We were talking Greek tragedy in the waiting if I didn't get out of that house. We were talking a story that was the bastard child of Arthur Miller and Henry Miller. I needed to be liberated from my mother's liberation.

I took another data entry job on the Upper West Side, after the one at the Empire State dried up. I worked for a huge law office, wandering around a maze of cubicles, delivering documents, answering phones. The lawyers were strange to look at, speaking their own language, yelling all the time. I kept my head down and tapped my keys, counting the hours. In the mornings, on the train from the East Village to the Upper West Side, I had a long time to think about what came next.

The other reason I moved to New York, besides needing to escape the moms, was to start a band. A band in the rich American indie rock tradition of the Flaming Lips, Guided by Voices, and Neutral Milk Hotel. I'd had three bands of my own: Gobbler's Knob in high school (ripping off Nirvana), the Chimps as a freshman in college (free jazz), and the School Board for junior and senior years (straight punk). I wasn't sure what shape the next one should take, the sound it should have. I was still thinking it through. But I'd spent the summer going to shows at Valentine's in Albany, as my friends from college called to tell me about their jobs in the insurance industry, or working at technology magazines, or doing technical writing. I had decided that you only get to be in your early twenties once. Cubicles were where you went to die.

At night, in the East Village, I'd stay awake and look at Carl and Keith's living room, which was well lit by street lamps and the glow of the aquarium, and I'd pretend that I was being interviewed by independent rock-oriented music magazines.

"What made you think you could succeed when so many have failed?" they'd ask.

"I just had faith, *Blender* magazine," I'd say. "I believed I could do it."

"Why?" they'd ask. "Why go to all the trouble?"

"You know, *Blender* magazine, there are two reasons to climb a mountain—"

"Because it's there—"

"And," I'd say, "because it gets you laid."

Four fifty-hour weeks later I was once again flush, with sore typing fingers and sixteen hundred dollars in my pocket. I gave a third to my roommates to ensure that I could stay with them a little longer, put away a third to pay down on an apartment in this faithless city, and took a bit for myself. I bought some groceries, made some long-distance calls to tell everyone how hard I was rocking out in New York, and bought some hair-care products. I tousled the legendary rich and full Benchley coif, and went to Pianos with a friend from college named Oliver.

It was some reading series at Pianos, and words are not rock. I didn't need to hear anyone else's sad story. So we headed down around the Manhattan Bridge to a place that Oliver knew about, a bar called Sketch, which was all white walls. A video projector was putting weird abstract shapes on the wall.

Oliver lusts but does not carpe the diem and I decided that he needed to witness my technique in action. The Benchley charm, once it's turned on, is a magical force, and you must see it to understand. It has no fear of rejection. It has no worries at all. In Albany, a river runs past an auditorium shaped like an egg. The entire city appears to be ovulating. It is a fecund place, a powerful place, even if it is a musical desert. And I was raised there, and women know it.

Also, I know that I am a handsome man, a smooth-skinned fellow with blue eyes and dark brown hair that almost, but not quite, hangs into his eyes. I am not perfect, you understand. Perhaps I should be six feet two instead of five feet eleven. Maybe I should have better-defined arm muscles. But I am perfectly within the range of acceptable for most situations.

Sure, there was snubbing. Two attempts at conversation failed, and Oliver laughed. But that was just as well, because I needed to get the juices flowing. The charm I have is not like a light switch, but more like a vintage tube amp. You turn it on and let it warm up, and then it sings like an angel. And so it was with Alyssa Illeander, the most pure expression of the feminine in the place, who listened as I told her of my plans, my goals, my life, and who laughed at my excellent jokes and repeatedly poked my shoulder. Oliver turned orange with jealousy, and tapped his fingers in boredom, and finally sulked away. Alyssa didn't even know he'd left. Then she said, a little drunk, maybe even drooling slightly—but still beautiful—"You love the Postal Service? I have to *kiss you*." And I gave a secret prayer of thanks to the god of indie rock, which is Lou Reed.

She gave me her phone number. A phone number, I reasoned, is a numerical form of rocking. A phone number is like a lottery ticket that's almost guaranteed to win, a mystical code that unlocks the safe to your future. A future that might involve fellatio.

And now I knew why I had to get my own apartment pronto. Whatever it took, I had to find my own place. Because without my own place, I could not be fellated while listening to Cat Power.

The bartender yelled out last call, right as someone had put the Dream Academy's cover of "Please Please Please Let Me Get What

I Want" on the jukebox. A perfect moment. Alyssa kissed me good night and whispered into my ear, "You're such a gentleman." I took a cab back up to the apartment.

It was quiet when I walked in. I flopped drunk into my air mattress, the phone number safely in my wallet, the light from the street lamps coming in through the bamboo blinds, and I thought: *I can make this work. There are many forms of rocking. Data entry is a path, not a destination.*

I did what was natural and true. I whispered Alyssa Illeander's name to the ceiling, and stroked and fondled the Benchley Beast, reaching a beautiful ecstatic peak, my body at one with New York City. I threw back the sheets and spanked drunkenly into the night, as if I was Eddie Van Halen and my penis was a guitar. And right at the moment of ecstatic release, as my pleasure was maximized and my mind was filled with the image of Alyssa's tender lips opening to accept my pearls of truth, Harris Glenn Milstead, Jr., leaped onto my penis, capturing it in his mouth, and viciously twisted his tiny head back and forth, growling furiously and drawing blood.

It was a noisy, angry moment, and a minute later Keith came out to find me in the bathroom, doubled over the sink gripping my private area. Benchley blood dripped onto the linoleum, and my pants were around my ankles.

GARY: Your fucking dog bit my dick!
KEITH: What were you *doing* to him?
HARRIS GLENN MILSTEAD, JR.: Bark!
GARY (*to Harris Glenn Milstead, Jr.*): Fuck you!
KEITH: No, fuck you! Don't yell at my dog!
GARY: He bit my dick!
HARRIS: Bark! Bark!

The rest of the night was long and painful, and I do not need to write about it. I thought about the morning bus from Port Authority, going north and home. The next morning, when Harris sat at my feet begging for some of my scrambled eggs, as if we were old friends, I put my hand over my crotch and thought again of leaving.

But then, should an attack by a wiener dog stop Gary Benchley? *No*, I vowed, *I am not going north. I am staying here, and this city is going to know who I am, no matter how much data I have to enter, no matter how many people try to stop me from rocking, and no matter how many creatures savage my penis.*

I'd developed a routine by the end of the second month with Carl and Keith. The Benchley day: 1) Wake up and roll off the air mattress; 2) Take the 6 train uptown; 3) Go to a skyscraper and take an elevator; 4) Enter the doors marked "Compliance and User Analysis"; 5) Enter data for ten hours, with thirty minutes for lunch; 6) Back at the apartment, check Yahoo! email for Craigslist responses regarding an apartment; 7) "You have 0 unread messages"; 8) Choose: suicide or television; 9) Television; 10) Sleep; 11) Repeat.

By now, I'd worked in the Upper East Side, the Financial District, Jersey City, downtown Brooklyn, and Chelsea. The city began to take shape. It wasn't just a huge pile of landmarks, like Central Park, the Empire State, or the Flatiron Building. The real city was in between those places, and much of what happened there was actually kind of boring. People went to jobs, did their work, and went home. It was a little less exciting than I'd hoped, which only stoked my need to get a band going, to make things happen.

The apartment situation was no better, and Alyssa Illeander had yet to return my calls. But one thing had improved: Keith had become cool. Yes, previously he was a true hyphenwad, that is, anything plus wad. But the night after his dog bit my penis, and he and I had our screaming match, I apologized. When you are sleeping on someone's floor, you must have respect. And Keith apologized, too, swayed by my charm and my humility, and maybe by the sight of my bare chest in a towel. After that, we started to watch TV together after work.

Of course, Keith was not really my first choice of friend. He didn't know Tortoise from the Turtles. And a good 80 percent of his conversation was about how incredibly unlaid he was, which got stale. But he was a human being in New York who knew the name Gary Benchley, and that was comforting.

"God, Matthew Perry is funny," he said one evening.

"Yeah," I said.

"And, you know, hot."

"Huh."

Keith paused, as the remarkable narrative that was *Friends* expanded on the screen. A little while later, he said, "God, I need to get laid."

"Well, if Matthew Perry is hot, maybe so."

"I just have a thing for straight boys."

It turned out that Keith hadn't gotten any play in eight months. It was a situation that I fully understood, and I commiserated.

"You're a good-looking guy," I said.

"You think?" he asked.

"Yeah, man. You're working the skin care."

Keith touched his face and winked. "I'm trying," he said.

I had to admit, it felt good to flirt with Keith. I'd been forced to slow down the Benchley flirtation machine, because simply walking out the door in the East Village after 9 P.M. costs about eighty dollars, and buying drinks for women would have to wait for better days.

So given the lack of easy social options, Keith and I got into a routine. He'd sit by me on the couch and we'd watch *Friends*. As long as Joey or Chandler weren't in the scene, Keith would complain about how little sex he got, and I would agree that yes, this sucked. Then he'd explain his incredible sexual technique, and how wasted it was. I would agree that yes, it was totally wasted. He would go on to explain how he only liked to give, never receive, he was totally into giving, he just loved to give, and then describe some of the ways he liked to give. I would nod, and murmur appreciatively.

On Friday night Carl came out of his bedroom with his knapsack on, to find us both on the couch. He put his hand on the door and said, "You know, Gary, I'm going over to Trina's. You should feel cool about crashing in my bed when I'm over there."

"Dude, bro," I said, "thanks."

The door closed behind him and I went straight to the phone and called the number Alyssa had given me, hoping she'd be home. With a bed instead of an air mattress, I could bring her back to the apartment. After two weeks of listening to Keith talking about incredible blow jobs, I was ready to explode. She picked up on her end, finally.

"I was buying a Death Cab bootleg at St. Mark's and I found your number in my wallet," I said, even though that was not true. "I was thinking, I'd love to go out for a drink with Alyssa again."

"That sounds really good," she said.

Exactly. 1) *Preparations—physical:* Double-brushed teeth, squared shoulders, carefully mussed hair, vigorous scrubbing of Benchley nethers; 2) *Preparations—environmental:* Hide Carl's Dave Matthews collection and assorted Internet-traded jam band CDs, sniff the sheets, plump both pillows, prophylactics with nonoxynol-9 under the bed, in reach; 3) *Preparations—emotional:* Achieve utter balance. As Beck says, put your hands on the wheel, let the golden age begin.

Two hours later, we met at a tiny SoHo bar with a tin ceiling— her choice. I'd picked out a dark booth in the back to allow for hand-brushing and smooching.

Alyssa wore a light gray top, woven through with something silver, and she had glitter on her eyelids. Under the track lighting she glowed, and I thought of the time I saw Guided by Voices (GBV to the true fans) in Buffalo. I was sitting in a balcony above the stage, and the spotlight caught the top of Robert Pollard's can of Budweiser, and it shone directly onto my part of the audience, right as Robert sang "Don't stop now, don't stop now."

Alyssa kissed me on the cheek and sat down. I asked her what she wanted, got up, and bought two pints. When I came back, she was crying.

It took ten minutes of questioning through the sobbing to find out what was up. The answer was: She was engaged to someone named Phil, and it wasn't going well.

"Gary, we met, and you were all I thought of the next day," she said. "And then you didn't call, and then you did. I got your message. I wanted to tell you to your face why I couldn't see you." She took my hand, and kept crying, and I realized that she was probably totally insane. I looked for exit options, and saw the nearly full beer near her hand. Alyssa, I realized, was a sipper. No more than a tablespoon of beer passed her pert, pink lips at a time. We had at least twenty minutes to go.

In that twenty minutes, she told me about: Phil who didn't love her; Phil the well-paid asshole with the gorgeous apartment; Phil who fucked her like a beast and then went out drinking with his friends (that's where he was right now, she told me). And warm, enthusiastic, broke-dick Gary, the true friend, sat in a dark booth, holding Alyssa's manicured hands, his balls turning to dust.

Watching her cry, I knew Benchley had hit bottom. I had reached the mythical state of total antirock, which I call "Train," after the band. When the head of every drum is torn, and all guitars out of tune, when the microphone melts in your hand, that's Train, and I was in Train all the way up to my drops of Jupiter.

Finally, the last sip of beer went down her throat, and she had to go meet Phil at a bar uptown. The crying was over. She went into the bathroom to reapply her makeup, and came back to kiss me good-bye. Since no one else was around to spill a huge bag of emotional shit into my lap, I went back to the apartment and collapsed onto Carl's mattress. I could hear the condoms under the bed, laughing at me.

But, because, as Moby says, God moves across the face of the waters, I found this in the morning:

From: Circleplayer13848@hotmail.com
To: garybenchleyrockstar@yahoo.com

Gary,
The place is right near the L train on Bedford. We need $1,800 for deposit and first month. Noones hear after 10, but if you can make it tomorrow night that would be cool. I can't make any promises, but it sounds like it will be cool.

Definitely (spelling aside). I just needed to scrape up the $1,800 and make it to December 1. No problem, if I skipped going home for Thanksgiving. I brushed my teeth and took a long look in the mirror.

GARY: Attention!

MIRROR GARY: Yes?

GARY: New policy is, eliminate the Train.

MIRROR GARY: Noted.

GARY: Get an apartment. People do it.

MIRROR GARY: Yes!

GARY: What doesn't kill Gary Benchley only makes him rock harder!

MIRROR GARY: (*Devil sign.*)

The devil sign was limp by my standards, but these were difficult times. I walked out of the bathroom to find Keith staring at me. "Talking to yourself?" he said.

"Hey, yeah," I said.

"That's cool," he said. "You want to hear something? You were in my dream last night."

"Was I playing guitar?"

"No, man. We were kissing."

Understand that the homosexual citizen has a true friend in Gary Benchley. When I was a student at one of the fine schools in the SUNY system, I was an active supporter of HOC, Homosexuals on Campus, as well as Q&A, the Queer Alliance, which split from HOC during my sophomore year. Later, I was also a supporter of OCLesGayTransBiActCo&Sup, the On-Campus Lesbian, Gay, Transsexual, and Bisexual Action Coalition and Supporters, which was created when HOC and Q&A came back together during my senior year. So I am fully aware of the complicated issues facing nonheterosexuals in today's society. But that said, the secrets of the Benchley bottom, by his own informed choice, were known only to Gary Benchley and a frisky girl in Albany named Gillian.

"Oh, hey," I said to Keith. "Kissing. How about that."

"Gar—"

"I'm just heading out," I said.

"I just have to ask you something," said Keith.

I stood in the doorway, waiting.

"Look," Keith said, "I know you're not gay."

"Yeah, bro."

"But I was thinking of you and, you know, your problem paying the rent, and—do you know what 'trade' is?"

"Like, a trade?"

"No, like *trade*."

I took a moment to think about it, to consider what that meant.

"Yeah, I know what trade is," I said. It was a difficult topic to discuss. It went around and around. But eventually Keith got his message across: He wanted to institute a blow-jobs-for-rent policy.

I just had to lie there, maybe yell at him a little, and when it was over, thank him. Not even any kissing.

"I mean, that's flattering," I said, "but. . . ."

He nodded and looked hurt. I got out of there, walked down to Battery Park, and sat on a bench in the rain, sipping a huge cup of coffee. Situation: Tomorrow I would go see an apartment in Williamsburg. That sounded promising. I needed $1,800, and I had almost that. I would have it by the first of the month if the temp work stayed solid. But I would not have it if I paid Carl and Keith the seven hundred dollars I owed them.

I definitely needed to give them some money. Carl would probably not care. He would probably tell me to forget it, or make it up to him later. But Keith didn't owe me anything. The upshot was, if I became, for just a short amount of time, a whore—a temporary whore, just as I was a temporary data-enterer—I could make New York work for me. And Keith, I reasoned, wasn't really that bad a guy, once you got past the whining about sex and the little dog.

Should Benchley leap the chasm? Was there a way back once it was leaped? I thought of my ex-girlfriend Cedilla, who'd introduced me to OCLesGayTransBiActCo&Sup when it was just HOC. She was bisexual, and it was a condition of dating her that I would support her alternative sexuality by attending meetings and on-campus rallies.

Cedilla could choose freely between steak or salad, but she lived in terror of her boyfriends ending up gay. She gave me regular "gay quizzes," asking what I thought about one passing man or another. "Nice ass," I'd say. She would make a face like a lemon exploding.

Once, before we broke up, I asked her, "What if a guy slept with a man, but it was just a one-time thing? Would you date him?"

She said, "I could, but there would have to be a grace period."

I asked her how long that would be, and she thought for a long time then said, "Five years."

Assume that most women shared Cedilla's distrust of the fully experienced man. That meant five years of keeping a secret. The alternative was God knows how long on the floor with Keith and Carl, if they let me stay.

No, last night was not Train. This morning was Train, and I was calling all angels. And as so many young men of my generation are likely to do in times of trouble, I asked myself, *What would Wayne Coyne of the Flaming Lips do?* I conjured him from my imagination and asked for counsel.

"Gary," said Wayne, "all you need in life, all you need, is a purpose."

"I've got a purpose, Wayne."

"What is that?" Wayne asked. I noticed that his white shoes were floating above the ground, not quite touching the asphalt.

"My purpose is to rock for the good of the people," I said.

"Well, goddamn," said Wayne. "There you go. Listen, Gary, as you know from countless articles on Pitchfork, I spent my entire adult life keeping the Flaming Lips together. Most of the time, *we didn't have dick.* I had to make sacrifices. But I never lost sight of my mission. You like *The Soft Bulletin?*"

"I love *The Soft Bulletin.*"

"What about *Yoshimi?*"

"Actually, I didn't really—"

"Look, Gary, we're talking about your *mission.*"

"My mission is to get my own place. I've got to get a place where I can rock out. That's the mission."

"See, I'm making a movie in my backyard about Christmas on Mars. I don't know a goddamned thing about moviemaking—"

"Wayne," I said, "this is about me."

"That's right, Gary. I'm just telling you."

"The mission," I said. "The new policy. *Pay the rent.*"

"You just stick to the mission," Wayne said. "Now I'm going to ascend into heaven in a golden chariot, lifted by a huge flock of doves, and throw confetti over the chariot's side."

"All right, then, Wayne. And thanks."

"I enjoyed our talk, Gary," Wayne said. He rose into the skies and yelled out, "Remember—pay the rent."

The oil massage felt pretty good. The oil smelled a little bit like lavender. Keith kept kissing my back, which was strange, but there are worse things. I was beginning to relax. Then I felt a man's fingers grip me where no man's fingers had gripped me before, in a tight circle. The moment was literally at hand. Benchley was about to make the trade.

"Gary, Gary. Turn over, baby." His voice was high, and kind of creepy. I shut my eyes, and suddenly I was outside myself, floating near the ceiling, looking down. I didn't really feel comfortable with what I saw, so I opened my eyes and stared at the wall.

To be honest, I expected better. Keith had promised that he was an expert at what he was about to do. I had figured it would be awful, but masterful, like Geddy Lee playing bass.

The summer of my sophomore year, I volunteered at a group home for the mentally challenged. One of the guys in the home was named Al. He was about forty-two, mentally four. Al lived for art therapy, when Mrs. Tornelle would arrive with sculpting clay or watercolors and brushes or, one time, origami paper.

Watching Al do origami was bad. He tore the edges. He licked the paper. He folded and unfolded, and he shredded. His hands shook and he was arthritic, among his other problems. When he was done, twenty sheets of square paper later, he had something that looked more like a garden slug than a paper crane, and he held it in the air and moved it in a circle, as if it was flying.

Keith's attention to my private area was like Al's attention to the origami paper. I have received about a dozen blow jobs in my life, and eleven of them were atrocious, so in the category of bad oral sex, I am an expert. But this was unique. It was more as if Keith was performing a tracheotomy instead of giving me ultimate pleasure. I was rapidly losing my steel. And, I knew, a lump of dough does not pay the rent. Reality wasn't going to be enough.

I leaned back and made a noise, and searched inside myself for an emergency fantasy, the darkest of the dark. I cycled through like I was shuffling cards: master of the harem, cheerleader slave colony, coked-up groupies. *Nothing. Go deeper.* The time I saw my babysitter go to town with a sofa pillow when I was eight. Jennifer Connelly in *Labyrinth. Pay the rent, Benchley, pay the rent. Wayne Coyne says pay the rent.*

Nothing.

And then I found something beautiful. I was onstage in a dark club, playing guitar for Cat Power. Who cares what happened to Chan's regular guitarist? What matters is that I am rocking, but gently. Chan is singing, and I can tell she wants to cut the song off, she's got that look on her face, she's singing "She Was a Friend of Mine"—no . . . she's singing "Rockets." And before she can stop, I take a little solo, totally unexpected. I look over at her, and she's laughing at me, but she's into it. Nothing brash; I mean, it's Cat Power, just a dozen bars, the words "Where do the rockets find planets?" echoing in my brain. Chan brings it back and finishes the song, and everyone is cheering.

Cut to after the show, we're all having a beer and a cigarette, and everyone wants to go out, and Chan tells us she's just really tired and is going to head back to her apartment. And she looks at me, and points to herself, and smiles. Because she keeps an apartment in the city, right?

Cut to her place, lots of recording equipment and Cat Power posters. We're talking, and she says, "God, Gary, I really had to just get away from everyone. I'm so glad you're here." She puts her hand on my arm. "You did such a good job playing guitar tonight. It was so totally *hot* just watching you. And I wanted to cut off that song, right then, before you came out with that solo."

"I know," I say, "and I'm so glad you didn't. And Chan, let's be honest, it's all about you at the piano, and that's why I'm up there with you. I'm just glad I could make that work for you." We're close, inches away from each other, and even though she's thirty, who cares? She just pushes her face into mine, and I put my hand on the waist of her jeans, and they're loose and come down a little, and I can feel her pubes, it's like that picture of her in the *New Yorker.*

She whispers into my ear, "Rock me, Gary," and we get into her queen-sized bed, under the comforter, and she bites my ear and says, "Take a solo, Gary, take a solo," and I say, "Chan, I just want this to last, I want it to be special, I want to go on tour with—"

And then I was gone from there, and back in the apartment, Keith leaning away from me with relief in his eyes and Benchley on his chin. I heard a shuffle, and looked over at Keith's wall to meet the dachshund eyes of Harris Glenn Milstead, Jr., who had watched it all in utter jealousy, and I beamed a thought directly into his tiny brain: *The rent is paid.*

I moved all my stuff to Williamsburg on a Monday, after my day at the temp mines. It took two trips on the 6 and L trains to lug my boxes to Brooklyn, using a luggage cart. Farewell, air mattress. Good-bye, Keith, needy young man. *Auf Wiedersehen,* Harris Glenn Milstead, Jr., cock-biting dachshund. I handed Carl his key and gave him an awkward man-hug, and gave Keith another hug, awkward in a different way. My prophetic vision of Wayne Coyne was becoming reality.

The new apartment was three bedrooms, one for each bachelor: David, Charles, and myself. It was decorated in an architectural style you could call grotesque asspaint, which comes to be when landlords kick out poor people from their homes, throw paint and plaster around, and double the rent. Moving in, I could hear my Anarchosyndicalist friends from college condemning me for my willing participation in the displacement of the impoverished, but no political theory could make me forsake my new bedroom, a thirteen-by-fifteen-foot space with a single dirty window, a wood floor, and a bare light bulb hanging from the ceiling. This was luxury.

I would sleep on the floor until I got a bed, and it would feel as soft as goose down. With my two suitcases and three boxes of CDs and books sat stacked against one wall, I locked the door, stripped off all my clothes, and stretched out naked on the bare floor. I lay there and breathed the sweet air of Williamsburg, inhaling independence. I had walked out of a metaphorical Joy Division show and straight into a Polyphonic Spree concert. I decided to cover the bulb with a round Chinese paper lantern.

It was cold on the floor, so I dressed and went out to the kitchen, where Charles was dicing carrots. Charles was tall and thin, maybe twenty-eight, with shaggy hair. He wore a lot of loose-fitting clothes made from natural fibers, and had that lopey way of speaking that I associate with California, but he was actually from Connecticut.

I struck up a conversation. He asked me whether I was allergic to incense. Apparently that was a major problem with the last roommate. I promised him I loved incense, and he nodded his head and said, "Cool." I asked what he did for a living.

"I'm a yoga and spiritual arts teacher," he said. "I run a class called the Ancient Art of Yogic Drumming. It's a new technique based on research I did while in India. We investigate yoga positions, and use them to enhance the receptive resonance of the body. Then we reinforce the yogic positioning with group drumming. It's partially based on Reichian theories."

I said, "Awesome."

"Do you know Wilhelm Reich?" he asked me.

"I'm not sure," I said.

For ten minutes, Charles talked about orgasms and something called an orgone accumulator, which can be used to control the weather. I asked him what orgone was, and why it accumulated.

"Reich called the primordial life energy that is in all things *orgone*," he told me. "Other people call it *qi*. You tap into it through your libido, through orgasm. The orgone accumulator collects that energy, and you can use that to change the environment."

"So it's like the Force," I said.

Apparently not. Twenty more fantastic minutes of orgone.

" . . . and I've converted each drum into an individual orgone accumulator," said Charles. "The drums are made from bodhi wood, so the drumming becomes a reinforcing orgone loop."

"So it's kind of like if Yoda was into drum circles," I said.

"Well . . . ," said Charles, about to continue, but Williamsburg beckoned. I excused myself.

As I walked out, Charles said, "Just for your information, the phrase 'The Ancient Art of Yogic Drumming' is trademark pending. I'd appreciate that when you talk about it, you let people know that." I told him I would definitely keep everyone in the loop.

Williamsburg deserves its reputation as the coolest part of New York. It's a parade that never ends: hipster men in tight shirts and big pants, with scraggly facial hair; pretty girls with short hair and elbows like razor blades, so thin you could blow them over; and cavernous, single-room stores with only a few racks of dresses. Nothing here is exactly as it seems: a coffee shop is not just a coffee shop *and* an art gallery, but it *also* sells baby clothes with ironic statements on them, like DON'T SHAKE ME! and BABY DOLL DYKE. A music store might not have any CDs, just vinyl, and then only twelve or thirteen records in thick plastic sleeves, and will sell the records next to leggings made from orange-dyed llama hair. There is a bar called Galapagos, which is also an art and performance space, and when you walk in there's a large black reflecting pool surrounded by a rail. At first the pool looks incredibly deep, almost bottomless, but it is actually shallow, and you can see your reflection in it. It is one of the most beautiful things I have ever seen. To me, that pool is Williamsburg.

Walking the streets, I thought of everything that had come before. The Yeah Yeah Yeahs' guitarist used to work at *this* furniture shop. One of the guys in Interpol worked at *that* used-clothing store. Norah Jones even lived here. It is one of the most historically rich neighborhoods in the city, a place with room for neopunk and adult contemporary, and everything between.

I drifted over to Galapagos, and took a long moment to look at my wavy face in the black pool. That night, Von Von Von was hosting the Floating Vaudeville Show. I felt uncomfortable being there alone, but I got into watching the show, and the trials and fears of the last two months lifted away.

Von Von Von pretends to be a sexy Euro-rocker from Amsterdam, and he sings songs about New York. His performance works on multiple levels. After doing a song called "Do the Von," and telling us how sexy he was, he introduced two women twirling batons, backed by a Journey song. They were followed by a woman with decorated breasts that she used as puppets. After her, a middle-aged man came up and sang show tunes, and then lay on the floor and asked women to come up and stomp on him.

I was surrounded by beautiful people, but I didn't feel as if I was one of them yet. Still, as I watched, I felt as light as a Pizzicato Five song, as ethereal as the Cocteau Twins, as grandiose as the guitar on My Bloody Valentine's *Loveless*. I had a thousand ideas for my own show. Should my band have a hot chick drummer, or a crazy drummer with his tongue out? Should the bassist be tall and smooth and detached, or short and jumpy, like a monkey? Should I play rhythm guitar and sing, or just sing? Questions for the ages—I wouldn't have my answer right away; I had to listen, and watch, and learn from the neighborhood.

When I got home, David was slouched on the couch, drinking a Budweiser with his shirt off and watching *24* on TiVo. He was surrounded by empty cans. I told him about my new job, and he told me what he did: something in finance that requires him to sit at a desk and answer phones. He moved the conversation over to our other roommate.

"All right, Gary," said David, "last month, Charles tried to make this a meat-free house. I'm coming in from work, he's right there at the door, just announces he's been thinking, right? And he's really tired of every time he opens the fridge, death stares him in the eye. And I thought, shit, it's like *Ghostbusters,* Gozer the Gozarian is in the fridge. But he's talking about a chicken breast. He wants it out. You're not vegetarian, right?"

"No. I like, you know, steak."

"Right. My uncle's a hunter, I'm going to get him to give me a whole deer next season. Don't skin it, just chop it up with an axe and stick it in the fridge—the head, everything. Here's some death staring you in the eye, asshole. Have a fucking hoof."

On the following Monday, I started my new job. Craigslist, which had once denied my every hope, had blessed me with an apartment, and now, a position (32-plus hours a week, $16.25 an hour, no benefits) in the growing field of phone answering and assistant office management, for BrandSolve, a "branding consultancy specializing in complete brand metrics and interactive brand experience," conveniently located in Chelsea, a short train ride and walk from my new digs. Most important, this job was not data entry. I needed only to find a way to rock out, and I would be back on my plan.

There were only twenty people in the company, and most of them seemed pretty cool. I was warned by Tom, the boss and founder, that I might be asked to stay on extra hours, to run errands, and to do web and photo research for people under deadline. I nodded, seeing the dollar signs add up, thinking of the guitar I could buy, the songs I could write.

The days went past in phone calls and filing. I got adjusted to BrandSolve's unique rhythms and learned the names of my cowork-

ers, and their jobs: designers, brand strategists, interactive special-
ists, vice presidents of et cetera. One night after a few weeks, Scott
Spark, Director of Interactive Services, asked if I could stay after
hours to help him with a project.

I liked Scott. He was in his early thirties, with well-tended skin
and hair, given to oxford shirts with high thread count. Some might
call him a metrosexual, but he preferred the more traditional "homosexual."

Following his directions, I spent an hour on a spreadsheet. I
watched the clock for another half hour, then emailed Scott the file
and wandered over to his desk. The office was empty except for the
two of us.

"That was fast," said Scott.

"I was inspired by the title of the program. 'Excel,' it said. I said,
'I will!' "

I scoped Scott's CD pile. It was good stuff. Pixies, TV on the
Radio, Aphex Twin, Love, Can. A logically consistent, respectful
collection of modern and historical relevance. With one exception.

"That, Gary," said Scott, "is a concept album."

"What does a band called Garden of Dragons sound like?" I
asked.

"Straight-up, no-apologies prog rock revival about an albino
dwarf messiah named Glordo."

"I thought so," I said.

Scott is a dedicated prog apologist. He told me the story of his
adolescence in Pennsylvania, playing xylophone in a marching
band. His descent into prog started with the gateway drugs, Pink
Floyd and Peter Gabriel. Before long, he was mainlining triple-disc
Emerson, Lake, and Palmer concert recordings. He saw Yes ("Not
Yes actually," he explained, "but Anderson Bruford Wakeman
Howe") the summer before he started college. At Columbia, he was
in two bands: God's Shadow, and another called Pink Noise, which
was with five synth players and a drummer.

"But I drifted away from prog," Scott said, "because all the other fans were dirty stoners. Just lately I've been going back in. You saw the Lou Barlow interview in the *Onion?*"

"I hate Sebadoh. I'd rather hear toddlers hit pans."

"Right," said Scott. "But they asked him, Lou, if you had all this stuff, all this cheap home studio equipment, what would you have done? And he said, 'If I'd had Pro Tools, I would have made these sprawling masterpieces.' And that's the spirit of prog."

At the beginning of our conversation, I was sure I could refute Scott's pro-prog bias, but the more he spoke, the more I realized that Scott, at least ten years older than I, with his own home studio, knew as much as I did about music—actually, more. Without intending to, he was telling me that everything I believed in was suspect. When I quoted a recent prog-mocking article from *Blender,* he accused *Blender* of snobbery, of fear of the old *and* new, and of "suspicion of ambition."

"The only difference between music writers and *Star Wars* nerds," he said, "is that you can't buy Steve Albini dolls on eBay. See, Gary, I just don't think kids in bands in college are thinking, 'How can I be more like Mission to Burma and Galaxie 500?' They're thinking, 'How can I plug Fruity Loops into Reason? How should I sample Radiohead? How can I make some orchestral shit?' Ted Leo and the Pharmacists is music for thirty-five-year-olds. Frank Black is just a middle-aged fat guy now. He's like an indie Stevie Nicks. And Elvis Costello and Burt Bacharach, together at last? Jack White and Loretta Lynn? It's like when Elvis sang 'My Way.' How can you be the voice of your generation when you dust off someone from the generation before?"

"Sid Vicious covered 'My Way,' " I said.

"But with ironic intent," said Scott. "It's an exception that proves the rule."

"What's Fruity Loops?"

"A sequencer," he said. "A drum machine, sort of. So is Reason."

Honestly, I was overwhelmed, lost in Scott's vision of a new age of MP3-downloaded neoprog lo-fi indie bedroom experimental electronic rock. I excused myself to get a drink of water, and came back a few moments later, stumbling with the possibilities.

"Sorry I went on," Scott said. "I've got a thing about prog."

"Look," I said. "I've thought about what you've been saying. My decision is clear."

Scott laughed. "What's that?" he asked.

"We have to start a band," I said.

I went to several independent guitar dealers the next evening, to search for the perfect guitar. Scott had laughed when I'd told him we were going to start a band, but I could see that he liked the idea. The old acoustic I had in my room wouldn't be enough. It was a worn, scratched Yamaha, and I was tired of it. I needed a serious instrument, one that would inspire me to great heights of musicianship.

I wanted a guitar that had personality and history, that had been touched by Dean Wareham or stolen from a Royal Trux show. I went to a store in the East Village, and another in the West Village, both places I had seen wandering through the city. Both of these stores closed at 6:30 P.M., it turned out. I could have returned the next day, I know, but I didn't want to go home without a guitar, so I went to Guitar Center, on Fourteenth Street, which is a mall for musicians. The place was filled with people with rock star dreams, men staring longingly at fiftieth anniversary Stratocasters and bright red POD 2 effects boxes.

But I didn't dawdle. I charged a new Fender DG-20CE acoustic-electric. Buying it, I promised myself that *this guitar would be different*. Because of all the guitars carried out of Guitar Center, only a few will ever be recorded; an even smaller fraction will ever go on tour. The merest sliver will ever be played on a major label release. Many more will be propped in corners or slid under beds, or find their ways onto online auctions.

Of course, the guitar is only the beginning. Then comes the amp, and the delay, the reverb, the Frampton talkbox, the condenser mic, the multitrack hard disc recorder, miles of unbalanced cable. Even then you're not done, because there is always a device more pure, something with expensive tubes and a single silver dial, the machine that will bring you closer to the pure essence of your own rock archetype, whether Hendrix, Zappa, or Richard Thompson. Your dreams pile up on monthly statements. There are nightmares, too, of being thrust onstage, naked, before an audience, with only a Chapman stick and no idea how to play it.

I pushed these thoughts away and decided that first I should learn how to play more than five chords. I took the guitar home and got to know it in my bedroom, savoring its glossed black curves, tapping it to listen to the resonance. I sat on the edge of my bed and plucked around until I got the opening of "Here Comes Your Man" and the "high and dry" part of "High and Dry." And I sang, and the guitar in my hands shone, reflecting the light hanging from the ceiling.

The next day I came home after work and, as he and I had discussed, I took my guitar to Scott's loft, only a dozen blocks away, a smooth space with lots of white chairs, so that we could jam. I was in awe, thinking of my empty room and my two roommates. How does someone afford to live this way, with all of these square feet?

"This is a *nice* place, Scott," I said.

"I had a serious Swedish furniture phase."

"That happens to the best of us," I said. "All you need is a big Ricola horn.

"Uh, that's Switzerland."

"Oh," I said. "Of course."

"Swiss is neutrality and chocolate. Sweden is a chair named Ingemar."

Scott had worked in Stockholm for a few months, it turned out. Everyone in New York City, besides me, has spent at least three seasons in Europe. I'm also the only person here who either 1) did not attend an Ivy League school or private liberal arts college; 2) speaks only one language; 3) never went on kibbutz.

Scott's apartment showed him to be a true equipment junkie, an addict. There was a wall piled high with equipment, a full-sized rack of glimmering devices, with a keyboard and PC below it. When I saw it, my eyes moistened.

As a synth player, Scott's addiction is more subtle than a guitarist's, driven as much by software and knobs as by the feel of nickel steel strings over a bird's-eye maple neck. For me, the pleasure of guitar has always been the ability to make a sound with my hands, but the synth player plans his fix, thinking in oscillators, dreaming of pitch bending and sine waves and portamento.

Putting down my guitar case, I pointed to a box with a blinking green LED.

"What's that?" I asked.

"That's my MOTU unit. It processes the audio coming out of the computer."

"What's a MOTU?"

"It stands for 'Mark of the Unicorn.' "

"And this one here? Is that the Foot of the Hobbit unit?"

"That's a military-surplus oscillator. It generates continuous sine waves. You just turn the big dial."

"You pick that up at the corner store?"

"I got it at the Poughkeepsie Hamfest, actually."

He caught my baffled look and said, "That's when ham radio folks get together to sell equipment."

"Wow. Saying you like to go to hamfests, that's like saying, 'I just got married as my character on Everquest.' "

"Cheap equipment," said Scott. "Did you play Everquest?"

"My roommate was really into those role-playing games," I said. "He had such a busy life as a cleric in the land of Mor'gathok that he kind of forgot to go to classes and got kicked out."

"It happens," said Scott.

The centerpiece of Scott's temple of digital sound is a Kurzweil 2600, a keyboard that looks like the monolith from *2001* turned on its side. I admired it, and Scott, the proud parent, said, "It arpeggiates like a star. Watch." He pressed a few buttons and hit a low C. Suddenly the room filled with a passable movie soundtrack, a big string sweep with a piano line and a gentle gonging.

"Dude," I said, both of us sitting in awe of the automated music machine. "It seems like cheating to be able to make that much music that easily."

"It's not cheating. It's just a shortcut. I was really into fractal music for a while. Don't make that face. But . . . I got back into songcraft. I had a big Beatles phase."

"Who's your favorite?"

"John," said Scott. "Who's your favorite?"

"John," I said.

We nodded in mutual approval, both having passed a test, and had the obligatory Beatles-worship conversation. As we spoke, I pulled out my new guitar from its plastic case and took a deep breath.

"Scott, I need to warn you, if we're talking smashing out chords and belting out some angry words, I'm your man. When it comes to bel canto singing over a prog riff, not so much."

"I'm sure you're fine," said Scott.

"I'm just saying, I grew up listening to Ween, not King Crimson."

"When I say 'D sharp diminished,' do you know what I'm talking about?"

"Mostly. I mean, I could look it up online."

We started in, talking out our ideas, playing scraps of sound and asking the other player to push back. It sounded truly atrocious, as bad as the last Soul Coughing album. But an hour of fiddling and knob twiddling later, with Scott showing me the fingerings on a few chords, we had something, a little one-minute riff with me humming, kind of folky. He recorded it into Pro Tools and played it back. I held out my hands low, and he slapped them.

SCOTT: Dude.
GARY: Bro.
SCOTT: *Dude.*
GARY: I know.
SCOTT: This is good for me. I've been spending too much of my life programming Java servlets.
GARY: Dude. You have no idea. I lived in Albany.

After our third session in as many weeks, with ten minutes of untitled song ideas multitracked onto Scott's hard drive, I told him we needed to think about getting a band together.

"Well, you know, this is fun, but I don't know if I want to go through all the stress of getting people together," said Scott.

I stared at him, silent.

"I'm just saying, it's a lot of work."

"Sure," I said. "I understand. Your time is better spent programming Java."

"No," said Scott, "but—"

"I mean," I said, "what'll be great is when you're on your bed of death, a ring of grandchildren around you—"

"Grandnephews and grandnieces—"

"Whatever," I said. "And the nurse is hooking up an IV to your arm, and you turn to the people in the room and with rheumy eyes, you can say, 'I die knowing my skills in object-oriented programming increased revenue for a branding consultancy.' "

"I'm just saying it's work to be in a band."

"Allow me, Scott, to draw you a picture."

Scott waited with exasperated patience as I drew a stick figure with whiskers coming out by its mouth. Then I drew a big circle around it and made a slash through the circle.

"OK, what's this?" he asked me.

"It means, don't be a pussy. It means carpe the fucking diem. I'm going to be in a band in Williamsburg unless I get hit by the B61 bus. I have nothing ahead of me but fantastic success or spectacular failure, so I'm not settling for anything in between."

Scott made a face. But a little later, not without more sighing, he signed on.

"No takebacks," I said. "You can't bitch out."

"I will not bitch out," said Scott.

Next I presented my plan for fleshing out the remaining open positions. "I go to the Mercury Lounge," I said, "and the bands are almost all white boys. It's boring."

"No argument there," said Scott.

"I've been giving it some thought. We have a straight white singer, and a gay white synth player. We're fusing prog and indie. So let's take it all the way. Let's have the most diverse band in the city," I rushed on before Scott could interrupt me. "I mean, we start with a hot chick drummer."

"Who can play," Scott suggested.

"Exactly. I'm not talking Meg White." Although, truth be told, I kind of liked Meg White's drumming. The White Stripes would just be a single Stripe without her.

"Now the bassist—in a wheelchair?" Scott was not taking me seriously.

"No, the bassist should be a black guy. Though he could be in a wheelchair, I don't care. Maybe if he had some sort of special mouth control for his effects box."

Scott looked out the window for a moment. "And what about a lead guitarist?"

"Are we getting a lead guitarist?" I asked.

"No insult, but it definitely isn't you."

"Maybe an Arab," I said.

"Sherpas are good too. They can lug the equipment."

It went on for another half hour, until Scott began to look tired, for him to agree that trying to build a diverse band was not such a bad idea.

"So," he asked me. "Do you *know* any hot chick drummers?"

"No."

"Well, there you go," he said.

"Bro," I said, "two words: Craigs. List. Dot org. And I'll put up posters. Williamsburg is hot chick drummer ground zero."

Scott definitely has a shrugging and sighing problem.

By now, New York had started to feel like home, a place I could call my own. I was comfortable, even, and I sometimes found myself wishing I could get rid of the urge to start a band, just live a normal life. Maybe, I thought, I should drop my dreams, go back to school, and get some computer skills. I could pick up one of those books in Barnes & Noble: *More Exploitable Wage Slavery in 21 Days*, or *Learn Java and Lose Friends*.

At night, notebook and rhyming dictionary in hand, I flopped down on my new futon mattress, humming improvised melodies to match the words I wrote. Like Jacob, I wrestled with the angel of rock, refusing to release him until he gave me his blessing. I wrote a song called "Abu Ghraib."

> *Have you heard*
> *From Abu Ghraib to Williamsburg,*
> *Can you see*
> *That all of us, we must be free.*

I decided that this would be the first thing I'd record, once we got the band together.

One night at work I sat browsing PitchforkMedia.com, thinking hard about the best way to find a hot chick drummer. The office had emptied out, and the rooms were ghostly and dark, except for the desk lamp over Para's computer. I was waiting for her to finish laying out a proposal so that I could run to the copy shop. Para was a designer, a foxy woman with big anime eyes and nice lips, and long slender fingers. Because she's my superior at work I can lust after her, and it isn't harassment.

At eight o'clock, she handed me a diskette and off I went. An hour later, I came back with bound proposals. She leafed through them, and told me we were done.

"God, it's eight," she said. "I have to meet some friends."

"Getting into something good?" I asked.

"Not really," she said. "Do you know what blogs are?"

"Yeah, sure," I said.

She looked embarrassed. "Well," she said, "I'm going to a blog party in Williamsburg."

"Bloggers have parties?" I wondered, *What do they have to celebrate?*

"It's just a chance to meet up, and not all be on email," she explained.

"So you have a blog?" I asked.

"Yeah," she said, apologetically.

"What's it called?" Maybe she had written something about me.

"It's boring," she said. "It's called Gowanus Research Society. Because I live in Gowanus, in Brooklyn. But I don't talk about it at work, you know?"

"Sure," I said.

Para invited me to the get-together, and since it was in Williamsburg, I figured it couldn't be all bad. For those who don't know, a weblog, or blog for short, is a personal website where people can post stories about their lives. I'd seen a bunch of blogs, and knew plenty of people in college who had them, but I don't really like reading online, except music reviews, so I'd missed the whole "blogging revolution."

Para had not. On the L train, she told me more about the exciting world of blogging. I tuned most of it out and just looked at her. She'd put on her lipstick before we left the office, and pulled her hair forward. She was sporting a cool, nerdy look, with big black glasses and clunky shoes.

From what she told me, the blog world sounded like any local band scene, where everyone is playing the same clubs and bitching jealously about each other. There is an A-list of bloggers who get the most readers, and some of the A-list royalty would be there tonight.

Para told me the biggest blog in New York is called Gawker .com, and it's about magazines. To me, this is really sad. It's like if you put together a band with the sole purpose of singing songs about the music industry. Unfortunately the Gawker guy was not going to be there that night (that would be like Bono showing up at CMJ Musicfest). Apparently it was a big deal to be invited to one of these things, and Para had actually gotten an e-vite, not just read about the party somewhere. She was acting like someone with a backstage pass to the Pixies reunion.

Personally, I was not so nervous. The party was at Royal Oak, on Union Avenue. It was a cool place, very big and old-fashioned looking. Para introduced me around to a group of people. There was an Indian guy who gave me his business card, and this couple who make blogging software who were clearly a big deal, who also gave out business cards, and someone who writes about Craigslist who apologized for not having a business card, and a number of people who were in the process of self-publishing books. They seemed to have their own language.

BLOGGER A: I mean, he's not even standards-compliant.
GARY: Yeah, that is the truth, isn't it?

BLOGGER B: She might as well have a Livejournal.
GARY: You are spot on the money, my man.

All the bloggers were really glad to meet you, and curious to know whether you knew who they were, and if you read their blog. If there is one word to describe bloggers, it is "vulnerable." Another word—well, phrase—might be "incredibly self-aware." Talking to them was like seeing Smiths songs come to life. The music was pretty loud, so the pressure to make conversation was low. Mostly you had to nod, and let the bloggers talk about themselves.

BLOGGER C: You might have read my blog, it's called Gathering Moss Slowly under Bridges.
GARY: Oh, totally. Your blog is awesome.
BLOGGER D: Who does Nick Denton think he's fooling?
GARY: Nobody, man, nobody at all.

Looking at the bloggers, I kept thinking of those fish that live way underwater, the ones that, when you bring them up to the surface, explode from the pressure change. I kept looking for the A-list, but it was kind of hard to tell who was on it. I asked Para to point out the A-listers, and she motioned to some people and mentioned their blogs—"There's Dinesh Patel, he does Patella. I just met him. And Morgan, who does New Morgania. I recognize her from her webcam. . . . Huh, Sue Gorsh, who does Invalid and Exposed. She's a genius designer." Even after she pointed them out, I couldn't really see what made them A-list. Para pointed out a guy who apparently writes a really important blog about blogging. I introduced myself, and struck up a conversation.

DUDE: I mean, Gawker links to you, but so what, right?
GARY: Yeah, what's it all mean, really?

DUDE: Do you read a lot of blogs?

GARY: No, but I read a lot of personal ads. That's kind of the same thing.

DUDE (*Someone taps his shoulder.*): I have to go. Here's my card.

GARY: I treasure it.

DUDE: I'd appreciate it if you didn't blog about meeting me, uh, . . .

GARY: Gary.

DUDE: It gets kind of circular.

GARY: Absolutely.

I picked up nine business cards that night. I was confused as to what I was supposed to do with them. Do I call these numbers when I need something blogged? *Hey, we met at Royal Oak, and I was thinking, Yo La Tengo is kind of boring. Can you blog that for me? You can? Awesome. Can you have that up in the next two hours? I might have something to say about Greg Dulli later, maybe you could blog that too? Terrific.*

I looked over to find Para deep in conversation with some fat guy in a suit jacket. He had that three-day beard growth that fat guys like because it makes their faces seem angular. Para was saying, "I just think what you've done with structure is amazing. And I love the redesign."

I didn't want to see any more blogger-buttering-up, so I tapped her shoulder and told her I was heading home. She didn't seem too worried to see me go. She kissed my cheek and asked if I'd had a good time.

"The best time," I said.

The next day at work I stopped by Para's desk and thanked her for taking me out. She was pretty excited to have spent all that quality time with all those bloggers.

"I was a little surprised to see all the business cards," I said. "I mean, I felt kind of stupid not having one."

"Oh, business cards are cheap. I could make you a business card. Seriously, we can do it right now."

"I can't really do it on office hours," I said. "I'm still new, you know?"

Para ended up inviting me to her place after work, where we could make my business card on her home computer. We took the F train to Gowanus. Her neighborhood was lots of pizza parlors and bodegas, kind of dark, no performance spaces, everyone looking as if they had worked all day instead of as though they were just waking up, and it made me realize how lucky I was to live in Williamsburg.

When we entered her apartment, she flicked on the lights and yelled out, "Butter!" I was confused for a moment, but Butter is her cat, a yellow tabby. He came out and eyed me, then propped himself up on her chair and ignored us. She apologized for the mess, but I didn't see anything out of order, unless you count the bed not being made. I don't even have a bed, so I can't judge. There were two museum prints on the wall. One was a sort of blobby picture of a face from the Chuck Close retrospective at MoMA, and the other was a big yellow shape thing by Ellsworth Kelley, from the Guggenheim.

Para got us both a drink of water and we got to work. Her Mac started up with its moaning noise, and her scanner went *ka-shaaa-kunk*. She opened some programs and moved the mouse with blinding speed, speaking while she worked. She seemed a little nervous to have me over.

Para said, "You know, I think you're a Frutiger kind of guy." For a weird moment, I thought she somehow knew about my episode with Keith, but then she brought up some text in Frutiger, which is a font, sort of like Arial, strong and manly.

"Adrian Frutiger did it for the Paris airport at Roissy. It's a good choice."

"You know," I said, "maybe not Frutiger." I pointed to the font menu. "How about that one?"

"Goudy Old Style," she said.

"Sorry. I thought it said 'old school.' "

"You know, I don't want to be too obvious, but we might want to use the Scala family. And Scala Sans."

"Well, I guess obvious is bad."

"They're the typefaces they use for the *New Left Review*," said Para. "Really reliable stuff. Just perfect, really—here, look at the descender on the 'g.' "

"That is one sweet descender."

After much discussion, we went with the Scala family, a happy and harmonious grouping of fonts with a rich history that I will not repeat here. I told Para what I wanted my business card to say ("Gary Benchley, Rock Star"), and she typed it in and moved some boxes around on the screen. Her fingers raced over the keyboard and mouse. She was pale, and as she flexed her hands, the veins showed through the skin. I realized, suddenly, that she was about twenty-six or twenty-seven, which surprised me, because most of the people I know are my age. It felt cool to be hanging out with an older woman.

"What are you doing now?" I asked.

"I'm kerning."

"What's that?"

What followed was a serious explanation of what kerns are, namely, little bits of lead that were used in Ye Olde Printing Shoppe of Yore. Para is as into fonts as I am into music.

My business card took shape. She added a red bar along the top of it, for no reason except that it looked cool. "It's awesome," I said. "You should do album covers."

"I've done some, actually. My friend Teri has a folk group."

I had to speak quickly, before she could pull out the CD and play it. "So, what do I do to get these made?" I asked.

"I'm going to burn this to a CD. You can take it to a printer, and he'll do them up."

"Wicked. Now let me buy you some pie."

"OK," she said. "I like pie."

Who doesn't? We had pie at a diner in her neighborhood, rhubarb for her and blueberry for me, heated up, with a scoop of vanilla ice cream for each. "I never eat pie," she said, "I don't let myself." She attacked the pie at first, two huge bites, hiding her ecstasy, and then began to eat it slowly, in small, polite forkfuls. Me, I just ate my pie.

Afterward she said she wanted to get home and write things for her blog. So I said good-bye and rode the G train to Metropolitan Avenue. I leaned back in the hard orange plastic seat and thought back through the last months.

New York City has tested me, made me kill its lions and clean its stables, and sent me to the brink of returning to Albany, but now, it had decided I could stay. The city had changed its mind, and now I had a room of my own, with a lock on the door. Yes, with a roommate who collects orgasms in drums, and another who wants to keep large game in our fridge, but who cares? Neither of them would ask me to trade sex for rent, and no small animal will ever again attack what my bathing suit covers. I had a job, and even a business card, or at least the digital equivalent of one, on a CD in my bag. And, I was not a blogger. And maybe, just maybe, it had presented me with a romantic opportunity re: Para. I definitely had that vibe.

Truly, I stood on the cusp of the age of Benchley. All that remained was to get the band together and stick to my mission. I was going to *produce* Williamsburg culture, not just consume it. The band would come into being—I knew it. I had the same feeling I had at Galapagos, that sense of victory, of rising above.

I let out a huge breath, as the train rolled toward Metropolitan Ave., toward Williamsburg, toward home.

*   *   *

I posted our ad for a hot chick drummer on Craigslist, and put up posters around my neighborhood.

URGENT!!!!!!!!!!!!!!!!!!!!!!
HOT CHICK DRUMMER
NEEDED FOR INDIE PROG BAND
EMAIL GARYBENCHLEYROCKSTAR@YAHOO.COM
IN STRICTEST CONFIDENCE
ALL HOT CHICK DRUMMERS WILL BE CONSIDERED
WE DO IT FOR LOVE, NOT MONEY!

Within three days we had four potential drummers. On the following Saturday, Scott and I got into his Honda Element and drove around Williamsburg, the East Village, and Fort Greene to meet and audition our potential bandmates.

WILLIAMSBURG WOMAN: I want to get into deejaying. So I can do that *and* be a model.

GARY: It's good to have skills.

SCOTT: You play drums, right?

WILLIAMSBURG WOMAN: Drum *machine*.

In the East Village we checked out another possibility.

EAST VILLAGE WOMAN: I've been taking classes at Tribal Soundz. I'm mostly into tantric rhythms.

SCOTT: Uh.

EAST VILLAGE WOMAN: Also, I don't do cocaine.

We drove to Fort Greene, where a woman explained that she was ready for us to teach her to play, if we'd provide the drums. All of these women *were* exceptionally attractive, but I had to agree with Scott that my plan might have been flawed with regard to actual drum playing. I thought back to my Theories of the Media class (honors), where I learned that we live in a world in which the surfaces of things take on more meaning than the things themselves. I tried to remember the French word for this process—I think it was *lexefierance.* In any case, it was disheartening that these women were clearly responding more to "hot chick" than to "drummer."

We had one more person to visit, but that wasn't until eight, so Scott dropped me off at my apartment for a few hours. Feeling a little despondent, I found the blinds drawn and my roommate Charles sitting on the couch next to a tallish woman, both of them in the lotus position. Charles tapped a long drum that he held between his folded legs.

"Gary," said Charles, "this is my friend Patmavadi."

She smiled at me, tilting her head to the right and turning her palm so it faced up. She had very pale white skin and dirty blond hair, with a bindi dot on her forehead. I sat down on the easy chair.

"Patmavadi just got back from Vietnam," said Charles.

"And Cambodia," said Patmavadi.

"How was it?" I asked.

"Amazing," said Patmavadi, shaking her head.

"It is an amazing place," said Charles.

"The people are so centered," said Patmavadi.

"Every time I went," said Charles, "it was a remarkable experience." He tapped his drum. "Of course, tourism is ruining everything."

"You've been there a lot?" I asked.

"Four times," said Charles. "The last time," he said, tapping his drum several times, quickly, "the last time, I had a residency at a monastery in Siemréab."

Patmavadi said, "People really are missing the point of Southeast Asia when they go there for tourism."

"Even in Burma there are tourists everywhere," said Charles, tapping his drum slowly, languorously.

"Western civilization chases you wherever you go," said Patmavadi.

"Chases you with its lies," said Charles, tappity-tapping.

Around then my other roommate David came in, holding a black trash bag. He sat down by the television and said hello to Patmavadi.

"Patmavadi just got back from Cambodia," I said.

"See any tigers?" David asked.

"No," she said.

"How about you, David?" Charles asked. "Any travel plans this year?"

Before David could answer, Patmavadi said, "It's really good to get out of the country right now. Everything is so conservative. Even Burma seems more open-minded than we are."

"If Bush wins, I'm leaving," said Charles.

"Exactly," said Patmavadi. "I'm so glad I have an Italian passport. Just having it keeps me sane."

David was fingering his black plastic bag, so I asked him what was inside. He pulled out a mounted animal head in poor repair. It looked like a tiny bear with a very angry face. Its mouth was open, showing sharp teeth. Charles's drum fell over.

Patmavadi looked disgusted. "What is that?" she asked.

"It's a wolverine head, right?" said David. "Coney Island junk shop. It was just crying out." He made a growling noise, stroking the wolverine's sharp teeth.

"It's hideous," said Charles.

"I figure it'll look good above the TV," said David.

David is a U of Michigan grad, given to blue and yellow sweatshirts. Even in May, I would learn, he was preparing for the next football season, telling me about the Wolverines' 1997 championship win.

"Look," said Charles, "I think it's fair to say no to dead wolverines in the room."

"Just from August to January," said David.

"Well, January's over. Gary," said Charles, "break this tie."

"I am seriously stepping out of the dead wolverine issue," I said.

"Dude," said David, "you can't be neutral." He held up the wolverine, which was missing an eye. "It's dead. It can't hurt anyone."

"I would be totally freaked out to have that thing staring at me," said Patmavadi.

"I'm pretty much saying no here," said Charles. "Please, no, thank you."

"One of these days," David said, "it's going up."

I excused myself to my room and dawdled for a while, reading and listening to the new P. J. Harvey album on my headphones. I've been reading *The Girls' Guide to Hunting and Fishing* on Para's recommendation. "I know it's weird, but this book is who I am," she'd said. Apparently who she is, deep inside, is a woman in publishing who visits St. Croix. I opened the book, began to skim, and luckily woke up right at 7:30. I went downstairs and, before long, Scott pulled up.

Our last hot chick drummer lived in one of those Brooklyn neighborhoods with lots of inspirational murals and memorial graffiti. The inspirational murals showed people overcoming bad situations without guns. The fact that no guns are involved was highlighted: PROBLEMS—SOLVED WITHOUT GUNS—IN THE COMMUNITY, one mural said, below pictures of children and dolphins. The memorial graffiti, in contrast, showed people who used guns to solve problems. RALPH 1978–1998, one said, with a picture of Ralph and his pit bull. We knocked on a heavy wooden door that had been painted in black and red stripes. Over the doorbell was a small sign that read PACKAGES FOR MONOTREME RING #4. A huge man dressed in leather pants and a rubber smock answered, wearing a welding helmet with the visor up.

"Yep," said the man.

"We're looking for Katherine Passerine," I said.

"Sure," said the man.

Inside was a workshop filled with welding equipment, band saws, and odd-shaped buckets. At the machines were four or five people who looked as if they might possibly have been to Burning Man. Or at least they had all watched *Junkyard Wars*. The man in the visor yelled out, "Spider!"

A man with tribal tattoos on his shoulders popped up from behind an old acoustic piano—it wasn't clear if he was wearing clothes—holding an enormous drill. The man in the visor asked him where Katherine was.

"Basement," Spider said and dropped back behind the piano.

Scott and I found the basement door. Downstairs, we met a small woman with a smudged face and long, dark hair. She was running silver lamé fabric through a large olive green sewing machine and wore a T-shirt with a picture of an angry chicken on it. The chicken was saying "$$$." Under the chicken was the word CHUNK.

"Scott and Gary?" she said. We all shook hands. She had a scratchy voice, bulging eyes, and a very little chin. "My kit is upstairs." We followed her up three flights to a small apartment.

"I like your shirt," I said. "What's Chunk?"

"Chunk is Chengwin's archenemy," said Katherine.

"Gotcha," I said. "Why is he talking in dollar signs?"

"Because he's evil," said Katherine.

"What *is* this place?" Scott asked.

"The Monotreme Institute for Extraordinary Art," she said.

"What kind of art do you do?" I asked.

"A lot of events, rides," said Katherine. "We make heavy use of propane."

"You guys did that nuclear thing in Williamsburg," said Scott.

"The Geiger Party," said Katherine.

"What was that?" I asked.

"Everyone was slightly irradiated," said Scott.

"It was just stuff you could find in a chemistry class," Katherine said. "It was the idea, not the gamma rays. It's kind of hard to explain that to the NYPD."

Her room was dirty, covered with clothes and papers. A small, dirty drum kit sat in a corner, with a black snare, a white bass drum, two bright red toms, and a surprising number of cymbals, rain sticks, and shakers, along with a gong.

"So," said Katherine, "prog rock?"

"It's kind of an umbrella term," said Scott.

"I mean, we want to rock first," I said. "But truly push the envelope. Reinvent what prog means for the new millennium."

"So maybe lots of electronica," said Scott.

"But keep it indie and not pure knob twiddling," I said.

"Not be bound down to any one sound," Scott said.

"You should talk to Kyle, downstairs," Katherine said. "The guy drilling the piano. He does a lot with MIDI. He made a MIDI bomb once."

"Wait—this is Spider?" asked Scott.

"Spider Kyle," said Katherine. "There's also Occasional Kyle, but he's only here on weekends."

"He made a bomb?" I asked.

"He made all these custom-tuned screamer fireworks," said Katherine, "and put them together to play chords when they went off. That hooked up to a keyboard via MIDI. We did it in Dresden."

"What songs do you play with a MIDI bomb?" I asked.

" 'Love Train,' " said Katherine.

"That's funny," I said. Scott was silent. "Scott, it's funny," I said.

"So," Katherine said, "let me get situated."

She straddled the stool in front of the kit and picked her sticks up from the floor, fishing them out from under a shirt. With one of the sticks she pushed a pair of dark blue panties off the top of the snare. "OK," she said, making a De Niro face. Then both arms went up and came down at once, reminding me of some kind of industrial robot, the sort they use to build cars. A sonic force from the deeps of the East River entered her body—the spirit of everything that has ever gone wrong in New York—and was unleashed in a kicking, pounding rage.

It was shock-and-awe drumming. It was like watching a lion spit firecrackers. She hammered the bass drum, sometimes simply kicking the drum head, and smashed the toms using every muscle in her small arms. The cymbals sounded like helicopters crashing into jungle gyms. Then, suddenly, it quieted as she tapped just one cymbal, gentle as a lamb gamboling over velvet. And when that stopped, the silence was as huge as the noise, and I had an erection.

"How long have you been drumming?" Scott asked.

"All my life," said Katherine.

We told her that we were still figuring out a bassist and a lead guitarist, and would call her when we knew what we were doing. Before we left, I asked her who her favorite Beatle was. She thought for a minute, then said, "Yoko."

We walked down and through the workshop. Outside, a woman with a leathery face came up and asked us for five dollars, and we shooed her away. We got into Scott's car.

"Fuckity," I said.

"She's not hot," said Scott. "She's almost homely."

"Why are we even discussing this?" I asked.

"I just want us to make an informed decision. I'm not saying she's not amazing, but she's not really a drummer. She's more like . . . a percussion wraith."

"Scott, when they discovered the Grand Canyon, did they say, 'If only it was a mountain'?"

"Also, she looks crazy."

"Did Newton," I asked, "when the apple fell on his head, move to another tree?"

"That's apocryphal," said Scott.

"Scott," I said, "I'm not talking about music. I'm talking about rock."

"Dude," said Scott, "I'm just thinking about the sound."

"Dude," I said, "look. You can differentiate between European countries with no effort. I know this. I respect it. But, frankly, there is no decision to be made."

"Dude," said Scott, "all I'm saying is, the music has to come first."

"Dude," I said, "OK. You need music for rocking, sure, or maybe music is a side effect of rocking. But rocking comes first. What we are searching for is the quality of awesomeness. That woman has awesomeness. She has *ineffable* awesomeness."

As we drove, I told Scott about the bands I'd seen lately. Bands at the Mercury Lounge with interchangeable names and inter-changeable members. I'd gone to Tonic and watched a group of three men in their twenties move mouse pointers as they looked at laptop screens, while a fourth man ran up and down scales on a saxophone. I told him that, with him on keyboards as a musical an-chor, me jumping up yelling and singing, and Katherine on drums, we would be on the way to revolutionizing the music of Williams-burg, and of the world.

"I think you forget that I'm a little older and settled," Scott said.

"Scott," I said.

"Quality control is important to me."

"Scott."

"Gary."

"Dude, Scott, bro."

"What?"

"Come on."

He sighed and nodded.

"Now we need a black bassist," I said, "and we're almost there."

"What," Scott asked, "are we going to put up a sign for cool black bass players on Bedford Avenue?"

"Probably not," I said. "But I'm sure there's a way."

Scott wanted to know my plan, but I only smiled and shrugged my shoulders. He wouldn't have approved if I'd told him. To his repeated questions, I just kept saying, "Give me some time and you'll see results." Because there is no arguing with results.

Now we needed only a cool black bass player, and a lead guitarist of undetermined (and perhaps even indeterminate) ethnicity and gender.

Some days later Scott and I went to lunch. Scott asked me how my search for a bassist was going, and I told him it was fine. He probed my methods, but I maintained a diligent silence. Finally, he gave up asking, and we began to talk about guitarists.

"Are we sure we need a lead guitarist?" asked Scott.

"You mean fill out the middle with keys?"

Scott shrugged.

"We'd be, like, the only band without a guitarist," I said. "It would be groundbreaking."

"Actually, Keane doesn't have a guitarist," said Scott.

"So we're riding the new no-guitar wave. Even better," I said.

"The Crazy World of Arthur Brown didn't have one either, and they were in the late sixties," said Scott.

"Who?" I asked.

"You ever heard a sample, goes, 'Fire, I bring you fire'?" Scott asked, singing in a big, low voice.

"I love that sample!" I said.

"That's them," said Scott.

"Cool," I said.

"I'm just thinking," said Scott, "if we're trying to break the indie mold, and really focus on a new sound, why not get rid of the guitar?"

"It's true," I said. "I've heard enough gay-ass guitar solos to last me a lifetime."

Scott frowned. My use of the word "gay" was a direct hit to a sore spot.

"It's really excellent," he said, "to have my sexual identity associated with all things that suck."

"Dude, everyone says 'gay,' " I said.

"I don't say 'gay,' " he said.

"Yeah, but everyone else does," I said. "It's not even offensive."

"Gary, not everyone thinks it's OK to call something that blows 'gay.' "

"But there's gay, like, I have sex with men, and then there's gay, like, I like Phish and can juggle. There's a clear distinction," I said.

"You sound like those phobes who get upset because they can't use the word 'gay' anymore," said Scott.

"Scott, I'm not a phobe," I said.

"I'm just saying, Gary," he said.

There was a pause as we looked at each other.

"How about if I use the word 'phobe' instead of 'gay'?" I asked.

"It's an improvement, but—"

"So, I'm like, 'Dude is totally phobe.' "

"Not good enough. You won't stick to it."

"Then . . . how about 'creed'? Like the band. 'Dude is creed'? I can make that happen. 'I've heard way too many creed guitar solos.' It works on multiple levels."

"That's better."

Safely out of the linguistic thicket, we talked about our newly guitar-free future. Personally, it was a relief. I thought back to my trip to Guitar Center and remembered the look of yearning on all the guitarists, the fractured egos hoping to be made whole by playing four-minute solos onstage. If we didn't have a lead guitar, we wouldn't have a lead guitarist. It only had upside. Scott had once again proved himself a genius.

The next day, Para and I also went out to lunch. I'd been thinking of her a lot. Actually, constantly. I looked at things in the street— a bakery window, a German shepherd, a half-naked homeless man—and wondered, *What would Para think of that?* My apartment had seemed like a palace when I moved in, but now it looked pathetic compared to her place with its lamp shades, window blinds, and cat. But I was getting no play, no pause, no rewind.

We'd been out once or twice since the blog party, but when we said good-bye it was always just another mouth peck. Had she decided I was just a half-employed, twenty-two-year-old rock wannabe, and not a man of great promise? Of course, that would be a fair assessment. I needed to pick up the pace.

When I came to New York, I was convinced that, as a dashing man of five feet eleven with a fine singing voice and musical ambitions, I could Casanova my way up the East River and down the Hudson. But after the incident with Keith and the utter flop with Alyssa, my optimism regarding my Albany-bred potency had faded and left me a vulnerable half-man. I'd tried. I'd gone out to a few bars in Williamsburg, talked to girls. But it was always friendly, and nothing was clicking. Even though I now had enough money to buy someone a drink.

The girls I met were my age, they worked in art galleries or coffee shops, and to be honest, they didn't have that much going on. I needed someone who could stimulate me in an intellectual way. Para had a career, an apartment of her own, she tended an animal (Butter) and thus had a relationship with nature. Like Scott, she was a real adult. Right now, that all seemed incredibly sexy.

At lunch, we didn't speak of love. Instead, Para ended up telling me about her knitting club. She was knitting a black hoodie for her friend's soon-to-be-born baby.

"You should see the yarn I got," she said. "It'll be perfect."

"I should see that yarn, definitely."

"This thing is going to be *adorable*."

"I can't wait to see it."

She and her friends were trying to name their knitting club. They didn't just want to call themselves Stitch 'n' Bitch like all the other knitting clubs, because they had a different philosophy of knitting.

"See, Gary, despite what these knitting clubs say, they reek of postfeminism, and we're *not* postfeminist," Para explained. "We're feminists who knit." Some of the names she'd come up with were Needle, Slip Knot, and Purlwise. These were, I thought, totally creed names.

I suggested they call the group Slits That Knit, but she didn't find that funny, and called me sexist. I explained that I was just being ironic, but she just looked at me. I apologized.

I knew the real rock star thing is to not be tied down to any one woman, or to date women of ill repute (Q: What does a stripper do with her asshole? A: Drop him off at band practice)—but the idea of a little domestic tranquility appealed to me. It would balance out the pressures of being a musician. I needed someone who could understand that.

One slow afternoon at work, I checked out Para's blog. I hadn't really been reading it, because it was all about design and filled with insider gossip about bloggers, which was deeply uninteresting. I wasn't sure if I was supposed to be reading or not, but it turned out she had been writing about me, and knowledge is power.

Youth

Coworker Youth & I went out to see Matty Charles and the Valentines in Red Hook. He liked the drummer. Afterwards, there was opportunity for a move to be made, but Youth is . . . a youth, big-eyed, & a little slow on the draw. (Still, nice that he doesn't know I'm easy.) So home he went to Youthburg.
4 comments.

Several people had commented on that post. One wrote, "Young ones always take a long time, or else they're quick on the draw, speaking from experience, so be glad you have a slow one." Another: "Sounds to me like he needs some patient teaching." I realized I had much to understand about women in their late twenties and early thirties. The most important lesson, the one I'd missed, was: They are ready to go.

My college experiences had not prepared me for that. When I was a junior, I went out with a sophomore named Kyla. She and I had radio shows in neighboring time slots, mine after hers. She called her show "Systers Themselves," heavy on Ani and Annie, DiFranco and Lennox. Mine was called "Gary Benchley's Unstoppable Rock Hour Destroys Monsters and Bullies."

For weeks, we just nodded to each other. Then, one night, when I opened my show with a Breeders song, we chatted about Kim Deal. After that, Kyla would hang out for a few minutes as my show started. She had met Ani DiFranco in Buffalo, and often mentioned how Ani was very cool, and not like a rock star at all.

Right before spring break, she stayed through my show, and I walked her back to her dorm. Kyla had very large, full breasts and a little belly, and kept her brown hair cropped to an inch long. We discussed our mutual dislike of the objectifying male gaze.

The relationship progressed to eating together in the cafeteria and going for walks in the woods. She sent me postcards through intracampus mail, with medical illustrations and torn-out bits of romance novels glued to them. We went to an art show in the student gallery, and the next week to a disco party at her friend's house. After the party, we sat on a bench in the brutal upstate cold, looking at the stream that ran near the art center.

"Are you cold?" I asked, teeth chattering.

"No, I'm fine," said Kyla, shivering.

"Are you sure?" I asked, hands going numb.

"I really like being out here talking with you," she said, through blue lips.

"Me too," I said, barely able to form words.

We talked about bands we'd seen and talked about books we hadn't read, like *Ulysses*. Finally, she put her hand on mine, her palm as warm as an oven. The next night she came over and I gave her a massage while we listened to Massive Attack. That night, finally, she said that it would be OK for us to change into sweatpants, get into bed, and hug.

Three weeks later we took off the sweatpants. A month later, she told me she had repeated sex fantasies about African American pirates. Not long after that, we broke up, with a great deal of weeping, got back together the next day, then broke up again a week later. She was a communications studies major.

And now, here I was looking at Para, and for whatever reason—whether because of Keith, or because I was still getting my NYC bearings—I'd regressed back to junior year. I was thinking, *I wonder when she'll let me give her a massage,* while she's waiting for me to ask if she prefers Astroglide or Wet Platinum. For women of her age, there are no sweatpants, and hugging is for the morning. Benchley had let anxiety steal his thunder—I had to make a move. I also needed to find a bassist, but you have to prioritize.

Opportunity appeared a few days later. Para's friend was showing a few digitally manipulated photos as part of a gallery show in

Chelsea called "Children and Buildings: the New Urban." Para invited me to come along. This was my plan: We would go to the show, then I would ask her out for a drink, and I would kiss her. Not at the bar, but right before we went in. I didn't want her to think I needed a beer to be interested; I wanted her to know I was sincere. And how did that go, you ask? As she wrote in her blog:

Movemaking

Youth made his move! We were leaving the Entropic Gallery, where Brian had exhibited yet more remarkable images, & Youth offered me a beer. On our way into Chelsea Social he stops, leans down to kiss me—but he did the open-mouthed thing with his eyes closed, in for the kill. Nice teeth. & I started to giggle, couldn't help it. He was like a cartoon fish blowing bubbles. He opened his eyes at my giggling & looked like a puppy when you hide a tennis ball behind your back.

I patted his hand & said, "Come on, I'll buy you a drink." He fidgeted through two vodka & tonics, poor thing, & I sent him home. Next time I'll stifle the giggle.

Comments?

The next time was that weekend, Sunday night. I rang her buzzer at eight. There was no show or art opening, no business card to be created, just us. We went out and drank steadily for three hours. She told me about her ex-boyfriend, Dan, whom she'd dumped a few months earlier after a five-year fling.

"See," she said, finishing her fourth beer, "your plans *could* be real. Maybe you *could* get a band together. But Dan—here's a forty-two-year-old man borrowing money from his mother to make a movie about snakes."

"I guess so," I said.

"If you want to be a rock star, right, go for it. It's not going to work. But seriously, I tried it. I'm glad I did."

"You were in a band?" I asked.

"No, but my own dream, I was going to be a photographer, from when I was fifteen, that's the big idea. You have to assist for years before you can even think about getting your own studio. I had to give it up."

Maybe Para was right. Maybe starting a band was a fantasy, something I needed to work through. Maybe it would be smart to give it up now, and focus my energies on something with a better payoff, see if I could work up the ranks at BrandSolve.

We took the short walk back to her apartment, both of us stumbling. Inside her place, we kissed hard, then she walked across the room and sat down hard on a chair. "Gary, look out," she said, and pulled off her shirt. "Wardrobe malfunction." Her bra was blue and shiny. She kicked off her shoes, the clunky heels hitting the wooden floor with two huge bangs. Her cat came over and rubbed her bare ankles.

PARA: So, is it sexual harassment for us to fool around?
GARY: Absolutely.
PARA: Good.

She got into bed and I followed, still dressed, and as you might expect when Benchley gets in bed, I performed a miracle: I removed her bra with one hand, no fumbling. Before me there were: nipples. Nipples! Brown, firm, warm, like the glass eyes on a teddy bear. Para began to arrange the half-dozen pillows on the bed, and then tucked in a sheet corner that had come undone. She reclined. I put my hand on her stomach, palm on her navel. "Yes," she said. *Indeed,* I thought.

The Benchley technique is one of small motions and great subtlety, and has shown itself about 75 percent effective in prior studies. I started Sigur Rós slow, then built up to a Joy Division tempo ("She's Lost Control"), and on to New Order (from "Blue Monday" through "Temptation"), and finally, to "She Is Beautiful" by Andrew W. K. Para began to yell out "goddamn" over and over, so I finished the performance with sixty-four bars at drum and bass speed. She collapsed into the pillows with a whoomph.

I flexed my sore index finger in victory and waited for sweet reciprocation. A minute later, she still hadn't moved, then another minute. It's hard to know exactly how long, because in that condition time is on pause, everything is frozen with anticipation. I bumped my hips against hers, softly.

"Oh, Gary, I'm sorry," she said. "What about you?" With sluggish movements she tried to undo my belt. I helped her with the buckle and had my pants off in a snare hit. She found me under the blankets, and a wave of warm relief ran through me. I was a man again, in full contact. Para jerked her wrist a few times and stopped. She let out a long sigh.

"In the morning, OK?" she said. "I'm so sorry. I promise."

"That's fine," I said.

"You're a gentleman," she said.

Within a moment she began to whistle gently through her nose. I, on the other hand, had plenty of energy and felt wide awake. I listened to buses run up and down the street, one every half hour. Finally, as the sparrows started up outside, I fell asleep.

I woke to hear her say, "Jesus!" She bounded out of bed and I caught a glimpse of naked before she vanished into the bathroom. I got up, wearing only a T-shirt, and put on my slacks. I opened the bathroom door with a cautious "Hello?"

"I'm totally late," she said from the shower. "I didn't set the alarm. I have a meeting in like an hour." Then, "Gary, can you feed Butter?" Para dressed in a hurry, blouse and slacks, and we made our way to the subway platform.

She kissed me, and put her hand on my side, and I put my hand on her back. Then I watched her get onto the F train, pressing into a pile of commuters. The doors closed.

The next day, I got in to work to find Para on her way out to lunch with some other designers. She smiled at me as we passed. She'd sent me an email.

From: para@brandsolve.com
To: gary@brandsolve.com

Mr. Benchley,

Last night was GREAT (sorry that it was so one-way though). Also, this is weird to write, but I've been thinking, I need to go really slow right now. For lots of reasons.

So just be patient with me, OK? I would like to keep hanging out and being friends, and maybe more than that. But I just need to test the waters.

—P

It was a little unsettling to get that message when she was a few feet away. But what could I do? I wrote back one word: "Definitely," and denied my impulse to wink when she returned from lunch. I reminded myself that sex wasn't always supposed to be about mutual gratification. Then I pulled my business card from my wallet and looked at my name and title. Later, I checked her blog. She had posted exactly one line:

Complexity

Sometimes complexity is a beautiful thing.

I had absolutely no idea what that meant. Was I the complexity? Was sex complex? After hours of pondering, I couldn't come up with a solution.

With Para busy healing her psychic wounds and writing cryptic blog posts, I had no excuse but to start my quest for a bassist. For three hours, I strolled around Williamsburg, trying to work up my nerve. Finally, I stopped in at Mugs and had three two-dollar pints, then went back out to the street and walked up to the first cool-looking black guy I saw. I reminded myself not to address him as "Bro" because that would seem too familiar.

GARY: Excuse me, I'm sorry—do you play bass guitar?
COOL-LOOKING BLACK GUY (*worn out, annoyed*): Uh, no.
GARY: Thank you.

I repeated this up and down Bedford. Most people just shook their heads, expecting me to ask them for money, or said, "No, I don't play bass guitar." A few of the people I stopped were hostile.

GARY: . . . bass guitar?
GUY: What the fuck is that supposed to mean?
GARY: I just was wondering.
GUY: Fuck you, man.

I found a guy, cool-looking with dreadlocks, who said that yes, he played bass, and also trumpet. My heart began to pound, but then he said he was already in a band, and gave me a flyer.

I went out again the next night. This time, I was even more anxious. I have a bad memory for faces, and I was worried I would ask the same guy twice, and he would think I was one of those white people who can't tell black people apart.

Before I left work, I told Scott how my search was going.

"Oh, my God," he said. "Tell me that you are not doing that."

"Why?" I said. "I'm committed to diversity."

"It's racial profiling," Scott said.

"It's affirmative rock action," I said.

"It's tokenism."

"You weren't freaked when it was a token hot chick drummer."

He thought about that for a moment. "OK. We live in a society that accepts sexism more than racism. But neither one is appropriate."

"Come on," I said. "It's like we're casting a play. We're creating a band that everyone can relate to."

"What about musical ability?"

"You're like a broken record. You have to trust me, Scott. We asked the universe for a hot chick drummer—"

"Actually, we asked Craigslist."

"And Bedford Avenue. And it provided."

Nineteen cool-looking black guys in their twenties later, outside of North Six, I met Jacob. He was standing alone and had an excellent cool-nerd look, wearing an untucked striped shirt and a pair of geek slacks. He was a little overweight, and all of it was topped off with a bushy goatee and thick black glasses. His hair came out six inches from his head.

JACOB (*surprised*): Yeah, I play bass guitar.

GARY: I knew you did.

JACOB: You did?

GARY: Absolutely. You have bass player all over you. The beard, the hair, the jacket.

JACOB (*confused*): So, uh . . .

GARY: Do you want to be in a band?

JACOB: (*Laughs*) Who doesn't want to be in a band?

After a little coaxing, he let me buy him a beer. And, miraculously, when he heard the words "indie prog," and my recounting of Scott's philosophy of music, he did not recoil in horror.

"That's actually not totally wrong," he said.

"I'm telling you, Jacob. The prog aesthetic, the indie vibe."

"But look," he said. "I've only been playing on and off for like two years. I'm not that good."

"Don't worry. We have effects processors."

We kept drinking. He was a very attentive guy, and at first he mostly listened. I told him about my road to Williamsburg, my struggle to get a band together, describing Scott and Katherine. In exchange, he gave me his story: He was twenty-seven and wrote for *Matchstick,* a magazine I knew and loved, a cooler version of *Blender* that reviewed not just music but graphic novels and anime and documentaries.

"Dude!" I said. *"Matchstick."*

"Yeah."

"That is like the best magazine. It was all I read in college."

"I'm kind of sorry to hear that," said Jacob.

"What's it like? I mean, do you guys just get any CD you want?"

"Mostly."

"And you're all just listening to music, all the time?"

He nodded. "It's not that big a deal."

"You're like, defining the musical consciousness of the entire country, man. It's a *huge* responsibility."

A song came over the jukebox. I didn't recognize it. Jacob told me it was Van Morrison, "Astral Weeks," and went on to talk about the album, using terms like "planned serendipity," "innate vagueness," and "zone of jazz-improvised chaos."

" . . . And Van recorded it when he was twenty-two."

"Same age as me," I said.

"Uh . . . yeah, I guess so."

We talked about the Beatles for a few minutes, as people do (he had no favorite, preferring to take them as a whole), and I asked Jacob how he'd come to playing bass. He told me he'd lived in New York for the last four years. Before that, he'd traveled around a lot, lived all over the place—London for six months, Seattle for a summer.

"I should put my money where my mouth is, right?" he said. "So my roommate sold me his bass."

"Awesome. But you're not in a band or anything now, right?"

"No," he said. "I kept trying to get something together. But I'm either too serious for people, or not good enough yet if they're serious."

I felt a wave of happiness rush over me and took a long drink. It was our fourth round, and we were talking a hundred bands a minute. Jacob suggested a game, making a list of all the groups that were named after animals. I had Cat Power, Counting Crows, and the Beastie Boys. He had Snoop Dogg, Super Furry Animals, Henry Cow, Le Tigre, the Jesus Lizard, Danger Mouse, Modest Mouse, Mouse on Mars, and 16 Horsepower. I gave him the last one after much debate. He also told me about Hatebeak, a metal band with a parrot on vocals, and Caninus, a grindcore band with pit bulls for singers, both honorable mentions.

"Enough animals," said Jacob. "Tell me about your guilty pleasures."

"Like, um, Internet porn?"

He laughed. "No, dude. I mean musically."

"I don't know," I said.

"Like, what music is embarrassing to you? I mean, I love Steve Winwood, 'Back in the High Life.' That's a great song."

I didn't know that one.

"Or that Christina Aguilera song," said Jacob, "the one—"

"God, no."

"Not even Alanis?" Jacob said. I shook my head.

"I guess I don't even need to ask you about Michael, then," said Jacob.

"Which Michael?" I asked.

It turned out he meant Michael Jackson. I had sudden concerns about someone joining my band who liked to listen to alleged pedophiles. Although actually I didn't suspect Jacob of condoning pedophilia, I was bothered that he liked the music's overproduction. But Scott was into prog, and that was turning out to be an asset. Maybe Jacob would bring a pop sensibility into the group. He had the look, and the attitude, and the knowledge of music. I made another pitch, hoping to seal the deal.

"Man," I said, "you have got to get involved with us. We're all in the same place. You'd be perfect."

"What's the name of the band?" he asked.

"We're still working that out," I said.

He definitely looked interested, and said he was probably up for a practice session, to see if it worked out. I couldn't ask for more.

"This is hilarious. Someone just picks me up off the street as a bass player. I have to do it."

"It'll work. I can tell."

"Come on," he asked. "How did you know I played bass?"

Confident in our growing relationship, I explained my method, and our goals for a diverse band. When I was finished, he stared at me for a long moment.

"So you racially profiled me as a bass player?"

I nodded, smiling.

"You accused me of Playing Bass While Black."

"Kind of."

He said, "That is some shit right there." His voice was very quiet.

"You just looked like a bass player," I said.

"Like a *black* bass player."

A moment before, Jacob had been an enthusiastic fellow indie rock aficionado, an animated and interested music nerd like me. Now he looked worn out, like a tired public school teacher facing a class of very slow-witted kids. He let out a long sigh that would have put Scott to shame.

"I am the most profiled man in the world," he said.

"This has happened before?"

"Well, not with bass playing."

"So, like, you get pulled over a lot when you're driving?"

"What, in a Cavalier?"

It turned out that his life had been filled with profiling, not only by police, but by everyone. People always wanted to include him in things. In high school, he said, "They were doing *Othello,* and they asked me to try out. So I auditioned for Iago. You could see them losing their minds." He was always asked to be in brochures, to contribute editorials to school papers, to speak at Student Diversity Day. Apparently he'd done really well on his SATs, and Harvard called him six times and arranged two personal visits. It turned out that being black in America put a lot of weird pressure on a person.

"So you went to Harvard?"

"Fuck that. You ever meet any Harvard grads?"

"No."

"Take one douchebag and shake hard."

Instead of Harvard, he'd gone to Bennington. I thought of Para, who'd grown up in Vermont. And thinking of her, I realized that in the space of two weeks, I'd managed to say something sexist to Para, offend Scott by using "gay" the wrong way, and racially profile Jacob. I'd always considered myself a white liberal, but maybe I wasn't liberal enough.

"So you're kind of caught between being black and being, uh—"

Jacob held up his palm. "No, dude, I'm black. I'm not caught between anything on that front. OK, when you saw me, the first thing you said was 'black guy,' right?"

"Not just that—"

"Just fess up. It's OK."

"Yes. I thought, there's a cool-looking black guy, I wonder if he plays bass."

"So maybe I'd love to play bass in your band, but now it's totally tied up in my skin color, and you're commoditizing my negritude."

"What exactly am I doing?"

"You're affirmatively activating me, but I'm already fully activated. I'm ready to go, no approval necessary."

I thought back to my conversation with Scott, when I'd proclaimed my dedication to "affirmative rock action." Jacob had a point.

"I still think you're perfect," I said. "All you have to do is bring your bass."

"You haven't heard me play."

"Trust me," I said. "It'll work."

Jacob told me he'd think about it, but I could see that he was lying, trying to get out of the conversation. He shook my hand firmly and told me that it had been interesting, shaking his head a little. I tried to apologize again, but he cut me off and turned to leave. I watched him go, and sat for a moment at the bar, the noise of Williamsburg around me.

I was relieved that Jacob was gone, because he'd started to make me feel like a racist. And I didn't like to think of myself that way, not even a little. Rather than getting Jacob completely enthused, sharing the vision, I'd pissed him off, made him defensive. I'd been acting from instinct, from the heart, and it felt weird to think that my heart could have weird ideas about black people.

But I still wanted him to meet Scott and Katherine. He had the right vibe, the right sense of what mattered in music. He wrote for the best music magazine in the world. Even if he wasn't cool and black, he was exactly what we needed.

I went home and turned on my creaking laptop, and googled "jacob matchstick" to see if I could find out his last name. There it was: a story he'd written comparing Kid Koala to Terminator X, with his email address at the bottom. With some drunken bravado, and without waiting for doubt to take over, I wrote him an email.

To: Jacob.Clinton@matchstickmagazine.com
From: garybenchleyrockstar@yahoo.com
Subject: Friendly neighborhood profiler

It's Gary. Dude, first, apologies. Second, I want you to give us a try. I don't care if you're black or white or puce. You have the vibe. Come over next Saturday. You can be whatever you want. If you want to bring your negritude, that will work, but we can just tell everyone that you're just really tan, or Canadian. What I really want is your Jacobtude.

I could hear Scott screaming at me: "We don't even know if he can *play bass*." But that wasn't what I cared about. I felt certain that Jacob would make us whole. A few minutes later, as I was about to sign off and go to bed, his response popped into my in-box.

Gary Benchley, you are a persistent profiling white man. That said, you actually listened when I schooled you on modern race relations. This is, sadly, a rare quality in a person. Also, I want to be in a band. So let us go forward in the spirit of brotherhood.
Read some Cornel West before rehearsal, and I'll bring my bass and my Jacobtude.
JC

I gave a quiet cheer, trying not to wake up my roommates, and searched the web for Cornel West, who turns out to be a Christianity-influenced Marxist transcendentalist pragmatist, as well as a hip-hop musician. I wrote another email to Scott, Katherine, and Jacob, introducing Jacob around, and we set up our first practice, a week from Saturday, at Katherine's place. The next day,

I went out and bought *The Cornel West Reader,* and got through a few paragraphs, then decided to save it for later.

I closed my eyes and saw a crowd, thousands of heads and bodies, and a huge, mystical voice recited the lineup. "Mr. Scott Spark on keyboards," it said. "Ms. Katherine Passerine on drums. Mr. Jacob Clinton on bass." Then the roar of the thousands went up as the voice said, "And Mr. Gary Benchley on rhythm guitar and vocals." The applause was so loud it was static. It went on for a full minute, until the scene dissolved, and I was back at my desk, in a room lit ghost-blue by the computer's screen-saver.

Nothing had changed in the world. The moon was half full, and the buses were running outside the window. I still had my job, my apartment. But even if you couldn't see it, something was different. The beginning was at hand. The hard work had just started. And where before there was nothing, there was now a band.

Schizopolis

The first rehearsal of our yet-to-be-named band was held at the Monotreme Institute for Extraordinary Art, and was not exactly a success. It had been a long week. At work, as clients called with urgent branding issues, I felt my rock gland shriveling, my indie secretions going dry. I needed an urgent dose of vitamin GBV.

Glooming up the workplace further was Para. She was perfectly nice, and would often touch my shoulder, but she was too busy to spend much time. She would pass my desk, on her way to the bathroom, but would give no acknowledgment that Gary Benchley sat mere feet away, chock-full of humble love.

My desk looks out at the bathrooms, so I had no choice but to sit and wait for the hiss of water through the pipes, followed by the quieter sound of the sink. Finally, the door opened to show Para's slender outline, framed by the fluorescent lights of the women's room. I winked to her, and she smiled thinly in return. It was like we were passing ships, and I was running up flags to signal: Para, the man you're ignoring has mapped your inward parts with the tip of his digits! Love him! But she wasn't looking. She only sailed back to her desk. The process would repeat later in the day. For the duration of those bathroom visits, I knew what she was excreting, and when. But I did not know her heart.

I decided not to let her slip through my fingers. I invited myself over to her place that night. But nothing came of it. We watched three hours of TV without saying much. Whatever was wrong, we didn't talk about it. She needed to get up at seven in the morning to fly to Pittsburgh for a meeting, and she'd been having trouble sleeping, so she said good night, and I went home on the G train.

Walking into my apartment at midnight, I heard strange grunts emerging from Charles's open door. Down the hall, David was leaning by the window smoking a cigarette, listening to the same noises. I walked gingerly past Charles's room, looking in long enough to see that, indeed, he was having sex. The woman in the bed looked like Patmavadi, but I wasn't sure.

"You've seen this?" David asked. I hadn't.

"He won't close the door," David explained. "He wants the sexual energy to be shared with the rest of the world. Closing the door ruins the communal human experience." David motioned down the hall. "Come on," he said.

We walked the few steps down the hall and stood quietly in the doorway, watching Charles's ass bob up and down. It was Patmavadi underneath him. Her eyes were closed, her mouth open, breathing hard. David exhaled a large plume of smoke through the open door and shrugged. The impassioned couple were lost in their own world, no idea they had an audience. After a minute, I followed David into his mostly empty room: a bed, a chair, and a desk, with a laptop and family pictures on the desk.

"That is disgusting," I said.

"Reminds me of college. I asked him to shut the door a year ago, and he gave me like a half-hour lecture on *qi*. So now I'm like, what the hell. Free entertainment."

"I can't believe we were watching that."

"Tantric shit. It goes on for hours."

"Hours?"

"Yep. Not me. If I wanted to have sex for hours my girlfriend would demand overtime. Want a cigarette?"

I turned him down and sat on the edge of his bed. We talked about his girlfriend; she also worked in finance. I'd never seen her, because he wouldn't bring her back to the apartment. "No need for her to see this place," he said. "She thinks I'm worth a damn."

I asked him about the photo on his desk. It was his mother and father, he told me. "They're the reason I live in this hole," he said. "My mom needs some help. So I hand them about three or four grand a month for meds and miscellaneous." The picture was framed in silver. In it, his mother wore a blue blouse with shoulder pads. His father was in an orange blazer with a red tie.

"That's a lot of money," I said.

"My dad hates it," he said. "Pride thing. But my mom is so proud of me. 'That's a good son,' you know? He writes the checks. Sometimes I think she got leukemia just to see if I really love her. But I do. I just love the moms." He put his hand on the picture frame.

I said, "I love my mom, too."

David nodded. "You have to love her. You were inside of her. I mean, think about that. You were just hanging out inside your mom's uterus for nine months."

"Come on."

"Seriously. How can you not love a woman when you've been inside of her for nine months?"

"It sounds like that's what Charles is aiming for right now."

"It's the ultimate," David said.

It surprised me when I blurted out that I loved my mom. She and I had been calling each other on the weekends, but those calls were just short summaries of events, everything-is-good-talk-to-you-soon. Now, suddenly, I wanted details. I wanted to know if the car was out of the shop, if my sister had landed that internship she wanted for the summer, how my brother was doing on his aircraft carrier. I wanted to know who was playing at Valentine's. I wanted her to wake me up in the morning and make me pancakes, and I wanted to tell her about Para and ask her advice.

David and I sat together, two men who didn't know each other very well, sharing a moment of mother-love.

"And what about your dad?" he asked.

"Well, he doesn't really get what I'm about," I said. "We don't talk much."

It felt odd to be talking about my family as sounds of tantric ecstasy resounded through the apartment. Charles and Patmavadi showed no signs of letting up, so I cleared out for a while. The night was warm and dry. At first I was heading for a drink, but none of the bars looked welcoming, so I kept walking, past the clubs and old warehouses, until I came to the water. There, in the company of other wandering silhouettes, I looked out at Midtown, and listened to the river as it lapped the mossy rocks.

Had anyone else ever been this lonely in New York?

But I didn't stay low for long. Looking at the buildings and lights rising over the dark of the East River made me feel bigger than my problems. The skyline reminded me of the way music looks in a mixing program on a computer. In Pro Tools, songs are shown as waves. Loud parts of a song are high peaks; quiet parts are valleys. Manhattan looked like that, peaks and valleys, a song thirteen miles long.

I tried to hum the buildings, remembering the parts of the city I couldn't see. The song opens very quietly, in the park at the Battery, but then gets Nirvana-huge with Wall Street's distortion and noise. Then it fades quickly, but only to build up to the climax of Midtown. There you come to the Empire State Building, huge and orchestrated: grand piano, drums, and acoustic bass. Still heading uptown, it gets a little quieter, with another loud moment for the Citibank building (that building is definitely a synthesizer solo).

Once you pass Midtown, the song begins to fade, all the way to Inwood.

The skyline was a song played at the biggest concert in the world. Listening to it from the shores of Williamsburg, I was both onstage, playing the New York song, and listening in the audience. A few feet behind me, a man said to his girlfriend, "Isn't this better than television?" I couldn't hear her response, but I nodded, and watched a tugboat steam south toward the Atlantic. I thought: That's a good job. You get off the land, wave good-bye to your depressed, distant girlfriend, and take to the rivers in your tug. You can forget everything that's happening on land, navigating by the lights of the buildings.

Still, you spend your life in service of the bigger boats. Sometimes I feel shame at not already being famous. Not ambition, but shame, as if I've failed. I wonder if that's something people have always felt, or if it's new.

I turned my back on that massive stage of river and skyscrapers, walking back to the streets, to the clubs and warehouses, the endless string of young Billburgians. Once more I was in the audience. The tugboat gave a good-bye toot behind me.

Rehearsal was on Saturday. On Friday night, my father called. We hadn't spoken in two or three months, but my father is a career politician, a state assemblyman, and just leaps into conversations without worrying about context.

GARY: I was just talking about you.
DAD: There you go. Me too. How's things?
GARY: Doing good. All great.
DAD: Your cash stream is OK?
GARY: Limited, you know. But I'm doing fine.
DAD: You're still a secretary?
GARY: Office assistant.

DAD: But you're still looking for something more permanent.

GARY: It's OK for now. I'm working on some other things.

DAD: You know, you're in the finance capital of the world. There are a lot of jobs in finance.

GARY: Oh, I know. My roommate works in finance.

DAD: Might want to get some advice from him.

My father told me about work, how much he was doing for the people in his district. There were zoning laws and budget planning. There was a quest for funds for a senior center and new rules regarding parking permits. He was already organizing barbecues with friends to coincide with the Democratic National Convention in the summer. His wife, Pat, was to be promoted to a senior position in IT at the NYS DMV ASAP, and her daughter, Kris, was away at science camp.

GARY: Sounds busy up there.

DAD: I tell you, Gary, you put a broomstick in my ass I could sweep the capitol floor.

GARY: (*False laughter*)

DAD: So how are things with the ladies?

GARY: Good.

DAD: Out there playing the field.

GARY: Yeah.

DAD: Met anyone special?

GARY: I think so.

DAD: Good for you. She has a name.

GARY: Para.

DAD: Nice name.

GARY: I'm working hard, Dad. I'm starting a band.

DAD: Excellent! Just as long as you keep your priorities. Bank account first, right?

Suddenly I was very tired, thinking of my bank account, the sad, small number that the ATM told me was my net worth whenever I put my card in the slot. I begged off the line and put the phone in its cradle. Nine hours later I woke up with the sunlight, with a knot in my stomach. First rehearsal.

Scott and I picked up Jacob with his bass and amp, which he threw into the back of Scott's Element, alongside Scott's smaller, portable Yamaha synth and my Fender. Scott and Jacob shook hands, and with a bootleg of the new Interpol on the CD player, we took off for Monotreme.

Katherine answered the buzzer. "Welcome, bitches," she said. We lugged our equipment up to her room. She had shoveled her clothes out of the way and moved her bed to make a rehearsal space around the drums. To start us off, Scott put a CD into Katherine's stereo and shared the music he and I had already created. Katherine began to giggle. Emboldened by her giggle, Jacob said, "I mean, I'm all for reverb, but . . ."

Scott made a sour face, put out by people impugning his studio wizardry. I began to panic. What if, after all the work to bring everyone together, no one got along?

I realized that throwing four people together—two of them strangers who'd never met, and one of them, Jacob, who thought I was a racist profiler—was not a recipe for instant rock greatness. I had that feeling you get when you take someone to see a movie you truly love. You've talked about this movie for days. And they agree to come, and you can't focus on the movie because you're so worried they won't like it. You watch them watch the film, and the movie starts to look terrible through your eyes. This had happened to me in college, when I took a date to see the movie *Old School*.

Now, looking at the three faces of my bandmates, I had that feeling at fifty thousand watts. I decided to reiterate the policy of true honesty.

"All right," I said, "Jacob says too much reverb. Excellent. Everyone needs to say exactly what they feel about this band. We have to have total freedom to be critical."

"Good. Because that sucked," said Katherine.

"Thanks, Katherine," I said. "Scott?"

"Yeah," said Scott, "thanks."

A long silence ensued. Jacob was the first to speak. He said, "So how do we get started?"

"Maybe we could play a cover," I said.

"What do we have in common?" asked Katherine.

Half an hour later, with a few dozen bands mentioned and discarded, Katherine went online and got the chords for "I Walk the Line," printing copies for each of us. Scott counted it off: "One, two, one, two." And then nothing happened. We all just looked at him.

We tried again, and this time everyone started to play. Scott was able to do something nice with the grand piano sound on his synth, and Katherine played a simple rhythm. Jacob and I struggled.

SCOTT: Let me . . . can I?

JACOB: Go ahead.

SCOTT: Let's see. It's (*playing synth*)—OK, F, G, A. Then . . . huh.

They worked together for a while, until Jacob had it down. At the same time, I looked at the tablature and tried to figure out the fingerings. Finally we gave it another try. What followed was the strangest, least competent cover ever attempted: as I stomped through the song (A, E7, A, repeat, A, D, A, then back to A, E7, A) on my Fender, Jacob picked up the bassline and began to play with confidence. He looked amused. I looked over to see Scott nodding at Jacob, and felt a huge sense of relief. Katherine was smiling.

Scott went to change some setting on his synth and accidentally triggered a preset, one we'd used before over at his place, called

"Computus Maximus," all saw waves and delay. Suddenly, "I Walk the Line" became IDM, and Katherine, inspired, began to hit the snare in a harsh, military rhythm. Jacob stuck to his bassline. I tried to sing as I played. But the combination was a bit much to handle. "For you I'd, uh, know, to tide. You're the line, the walk I tide," I sang.

It ended, sort of, and Jacob laughed.

"That was fantastic," he said. "Johnny Cash on Mars. Keep that synth sound."

"Kind of not bad, right?" I said.

"Industrial Johnny Cash works for me," said Katherine.

"Except for the music part," said Scott.

"But we'll get that," I said. I could tell that even Scott, though still grumpy, was engaged. This was something we could build on. We tried it again, and the song came into more focus, everyone figuring out their place. And in the middle of the sounds, I thought of the phone call with my father. Here at Katherine's apartment, we were creating something new. Working in finance, how often did you get to create something totally new?

Actually, we were playing a cover of a forty-eight-year-old song. But the point is that something was happening. Where before there was nothing, there was now music. Yes, it sounded like a giant robot attacking a bag of marshmallows. Yes, we were turning one of the most essential, minimalist songs of the last fifty years into a cross between the Butthole Surfers and Vangelis. But it was a start.

We decided covers would be the way to go while we got used to one another, and picked out a few more to prepare: "Hotel Yorba" by the White Stripes, "What Is the Light" by the Flaming Lips, and "Year of the Cat" by Al Stewart. The last was Scott's suggestion, because it lent itself to long synth solos.

"So what are we calling this thing?" asked Jacob.

"I've been giving it a lot of thought," I said.

"Me too," said Katherine.

Awkward silence. No one wanted to go first. Secretly, I wanted to call the band the Gary Benchley Rock Experience, but I didn't think that demonstrated a proper community spirit.

"I was thinking we could call it No More Bullies," I said.

"Why?" Jacob asked.

"I don't know," I said.

"How about the Yellow Skulls?" said Scott. "I think it would make for cool posters."

"It sucks," said Katherine. "I always thought there should be a band called Porn Biscuit."

"Why that?" Scott asked.

"It's two things everyone likes," said Katherine.

"There's already a New Pornographers," said Jacob.

"But they lack biscuits," said Katherine.

"I'm antiporn," said Jacob.

"Why's that?" Katherine asked.

"Because it's exploitative," said Jacob.

"I like looking at cocks," said Katherine.

There was a moment of quiet as we absorbed the conversation. I stared at Katherine, not sure how to respond, then looked over at Scott.

SCOTT: What?

GARY: Nothing.

SCOTT: Yes, Gary, I like looking at cocks, too.

KATHERINE: Good for you.

JACOB: I'm just saying—

KATHERINE: That you're a self-hating cock-haver. I know the type. Oh, my God, I do.

With the conversation moving toward genitals, Scott suggested that we table the band name discussion and come to the next rehearsal with lists of ideas. We went through "I Walk the Line" again, without much improvement. Finally we called it an afternoon, and Scott, Jacob, and I said good-bye to Katherine and went down to the car.

I asked Scott for the time, and he told me it was 4:50. That meant that I had exactly ten minutes to get to my destination, which was my first official "date" with Para. This meant that I had already screwed up.

The other day, I'd decided that I had to stop thinking about Para and move on with my life. I'd been checking her blog, which, between the postings about new Flash scripts and the thrilling dramas of the blog world, was interspersed with more cryptic, brief entries that made me slightly insane to contemplate. Like:

Changing
There are worse things than being in the middle of something. At least the gray times are kept at bay.

Or:

Transition
Maybe it's time. I think that, and then I think something else. I don't know which direction to go. Too many paths to take, not all of them clear.

Reading these, I figured I was better off not going out with her. It would be like dating a sphinx. I decided to tell her this, that I wanted to stay friends and not worry too much about what happened, so I walked her to the train after work, and she kissed me on the lips.

"I want to spend more time with you," she said. "I think I'm wasting my time if I don't."

"I agree," I'd said. "I feel exactly the same way."

"I want to go on a date," she'd said. "I want to do it right."

"Definitely," I'd said.

We set our first date for Saturday; I figured it would be a perfect day. I'd go to rehearsal, then meet my new girlfriend at a movie theater in Brooklyn. Then, I'd hoped, we would go for a walk in the chilly air, and talk seriously about the relationship and what it meant to us.

I called her cell, and she picked up, explaining the situation. "I'm standing here," she said, and the cell phone connection cut her voice down to a snake's hiss. I promised speed.

"Scott, where is the Pavilion Theater?" I asked.

"The Pavilion?"

"Yes."

"It's like half an hour away. It's way the hell out by Coney Island," he said.

"What?" The buzz from the rehearsal was gone. "Moviefone said it was . . . what, do I take the train? Is there a cab here? I am in such shit."

"What the hell were you thinking?" Scott asked. "Why would you say you'd meet her out there?"

I saw that Jacob was laughing. Scott then told me that the Pavilion was about three minutes away. "Get in the car," he said.

I counted the blocks as we drove, desperately searching the streets for a movie marquee. Scott and Jacob made fun of me the whole way, bonding over my nerves. Finally we pulled up.

"There she is," said Scott.

"By the look on her face, someone fucked up," said Jacob.

"Not me," said Scott. "I know how to use a clock to keep track of time."

"Me too," said Jacob. "The big hand is over the little hand. Just like at Michael Jackson's house."

"Jacob, I don't know you that well, but you're an asshole," I said. Jacob gave a huge smile.

"What about me?" asked Scott.

"You're an asshole, too," I said. I jumped out and Para watched me pull my Fender from the back of Scott's car.

"The guitar is coming to the movie, too?" she said. She turned her head to look at nothing, as if looking at me was just too awful at the moment. Walking to the window, guitar in hand, I prayed to God the movie wasn't sold out.

The film was about a young couple who couldn't make their relationship work, no matter how hard they tried; the man kept cheating on the woman, who finally cheated in revenge, and then there was a stabbing. At a certain point in the film, I reached over and put my hand on Para's knee and squeezed. But she didn't squeeze back. She just looked at the screen. No reaction, no moment of connection. For a first date, it was going kind of poorly, especially when you consider that she and I had already had relations.

The movie ended, and we left. I was glad to be back outside. On-screen, everything had crumbled into ashes, but here, in Brooklyn, near the entrance to Prospect Park, the sun had just set and cars tootled by with music coming out of their stereos.

GARY: You want to go for a walk?
PARA: God, that made me want to kill myself.
GARY: The weather is really not bad.

I'd only wandered through Prospect Park once before. It was amazingly quiet compared to the street. I could hear my guitar case knocking against my knee, and Para's shoes paddling over the asphalt. To fill the silence, I said, "I don't know if I like Prospect Park as much as Central Park."

"I didn't know it was a competition," said Para.

"Maybe the parks could have a battle," I said, starting to ramble. "Central Park would be like, 'My fountain is bigger, motherfucker,' and Prospect Park would be like, 'Hey, I am so much better for bicyclists,' and Central Park would say, 'How many movies have you been in?' and Prospect Park's all like, 'Maybe I could come over and jog around your reservoir, Central Park, except for the part where I get raped and beheaded.' And Central Park would be like—"

"Gary," Para said, taking my hand. I smiled and went quiet at her touch.

She took a deep breath. "That movie made me upset," she said.

Talking about Central Park brought to mind the Republican National Convention coming up in the summer. There was a huge antiwar march that was forbidden to go to Central Park. Para is a serious marcher, and keeps tabs on these things. I'm a marcher in theory, but the opportunities in upstate New York were limited. During college, I had taken back the night a few times, and with a few dozen peers, I'd yelled angry words at the provost's window regarding free trade. But that wasn't the same as big-city activism. Para's friends, many of whom she has met via her blog, were already planning large-scale activities involving balloons and puppets, months before the actual event.

As we walked up a hill in the park, in the dark, a steady stream of bike nerds passed us, all in Spandex. What golf is to the suburbs, bicycles are to Brooklyn, and these men were in the race of their lives. In contrast, I was tired just from watching their legs pump, tired from band practice earlier that day, tired from the lamentations of the movie.

"I forgot to ask," Para said, "how was rehearsal?"

"It was awesome," I said. "That's why I was late."

"Is the band going to work?"

"Absolutely!" I said.

"What are you working on?"

Para thinks my music career is a joke, so I didn't want to push my luck with stories of potential tours or Johnny Cash covers. I looked around for something to change the drift of the conversation and spied four men in black-and-yellow bumblebee suits riding by, flying down the hill.

"Look!" I said. "It's Stryper! They ride bicycles now."

"How do you know Stryper? That was before your time."

My older brother had been a huge Stryper fan, I explained, and Stryper was a major part of my burgeoning rock consciousness. When I was nine I gazed up at his large Stryper poster (next to the more secular Pink Floyd "Momentary Lapse of Reason" poster), and asked, "Who is that girl?" That girl, my brother explained with a sneer, was Oz Fox, a master of the double-necked guitar, dedicated to both pyrotechnics and Christ.

"Wow," said Para. "I only made fun of Stryper. There were these fundamentalist kids in my high school who loved them, and the T-shirts were just amazing. I never heard any of their music."

"It's some remarkable music."

"Does he still listen to them? Your brother?"

"Not anymore. He has pretty good taste, if you discount the Steve Miller."

"Where is he, again?"

"San Diego."

"But he's not going to Iraq."

"I don't think so."

My brother *could* be sent to Iraq, but I wasn't too worried. As a junior lieutenant on one of the largest aircraft carriers in the world, the USS *Ronald Reagan* (motto: "Peace through strength"), he is rarely put in front of bullets. He's in charge of loading things into other things—like plane engines, or crates of food, or bombs.

"Does it freak you out to have a brother in the navy?" Para asked.

"What do you mean?" I asked.

"Like, you're kind of against Bush."

"Oh. No, that's fine. My brother is a Democrat."

Para was raised by agnostic high school teachers in Vermont. Her father taught science, and her mother taught English. (Her folks were divorced during her freshman year in college.) When she was fifteen, Para had serious conversations about menstruation and civil rights with her mother, and she rode horses. When I was fifteen, I was going to Presbyterian youth group and listening to Seattle grunge.

"We're liberal Presbyterians," I said.

"Which ones are the Presbyterians?" Para asked. "Different than Catholics?"

"The Catholics eat evil cookies and worship a man in a hat," I said.

"Presbyterians believe that?" Para asked.

"No, we're—they're usually very tolerant. That is, Church of Pres USA is tolerant. There are also Evangelical Presbyterians, and they're more about Bible lovin'," I said.

We came to a big pond. There was still some snow on the ground. I thought for a moment about religion, about my own spiritual path. I wondered what my bandmates believed in. Was I playing guitar with atheists? Was someone practicing Zen? I could see Scott going in for Zen. Jacob seemed the atheist type, but he could also have something weird going on—maybe he's a Zoroastrian. As for Katherine, I had no idea. No religion was an obvious fit.

I had been raised to be a churchgoer. It turned out that Para hadn't been. She knew a lot about Zen from books and living in Vermont, and had divined her future from both tarot cards and I Ching hexagrams. She knew that Catholics hate abortion, and that there are fundamentalists, and Baptists, and that they are bad. But she didn't really understand the huge variety of experience that is American Protestantism. She never read an annotated, kid-friendly

New Testament, or drank apple cider on a hayride while a twenty-two-year-old youth pastor sang Harry Chapin songs. She never was asked to commit her life to Jesus, at age fourteen, as I was. (It was a beautiful September day. I took my Bible, sang a hymn, was welcomed into the church, and then I went home and cranked "Iron Man" by Sabbath.)

But, Para told me, she believed in God. Or rather, she believed in a magical benevolent force that moves through the universe, a sort of Jedi/Zen/Edie Brickell theology. Whereas I, who know the Apostles' Creed and a miscellany of other prayers, psalms, and hymns by heart, and can sing a rousing version of "40" by U2—I don't believe in God at all.

I lost my faith when I was nineteen. One day I was down in the dorm basement, doing laundry, tapping out the rhythm to "Cocoon" off of *Vespertine* as I sat on the washer. In my heart, I felt the world was a good place, and that things would work out. Then, suddenly, the washer kicked into the spin cycle, and a quiet, inner voice spoke to me. It didn't speak to me in words, but in impressions and emotions, but what it said was something like: "Gary, the world is not good or evil, it's indifferent. God has no plan for you. Also, snakes don't talk, and God has no children." I looked around, but nothing had changed. The washing machine kept spinning.

It was a truly blessed moment for me, and I definitely felt called to atheism. Atheism was something that finally made sense. Before I converted, I would see the Christ on Campus guys with their iron crucifix necklaces, and feel a sense of guilt for being such a poor Christian, for all of my doubts and my resistance to churchgoing. But after I came to atheism, I simply wished them well in their own journeys. I got heavily into science, and learned about the heat death of the universe. I stopped listening to Slayer for the lyrics, and began to enjoy how much they truly rocked musically.

I thought of all this while I held hands with Para. And then, without saying much, we wandered back to her place. Surprisingly, we had sex, or rather, I had sex, and she wiggled around in an accommodating, comforting way. It felt right, like we'd completed the circle. It had taken six weeks, but here we were, dating. Afterward she told me that she had been feeling depressed lately. I had guessed this because, in her bathroom, there was a big sign inside the medicine cabinet that said DO NOT FORGET MEDICATION.

GARY: I knew something was wrong.

PARA: I just get this thing.

GARY (*growing closer, feeling his heart expand*): Depression?

PARA: It's really rough. I can't remember which socks to wear. I forget to eat.

GARY: I'll remind you to eat.

PARA: Sometimes I don't eat for, like, three days.

GARY: You should keep pie on hand.

PARA: That would work.

GARY: Emergency pie.

PARA: And so I went back to my therapist.

GARY: Who is . . . ?

PARA: Dr. Adams.

GARY: He or she?

PARA: She. And she put me back on meds, and they are definitely helping.

GARY: How can I help?

PARA: This was nice, just spending some time.

GARY: You know, I really do love you.

Suddenly the air was gone from the room, as if a thunderstorm had rolled in. The words had slipped out of me. I'd had no intention of uttering them. But there they were.

The thing is, I had been feeling a strong, loving feeling toward Para in the preceding weeks. I could feel her trying to work things out, and I wanted to help her, to support her, and make things work for her, as long as I could be part of the process. If that's not love, what is?

But in New York, love is a huge deal, as complex as real estate. A confession of love in Albany is no big problem. You go to a few movies, you make out, you confess love. If I'd been dating Para in Albany, this wouldn't have been a big deal. Love in New York, however, meant all sorts of things. Because I was always going to leave Albany. Nothing was going to last forever, there. But I was here, working in Manhattan and living in Williamsburg, indefinitely. Maybe for the remainder of my life. And so every decision I could make had ramifications far into the future. And this love would follow me on tour. It branched out across the country. Being in love in New York meant that I'd have to turn down offers of sex in Austin, even if aforesaid offers were delivered by tattooed coeds with purple-dyed pigtails wearing Hard Candy nail polish and baby-doll dresses. And yet, there it was. The words were out there. I could do nothing but listen, and see if she felt the same way, assuming I felt the way I thought I felt.

"Huh," said Para. She paused for a moment. "Thank you."

What comes after you confess your love to your pill-using depressed semi-girlfriend, and she says "Thank you"? What is the correct next step? I had no idea, and no one to guide me.

Para fell asleep, drifting off like a leaf in the breeze. And normally it takes very little for me to fall asleep, but the idea of love was there in the room like some sort of unexploded explosive device, humming. The love bomb squad would have to be called in to defuse it.

Or maybe it would just stay there, a ten-ton killing machine ticking under the bed. I looked at it, and wondered: Did I mean that? Did I love Para? Or, did I want to be in love? Maybe, I thought, in a hundred years, when all of these buildings have given way to the wildflowers, when people live in antigravity castles in the air, someone will wander by. Some young couple with microchips in their spines. They'll walk right over this exact spot, and the love bomb that I dropped tonight will finally go off. And for a moment, the world will be choked with love. The rat will lie down with the pigeon. The exterminator will embrace the cockroach. And the beggar will throw his quarters into the air and dance in a fountain with the cops.

By mid-August we had written three songs. It was time to name our band and book our first gig. New York stank terribly. In Williamsburg, I would wake up, not sure I'd even slept, covered in a foul-smelling grime that blew through the chuffing, useless fan propped in my window. The hallways of my apartment building smelled of fish, and the streets smelled like opening a broken refrigerator. The subway tunnels were dank and hot, and it was plain that the MTA had stopped cleaning them with soap, and started using warm urine instead.

SCOTT: I don't even notice the smell any more.
GARY: How do people live here?
SCOTT: You know, this isn't even a bad summer. This is a nice summer.

Despite the heat and funk, rehearsals had been going well, and Para and I were in a gentle place, talking a lot about nothing, going for walks, and watching TV. I was in a zone of peace, feeling optimistic.

I wanted an air conditioner, but times were tighter than a Tony Levin bassline, and my credit card squeaked in my wallet. My money was already spent on a guitar, on rent, and on snacks. So I slept with the fan on high and regarded my roommates, both asleep in air-conditioned rooms, with raw jealousy.

The air-conditioning habits of Charles, the master of Yogic

Drumming™, chafed me. One night, Charles opened his door as I was getting home. I caught a glimpse of batik wall hangings and felt a blast of cold air strong enough to maintain a glacier, accompanied by the smell of burning incense. Charles would share his sexual energy with the rest of the world, but not his Freon.

My roommate David was much more generous. He would come home to find me sitting on the couch in our living room, and after a few moments of chatting, he'd say, "For Christ's sake, come to my room where it isn't a barbecue." Then we'd talk: about his mother; about my sister, who'd been up to visit and stayed the night; and about the president.

"My friend Fred, middle school friend," he said, "he's over there, in the army. He's into weird stuff, like swimming from Korea to Iraq on the back of a computerized dolphin with microfilm up his ass."

"No shit."

"So I wrote him an email, 'What's up, don't let any camels hump you late at night.' And he writes back, he's just totally disgusted, he's like, you have no idea how stupid this thing is, this is bullshit A to Z, vote Kerry. Your brother's in the navy, right?"

"USS *Ronald Reagan*."

"Shit, Reagan got a boat already?"

"A carrier. They're in San Diego right now."

"Damn. I bet Nancy set that up. I bet Nancy was giving it out to every sailor she could find to get that boat set up. There were a lot of grinning admirals at Reagan's funeral, I bet you."

"There's that possibility, absolutely."

"So is your brother, like, greasing his mizzlemast, or whatever?"

"He's got a girlfriend onshore. I haven't met her. She manages a bookstore."

"And your sister, she's in Pittsburgh?"

"Almost graduated."

"Twenty-one?"

"Twenty. She's graduating early."

"I can't believe she's a geek."

A few weeks ago my sister had crashed on our couch for a night. She'd appeared in a black tank top with blue fringes in her hair, full of winks for David, and jumping into conversation, asking him about the Linux networks at his job, touching his shoulder. After catching sight of her, David had been gathering intelligence.

Now he kept working her into conversation, in order to learn where she lived (she was at school at CMU, and had an internship at the school), what she was like growing up (a whiner), if she had any pets (no), and what she did (a computer geek).

My sister had been in town for a hacker conference where she could build networks and talk about our robot overlords or whatever. She was excited because Jello Biafra, the singer for the Dead Kennedys, was speaking. We'd barely had a conversation, and hadn't even gone out for a drink.

It was strange to see her walk through the door, confident, hair smooth and straight, stomach flat, with the traditional Benchley bosom. My sister had been a sullen girl, always chatting on AOL— someone my friends and I passed by on the way to my room to play Sim City. Now she was much, much cooler than I. After the conference, she left on the midnight bus to Pittsburgh, promising to visit again before long.

"She's a total geek," I said. "She wrote her own Nintendo game when she was twelve."

"What was it called?" David asked.

"Savage Garden," I said.

"Like the band?"

"Yeah, she had a big crush on Savage Garden."

"So what kind of game?"

"You moved the guys from Savage Garden around and they picked up bunches of bananas and shit, and then they could trade them for plane tickets, and that way they could get to their concert."

"Wow," said David. "That sounds like the most boring game imaginable."

"Yeah, but I mean, she was twelve. I had to play-test it like nine thousand times. And I was like, why the bananas?"

"I know why the bananas, man."

"That's my sister, David."

"I got nothing but respect, believe me."

David and I finished our beer. It was time for me to return to the thick warmth of my room, smelling of kielbasa from the sausage factory around the corner.

"You know, I'd let you sleep here," said David.

"Nah."

"But it'd be kind of super gay."

"I understand," I said. "My fan's doing the job."

I went to my room and settled back into my hot pillow, trying to tune out the street noise, the buses going by. I had a Bonnie "Prince" Billy song in my head, about being a cinematographer, and I kept thinking about the draft, since they're supposed to bring it back in 2005. I don't know if Baghdad is as humid as New York, or if it's a dry heat, like Arizona. But I don't want to go in any case.

I guess I should feel some patriotism, some desire to help. My father, the state assemblyman, used to give me lectures about public service, usually when my grades slipped down to B's, and at one point he offered to pass my name up the ranks in case I wanted the governor's recommendation for the Naval Academy (I did not). But I just want to do my crappy job and play a few gigs. I want my sister to come to a show, to see me sing. And I want our album to be released on Sub Pop, and given an 8.9 or better by Pitchfork.

I fell asleep, and had a dream I was back in high school, and then I was in an aquarium, and then I was at BrandSolve, except I'd been promoted to manager.

Katherine invited Scott, Jacob, and me to a party at the Monotreme Institute for Extraordinary Art. We combined it with a practice in Katherine's huge bedroom, above Monotreme. She had carved out a space, ten by ten, on the floor. Around us was a chaos of dirty clothes and weird metal sculptures, but our practice space was tidy and pleasant, an island of sound.

Originally we'd started with the idea we would be indie prog, taking the most advanced music of the 1970s and the most progressive of today, and combining them into a compelling sonic stew. But we didn't sound much like Rush or Yes, or Spock's Beard. We sounded more like the Pixies crossed with the Flaming Lips, run through an IDM blender thanks to Scott's synth chops.

Our songs were about walking across the Brooklyn Bridge ("Tugboat"), living in Williamsburg ("Galapagos"), and coffee shops ("We're All Annoying Together"). Jacob helped with the lyrics, taking my ideas and helping me make them "less obnoxious," in his words. He's taught me that I can be a bit pretentious if I'm not careful.

After a good rehearsal, one in which my voice did not split into ten thousand pieces during the performance of "Tugboat," we went downstairs to the party. It was just beginning. The guy who runs Monotreme, who wears leather pants and likes to weld, was setting up a keg. I don't know his real name; everyone calls him Squid.

"Katherine!" Squid said. "Will this band be ready to play in late August?"

"No way," said Jacob.

"Not really," said Scott.

"Absolutely," I said.

"Because maybe for the convention party," said Squid.

"What party?" I asked.

"We're doing a three-day party for the convention," said Squid.

"The theme is 'Police State Fair'," said Katherine.

"Like a police state," said Squid, "but a fair."

"Yeah," said Jacob. "I put that together."

"We have a donkey," said Katherine.

"A real donkey?" Jacob asked.

"No," said Katherine, "a guy dressed as a donkey. It's no fun to nail the tail on a real donkey."

"Nail?" said Scott.

"And lots of rides," said Squid. "But we definitely need music."

"We'll do it," I said. "We'll be ready."

"Katherine tells me you rock," said Squid.

"We rock," I said.

"Katherine rocks," said Squid. "We are in the process of rocking."

"It is feasible that one day we'll rock in unison," Jacob said.

"You know," Squid said, "the Bush regime was supposed to be the catalyst for music not to suck again. And that hasn't happened. At all. Instead, we have Pink."

"I like Pink," said Scott.

"So do I," said Jacob. "She's Missundaztood."

"So what happened to the future of punk rock?" asked Katherine.

"Electroclash," I said.

"Blogging," said Jacob.

Everyone laughed at the word "blogging."

"Come on," I said, "my girlfriend's a blogger."

I said this expecting them to tease me, but instead they all smiled and looked away, as if they knew something I did not. Squid walked off.

Names were thrown out, some of them better than others, but none great: the Fishes, Red Wagon, Stevie Wondermints, and (from Katherine) "Kate Chopin's the Awakening, Part 2: The Awakening," which left us all a little baffled. We tabled the discussion. The party got under way, and for some reason—perhaps because of that awkward silence after I mentioned Para's blogging, or because I drink too much—I drank too much. I also smoked some marijuana. They have a beer vending machine at Monotreme—fifty cents per can—and a change machine. It's a dangerous combination.

Awhile into the party, I was talking to a woman in open-toed sandals with high breasts. She smelled like a waterfall. As I was talking, I thought how lucky I was to have a committed relationship so I wouldn't have to fall in love with this woman, and rub her toes for hours using expensive lotion. Feeling confident and open, I told her exactly what I was thinking. She walked away. Scott came up and pulled me out to the backyard.

Someone had set up a large screen and a video projector, and a number of benches, chairs, and large stones had turned the small, concrete rectangle into a postapocalyptic cineplex. The rest of the band were there, beers in hand. "Check it out," said Scott. "They're showing *Schizopolis*. This is my favorite movie." On the screen, a man dressed as an exterminator said, "Nose army." A woman replied, "Beef diaper."

"Let's call the band Nose Army," I said to the air. Then a man who looked like Bert from *Sesame Street* masturbated in the bathroom of his office. I have asked Scott if my memory of this film is accurate, and he tells me I remember it correctly, and that the masturbating man was Steven Soderbergh. I do not think the film featured naked white men with dreadlocks, in some gigantic, flat desert place, setting a huge wooden octopus on fire. I think that was Burning Man footage. Because later, someone with a competing video projector projected another film on top of *Schizopolis*, and I have no idea which movie was which. I simply know it was the best film I had ever seen.

When the movie ended, I urgently needed to tell Scott what an amazing person he was.

"Dude, you are, like, a total genius star awesome genius," I said.

"Thanks, Gary," said Scott.

"No, you are like, what chord goes here, and then you have the chord, and wow."

"It's just theory."

"No, like, you know where the bridge goes."

"Sure."

"Like, if it was a real bridge, instead of a musical bridge, like the Williamsburg Bridge, I'd put it in Queens. I'd put it in the Atlantic Ocean. That's where I'd put the bridge. Whoa."

"Yep. A bridge connects the verse and the chorus."

"So Brooklyn is the chorus and Manhattan is the verse."

"Yep. Yep, yep."

"Gary," said Jacob, "you're making music out of architecture. It's almost as good as dancing about architecture. Elvis Costello would be proud."

"Who's Elvis Costello?" I asked.

Jacob and Scott exchanged one of their glances.

"Assholes! I know who Elvis Costello is! You all think I'm stupid and immature. What does Elvis Costello have to do with any of this?"

"Elvis Costello said that writing about music is like dancing about architecture," said Scott.

"Actually, no one is sure who said it. Some think it could be Eno," said Jacob.

"No one dances about architecture," I said.

"You were talking about music as if it was architecture," said Jacob.

"Swan Lake is not man-made," I said. "But wait! Wait! Oh, my God!"

Everyone waited.

"The name of our band is Schizopolis," I said.

"Just like that?" Jacob asked.

"And the title of our first album is *Dancing about Architecture*. It's a concept album about life in New York."

There was a moment of quiet. Jacob said, "Huh." Katherine nodded. Scott said, "OK then." I said: "Exactly."

The party was winding down around us, the music low.

"There's some other band called Schizopolis," said Jacob. "I think."

"We can search," said Scott.

"Right now?" said Katherine. "You want to?"

We ran upstairs, excited, and waited for the modem to complete its mating cry. Before anyone else could sit down Scott was tapping in search terms, annotating them with special squiggles and quotes in order to achieve the highest level of exactitude, visiting the government's trademark database, all of us nervous, knowing that at any moment the idea could be taken away.

But there was nothing, no list of matches, no other band popping up with the same name. There was likely another album called *Dancing about Architecture*, but titles can't be copyrighted. It didn't matter. A few minutes earlier, I was Gary Benchley. Now I was Gary Benchley, lead singer and rhythm guitarist for Schizopolis, and please call my publicist if you'd like to interview me.

We scheduled intensive rehearsals over the next two weeks. It was only to be a party in Monotreme's backyard, but it was also a real gig, with strangers in attendance. We had to accentuate the rock, and mitigate the suck.

"We're going to go right out on the tightrope," I said during one rehearsal. "We're not going to fuck this up."

"Yeah," said Scott.

"I need to practice," said Jacob.

We turned to Katherine, who had a thoughtful, distant look on her face, biting her lower lip, off visiting her own planet. She said nothing for a long moment. Then she said, "I want to use fireworks."

Knowing we would soon play live in front of strangers, Schizopolis became a band with a mission. These were the facts: We were playing a party, the Police State Fair, at the Monotreme Institute for Extraordinary Art in Brooklyn. The party was to take place on August twenty-ninth after a huge protest against the Republican National Convention in Manhattan. The plan was for everyone who didn't get arrested to come back to Brooklyn and go insane, while listening to Schizopolis and three or four other bands.

So we had two weeks—six rehearsals of three hours each. It presented a terrible conundrum: how could we achieve rock greatness in eighteen hours? Was it possible? I took Scott aside at work.

"How the hell are we going to do this?" I asked.

"It's a good sign to fear failure."

"Then I am in fine shape."

"Don't concentrate on being a musical genius. Concentrate on being interesting."

We shared a friendly man-hug. It's odd, I think, that I can embrace Scott at work, but not Para.

After hugging Scott, I returned to my desk and contemplated his comment: what was *interesting*? G. G. Allin was interesting, but he threw his own feces on the crowd. Wayne Coyne is interesting, but he travels in a giant plastic hamster ball above an audience of fifty thousand screaming acolytes. That was off-limits given our current budget of negative many dollars and our current wide exposure to no one. The band The Arcade Fire was Jacob's new love; he'd burned us each a prerelease bootleg of their forthcoming album, evangelizing about it like a fundamentalist. I liked the album; it was quirky. But is The Arcade Fire *interesting,* or just Canadian?

Rehearsals were suddenly serious. We were focused on learning

our parts, all of us worried about screwing up. I had the lyrics
down for "Tugboat" and the guitar part for "Galapagos" was in
good shape. Another song, "We're All Annoying Together," was
still a mess. Scott wanted me to drop an octave on the first line, and
then go up half an octave on the second, and I kept switching that
around.

"So we concentrate on sheer, pure energy," I said. "We don't
worry if we're not perfect musicians. We just keep going."

"Yes," said Scott. "But you should still learn the part."

"Absolutely," I said. "But I'm just saying, the show must go on."

"Right," he said. "We absolutely never, ever stop playing."

Our indie prog ideals had been dropped, temporarily, due to
incompetence, and what we now played was a sort of pop-punk-
plus-synth with monster drums. I don't know how to describe
the sound, exactly. When we get an album out, and Pitchfork
writes the impossible-to-understand review, maybe then we'll
have a better understanding. Would our sound be called arching?
Or sweeping? Grand, small, or both at once? Would we score a
2.0, or a 9.5? Thinking about it, I knew how Olympic gymnasts
must feel.

I went over to Para's that night and bought an orange at a
bodega on the way. As I walked toward her building, I wrote a
song called "At Frank's Grocery It Is a Dollar for an Orange."
(Originally, that was the first line of the song, but "orange"
doesn't rhyme with much, so I made it the title.) I'd been doing a
lot of this, looking around for poetry, trying to make up songs
everywhere I went. Para's neighborhood is kind of low on inspi-
ration, but I did see some barbed wire, stretched along the top of
a warehouse wall. It was stretched in such a way that it looked
like a sine wave.

I travel through a line of moving caves (note: this is the subway)
And find you near the barbed wire sine waves

I sang this out loud as I walked. A bus drove by and I harmonized with it. Most buses run on B flat, Scott had once said; I didn't know exactly what to do with that information, but it did make buses more interesting.

All of us were nervous. Katherine, for instance, was flicking Jacob's ear and giggling. Jacob was pretending she wasn't doing it. Scott fingered his shirt collar. I mumbled the lyrics to our songs over and over.

A guy at the grill handed me a hot dog, then asked to see my hand stamp. I started to mumble something, but he looked at me and said, "Oh, you're in the band with Katherine." He smiled. The hot dog was my reward for being an artist, and I ate it with (emotional) relish. Then I went upstairs to Katherine's apartment. Scott emerged from the bathroom with his hair slicked back, as shiny as a classic car. "So fancy!" said Katherine. Scott just smiled.

We had each dressed up in our own way. Scott looked crisp, in an oxford shirt, tan slacks, and black shoes, with his hair smooth and shining. Katherine wore a T-shirt that said NYPD PLUMBING SQUAD with a picture of a plunger underneath the words (I didn't get what that was about) and a tight pair of jeans. Jacob wore a simple black polo. I was in jeans and a snug striped shirt, hair combed, then strategically roughed up, as handsome as I could be.

We had two hours before we had to go on, so I wandered through the party. There was, as had been promised, a man dressed in a donkey outfit, and another guy with a long elephant trunk that shot flames from its nostrils. The elephant kept chasing the donkey, both of them running through the crowd braying and trumpeting. There were two women dressed as cops behind a makeshift bar selling Jell-O shots. They had batons, and a dozen donuts on each baton. You could buy a donut with your Jell-O for a dollar inclusive. They screamed at anyone who came their way, "Filthy longhair! Go back where you came from!" Which was entertaining, because only the girls had long hair, with the exception of a few people with dreads. Above us all, someone had hung a banner with a huge eye-in-the-pyramid on it. After a while, Jacob came up to me and tapped my shoulder. "It's time for us to go on," he said. I followed him out to the stage.

There were maybe fifty people in the audience, most of them facing away from us with drinks in hand. Someone had put up lights so I couldn't see much past the stage. I looked around at my bandmates, all assembled and ready to play. I kept waiting for someone to give me permission, for a light to go on, but it appeared to be up to me alone to set things off. This was it, I thought; time for the all-important introductory stage banter.

"Hello," I said. "We're a band—"

"No shit," said an invisible drunk.

You have to start somewhere. "We're Schizopolis," I said.

Someone, possibly the drunk, made hooting noises. I turned to Katherine and nodded.

"One, two, three, four," she said, and her arms went up and down like pistons. I stepped up to the microphone. Our first song, "Tugboat," doesn't call for any rhythm guitar, so I left my guitar on its stand.

But before I could sing the first few words, fireworks went off, about a dozen very bright, noisy, whistling rockets. For a moment, in the streaking light, I could see the audience, lots of whom were ducking and hiding their eyes. Most of the rockets went into the air, but one veered left and passed right over Scott's hair.

Scott waved his hands wildly and people in the crowd screamed. Afterward, I learned his hair had caught fire, but at the time I was too confused to pay attention. It turns out his citrus-smelling hair product was highly flammable. I remembered Scott's words: never stop playing.

"My knee hit the trigger," yelled Katherine. "Sorry." Though I didn't understand this at the time, Katherine had rigged up a tom with about a dozen rockets and a complex triggering mechanism. Jacob looked on serenely.

There was a moment of silence and weird yells from the audience. Scott looked singed and hurt, but his fingers were on the keyboard. His high-thread-count oxford shirt had dark handprints—he'd put out his smoking hair with his hands, and then rubbed them on his chest. I turned to the mic and said, "Here we go," and I looked at Katherine again. She counted off once more, and there were no explosions.

We played our set straight through. I remember only a few things: I was so nervous that my leg was shaking, and I sang the chorus on "Tugboat" twice. The shapes in the audience kept moving, people going to get more beer or see what else was happening at the party. At the end, my throat hurt and my top three shirt buttons were undone although I don't remember undoing them, and I said, "Thank you, we're Schizopolis." The applause was indifferent and quiet; you could hear the individual hands pressing together.

Before we could leave the stage, the next band—three men in their thirties, guitar-bass-drums—began to edge in. I didn't know what to feel. Right then, an attractive girl was supposed to come over and tell me how great I had done. But the universe gave me none of it. I pulled my guitar and a mic stand through a crowd that had already forgotten I existed.

I felt a hand on my shoulder.

"Dude, that was kind of . . . an awesome show," said a short, homely, stout man, a stranger. He was definitely not an attractive, affirming woman. He had a beard with no mustache, like the Amish.

"There was kind of . . . a fire," I said. "It was pretty creed."

"That's what made it great," he said. "You kept it going. I admired it."

"Do you have any throat lozenges?" I asked.

"I'm sorry, no," he said.

I almost told him how it didn't work out at all, how it had been pretty weak, how we were really a much better band than you might think. But instead I shook his hand, and said, "I wish I had a flyer to give you." He shook my hand back, hard.

"I wish you did, too. I'd love to see you play again."

"I'm Gary Benchley," I said.

"I know," he said. "You introduced yourself onstage."

You know how every annoying actor or musician goes on talk shows and says, "It doesn't matter what people say, it doesn't matter who comes to the show, because if I reached one person, it was worth it"? I always thought that was self-serving bullshit, but it turns out they're telling the truth. That shred of validation, the Amish-bearded man who actually cared that I existed, redeemed the evening. I went back to help pack up Katherine's drums, and scanned the crowd for Para. But, just like earlier, at the protest, she was nowhere to be found.

We packed up after the show was over and Katherine hugged me good-bye. Jacob was kneeling, putting his bass in its cloth case, and he stood up to shake my hand. "Gary, don't sweat things. It was what it was," he said. "It was fine."

But it hadn't been fine. Schizopolis's first concert had failed. It had been like playing a concert for the stone faces on Easter Island. The *quietness* at the end of the show—I kept going back to that moment of near silence, as the last note faded, when all I could hear was amplifier hum, beer cans opening, and soft, polite applause.

Scott drove me home. It was still only ten; it felt like I hadn't slept in days.

"I'm sorry you caught fire," I said. "And that your shirt was ruined."

"It happens. Katherine apologized to me."

I bumped my head against the car window. I told Scott about

the one Amish-looking guy who liked the show, who'd come up after to congratulate me.

"See?" Scott said. "You got someone. He'll tell someone else. It'll work out." He dropped me off, and I trudged up the stairs to my apartment, counting the steps as I went—thirty-six. There was no one in the living room, for which I was grateful. I put the guitar case down inside the door to my bedroom and flopped on my bed.

I needed affirmation, a huge, direct infusion of it, so I called Para, but she wasn't home. Then I called my mother.

"Gobbums!" yelled my mother. That was her nickname for me when I was a wee Benchley in arms. "We were just talking about you. What's going on?"

Five minutes of random chitchat passed, and then I told her about the band, about this new day of Train. "And we played, and we totally sucked."

"You've just got high standards, honey."

Exactly. It's high standards that made me feel that I failed, not lack of talent. I knew Moms would understand. She said that I was her incredibly talented Gary William Benchley and I would be able to do anything if I just gave it time. I went out to the living room, where David was sitting, sat on the couch, and sighed. I told David everything that had happened.

"Gary," he said, "you and I need to smoke a cigar and drink a beer."

"I've never smoked a cigar."

"Oh, my God!" said David.

We went into his room and opened a window. He gave a brief lecture on humidors (his was Tupperware), and handed me my own cigar. It tasted like burning pepper, but the buzz was pleasant. The entire day had been an exhausting blur. Anything before noon was ancient history. I told David more about Schizopolis's concert.

"His hair was on fire?"

"Just for a minute," I said.

"I'm miserable too, if that helps."

It turned out that Sue, his girlfriend, had come to some conclusions regarding their relationship. After two years of dating David, at thirty-two years of age, she'd decided that David was either going to take steps involving a ring and a viable fetus or she was going to find other options.

"I wish she'd just forget to take the pill, and whoops," said David. "That's the old-fashioned way."

"You want that?"

"Well, if it happened, I'd be OK with it. That's what I'm saying. I don't want to sit around making big decisions about whether or not to move to Westchester."

"I can't figure out what my girlfriend wants," I said. "Or really if she's even my girlfriend."

The room was filled with smoke and I was catching the hang of the cigar, puffing every few seconds, getting a buzz, until the cigar had burned down to its label, and then I said good night.

I went out with some friends for my birthday, on a Tuesday night. Para and I had discussed the night, and decided that I should go out with my friends, then she'd take me out for dinner on the weekend. Carl, long-lost friend from the East Village, came out, and my friend Oliver. We ended up at a bar on Sixteenth Street. I let my friends buy the rounds, and the bartender slid me a flaming drink, on the house. I threw it back as everyone sang "Happy Birthday," out of tune. It was 2 A.M., and time for birthday hugs from my bros, who went on their way as I headed out toward the L train, pulling out *This Business of Music*. I realized that I was a little more drunk than I'd known, and the train ride became kind of impressionistic and confusing. It took me ten minutes to unlock the front door of our building.

Climbing on my hands and knees, the stairs to my apartment took a long time. I had to take a few breaks, and it was hard to

find the keys. But finally I found my bed and fell quickly asleep—
to wake three hours later, for the first day of my new adulthood,
into the dawn of a new age of Benchley, with a hangover the size
of Texas and the alarm reminding me that I had scheduled a full
day at BrandSolve, since the other part-time office manager was
on vacation.

I am a healthy young man, at least I think so (I can't afford a
doctor's opinion). But I've been drinking a lot, and maybe smoking
too much, cadging cigarettes here and there from my puffing
friends. After my birthday I was hungover for most of three days.
And then, one morning, the elevator at work was slow and the
door to the stairs was open. I thought, *Why not?* After seven
flights, I saw lights dancing in my eyes.

"I can't climb the stairs," I said to Scott.

"You should go to the gym."

I sighed. "That's not a bad idea."

It turns out that, while I don't get health insurance, BrandSolve
gives me a good discount at City Athletics, which is about four
blocks from the office (Scott doesn't work out there; he goes to
Equinox, a gym for fancy people). I walked over one evening after
work, imagining what it would be like to get in shape.

MONTAGE: "Benchley at the Gym"
MUSIC: Johnny Marr, "Down on the Corner"

Gary enters City Athletic, looking lost and confused. CUT TO:
Flashbulb goes off as he gets his membership card. CUT TO:
Benchley lifting weights, exhausted, puffing. CUT TO: Benchley
falling off elliptical training machine. ~~CUT TO: Benchley masturbating furiously looking at pictures of rats.~~ CUT TO: Benchley lifting weights, pushing hard, *succeeding*. CUT TO: Benchley
on the treadmill. He's flagging. His head is down. Suddenly—
eye of the tiger—he tosses back his head, and his shaggy, almost-

black hair, which has heretofore been covering his dashing blue eyes, flies back. SLOW MOTION, HIGH CONTRAST: Benchley looks left, then right, sweat fleeing away from him. His five-foot-eleven frame comes uncoiled, releasing some deep source of pure energy. CUT TO: End of the New York City marathon, where Benchley breaks the ribbon, arms out, smiling, trailing Kenyans.

That night, my freshly minted membership card in hand, I got my little towel from the towel handler and hopped on the treadmill for a thirty-minute jog. After thirty seconds, the hurt started, and four minutes later I was wondering if my legs could actually explode. Then a tiny woman of mixed Chinese American heritage climbed on the treadmill next to mine and jogged nineteen miles in six minutes while listening to Belle and Sebastian on her iPod and reading a typescript manuscript from her job at *Elle*. I gasped like a drowning smoker, counting the seconds until it was over, ending my jog at 2.3 mph. New York sometimes makes it really clear that amateurs aren't welcome.

But I went back, and it got easier. And I'm able to catch up on my CNN, although after you've seen one enormous rocket smash into some vaguely outlined mosque, you don't really need to see it again. So I find myself looking at the different people. There are the fatties, and they're interesting in a this-could-happen-to-you way. There are the gay men, working hard and with total seriousness. There are the men in their late forties who don't want to lose their twenty-eight-year-old girlfriends. And the trainers, some with Vietnam stares, watching, observing, shouting at their charges. "Five more! Four more! Breathe!"

And then there are the women, who outnumber the men three to one. The sweat pours through their sports bras while they punch their iPods; they bend their backs over giant inflatable balls and stretch their legs. Some of them do it cheerfully, with apple cheeks, and others seem to hate every moment. I watch them, moving my legs and arms on the cross trainer, going through the motions.

With spending time at the gym, with preparations for the next show, with picking up more hours at work, I saw a little less of Para. But I was somehow seeing more of Katherine.

It happened like this: she was complaining, after practice one day, about having to carry a number of boxes from the basement up to the street by herself, since no one in the arts cooperative would help, her arts peers being self-interested bastards, et cetera. Scott and Jacob just smiled and left. Then:

"I can help you with the boxes," I said.

"No, you don't have to help me."

"I'd rather help than listen to you whine."

"Well . . . that seems OK."

So I helped with the boxes, climbing the stairs behind Katherine and enjoying the view. She is not conventionally pretty, and maybe she doesn't have the smallest nose. Her hair was long when we first met, but now it's about two inches off her head and goes in every direction. And her fingernails aren't clean. But she is definitely a cool-looking girl. She has a huge spiral-pattern tattoo on her right shoulder.

"That really wasn't bad," I said. "Of course, I've been working out."

Katherine rolled her eyes. "I can tell," she said. "You want to get some food?"

"I'm a big food fan," I said. "But I should go."

"Why?" Katherine asked. "Is there someone you like better?"

So we went out, and I was regaled with Burning Man stories, and tales of that glorious land beyond the mountains, San Francisco, where both Spider and Katherine had spent their early twenties, riding out the very tail end of the Internet revolution, making a great deal of money before the world decided that the dot-coms were stupid.

I went home and my cell phone rang. It was Para.

"I miss you," she said. "Where is my boyfriend?"

That was nice to hear. "Once this show is over," I said, "I'll be right there. I just need to keep my head down."

"I'm coming, you know," she said. "I won't miss it."

"Excellent," I said.

It was strange to contrast the two women. I'd go over to Para's, and help her make risotto stuffed into bell peppers, and we'd watch TV. At Katherine's it was burned grilled cheese and tomato soup, and that seemed better for me, somehow.

One afternoon, Scott said, "I notice you stay after practice a lot." I nodded.

"And I noted that you and Katherine are getting to be friends."

"We're just hanging out," I said.

"Hanging out like hanging out?" Scott asked. "Or hanging out like, I put my penis inside her vagina?"

"The former."

"Because, Gary, it's not my business. I just want to prepare for total catastrophe if the singer in my band who's dating my coworker starts fucking the band's drummer on the side."

"I can understand your concern, definitely. But we're chaste like Mormons."

On Para's blog, I was no longer "youth." I'd been promoted to "boy." I would go over to her place twice a week, and we would watch TV, and as I watched, I'd hum the songs Schizopolis had written, quietly, hoping I could hit the high notes, and I'd pet Butter the cat.

One Saturday morning, a week before our second show, Katherine called.

"Benchley," she said, "would you like to come with me to visit my brother in New Paltz and pick up electronic devices?"

I was exhausted from the week, and I'd planned on sitting around the house in my underwear, but going somewhere outside of New York, in a car, sounded exciting. "OK," I said.

An hour later, she pulled up in a huge brown truck, which belongs to the Monotreme Institute. Her brother, who was some sort of multimedia artist electronics guy, had a huge pile of electronic geegaws that he didn't want. He was giving them to Katherine so that people at Monotreme could use them in their art. As we drove, we talked about Katherine's work: part-time jobs on about a dozen different projects. For the most part she builds or finds things for movie sets. She told me that she built a desk for *Zoolander*.

"That's awesome," I said.

"And I helped them find the kitchen table for *Elf*."

"No shit!" I said. "Do you feel totally famous?"

"Sometimes, a little, when I see my stuff in the movies. I did this huge decorative wall hanging for *Catch Me If You Can*, but it got cut."

"Were you bummed?"

"I was totally bummed."

We talked about her younger brother, and about my brother, who had just called me out of the blue. He and I hadn't spoken in months. He filled me in on his life, his girlfriend. He was trying to decide whether to reenlist (he called it "re-upping" and I couldn't figure out what he was talking about at first). Apparently the pressure to stay in the navy is pretty huge right now.

"Anyway," I said, "I told him about Schizopolis playing out in Brooklyn, and he thought it was the coolest thing he'd ever heard. I thought he'd rag me. I almost didn't tell him."

"See, it's that older-sibling thing. Like, the approval just means a huge amount, right?"

"It shouldn't, but it does."

"I know. I should remember that when I'm talking to Danny.

But there's also a part of me that doesn't want him to get too far ahead, you know? Not really, but it's still there."

"Well, you know," I said, "that probably just makes him try harder."

We arrived after two hours' driving, and I realized that I was halfway to Albany. Part of me wanted to keep going and see my mom.

Katherine and Danny looked alike, and acted like best friends. I felt weird watching them. My siblings and I aren't at all like that; we don't do the same things, whereas Katherine and Danny were both into weird art and even had friends in common. Danny made flexible geometrical structures embedded with LED lights, which apparently sold OK at local galleries.

Danny kept eyeing me, trying to figure out my place in Katherine's life. There was no comfortable way to say "I'm not her boyfriend," so I said nothing and looked appreciatively at his strange gallery: things that blooped, machines made from tape recorders and baby doll arms painted silver, and tiny video screens embedded into varnished wood boxes. Some of it was pretty boring, but a lot of it was cool. I wanted to take all of his stuff apart and put it back together, like LEGOs.

Danny made us some lunch, peanut butter and jelly sandwiches on incredibly dense hippie bread, which he toasted. It was great, up there in his weird factory-space apartment, eating out of our hands, with the draft coming in through the chinks in the brick walls. We loaded up the truck with various rods and tubes, and white cardboard boxes that had numbers on the outside.

"Anything, uh, *interesting*?" Katherine asked, emphasizing the word.

"Nothing too *interesting*. All the *interesting* stuff is a lot harder to find."

She nodded.

"What defines *interesting*?" I asked.

"Interesting things tend to explode under some circumstances," said Danny. "But the political climate means we're way more careful about things like that than we used to be."

Katherine and Danny talked about a jet bike that had been set off at Monotreme Institute a few nights earlier. It was a motorcycle frame with a simple hand-hewn jet engine attached, and it ran on propane. The metal of the jet glowed bright red. It only went about two blocks, but it made an enormous, sonic boom–quality noise when operated. Twice it had brought out the Brooklyn fire department. Katherine wanted to bring the jet bike up to New Paltz and find a place where sonic booms weren't such a big deal.

I left them to art chatter and went over to look through Danny's books. I picked up an electronics manual written by someone named Forrest C. Mims, published by Radio Shack.

"I've got the entire Radio Shack library," Danny yelled out.

"How about that," I said.

The conversation shifted back to family matters, and before long it was time to go. I shook Danny's hand, and I could feel him appraising me as possible sister's-boyfriend material, but his face didn't reveal any opinion. Katherine and I got back into the truck.

"He's cool, right?" she said.

I agreed that he was.

"Isn't his art great?" she asked. "That's my little brother."

The conversation moved on to Para. We had barely talked about her before. Katherine was curious as to how serious the relationship was, what the sex was like. I answered her honestly that the sex was not that good but we were still figuring it out.

"You're going to meet her," I said, "so . . ."

"No, I promise," said Katherine. "Don't worry. But she's thirty?"

I told her that Para was thirty-one.

"Tick, tick, tick," said Katherine.

"I know," I said. "What about you? Are you ticking?"

"I don't even wear a watch," she said.

It was getting dark, and the truck rattled in a comforting way, the boxes in the back shifting, wind sneaking in through holes in the insulation around the windows. It felt wonderful to be in a pickup at night, driving back to New York, and I had a moment out of time, when I didn't have to worry about my band or making rent, or going to the gym, and a huge wave of cool relief came over me. I hadn't even realized I'd been stressed.

Then we were stopped at a light, and I looked over at Katherine, and she was looking at me, and our eyes locked, and neither one looked away. The light changed, and she drove on. That was it. But I kept thinking about that moment. When we got back to Monotreme, I helped her unload the electronics, and drag them down to her basement, into storage bins. I followed her up to her room, where we'd rehearsed now dozens of times. She thanked me for helping.

"I should go," I said.

"OK," she said. "But if you want to have dinner . . ."

"No," I said, "that's OK. I need to go."

"All right," she said. I leaned down and hugged her, and the hug went on a few seconds too long. The smell of Katherine's hair—the gasoline smell of the truck, and some distant shampoo—rose up through my nose. When I pulled back from her, I could see the bed in the corner. She was smiling at me, and gave me a kiss on the cheek. I walked out to the G train, trying to decide whether I was a good person or a bad one.

In September everyone in my life had caught election fever. Scott created a spreadsheet with his own electoral college statistics. Jacob went to Philadelphia, to knock on doors and get out the vote. Katherine gave out beets with BUSH stickers on them. ("Beet Bush," she said. "Get it? Plus, I'm a drummer.") And Para went out of control, making web banners for her blog with vague slogans like "Defeat the Hegemony of Evil" and "No Monsters in 2004," emailing them to her blogger friends.

She showed them to me, and showed me other blogs where her banners posted. I nodded with approval, and kept nodding as she complained about electronic voting machine interface designs. At work, she emailed me five times a day, pointing to sites with names like Counterpunch and Talking Points Memo, and at night she read to me from articles in the *Nation* and *Harper's*. "I'm feeling human again," she said one day. Apparently the meds were kicking in.

"George W. Bush has given meaning to your life," I said.

"You're a patient friend," she said. Then she invited me over to her place, and when we got there, we talked for a while, until she took my hand, and then we got into bed.

I'd expected another night of amiable snuggling. There were a lot of those, and about one in four turned into sex. But without warning, Para was interested in some action. A few minutes later, when we were both in underwear, she whispered, "Gary, what do you fantasize about?"

This question has come up before, and it's a risky one. Example: During college, as I mentioned earlier, I dated a woman named Gillian. One night, she asked me about my fantasies, and after I gave her an evasive answer, she said, "For me, I think a lot about having a really big dick." After that there was a lot of weird discussion, and an electric leg razor, and certain parts of me that were normally rough and dark became smooth and white, and I had red marks on my forehead the next morning from being smacked into the headboard of her bed. When I got home, I had to really think hard about what kind of man I was. I had to rent *Raiders of the Lost Ark* and watch it a couple of times before I felt better.

So when Para asked me about my fantasies, with her hand on my thigh, I thought immediately of that night with Gillian. I real-

ized that I had never really fantasized about Para. I tried to, sometimes. But I could never stay focused all the way through.

Even worse, the night before, I'd had a dream about Katherine.
It had been vivid, taking place on her large messy bed, next to her
drums. Every detail was perfect, including the sound of the condom
wrapper tearing open, and in the dream I'd rationalized that it was
for the good of the band—anything that made us a tighter unit was
a good thing.

So I shrugged. "Just stuff," I said to Para. "You know, I fantasize about regular stuff." She smiled at this, and curled up next
to me. The cat sat between us, all three of us breathing together.
"What about you?"

"Honestly? I think a lot about being pregnant. It just seems so
awesome. Like, you've got this thing inside of you. You're making
this completely new life."

I made a "Go on" noise.

"Like, I think a lot about unsafe sex. Just not worrying about
it. Does that totally freak you out?"

"I am not freaked out at all," I said, totally freaked out.

"And also, sex when you're pregnant. I think about that."

"Totally," I said.

Luckily, it was dark, or she would have seen my eyes open as
wide as half-dollars. We'd already had the what-if-I-get-pregnant
discussion (where "I" equals "Para"), months before. "I don't
know what I'd do," I'd said, and she said, "I don't know either."
I'd thought we were in agreement, but now I wondered if our "I
don't knows" meant radically different things. She seemed to be
thinking "Poppa Don't Preach," whereas I was coming more from
a Ben Folds Five "Brick" sort of place. I'm out there planting a field
of wheat, and she was thinking about the hard, expensive buns that
come out of the oven nine months later.

But while I was hiding my agitation, wondering what it would
be like to be a dad, Para jumped on me as if I were a pony. I put

aside my fears and guilt (with the exception of the moment when Para ripped the condom wrapper, which put me back in mind of Katherine), and in the morning our discussion was forgotten in the regular activities of finding my socks and making coffee.

I left when Para started to read me an editorial from the *Times*. Democracy is all well and good, but I needed to keep my eye on the rock, especially after the nightmare of our first performance. Luckily, everyone in Schizopolis acknowledged that our first show had blown utterly, and our rehearsals had grown serious. That we began to sound genuinely OK helped, too.

When you're in a band, and you're ambitious, you have to be two people. You have to be the true believer and also a serious, objective critic. Believer Benchley had been beat down pretty hard by our performance, but Objective Benchley was still intact, and when he listened to Schizopolis rehearse, he acknowledged something was growing, getting better. And the band was growing closer, not just in my dreams. We were talking more, focusing on the music, talking about our performance ideas.

Not that there weren't difficulties. Jacob was usually late, by ten minutes or half an hour. And sometimes our focus drifted. Katherine wanted to use her smoke machine. Scott liked to talk about his video-projection ideas. But, in the end, we always decided to focus on the music and worry about special effects later, and Katherine even promised to hold off on the fireworks. I began to feel confident in my own voice. I noticed things about the songs we'd written that I'd never noticed before. Mostly, I'd forgotten about dynamics, and I felt very guilty when I realized that. I'd been singing at two volumes—*forteforte* and *forteforteforte,* like I was singing along with Slayer. Here I was, twenty-three, aspiring musician, and I'd forgotten about dynamics.

Jacob didn't care about the theatrics, but he often came with CDs in hand and insisted we listen to them. One day it was a Suede rip-off named Flinch, the next, an old Eugenius disc. One

Saturday, he popped in an especially annoying CD by a band called Slake. "They're going to be the next Radiohead," he said, nodding knowingly. So we listened, Jacob skipping through the tracks and narrating—or, rather, lecturing—about what we needed to hear: this drum part, that bass line, this synth line.

We had good reason to humor Jacob's listening habits: he had set us up with a second gig. Due to his influence, we were opening for the Crothers Scatmen in early October. They were a Brooklyn punk band ("They play with Japanther," Jacob explained), and the concert was part of the *Matchstick* Magazine Showcase, which was focused this year on Brooklyn bands. "We're just opening," he said. "But it'll be a real audience." It felt like redemption, a chance to put things right so soon after failure. I felt truly lucky.

Because I *am* lucky. I live in Williamsburg, which is still the finest neighborhood in the world. I'm in a promising local band, and I just turned twenty-three at the beginning of September, marking a full year of living in New York. I'd hunted apartments and jobs, and captured both; I'd been with the same woman for over half a year, and Albany was out of my system. Albany was where my mom and dad lived. New York City was my home.

I thought only of the next show. In three days we were opening for the Crothers Scatmen. There was even a website for the venue, a bar called Red Light Brooklyn, in Red Hook, with our name on it: "SAT OCT 2 MATCHSTICK SHOWCASE Crothers Scatmen (11PM) w/Schizopolis (10PM) $10," it said.

Scott had recorded a rehearsal session on his MiniDisc and burned it to a CD for me, so I had been listening to that on my headphones on the train, or in my room, humming along, alternating it with a Long Winters CD. In a perpetual state of flipout, I made constant mental checklists.

- Decrescendo on "Cobble Hill."
- Face the audience.
- Look for cue from Scott on "August."
- Don't suck.

I sat on my bed, imagining being onstage. I made a limp devil sign into the dirty glass of my window, frowning. It was getting dark early. I truly, deeply did not want to fail again, and that desire made me nervous. But in the back of my thoughts I felt a certain faith returning, a mustard seed of faith, the sort of faith Bono has. Everything is going to be all right, I told myself. Find the flow with which to go, and go with it.

New York is almost pleasant in the fall. The smell of urine fades as the days grow colder. Para and I went for long walks, joking and laughing. She seemed to be cheered up by the fall, talking about work and wondering whether she should quit BrandSolve and go work for a magazine instead. She wanted to be an art director. "You have to follow the dream, man," I'd say, and she'd kiss me, encouraged by my optimism.

I still thought of Katherine too often. I thought of the way her eyes scrunched when she smiled, and the way she laughed, and the story she told about drilling a hole through concrete using an industrial-strength laser. When I wrote emails to the band, I edited them compulsively, imagining Katherine reading them, and trying to impress her with my succinct wit and proper punctuation. Then, as I noticed myself doing this, I'd repeat the words "bandmate, not girlfriend" over and over to myself, and that seemed to help.

We arrived at nine, to an empty room. The main act wasn't there yet, and rock club protocol says they soundcheck first. So we sat around, not talking, opening our instrument cases and then shutting them. Finally the Crothers Scatmen arrived, shook our hands, slapped Jacob on the back, and went deep into engineering talk with the bandanna-wearing sound guy. The Crothers Scatmen were calm and cool-looking; the lead singer was a bald man in his early thirties, and the bassist and drummer were normal-looking, hairy, white, indie rock guys. Surprisingly, a trumpet player and a cello player were onstage as well. I watched them without hearing what they were saying, and my hands shook.

After the Scatmen were finished, the sound guy came over and introduced himself. "I'm Steve," he said. We introduced ourselves. "So what we got?"

"Nothing surprising," I said.

"Synth, bass, drums, vocal, and acoustic," said Scott.

"What's coming out of the synth?" Steve asked.

"A maple syrup G-98 grounded camisole," said Scott. Or something like that; I had no idea what he was talking about. Steve watched and listened as we pointed to Jacob's amp and Katherine's drums, and then they got to me, and my acoustic-electric Fender guitar.

"You have a direct box?" asked Steve, and his words magically transported me back to my apartment in Williamsburg, where my bright red direct box, which amplifies an electric-acoustic guitar so that it can go straight into the soundboard, was resting peacefully on "Gustav," my plywood-laminated, Ikea-brand, three-drawer dresser. Forty-five minutes of travel spanned the distance between the club and my apartment. The direct box might as well have been at the bottom of the sea.

"Oh, shit," I said.

"We might have another one," he said. He walked across the room and opened a closet, and emerged a few moments later.

"No luck," he said.

"Where could I get one?" I asked. They're not expensive.

He gave a whistle. "Not much open at nine thirty. We've got our spare on the back line—the one I was thinking of is on the cello."

As my world melted, my bandmates watched to see how I'd react. I called my home number, hoping that David might be there—wondering if I could ask him for a favor. But nothing. I was screwed.

"You know," said Jacob, "my friend Bee is coming tonight. He plays the fiddle in Crabwalk. I'm sure he's got one."

"Oh, shit," I said. "You think?" I watched Jacob dial a number on his cell, and I began to sweat. He spoke into the phone for an eternal minute, and then hung up.

"We're good," he said. "His regular box is over at his friend's, but he's got a spare."

"And he can make it?"

"I told him you'd buy him a beer if he got here in the next hour."

"I'll buy him, like, sixty beers," I said.

So we took the stage, and with Steve's help we sculpted our sound, the unique, simple, evocative, electric-guitar-free indie-pop (with prog leanings) sound of Schizopolis. It was powerful to hear myself sing in the monitors, speakers at my feet giving me my voice back to myself. Our first show had been random speakers and a Radio Shack mixing board, but this was for real.

We ran through "August," a few people already filing in— girlfriends of the Scatmen, as far as I could work out—and stepped off the stage with little to do for the next hour. I stared at the clock on my cell phone every ten seconds, until finally a lanky guy in jeans and a T-shirt, under a Carhartt jacket, came up to shake Jacob's hand.

"Here you go," he said. "I brought you some cable, too."

"God bless you," I said and bought Bee a beer, and one for my-self, then another a few minutes later until I remembered to slow down and pace myself. As time passed, the knot in my stomach un-wound. Katherine came up behind me and rubbed my shoulders, and for a moment I froze, wondering if Para had arrived yet, but she hadn't.

"You got your box," Katherine said.

"It's all good."

"Thank God. There, see, it all worked out," she said. "It's all fine."

I leaned back into her fingers. "Yes," I said.

Scott came over and announced, "There is nothing more disgusting than watching people give massage." Katherine responded by rubbing his shoulders for a moment, which he accepted gladly, and I closed my eyes and exhaled for a long moment, opening them to see Para walking across the room. I was worried she'd seen Katherine giving the massage, but even if she had, Katherine had moved directly over to Scott, so I was in the clear—

"You ready?" said Para.

"I'm ready!" I kissed her, and embraced her, to see, over Para's shoulder, Katherine mouthing the words, "Is that her?" to Scott.

I introduced Para to Katherine.

"He talks about you always," Katherine said.

"All good stuff, right?" said Para, punching my side.

There were at least fifty people in the club. A minute later I took the stage with the rest of Schizopolis. I plugged the cord coming out of the direct box into my guitar, and a huge humming, like a plague of locusts, filled the room.

I strummed a bit, hoping to tune, but the sound was buried in the humming. Finally the humming faded, but when I strummed, there was nothing, no sound at all from the guitar.

"Your DB doesn't have ground lifting," yelled Steve from across the room. "The lights are on the same circuit." I nodded, and looked at my bandmates. Scott was nodding. To him those words—"ground lifting" and "lights on the same circuit"—made sense.

"I guess it's just vocals," said Jacob.

"Gary, who cares?" yelled Katherine. "Fuck it!"

"OK," I said. "Works for me." It was me and a microphone. I put down the acoustic and felt exposed and cold. The lights were up and everyone in front of the stage was a silhouette, a shape. I had one hour to earn the love of these ghosts.

"Hello," I said, "we're Schizopolis. This song is called 'Jesus Was a Union Man.' "

Applause, real, and someone shouting "Schizopolis!" And then the lights came back up, and we were done. I was exhausted, half-aware of my surroundings. I smiled to the room, faces suddenly apparent. The group had grown over the set to about 250, here for the main event.

We'd done it right, this time. I'd gone wild onstage, yelling, tearing up my voice as if I had a few dozen voices in store. Scott had played with crisp precision, Jacob with steady intensity, and Katherine had once again proved herself some kind of primitive goddess, thrashing away on her toms. According to protocol, we removed ourselves from the stage in an efficient, polite manner, making way for the main act. I packed up my dead guitar and wrapped Bee's DB in its cable, and then went to help Katherine with her drums.

"Pretty cool," she said to me, quietly, as I lifted a cymbal.

"I know, right?"

We were the opening band. There was no poster to commemorate the event, just a line on a website, and that line would soon be deleted. Two hundred of the 250 people now crowding the venue were here to see someone else. But as Para embraced me, and a random stranger shook my hand, I felt as if I had climbed a ladder through the clouds and touched the sun.

The random stranger was a tall man in his early forties, wearing black denim and a sweater. He had a ponytail and a tribal tattoo poked out from under his right shirt cuff. "I'm Lou Tremolo," he said. "I liked your set."

Liked, I thought. *Liked is not loved.* "It's a cool place," I said.

"I'm the manager for the Scatmen," he said.

"They're great," I said, not sure if I felt that way at all.

"Is Schizopolis under management?"

"No," I said. I paused, and introduced him to Para; they shook hands. "I mean, we've spoken with a few people, but nothing has really gelled," I lied.

"Well, if you want to talk—"

"Sure, but let me bring everyone over."

SCOTT: He wants to manage us?

GARY: No, he wants to talk.

JACOB (*pointing to the stage*): And he manages these guys?

GARY: Unless he was lying.

KATHERINE: Did he say, "I want to manage you"?

GARY: He said, "I would like to talk to you about your management."

JACOB: Meaning that it could go either way.

GARY: There are definitely many ways it could go.

SCOTT: It could mean nothing.

GARY: That is one distinct possibility. My suggestion is that we all go over and say hello to him.

KATHERINE: What does a manager do?

SCOTT: He manages—

KATHERINE: Jesus Christ, Scott. For God's sake.

SCOTT: I'm trying to say, he builds relationships for the band.

GARY: I think that's right.

JACOB: A manager makes the phone calls.

SCOTT: I thought that was a publicist.

JACOB: It can also be a booking agent.

KATHERINE: Do we need a manager?

GARY: I would say, yes, because if we knew what managers did, then we'd be doing it, and as we don't, we should probably have one.

KATHERINE: Does Fugazi have a manager?

SCOTT: Why Fugazi?

KATHERINE: Because they do everything themselves.

SCOTT: Then probably not.

GARY: U2 has a manager.

JACOB: So we're like U2?

GARY: The Beatles had a manager.

KATHERINE: He killed himself.

JACOB: But he was homosexual.

SCOTT: I am homosexual, and I have yet to kill myself.

GARY: This guy is not homosexual.

SCOTT: How do you know that?

GARY: See his ponytail?

We introduced ourselves.

"You've got a good presence," he said, weaving a little. "Do you have a demo yet?"

"We're working on a demo," said Scott. I waited for someone to blurt out, "We are?" But no one did.

The Scatmen tore into their first song, something extremely angry and loud, and we all began to yell above them.

"Well, look, I think I have a guy who would want to talk to you. He runs a label called Parakeet Records. In Brooklyn Heights." He paused. "I hate yelling. Let's go out sometime and get a beer. Do you all live in Brooklyn?"

"In Williamsburg," Scott shouted.

"Fine, wherever. Send me an email. You have email?"

"We definitely have email," I yelled.

"You'd be surprised who doesn't have email," he said.

He opened his wallet and handed out four cards. LOU TREMOLO, ARTIST MANAGEMENT. "I have a card, too," I said and pulled out my wallet. GARY BENCHLEY, ROCK STAR. Address and cell. He took it and read it, and laughed. "Para made that," I said into his ear, pointing to her.

"Looks good," he said. We all shook hands, then we drifted

into the crowd to watch the Scatmen play, loud power-pop, and
Para stood in front of me, bobbing up and down, finally leaning
back into me as people stood around us, bathed in bass and noise.

Para and I went home together afterward. I showered and we
fooled around. I pushed my thoughts of Katherine away. Para fell
asleep, breathing loudly, but I was still filled with energy from the
show. "OK," I said out loud, but quietly. "OK. This is what you
do." And then I started in on my list.

*You create your demo. You sign with a manager. You talk to
a label, and they give you some money. You record an album.
Then you tour. The label gives you tour support. You make a
video. You get in a van. Scott and Jacob and you and Katherine.
You drive across the country, usually in support of another band.
That is your foundation. You build on that. You quit your job.
You play Valentine's in Albany, and everyone says, Gary Benchley, no way, Gary Benchley from Delmar is on tour in a multi-
cultural, multiracial, multigender New York City band. He has
done something with his life at the age of twenty-three.* Go,
Benchley, go.

Katherine booked us another show in New Paltz two weeks
after our performance in Red Hook, at a huge benefit party organized by her brother for his art collective. "And we get paid," she
said. "Fifty dollars."

"No kidding," said Scott. "That'll cover gas."

With more gigs coming in, with a manager interested, it was
time to get serious. Not just somewhat serious, like before, but genuinely serious. Maybe it was time to print flyers.

"I'm thinking I should bring some gear over here," said Scott,
"just the Digi 002. So that we can do the demo."

"Not get a studio?" asked Jacob.

"That's fifty dollars an hour," said Scott. "At least."

"I don't have any money," said Katherine.

"I don't either," said Jacob.

"I forget what money looks like," I said.

So Scott would engineer. Later in the week I helped him pile his silver Macintosh and a few other electronic devices and speakers into his Element, so that we could drive them to Katherine's. He wrapped the Macintosh in a blanket. "Just like a baby," I said.

"That's right," he said. "Keep it safe." We drove for a bit.

"What do you think of Jacob?" Scott asked.

"I think he's getting to be a good bassist," I said. Jacob's chops had definitely improved. "I mean, 'August' sounds *tight*."

"Yeah, he's definitely improved," Scott said. "I just wish he'd be a little more involved."

"He told me he was practicing all the time," I said.

"I know," said Scott. "I don't want to bitch."

"Also, he's got a writing career," I said. Jacob had been stringing for a variety of music newspapers and writing about shows for the *Village Voice*.

"I have a career, too," said Scott. "And I'm at practice on time."

"But come on, you work for BrandSolve," I said.

"And your point is?"

"You *really* care about building brand intranets?"

"It's not evil," he said. "I mean, advertising moves the world forward. You couldn't have the United States without it."

"If you say so."

Scott shrugged. "All right," he said. "Clearly you think little of me for taking my career seriously."

"It's not that," I said. "Of course I respect your career." Although I didn't, not at all. What Scott did for a living seemed soul-numbing to me, the archetypal day job, clicking a mouse from nine to six. "But is that all you want?"

"Of course not. I never said it was. But it's not just something I do to pass the time."

"No, I know that," I said, lying further. "I just think of you as the brains behind Schizopolis, not Scott Spark, senior developer."

"I think I can handle both pretty well," he said.

"I worry," I said. "I worry that you're not going to have time for this band. I mean, we met Lou—"

"I don't put much stock in Lou," said Scott. "I googled him and got nothing. Not the best sign."

"Yeah, well, still. I guess what I'm wondering is, you're still signed on, right? Like—" It was hard to ask this; I was afraid of the answer. "What if we get a record deal and go on tour? What would happen then?"

"I've thought about that," said Scott. "I've got about twelve weeks of vacation coming to me. So I'd just take that."

"Twelve weeks? Really?"

"I mean, I shouldn't take them all at once. But I could."

That was enough time to record an album and go on a nationwide tour, plus some extra. I told Scott as much. "Look, this band can't be my only priority," he said. "That's just not possible for me. But I can be as involved as I have been."

"Of course," I said. "Totally." I wondered what it was like, to live a life in which Schizopolis was not the first word he said in the morning, did not show up in his dreams.

"And Gary, the odds are atrocious. There are eight million people in New York, and twelve million bands. I mean, I don't play the lottery, either."

"I just started playing," I said. It was true. I'd bought my first ticket two days ago, when the pot reached $33 million.

"You're *not* playing the lottery."

"A little." My mom had loved scratch-and-win when I was a kid, and something about the pink and white tickets had appealed to me a few nights ago, as I waited in line to buy a six-pack. I hadn't won.

Scott shook his head, and went on to explain the statistics involved, but I tuned him out and thought about what I'd have done with my 33 million, had I won. The Gary Benchley Foundation was one option. What could it do? Something with troubled teenagers—that was the way to make the world better. Then I'd make a documentary about the work the Benchley Foundation was doing. Or better, I could hire all the people I'd met who were making documentaries. Or even better than that, I could hire those people to help the troubled teens to make their *own* documentaries. Was that enough to help the troubled teens? Maybe I just give them guitars. Or start a label, and produce albums by troubled teens, and work with them to make documentaries about their experiences in the studio.

I cut Scott off; he was rambling on about something called "naïve probability." "So we're playing the odds," I said. "We'll put down a demo and see where it goes."

"I'm just saying, Schizopolis needs to be part of my life, not my whole life. This demo is probably going to be my whole life for a while."

"Can I help with the demo?" I asked, and Scott made a snorting noise in reply. He turned onto Katherine's street and found a place to park.

Upstairs, I deposited Scott's blue monitor speakers onto Katherine's bed and watched as he began to assemble his studio, plugging wires from a green box into a black one. Katherine was in a good mood, hair back, eyes shining.

"I just got a new job," she said. "Like an hour ago."

I asked her to tell me about it, worried that it would be a full-time gig, that there would be three people trying to balance work with Schizopolis. "They're making a movie where Christopher Walken is in the war in Iraq," she said, "and he sees something really awful, like his best friend is castrated or something, and when he comes home, he decides he's a bug. So he builds a giant persimmon. And they need someone to build out the inside of the persimmon. Like, it's really beautiful inside of it, all silky. He's made this gorgeous persimmon to live out his fantasies of being a bug. And it's half-buried on a farm. So I'm building the persimmon."

"That's the movie?"

"It's a love story," she said. "A woman has to love him enough to help him out of the persimmon. I think Spike Jonze is directing it."

"Spike Jonze has a creamy center," said Scott, twiddling with his computer.

"And is recently divorced," said Katherine.

"And heir to a massive fortune," said Scott.

"And straight," I said.

"Oh, please," said Scott. "He produced *Jackass*. He's definitely looked fondly on another man's buttocks."

"I loved that movie," said Katherine.

"Me too," said Scott. "It was like John Waters, but with straight boys begging to be led astray."

"That's really the fantasy, isn't it?" I asked. "Seducing a straight boy?"

"Oh, Gary, of course not," said Scott. "Now take off your pants." Katherine snorted, like a horse. "No, it's not really the fantasy," continued Scott. "Straight boys are a nightmare from which I long struggled to awaken."

"I'm still not done with them," said Katherine. "So, Gary, take off your pants."

I reached for my belt buckle, and saw Scott arch his eyebrows. I remembered our conversation about not having sexual intercourse with other band members, and the wisdom of his counsel.

"I can sue you for this," I said to Scott. "You have seniority. You can only touch me where my bathing suit doesn't cover."

"That leaves nipples," said Katherine.

"Actually, Gary, the law doesn't apply in that case."

"It doesn't?"

"Nope. We're in different departments," he said. "In so many ways. And I have no power over your career. I would have thought that, given your girlfriend is a coworker, you would have investigated the relevant law."

"Maybe if Para gets promoted I can get a raise," I said.

Katherine and I watched Scott put together his setup, listening to him bitch about some software program called Logic.

"Can you make me sound like John Bonham?" Katherine asked, tapping a cymbal.

"No," said Scott, squinting. "I'm not used to setting things up for a band. It's a little harder than plain MIDI."

"Why don't you just get it set up so we can start?" I said, fucking with him. "I mean, what's the hold-up?"

"Gary, I think—"

"Scott, isn't it too late for excuses? You insist you're a professional, and it's been nearly twenty minutes. Are we going to record a demo or not? I can't work under these conditions."

"Where's your direct box, shithead?"

"Right in my bag," I said. "I carry it with me everywhere now. Even into the bathroom."

The buzzer rang, and Katherine let in Jacob.

"Scott's setting up for the demo," I said. "It's really boring. I told him we could just do it on a four-track."

"I have twelve tracks, digitally," Scott said.

"Ah, well, twelve tracks. But there are only four musicians."

"Jesus Christ," said Scott.

"The Beatles recorded *Sgt. Pepper* on a four-track," I said.

"They recorded it on three linked-together four-tracks," said Scott.

"But they did it using analog technology, not digital," I said.

"Can't you do something instead of annoy me?" asked Scott. "Like hit the high note in 'Hoyt-Schemerhorn'? That would be nice."

"Ouch," said Katherine.

"Of course, we could always get you Auto-Tune," said Scott, "and then you can sound like Cher."

Scott estimated twenty more minutes to set things up, so we went downstairs to Monotreme, where a lone man was boring a hole into a female mannequin's crotch; across the mannequin's chest were the words TOY PARTY. Outside, Jacob lit up a cigarette.

"I didn't know you smoked," said Katherine.

"I have a cigarette from time to time," said Jacob. I asked him for one.

"Gary," said Katherine, "don't smoke."

"Jacob can smoke," I said.

"He's an adult."

I pulled the smoke as far into my lungs as it could go, letting the nicotine do its trick, getting light-headed as a result. I was definitely getting into smoking lately. I'd bought my first pack of Parliaments the other day, and it felt good to have them at home, safe in a drawer. Jacob and Katherine talked about Jacob's new girlfriend, and I thought about all the sex Para had had before me. We talked about it sometimes. Her stories would start, "I had this boyfriend once," and after a few dozen such stories I began to index the boyfriends. There were at least four major ones, and a countless number of short-termers.

As I led the way upstairs, Katherine asked me about the gym.

"Oh, God, I need to go," I said. "I've totally screwed up."

"That's how they get you," said Jacob. "I haven't been in, like, six months."

"We just need to gig more," I said. "I get a workout onstage."

I vowed to myself to go back the next day.

Upstairs, Scott was nodding to his computer. "I think if we do something quieter, like 'Hoyt-Schemerhorn,' I can make it work," he said.

"Ready," I said, picking up my acoustic.

The next afternoon, I called the number on Lou's business card, to see when he wanted to meet to discuss the future of Schizopolis.

"So you think we should still meet with Parakeet?"

"Parakeet? No, no, I don't think you're right for them at all."

"No? Because at the show at Red Light, you thought that maybe . . ."

"Oh, I'm sorry," he said, his voice narrowed down by the cell phone into a series of skips and pops, like an old 78 record. "I was just thinking out loud."

"So, not Parakeet Records."

"No, you're better off. They would have screwed it up anyway. They're knuckleheads."

"Then that's good."

"Yeah, you're better off," he said.

"Cool," I said. No one said anything for a long moment. I heard the sound of honking from Lou's end. "So when should we meet up?"

"Yeah, OK. This is a hard week for me."

"We're in no hurry," I said.

"That's good," said Lou. "Hey, Gary! I'm going into the tunnel."

"All right," I said. "I'll check in."

"Yeah, give me a call in, when, um . . . Schizopolis, right?" he said.

"We've got a gig in New Paltz next week, and we're putting down the demo—"

"Good," he said, cutting me off. "It's a plan."

I left my desk to tell Scott about this conversation.

"Well, that was that," said Scott.

"I don't think it's a wash," I said. "I mean, he definitely showed interest. He seemed pretty excited at the show."

"He seemed pretty *drunk*," said Scott. That was a good point.

Could someone be excited about a band while drunk, and then less excited when they woke up? Could Lou have been beer-goggling? Or rather, band-goggling?

It stung to see our glorious road straight into the studio torn up, with a big detour sign put in place where before there had only been open highway. Still, whatever happened with Lou, his interest had given us enough momentum to start on the demo, and that night, Scott sent each of us an MP3 mix of "Hoyt-Schemerhorn."

In his email, he explained that he'd had to use some extra reverb because he had to time-shift Katherine's drums in order to match them up with Jacob's bassline, and the reverb covered up the "fringing." As a result, it sounded like we were playing in a cave, but then again, that made sense, because "Hoyt-Schemerhorn" is about a subway station. It's about transferring from the A train to the G, and what it's like to be standing at a station late at night, waiting for a light to appear in the tunnel. I wrote the first verse, which goes:

> *I came from a blue line,*
> *Looking for a green dot.*
> *Heading for a gray line.*
> *I plan to keep switching*
> *Until I get home.*

The colors refer to different trains—the blue A, the green G, and the gray L, which takes me home. And there was now a bit of digital substance, three minutes and twenty-nine seconds, where before there was nothing. It didn't count for much, maybe, given the 9 trillion MP3s spinning around out there in the wide world, but it still counted.

We played the gig in New Paltz, the one that Katherine had set up with her brother. It was just a noisy party in a warehouse, which meant we sounded like we were underwater, but people were generally appreciative, in an offhand way. After the show, someone said, "Sounded good." That was about it.

This was one of the hardest lessons to learn about being a musician: people don't really care much about you and your needs, unless you're actually famous. You're just there to make interesting noises and amuse them, and they don't care if your mother just died, or your girlfriend just dumped you. You go up onstage to wrestle with the demon muse, but they simply look on nodding, holding plastic cups filled with beer. Roman gladiators probably felt this way, looking into the crowd.

I guess I'd expected more glory from playing out as a band, but I vowed not to become bitter, at least not until we had a record deal. And there was *some* glory, it was just fractional. Like when Katherine's brother, who'd organized the party in New Paltz, came around to pay the band. It felt good to be remunerated for our hard work, our discipline, our careful attention to stage presence.

JACOB: How do you divide fifty dollars four ways?
SCOTT: You put aside twenty for gas and buy beer with what's left over.

After New Paltz, we got down to work on the demo, slaving away. For the first week. But Scott was busy at work, and Jacob had to keep canceling rehearsals, and Katherine was working hard to build a huge persimmon for a film set. So we made a group decision to slow down on the demo, while we each pursued our individual goals. We'd still rehearse once a week, to keep our skills fresh, and to discuss the demo, and when we had a little more time, we'd buckle down and record.

I felt a little awkward, because I didn't really have any individual goals besides making Schizopolis work, but I couldn't expect everyone to give up their careers, either. So I found myself with a lot of time to read, and think, and work on my unique vocal stylings. I didn't do any of these things, though, because of cable television.

I was sitting around at home one night when my roommate David burst through the door. "How are you doing?" he asked.

I tried to answer but he cut me off. "That's very interesting, because I'm getting married."

"Holy shit!" I said. "You're getting married. When?"

"Late 2005," said David. "Not before. I gave Sue the ring yesterday."

"You did? What kind of ring."

"An . . . engagement ring."

"But, like, with a diamond?"

"No," David said, "it's made from tires."

"She said yes?"

David shook his head at me. "Do you know what marriage is? When two people exchange vows and decide to share their fortunes?"

"Am I invited?"

"Probably."

"Great."

We got beers. David sat on his bed, and I took his desk chair. The ring had cost him $12,500, several months' salary for me. I had to stop and remember that David was making $100,000 a year and living cheaply so that he could help out his parents with their medical bills.

"So my mom cried for like an hour," he said. "I told her, and she just started crying, and then she kissed me about twenty times. It was tears everywhere. It was like the time I saw *Philadelphia* in the Village. And my father comes in, right, and my mother screams it to him—shrieks, 'David's getting married!—and then she says, 'You boys take some time,' and goes upstairs. So Dad takes me out to the backyard, and we light up a cigar, and he's like, tell me about your plans."

"Some good Dad time," I said.

"So we sit for a while. He doesn't say much, you know? And he says to me, 'Son, I know you've been helping us out a lot here. But you're going to need to stop that.' And he puts his hand on my arm, and says, 'Don't you worry about us. The best gift you can give us is to have a family of your own.' "

"Wow," I said. "Your dad calls you 'son'."

"And you know, I was about to start crying again, but you can't cry in front of your dad."

"No," I said. "You can't. If he'd wanted tears, he'd have had a daughter."

"So I said, 'Do you want to talk about the Mets?' "

"That's what you said?"

"Yes. So we talked about the Mets."

David went on to tell me that he was planning to move out soon, once a few details were worked out. Sue had a beautiful apartment on Mott Street, in the city. And David was still going to help his parents out with expenses. "Unless we have kids," he said. "But that's a year or two off."

We talked about the ring. He'd bought it from men in skullcaps, in a busy jewelry store in the Diamond District. He impersonated the man who sold him the diamond, doing a Yiddish accent: "You want a *beautiful* diamond? How beautiful is this woman? Because too beautiful a diamond isn't good for a woman if she's not that beautiful." Which of course had led David to go five thousand dollars above his budget.

He told the story in slow motion, moving his hands to show how he slid the jewelry box across the restaurant table, a gray metal box with an inlaid silver top, and then she opened it to see black velvet with the gold inside. Sue immediately started to cry, then put it on; the fit was perfect, David said, and the ring caught the light, glowing.

"The ring, man," he said. "It's like the most powerful symbol in the universe."

When I wasn't working, rehearsing, or sitting around aimlessly, I went out with Para. Her conversations increasingly left me baffled. She was angry and worried about the election, a woman's right to choose, copyright law, and the recent design trends. "I mean, the Dutch all are well and good," she said. "But there are other places to look for ideas."

"I agree," I said. On the plus side, she seemed to be coming around to Schizopolis. She told me that it was fun to date a young lead singer, and her friends were jealous. "I saw you onstage," she said, "and I was worried that girls would snatch you away."

"I am unsnatchable," I said.

"Everyone is snatchable," she said.

"Gary Benchley is the portrait of fidelity."

"Have you been tested?" Para asked.

"For . . . HIV?"

"No, although that wouldn't be a bad idea. For fidelity."

I thought about it for a moment, considering Katherine. I admitted that I *had* been tested.

This led to a quick round of questions. Para wanted to know who had done the testing, so I immediately lied and told her it was just someone I'd met out one night. Then Para wanted to know if the girl was cute or not. No, I told Para, she was not cute.

So I went from truthfulness to total falsehood in two sentences— a Benchley record. Then, I realized, if this imaginary girl-who-is-not-Katherine (let's call her X) wasn't attractive, then it wasn't a big deal to turn her down, and I hadn't scored any fidelity points.

So I amended my statement and said, actually, yes, the girl was pretty cute.

Then Para wanted X's name, so I pulled out "Liz," which is what some people call my sister. This was a mistake, because now I was talking about being attracted to my sister, and it felt kind of nasty. "Was there any kissing?" Para asked, and of course there hadn't been, because who makes out with their sister? So I said, no, my lips belonged only to Para, and I had engaged in absolutely no extracurricular smooching.

PARA: Good. That was the right choice.

GARY: It was the only choice.

PARA: I was a little worried about that girl in your band.

GARY: Katherine, or Scott?

PARA: Katherine. You never talk about her.

GARY: She's pretty funny. She says raunchy stuff.

PARA: Like what?

GARY: Like, with Scott. They're like two girls. They talk about cock. I can't really convey it.

PARA: Uh-huh.

GARY (*nervous*): She's a crazy drummer.

PARA: Do you think she's pretty?

GARY: Oh, no. Of course not. She's my bandmate.

PARA: Because her nose is definitely not the smallest.

"No," I said, not sure who I was betraying. "It's not the smallest nose."

Para's birthday was October 31, and we set out to do some camping. Para is from Vermont, so she thinks, incorrectly, that winter is a good time to do things outside. Growing up in Albany, I never went camping in the winter. Winter was the time when your hair gel froze to your head while you waited for the school bus. But winter, for Para, was long hikes and Christmas trees, and pancake breakfasts with maple syrup. Technically perhaps it wasn't winter yet, but the last day of October in Vermont qualifies in my book.

We were leaving on Saturday morning so we could enjoy the drive, and both of us were taking off from work on Monday. We were going to meet Para's mother, and stay at her house on Saturday night, then camp on Sunday night.

"Will your mom hate me?" I asked.

"No, she'll like you," said Para. "You're much nicer than most of the boys I've brought home."

I tried not to think about how many boys that might have been. "Am I on the couch?"

Para laughed. "No, of course not. It's all very modern. You're in a bed."

"Your bed, right? It would be weird if it was your mom's bed."

Para made a disgusted noise and refused to respond.

"Unless," I said, "you, your mom, and I had a three-way." In response, Para kept her eyes on the road and her face somber, refusing to acknowledge I existed. A moment later, though, she'd forgotten about my observations, and began to hop up and down in her seat.

"Gary, look at this beautiful nature," she said. "I don't know why I live in the city. I want to live in a tent." Going north had released Para's inner hippie. "What I always wanted to do," she went on, "and what I am going to do someday, is run a horse farm."

"And raise organic horses?"

"I rode so many horses," she said. Para loves the horses. On the mantle of the defunct fireplace in her apartment was a set of small plastic horse figurines, and in an album under her bed there were photos of her riding, twelve years old and light as a leaf. I asked for the name of her horse.

"There was Sunshine," said Para. "And Maplewood, and Bill."

"What was Bill like?"

"He was *beautiful*."

"What is it with horses and women?" I asked.

"You don't like horses?"

"They look hungry."

"Riding horses is the best thing in the world. It's better than pie."

"I'm sure it's the best thing in the world to straddle a giant throbbing beast and ride it around," I said. "Clearly it's gotten a lot of girls through middle school."

"Oh, God," said Para. "I worked at a stable in high school, and there was this one nag that we used to put all the little girls on. We called him 'the hymen buster.' "

"You did?"

"His name was Chief."

Para told me she could have me on a horse within three hours. I said she was sensing urgency where none existed. But it turned out her childhood friend Kenyon and his wife, Piper, had a stable on their property, a few minutes from Para's mother's place. Para had an open invitation to come by and ride any time she wanted. It would only take a phone call.

She pulled her cell from her purse. I demurred. She insisted. I demurred again. She couldn't believe I wouldn't ride a horse. "I'm not in the mood," I said.

She pitched her voice high, and said, " 'I'm Gary Benchley, and I'm not in the mood.' You're a total little girl."

I cracked the window, breathed deeply, and found that, unlike the city, the air here did not taste like socks.

"Horses love you," said Para. "Come on, Gary."

"OK," I said. "I'll ride."

Para made the call. Yes, Kenyon and Piper were home. In fact, they were working on their Christmas decorations at the moment, because their home was going to be on the countywide local Christmas tour, and you can't get too early a start. And, yes, *definitely*, they were glad to open their stable to us for a casual ride through a wooded glen. I heard a shrill, laughing voice come through the cell phone—Piper, I guessed—saying, "He's never ridden a horse?!"

So it was decided; I was going to have my equine cherry popped within two hours. Para, already hopping with Vermont excitement, began to grin like a madwoman. "Gary Benchley is going to ride a horse," she said.

"And meet your mom," I said. This trip was turning into a huge, anxious horror.

Para had known Kenyon in high school. They had met up again in New York, where Kenyon had worked in an extreme money situation. Kenyon had made millions, married Piper, and, two years before, at twenty-eight years of age, come back to his Vermont roots to retire and restore this house.

Kenyon and Piper lived in a many-gabled, large-garaged, eaves-ridden home with two gazebos, one for emergencies. A bit away from the house, across a field, was the stable. Three horses stood there, munching. We got out of the car.

"Did you guys date?" I asked.

"Oh, you know," said Para. "You've got nothing to worry about."

"Gary!" said Kenyon. "Our first-time rider! Nice to meet you!" He shook my hand heartily, and shepherded Para and me through the foyer to the first dining room. Kenyon was blond; even his pants were blond. The cream walls inside his house were decorated with signed hand-numbered framed etchings of local barns.

The limousine-sized dining room table was piled high with ivy cuttings and dried wildflowers, and beyond the table sat small, blond Piper. A German shepherd lay curled at her feet. The shepherd came over and inquisitively shoved its nose directly into my crotch.

"Deepak!" said Kenyon. "He does that." She called the dog's

name once more, and Deepak the German shepherd sauntered back to Piper. I felt rejected.

"As you can see, I'm just trimming," said Piper, snipping a vine with some garden shears.

"It smells wonderful," said Para.

"Well, it's so competitive, the Christmas house tour. You have no idea. We're getting a head start. Isn't that ridiculous? In October?"

"That is, like, so crazy," I said.

"Gary," said Para, "if you'd seen this place when they moved in, you'd be shocked."

"I'm shocked already," I said.

"You have to see the upstairs," said Piper.

There was more refurbishing chat, about masonry trim. A South American woman in a Ben & Jerry's T-shirt walked into the room with an unplugged vacuum cleaner, then apologized and walked out. No one seemed to notice.

Kenyon asked what I did for a living.

"I work with Para," I said.

"Ooh, office romance," said Piper. "Well, I'm glad you've come to visit."

I thanked her, and thought of my little room in Williamsburg, one-fifth the size of their dining room.

"Gary's also a musician," said Para.

"It's just a hobby," I said.

"What sort of music?" asked Kenyon.

"Oh, you know," I said.

"Indie rock," said Para.

"Do you know Galaxie 500?" asked Kenyon.

"I love them," I said.

"I have a real connection to them because of school," said Kenyon. This, I realized after a moment, was code for "I went to

Harvard, like the members of Galaxie 500." I decided that Kenyon did not rock.

"You know, I *don't* want to cut this off," said Para. "But before you two share indie music stories, I want to put Gary on a horse."

"Of course," said Kenyon.

"You've really never ridden, Gary?" Piper asked.

I had the sense Piper would be shocked by some of the things I'd never done. I'd never yachted, for instance, or eaten off real silver, or owned a chain of hotels.

"Not a lot of riding in Albany," I said.

"Oh, that is so not true!" said Piper. "I went to *at least* a dozen equestrian events in Saratoga."

"Piper was equestrian at Wellesley," said Para.

"Oh," I said. "There you go."

Kenyon and Piper left us to find our own way to the stable, because they were too involved with snipping ivy and exploiting South American housekeepers to join us in the stables.

"What do I do?" I asked. "Do I have to wear those hats? Or jodhpurs? What are jodhpurs?"

"I would love to see you in a riding hat," said Para. "But it's not required." She unlatched a fence and pointed me to a gelded dappled white Arabian roan stallion horse, or whatever. His name was Santa.

"Make friends," Para said. On cue, Santa snorted and looked over at me. A small blast of steam came out of his nostrils, like an angry dragon.

I went up to him. I put a hand on his side, tentatively. It was warm, and his muscled sides flinched at my touch. "Hey there, Santa," I said. "You like the Pixies?"

Hearing a quiet thump, I looked back to find Para already mounted.

"How'd you get up there?" I asked.

"Lead him over to the mounting block."

"Lead him . . . using my natural leadership skills?"

"Take the bridle," Para said.

"Is this the bridle? Stop laughing."

"Yes, that's the bridle. Now lead him over to the big piece of wood."

I led Santa over to the block, and was relieved that he stopped walking when I did. I got up on the block. He licked my hand. "He's moist," I said. "Is that good?"

"Yes," said Para. "Now one leg, then the other."

I stopped counting after my seven hundred and ninety-eighth mounting attempt. Finally, Para dismounted, came over, and pushed me onto the horse, which took seven more tries. God, I wanted a cigarette. I hadn't brought any along because officially, I didn't smoke.

Finally, I got on Santa, and leaned forward, trying to find my balance.

"I think I have this," I said.

"Great," said Para.

"What's your horse's name?" I asked.

"Oscar," she said. "He's a Dutch warmblood." She patted his neck. "And so very handsome."

"I feel jealous," I said. "Particularly given the hymen-buster conversation."

"Take the reins," Para said, suddenly no-nonsense. I picked up the reins, feeling a little more in control, but still wobbly.

"OK," I said. "So where's the ignition?"

"Just kick him," she said.

I brushed my feet against Santa's sides. Nothing. I tried a few more times, finally delivering a solid thump, and Santa began to move forward, toward the fence.

"There you go," said Para. "You're riding a horse."

Para led the way on Oscar, and Santa followed. I began to get the hang of it. After we got out of the yard, or field, or corral, she had her horse double around, and she kicked a red button that automatically closed the fence gate.

Santa turned to follow Para, which surprised me. I said, "Whoa." Santa stopped.

"Check that out," I said. "I say 'whoa,' and he understands me. That's where 'whoa' comes from."

"You ready?" Para asked. "We're going to take a trail through the woods."

"Sure," I said. "Let's kill us some Injuns."

Santa followed Oscar through the woods. The forest rose up around us, a carpet of leaves below, with a few still left on the trees. It was a fairy tale, a Stevie Nicks song come to life.

"This isn't so bad," I yelled to Para. Being on the horse, I had the same kind of high I get from being onstage, a sense of conquering my fears. I wished I could ride a horse onstage. That would be compelling rock theater.

Para brought Oscar up next to Santa. I tried to lean over to kiss her, like in a movie, but nearly fell off.

"Careful, man," she said. "Don't lose your balance."

"I am so balanced," I said. "Balance is all I've got. I'm in Vermont on a horse with my beautiful girlfriend for her birthday. This is exactly what I need. Just Para and Gary."

I was looking forward to the moment, later, when I'd give Para her birthday book, which was a book by someone named Jan Tschichold, called *Essays on the Morality of Good Design*. Thrilling. But Jan was apparently *the shit* when it came to graphic arts.

Para had coveted this book one day in a used bookstore, but apparently it was rare, and cost $150, so she'd decided against getting it. I'd gone back and bought it, and now it was wrapped in my duffel bag in the trunk of the car.

I leaned back and put out my arms, taking a deep breath, pulling in as much of Vermont as I could. High above the ground, on this beast, the cold cutting through my jacket—I felt as if I could stay here for eternity, free of Pro Tools and demos, under wispy clouds at the edge of dusk.

Then I fell from the horse, like this: whump.

I was winded, but I got up feeling jubilant. Who cares if you fall? I was here trying something totally new, experiencing something fresh. I dusted myself off, promising Para I was fine, I was *really* OK, I was more than fine. Then I stepped back over to Santa, trying to figure out how I'd mount him without a big piece of wood, and in that single step, I caught my foot on a fallen branch, fell over, and sprained my right ankle.

The mother of agony shot from my ankle. *It was like this for Christopher Reeve,* I thought.

Para hopped off Oscar, urging me to stay still. The horses stood without moving, unconcerned.

"Let me see," she said, taking my hand. I hopped up on one leg.

"I just totally ruined our horse time," I said.

"Is it doctor bad?"

"Ice pack bad," I said. I didn't have any insurance, which meant that nothing short of a missing foot was doctor bad.

"Can you walk at all?"

"A little." I hopped in a circle, putting a few ounces of pressure on my right side. The results were disappointing. After a bit of stumbling, with Para supporting me, we decided to go back. Except, as I had noted, there was no mounting block this time.

"This is going to be hard," I said. Para helped, pushing hard to get my body up on the horse. My bad ankle sent bursts of fresh pain every time I flailed.

Finally Para said, "Just grab on. He won't mind." This was true. I climbed Santa like he was a mountain, pulling myself up stomach over saddle, and slowly, slowly righted myself.

Don't cry, I thought. *Do not cry.*

"It could have happened to anyone," said Para, hopping onto her own horse, as if the horse was just a fairly high-up sofa.

"But it definitely happened to me," I said. We rode back to the stable, and Para got off of Oscar and led Santa to the mounting block, then came around to help me dismount. I moved very carefully and very slowly. The ankle throbbed—definitely good and sprained, probably crutchworthy.

We stumbled back to the house, finding the door open. Hearing us enter, Piper yelled, "I hope you both like Brie!" Then she saw us, as Para helped me through the long, parquet-tiled hallway.

"Oh, God, what happened?"

"I fell off Santa," I said, "and then I fell down. I'm kind of special."

"Do we need a doctor?" asked Kenyon, appearing from a side room. "I know some people at the UVM sports medicine center." It sounded like a brag.

"No," I said. "Just a sprain."

Piper prepared a place for me on an enormous couch, and put a needlepoint pillow, decorated with an embroidered stallion, on the coffee table, on which I rested my foot. No one mentioned my scruffy socks. Kenyon, an athletic man, had a wide variety of ice packs and bandages, which he handed to Para, and which she helped me apply.

Some Vicodin (left over, Piper said, from the treatment for a recent tennis injury) soothed me before I could start to feel like too much of an idiot. And everyone spoke comforting words, asking me what I wanted to do, what would make me comfortable. What I wanted to do, I decided, was turn on the massive plasma television and watch some HBO, and drink a bottle of wine. But instead I asked for a drink of water.

"God, we're supposed to go to my mother's," said Para.

"Sure," I said. "Let's go."

"You relax for a while," said Para. "There's no hurry."

"I was really having fun," I said.

"I know," she said.

"Maybe we can still go camping," I said.

Para shook her head. "It's OK," she said.

So we all sat around the living room, on seats of great plushness, and talked of many things. We spoke of horses and injuries, and Kenyon listed the worst accidents in his life of sport, which included a torn shoulder from rugby, a lacrosse ball concussion, swimmer's ear, and rope burns from sailing. Piper countered with tennis elbow, a cracked rib when a horse "went spooky" on her (I had the image of a horse reeling up and saying *"Mwa-ha-ha-ha-ha!"*), during a freestyle dressage competition turned tragic, and—she said this as if it was dirty—a bruised breast playing polo.

"Smacked her tit!" said Kenyon.

"Kenyon!" said Piper. "Gary, are you sure you don't want a doctor?"

I smiled, feeling a little detached, and insisted I was fine. A little later, after complimenting Kenyon and Piper on their glorious home and their hospitality, their generosity regarding horses, I hobbled out to the car on Para's arm. Kenyon told us that he'd be in New York soon for some consulting work and wanted to take us out to dinner. Then he embraced Para, and I thought I saw him sniff her, but I wasn't certain.

We drove the half hour to Para's mother's. At every bump and pothole, Para apologized, and I in turn told her not to worry, although the pain was returning despite the Vicodin.

Para's mother had gray hair tied in a ponytail. She'd been warned by phone of my condition.

"Hi," I said, shaking her hand. "I'm your daughter's broken boyfriend."

"Call me Eileen," she said.

She led me in and propped me on the couch. Eileen's house was much more my speed: two stories, no stable, no gazebos, and books everywhere—which made sense, as she was a librarian. Nice and middle-classed. There was a smell of roasting chicken. "You eat meat, right, Gary?" she asked. "If you're up for eating."

"I could eat," I said.

"Para?"

"I don't know if I'm hungry," said Para.

We had dinner. Between bites, I said that I worked with Para; I was in a band; yes, it was exciting; yes, I enjoyed going to art galleries with Para; no, I had never been to Vermont before.

Para's mother told me about her job as a senior librarian at UVM, and told a story about how the young activist girls at the college had lately been leaving angry notes in the library suggestion box, because the library received *Playboy,* on microfilm, but not *Playgirl.*

"And for God's sake, Gary," said Eileen, "you don't know this about me, but I'm ninety times the feminist of any of these little girls. I wrote fan mail to Bella Abzug."

"You too?" I said.

Later, Para and I went upstairs, and, as Para had told me, it wasn't a question that we'd sleep in the same bed, which was a relief, although it made me think of all the other men that Para had brought home and been allowed to have sex with under her mother's eye.

"Your mom is pretty serious about library stuff," I said.

" 'Libraries are the boundary between civilization and chaos,' " said Para. "That's a quote."

"Well, there are some other boundaries," I said. "Like pants. Without pants, chaos."

"Mom would put pants after libraries," said Para.

"Maybe she has a point," I said. We reclined, and I sighed. It felt good to be under covers and still, after this day of horses and mothers.

After a while, Para said, "You know, I'm bummed. I kind of wanted to do it in my childhood bed."

"This is your childhood bed? It's queen-sized. How big was your crib?"

"Actually, no, this is a guest bed. But you know."

"I'm sorry," I said. "I mean, I could get something going."

This was true. Even if I'd had my arms chopped off and a case of rickets, if sex was called for, I could muster the energy. There was no reason a sprained ankle should drop the curtain on some play.

"Just relax, big fella," said Para. "It'll wait."

She was right; I needed to rest. But I had to tell my brain, which had become excited about the slim potential of sex, that there wasn't going to be any after all.

My brain was upset for a moment, and then it said, *Well, that's probably for the best.* Then I fell asleep like I'd been hit on the head by a Pink Floyd hammer.

I woke alone to serious, but diminished, ankle pain and the smell of blueberry pancakes. I went downstairs to a mother-daughter argument.

PARA: I'll tell you about Christmas when I make my mind up. I don't know what I'm doing this year.

PARA'S MOM: Hello, Gary. Para, honey, I just think it would be nice to have you here one time. We could decorate the tree.

PARA: I just don't know. We'll see.

PARA'S MOM: "We'll see." Gary, my daughter is incapable of making plans.

PARA: I make plans all the time.

GARY: Those pancakes smell tasty.

For breakfast there were pancakes with maple syrup and bickering. I ate several helpings of the pancakes and stayed out of the bickering. I noticed that Eileen, like her daughter, did not really eat food, but rather looked at it, and nibbled at the edges. Instead of eating, she made cutting statements about Para never visiting, and Para's lack of ambition.

These weren't direct hits. Rather, Eileen might just be talking away about her friend Doug, another librarian, who was preparing a book-length bibliography on the Vietnam War, and she'd say, "He works hard. But of course, Para, you like to relax."

Para would take the bait, and say, "I work *very* hard." Then her mother would say, "Gary, you work with Para. Is she a hard worker?" And I would say, "Para is like an incredible motor that never stops." Then Eileen would say, "Well, that's good, because in high school, she would never wake up in the morning." And Para would huff.

After a long half hour of that, I offered to help with the dishes, but was refused and directed to the living room instead. There, I stretched barefoot on the couch and Eileen instructed Para on the right way to fill the dishwasher, to which Para snapped, "I know how to fill up a goddamned dishwasher." I turned on the TV and watched a show where people play competitive video games. It was strangely interesting, and took my mind off my ankle.

At noon, we sang "Happy Birthday" to Para and had some cake. It was all a little tense and hurried, so in the rush to blow out the candles, I forgot about Para's gift. We put the plates in the sink ("I'll deal with the dishwasher, honey," said Eileen). Para told me we were leaving.

In the car on the way home, Para spent a good hour surfing a huge wave of mother-frustration, whining like a saw cutting through steel. I looked at trees and tried not to move my foot.

"Breathe that air," I said. The mother-whining and the swelling were hard to take all at once.

"You're right," said Para. "I need to breathe." She rolled her own window down and we drove on, toward home.

* * *

"Gary," said Charles, sitting on the couch with Patmavadi. I'd come in on them, sitting on the floor of the kitchen, with Charles wrapped around her, hugging. "What happened to you?"

"I took a fall off a horse," I said, dropping with a thump into the easy chair.

"Did you break something?"

"It's sprained," I said.

"Did you go to the emergency room?" Charles asked.

"No health insurance," I said.

"That's just as well," said Patmavadi. "Western medicine."

"Do you want me to look at it?" asked Charles.

"Look at it?"

"You know I'm a healer," said Charles. He held up his hands. "I promise to be gentle."

"Oh, I'm fine," I said.

"Gary, seriously," said Patmavadi. "I threw out my back at the potter's wheel, and Charles made me whole again."

"I just move the muscle groups," he said. "After fifteen years of yoga, I can usually find a way to make things better."

What did I have to lose? I assented. Charles instructed me to lie on the floor and remove my shoe. Luckily, my right sock was intact.

"You banged it up good," he said.

"I didn't actually fall off a horse," I said. "Actually, I fell off a horse, and then fell down."

"God, I love watching this," said Patmavadi. "It's inspiring."

Charles began to move his hands over my ankle, touching it lightly. He began to chant, a little humming chant. "Umm-umm-umm-ummmmmm," he said.

"Do you feel it?" asked Patmavadi.

"I do feel something," I said. Charles had a surprisingly light touch, and somehow the pain was lessened. I realized I'd been suffering for hours. I leaned back and let a man stroke my ankle.

"That's better, right?" said Charles. "Just let me do my work."

"You know, it's much better."

"Before long we'll have you doing yoga," said Charles.

"Oh, Gary, you should," said Patmavadi. "You would be so much happier."

The door opened, and we all looked over to see David, silhouetted by the bright fluorescent light of the hallway. There was a long silence.

"This is the kinkiest thing I've ever seen," said David.

"Charles is helping my foot," I said, knowing that nothing would excuse the scene in David's mind. He was going to rag my ass for years.

David put down his bag and sat. "Don't mind me."

Charles began to hum again, and I could feel David's mind working, critical opinions growing in his mind.

"Gary, now, you're not used to this," said Charles. "But I just want you to let go, just let yourself wander. Try to clear your mind."

"Think of a star," said Patmavadi. "A single star. That always helps me."

"Don't think of my balls," said David. "That won't help you at all."

Patmavadi huffed.

"David, please," said Charles. "Please. I know you don't take this seriously."

"I do," said David. "I really do." He nodded and smiled. "In fact, I just shaved them yesterday."

All I could think of were David's testicles, shorn and smooth. In my mind they hung remarkably low.

"I was riding a horse," I said.

"Wow. You are truly a fuckup," said David.

"David, let Charles try," said Patmavadi.

"Gary," said Charles, "take a moment. Is your mind free?"

"It's free," I said, desperate to limp to my bedroom, where I could hide and cry.

"I'm going to put things back together," Charles said. "It might hurt a little."

There was a crunch, and a single, hot tear came from my ducts, unsolicited, and raced down my face. "Ah," I said. "Ah-ah-ha-ha-ah."

"There you go," said Patmavadi. "That's what you want."

"Oh, yeah," I said, "that's much better." It was so much worse. "Oh, that's great." I got up, trying to hide the fact that, if my foot touched the ground, the world would end. "I just want to get to bed."

"Sure," said Patmavadi. "You need sleep."

"Twelve hours a day during the winter," said Charles. "You know that, right?"

"Sure," I said, with no idea what he was talking about.

"And orgasms," said Patmavadi. "Give yourself an orgasm before you go to bed."

"He will," said David. "Rest assured."

I made it to the hallway, and then hopped as quietly as I could back to the bedroom. Charles had messed me up bad. Maybe my mind hadn't been free enough. Maybe the sudden appearance of David's testicles had ruined my psychic healing aura. I wondered if this often happened, if people pretended to be healed by their gurus in order to not hurt their feelings.

I went in and lay down on the bed, gasping until the pain finally subsided. It was almost back to normal.

A few minutes later there was a knock at the door, and I yelled that it was open. David came in. "Mind if I turn on the light?" he asked.

"Sit down," I said. He sat on the rickety wooden chair I'd fished from the trash. "How's your ankle?"

"Just get it over with," I said. "Have your say and let me die in peace."

"Did Krishna help you at all?"

"It's, like, twice as bad."

"That's what you get," he said. "That girlfriend of his is a piece. I'd give her an orgasm."

"Yeah," I said, not interested in anything but the relief of suffering. "I had some Vicodin last night. It helped."

"That's the sweetness of life," said David. "You ever snort it?"

"No," I said. I didn't know you *could* snort Vicodin. I told him my story of horsemanship, and he listened patiently, nodding. As I described the way Para had patiently driven me home, I noticed that he was moving around in his chair, and patting his pocket over and over again, so I asked him how he was doing.

"Want to see something?" he asked, reaching into his pocket and pulling out a jewelry box. "Check this out." He handed me the box. I opened it. Inside was a huge, gorgeous, shining diamond.

"This is it!" I said, temporarily forgetting my own pain. "You gave it to her."

"I did," he said.

"It didn't fit?" I asked.

"You could say that," he said.

"Oh, no," I said, catching on.

"Check that shit out," he said, shaking his head. " 'Maybe later, but not now.' That's what she told me. I guess you don't want to hear about it now, though," he said. "Given your infirm condition."

"Actually, it makes me feel better," I said. "I mean, I thought I was a screwup."

David sighed, and told his story. It was a story I knew, one I'd heard from countless friends, and lived out myself. Although the versions I knew never involved a $12,500 diamond ring. He looked

exhausted and frustrated, like he'd been listening to Alanis Moris-
sette albums for days on end.

He concluded his story with Sue handing him the ring across a
table, saying, "I know I asked for this. But I don't think it's the
right time."

"I have to admit," he said, "coming in to find you on the floor
making love with Charles cheered me up, no end."

"I'm glad I could help," I said. "God, I'll have to go onstage with
a crutch." Not that we had anything lined up at the moment. I reached
down to rub my ankle. "So what the hell do you do?" I asked David.

"Drink," he said. "Smoke. Sit around and watch TV. Also, tell
my mom. And then, I think, the best thing to do is kill myself."

"It's good to have a plan," I said. "I'd suggest heroin overdose."

"Freezing to death is supposed to be nice," he said. "But that
won't work for a couple months."

"Besides, if you kill yourself, I only have one roommate."

"Oh, don't worry," he said. "We'll have lots of time to hang out."

"Definitely."

"And I can date," he said.

"It's like that?"

"I don't know," he said. "Sue wants to be free to make her own
choices. Quote unquote. I don't even want to consider the ramifications of that statement."

"It stings, huh, bro?"

"You have no idea. Is your sister coming back to town any time
soon?"

"Not that I know about."

"Ah, well."

I felt bad for David, supporting his folks, losing his fiancée, but
I had no intention of letting him anywhere near my sister.

"Luckily I didn't tell anyone at work," he said. "So I don't have
to face that."

"Well, at least you didn't fall off a horse," I said, expecting him to at least nod and smile, but he just sat there, shadowy under the light that a seventy-five-watt bulb cast through a paper lantern, and bit his lip.

After some further mumbling conversation, he left me alone to my suffering. Later in the night, sleeping lightly due to the throbbing in my ankle, I woke to a thrashing sound from his room, and then some crying, snatches of anguish rising up loud enough to penetrate the walls. I filed those sounds away. He never wanted anyone to hear them, and as far as I was concerned, they never happened.

With the demo on slowdown, and nothing much to do, I checked Para's blog.

Jan

Boy gave me a copy of Tschichold's opus, very thoughtful. We had a horseful and eventful weekend which ended in Boy spraining his ankle. But also caught up with some good old friends, and renewed an old connection.

Not much to learn from that. I gave up on browsing the web and decided to see if I could get some more work. I asked Tom, the big boss at BrandSolve, if he had any extra hours for me. He told me to talk to Scott.

"Hey, synth dork," I said. "Do you want to give me any work?"

Scott thought for a moment. "You can break up a Word file for me, paste it into a web browser. Do you know HTML?"

"No," I said. "Can you teach me?"

"Some of it," he said. He told me about the tags that wrap text, how to make paragraphs and italics. It only took about twenty minutes.

"That's it?" I asked. "That's the web?"

"A big piece of it. It gets a little bit harder after that." I went back to my desk and proceeded to follow orders. After an hour, Tom came out of his office, bags under his eyes.

"Hey, Gary," he said. "What you doing?"

"HTML," I said.

"Excellent," he said. "Keep it up."

That felt good, to get the boss to notice my hard work. I finished the job and headed home. A few weeks of filing, answering phones, and HTMLing went by, until one day Scott said, "I want to get back to the demo."

"Me too," I said, thanking God. "I think it's time."

"Do you want to call everyone?" Scott asked, and of course I did. I went to the phones and found that both Katherine and Jacob were ready to jump back into recording.

The first problem we faced was all the reverb. The first two songs sounded as if they'd been performed at the bottom of a chasm.

"I have to make them wet," said Scott. "Otherwise . . . well, it's just not possible otherwise."

"Eh," said Jacob. "We sound like we're spelunking."

"That's because slot A doesn't fit into tab B," said Scott. "Gary comes in late on 'August,' so I pitch-shift his voice, and then Katherine hits a beat late, and so forth, et cetera. It hides the flaw. The other option is to practice, and get it right."

"I want to get it right," said Katherine. I was also for getting it right.

"I have no time," said Jacob. "I mean, I don't know how much I can give to this band. I haven't wanted to say anything about it."

"You have a new girlfriend," said Katherine.

"This is true. She has needs."

"OK," I said, "so this is a crossroads. This is a decision point."

"I'm trying to make it work," said Jacob. "I don't like being late. But I've got seven things going at once."

"And, let's be completely honest here," said Scott. "You are not a brilliant time manager."

"I know," said Jacob, looking forlorn. "I truly do. Look. I'll just sleep less. And I'll tell Paula what's up. She's a dancer. She understands rehearsal schedules."

"OK," said Scott. "But is that going to work?"

"I'll just get up early," said Jacob. "And I'll tell my editors when I can't meet a deadline."

"That sounds like a recipe for awfulness," said Scott.

"No, I think Jacob could make it work," I said.

"You know, when I get a writing gig, I just see dollar signs," said Jacob. "It's hard to say no."

"I'm the same way," said Katherine. "I mean, next week I've got a gig and I'll probably be hard to reach."

"Look," I said, "we all have lives." Except for me, but I glossed over that point. "And I think this is a good sign, that we're hitting a point where hard work means something. I mean, if we need to practice harder, or individually, or . . ."

"Like I said, I'll be here," said Jacob. "I'll make it work."

And he did make it work, although he showed up with hair in fifty directions, and sometimes he looked like he was going to pass out over his bass. Scott became a serious taskmaster. When I was off-pitch, he'd sing the note until I matched him, over and over, until I could nail the songs. He made Jacob and Katherine practice together, with no other instrumentation, until they could keep the beat without flaw. Or without many flaws.

Even though he was the most time-starved of all of us, Jacob found it easier to pick up what Scott was after. He would just nod, look at the bass, and try whatever Scott advised him to do, until he got it. Katherine, who was used to just thrashing the drums like a madwoman, had a harder road.

"All right, come on," Scott would say. "Watch me. Triplets. Tum-tum-tum, tum-tum-tum."

"I know what *triplets* are," she'd say.

"Prove your knowledge," Scott would say, and Katherine would try, but it didn't always work. It didn't help that Scott had written a song, called "Christmas," in 7/4 that switched to waltz tempo halfway through. I always missed my cue coming in after the bridge. He still was holding on to the fantasy that we were, deep down, a prog band.

Still, slow and steady, we piled up the tracks. "August," "Hoyt-Schemerhorn," "Jesus Was a Union Man"—each one came into its own on Scott's hard drive. It was a very different feeling from playing a stage. When you perform, you're in the moment, trying to communicate with the audience however you can. But recording an album (well, a demo) is different. So, while live, we were kind of noisy and sloppy, on the demo we became crisp and rehearsed, with a sort of power-pop sound in parts. Katherine's drumming took on some subtlety. Jacob's bass was big and badass. My voice changed pitch and dynamics *at once*. And Scott played interminably long synth solos, each a minute or more, on six of the songs. Since he was doing the mixing, it was his prerogative.

The goal was to create something that people would listen to again and again, something that would sink into their brains, and that would eventually draw them to Schizopolis shows even if they *didn't* personally know any members of the band. Were we doing that with the demo? I honestly didn't know. My instinct was: yes, we were. And if I was right, that meant we could get back in touch with Lou Tremolo and talk about a label deal. And then, well— we'd have to rerecord the album. But then—then, we'd go on tour to support our new album, and Schizopolis would turn from a hobby into something real, and I could turn to the people who doubted me—my dad and my brother especially, and everyone in high school who ever winged a Tater Tot off the back of my head— and say, "Look. I made this work. I am one of the few, the proud, the brave, the indie."

*   *   *

Para went home for Thanksgiving. I wasn't too sad about spending some time away, because she'd been down in the dumps ever since the birthday trip to Vermont.

I decided to go home, too, and braved Penn Station's insane crush of holiday commuters. It felt strange to see the paramilitaries there, men and women in camouflage, keeping us safe from terrorists. There were other people in uniform, carrying duffel bags, soldiers on their way home for the holiday. I wondered what that was like, shuttling between army bases and Iraq. Then my train number popped up on the big board.

The plan was for me to stay at my father's on Wednesday evening, then head to my mom's on the day itself. This was the ritual way in which I observed Thanksgiving. I never told my father, of course, but I preferred my mother's half-assed observation of Thanksgiving to the perfectly glazed turkey that emerged from my stepmom Pat's oven.

Exactly as planned, I stepped onto Albany's ugly, squat train station, and there was my father's gray Mercury, not far from the station entrance. I threw my bag into the backseat and took my place in the front, giving him an awkward hug across the gearshift.

DAD: Good ride?
GARY: Fine ride.
DAD: Excellent.
GARY: Exactly.
DAD: Cold.
GARY: True.
DAD: Job going good?
GARY: Job is fine. I think they want to promote me.
DAD: Take it.
GARY: I might.
DAD: What's the holdup?

GARY: Just trying to make the band work, too.

DAD: Schizopolis. But don't count unhatched chickens.

GARY: I count only chickens that are there.

DAD: Those are the chickens that matter. Because you want to retire someday.

GARY: Definitely, within the next forty or fifty years, I want to retire.

DAD: Then you have a plan.

GARY: A detailed plan. With maps.

My father was big on plans. When I was twenty, and the bill came for my junior year at school, he asked me to create a Power-Point presentation to outline my future plans. He said it was only fair, as he was investing so much in my future, that he know exactly what that future entailed. I did so, using a campus computer lab, and presented it to him over Christmas. Slide one was:

1. GARY BENCHLEY, ENGLISH MAJOR

DATE OF GRADUATION: MAY 2003
GPA: 3.68
POSSIBILITIES: UNLIMITED

Slide two was "Applications of the English Major." Creating the presentation, I felt like a massive idiot, but when it was over, my father applauded, and I was once again a champion. His handshake and compliments were as potent as the gold stars he used to put on the fridge.

So I spent an evening sipping wine with my father and Pat, urbane and pleasant.

DAD: Joke?

GARY: Sure.

PAT: Oh, no! Your father's jokes.

DAD (*six hours later*): . . . And the bear said, "Let me paws for consideration."

GARY: *Ho! My!*

PAT: You guys!

DAD: I thought you might enjoy that.

Being at my father's was always a polite, distant affair, in the temperature-controlled house with central vacuum. With my mother, everything was more direct. When she rambled on, I just told her to shut up, and she threw things at my head, all very playful. But to tell my father to shut up—it's not like he'd pick up a lamp and smash me in the head with it, or disown me; it just didn't happen; saying that sort of thing was just not possible. It felt like, if I confronted him, or said something wrong, the world would end and the universe would die.

Pat's daughter, Kris, was out with friends, so I didn't see her. Which was just as well, as we had absolutely nothing to talk about, my interest in lacrosse being minimal, and her album collection consisting of the "Now That's What I Call Music" CD series. I went to bed in the spare bedroom, noting the huge headboard and the collection of porcelain and pewter knickknacks left on the bedside table.

The next day my father dropped me off at my mother's, and came in to say hello and tender his holiday greetings. Jad excused himself. My mom had poisoned Jad against my father, so while she could be perfectly pleasant to Dad, it was harder for Jad.

DAD: Gary here is making an impression at his job.

MOM: No! I had no idea.

GARY: I'm learning HTML.

The sound of hammering came from far away, Jad pounding something in anger.

DAD: He's coming up in the world, our Gary.

MOM: Of course he is.

DAD: Some sort of hammering?

MOM: Jad's workshop.

DAD: Oh, you know, that's right—I need to ask him about getting a new drill.

Mom directed him to the garage, shrugging her shoulders. My father liked to ask Jad tool-related questions, in as condescending a tone as possible, and then say things like, "Well, those of us with law degrees, what do we know about hardware?" I always expected Jad, who had strong emotions, to stab my father through the heart with a Philips-head screwdriver.

In the living room, I found my brother and sister watching TV. Elizabeth had taken a bus up a few days before, and Bill had flown in from San Diego for a few days.

"When'd you get in?" asked my brother. I told him about the train ride up. I bragged about going to the gym, even though I hadn't been in months, and left out anything about smoking. Then we watched TV for a while, sharing that special togetherness that only sitting on a couch watching VH1 can bring, until it was time for the turkey. Before he left, my dad had come in and asked Bill and Elizabeth when they were coming over, and they both promised to swing by that night.

We circled the table, ravenous. Mom asked God to watch over each of us, mentioning our special accomplishments over the year. Bill had been promoted to Lieutenant Junior Grade. Elizabeth had achieved honors in her classes, had had an excellent paying internship over the summer, and now was likely to achieve another 4.0 average at CMU. And Gary, well, he had moved to New York, and was doing very well. I waited to see if there might be a mention of Schizopolis, but none was there.

Jad carved the turkey with an electric knife, and we set to eating, mostly in silence except for the obligatory compliments to my mother, who had opened many a can to make the feast a reality. There wasn't enough stuffing, particularly after my brother took a nine-person-sized helping, but otherwise it was an ideal, starchy meal. Eventually, I arrived at the comfortable numb, engorged Thanksgiving sensation. Which meant that it was time for the siblings to start screwing with each other.

"I'm looking forward to some pumpkin pie," said my brother.

"That's interesting," I said. "I thought navy guys liked fudge."

"Oh, Bill, do you get good desserts on the ship?" asked my mother.

"When I was in the army," Jad said, "we had to eat frozen cake. They used to serve it frozen. Put it on the plate. Like a brick."

"The desserts on board are really good," said my brother, shaking his head at me. His look said, "Later, I will beat your ass at football."

"I asked specifically about fudge," I said. Elizabeth shook her head as well.

"How's your band?" asked Bill. "I was listening to the radio the other day, and I didn't hear you."

"That's because we're not on the classic rock station," I said.

"Gary? You're on the radio?" asked my mother.

"Yes, Gary," asked my brother, "where can I tune in to hear Schizodopomolopis?"

"Is that a Greek name?" asked Jad.

"Schizopolis," I said. "That's the name of our band."

"That's *creative*," said my mother.

"You're lead vocals, right?" asked my sister. "Is it going OK?"

"And rhythm guitar," I said.

"That means you can't play guitar for real, right?" asked Bill.

"That's what it means," I said. "But in response to Elizabeth's question, we're getting a demo together, and we've got a manager," I said. "So bit by bit."

"What does that mean, a manager?" asked my mother.

"He'll sell the album," I said.

"In stores?" my mother asked.

"No, Mom," said Elizabeth. "He represents the band to the label. He's like an agent."

"Sounds real promising," said Bill.

"Bill, I've been meaning to ask you," I said, "does it get lonely on the carrier? Sometimes you just need a hug, right?"

"Gary," said Elizabeth, "I hate to rain on this, but the navy is coed now."

That was very disappointing. I'd been thinking of ways to imply that my brother was a homosexual for the entire train ride.

"Really?" I asked.

"Yes," said my brother. "The navy is a very progressive organization."

We ate until we were all a little sickly, then sat around a bit, and helped with the dishes. Following this came the obligatory football-passing. In moments, the game went full tackle, and a minute later I was aware that my brother was standing over my prostrate form, yelling, in a drill-sergeant voice, "Get up, muddy bitch pussy-boy, so I can beat you down again."

I stood up, wet mud covering my slacks and sweater, an ache in my bad ankle, and Elizabeth laughed until she doubled over. "Bitches have a lesson to learn," I yelled, tearing toward him as fast as my boots would let me. I leaped from almost a yard away, en-joying a moment of flight, and took him to the ground with a crunch.

"Not bad for New York," he said.

We stood up together and I said, "Elizabeth doesn't have any mud on her at all."

"Come on," she said, "seriously, don't."

"Ooh," I said. "I hate when she uses her whiny voice."

"I know," said Bill. "Come on." He and I chased Elizabeth

around the backyard, out into the street, then back into the yard, finally taking her down to the ground. She yelled out the words "you assholes" over and over, laughing hysterically. Then we went back into the house, all three of us filthy, for some pumpkin pie.

The demo was done by the first week of December. There were nine songs, three newly added by Jacob. After what felt like far too much time, everything was wrapped up and placed on cheap, shiny CDs burned straight from Scott's computer. And it sounded great, twenty minutes and thirty-two seconds of clean sound. It rocked out, as it should have. Having it done was an essential part of the plan. Of course, there was still some reverb, and Scott had sequenced a drum track on "Times Square," but effects were judiciously used.

Live, I could get through most of the songs pretty well, but it turned out that I was often a half-step flat, and so I learned to thank God, in the guise of Scott, for Auto-Tune. If we went on tour, I decided, I'd find a way to buy an outboard Auto-Tune box for live performance.

We sent out the demo, we gave it to friends, and we put up MP3s in a password-protected directory. Absolutely nothing came of this. I sent a copy to Lou Tremolo, and received no response. Jacob gave it to his music-writer friends, and reported back that they were suitably impressed. Not enough to write about it—after all, it was just a demo. But the word was good.

And we began to get more gigs. They came through word of mouth, from people who knew people, not as a result of the demo. We played Fishkill in Brooklyn, and the Mighty Caw in Manhattan. We played McMallister's Pub in Queens one Friday, and Tom's Deli in Brooklyn the next night. For that last event we had a listing in the *Onion* events section, which felt like a true victory. I cut out the listing and Scotch-taped it to my wall, next to my picture of

Wayne Coyne being carried across a crowd inside a giant plastic bubble.

It was only a matter of time before we'd be interviewed, so I got back on the wagon and started practicing my interview technique again. "Well, we started out with a prog feeling," I planned to say, "but then we decided to get back to something simpler, but now we're definitely picking that up again. We want to bring a sense of musical creativity back to the scene." At my words, the attractive reporter from the *New York Times* would nod and write on a steno pad. "That's exactly what I'm looking for," she'd say. "Now, Gary, do you mind being a sex symbol, or is it a burden?"

"It has its ups and downs," I'd say.

Tom, the big boss at BrandSolve, called me into his office. *This is it,* I thought. *I'm getting fired.*

"Just wanted to take a moment and catch up," he said.

"It's good," I said. "The phones are ringing."

"And you're answering them!" he said, smiling. Tom was a nice guy, mostly, although he could get very pissed off when someone missed a deadline; then he'd stomp through the office. That rarely came down on me, though. He was maybe thirty-six, and had decorated the wall by his chair with photos of his two children and prints of paintings of sailboats. He saw me looking at the pictures.

"No boat yet," he said. "Someday."

"Definitely," I said. "Who doesn't love a nice yacht?"

He smiled; praising yachts had scored a point. "What I want to talk to you about is, you've really made a place for yourself here, at BrandSolve—"

I told him I was glad to hear that.

"—No, everyone thinks very well of you. Working is a lot more than just answering the phone and dealing with spreadsheets. There's a lot of personal give-and-take, a lot of interaction. A lot of synergy."

"I'm a big fan of synergy."

"So I wanted to know what your plans were. What comes next?"

"My plans?"

"For a career, for life, anything. I mean, it's clear you're not going to answer phones forever."

"Well, I've got this music thing I do in my spare time," I said.

"With Scott," he said. "I've heard it. It's great. I don't have any musical knowledge, I mean, I don't even listen to the radio anymore. But real energy."

"You've heard it?"

"Totally. Scott gave me the demo. I respect it."

"Well, thank you," I said.

"I used to play trombone in high school, and I know how hard it is to do what you've done. But I guess what I'm asking is, what else do you want to do?"

"I'm just really seeing where the demo leads," I said. "You know?"

"What I want to say here is that if you'd like some new skills— I saw you with Scott doing HTML, and if you'd like to talk about some other work you could do, and think about full-time, we could do that."

It finally made sense what he was talking about, the reason he'd called me into the office: Full time! Full time with benefits! Benefits! The only thing that rocks more than rock is health care. I could hear the call to my father, telling him how I was on a career track. I could see money, money piling up in my bank account, and never again thinking the word "overdraft." I could buy Para a meal at a restaurant that fused French, Spanish, and Chinese cuisines. And with these visions came a sudden change in perceptions. I suddenly saw Schizopolis in a completely different light: as a millstone, a huge weight holding me back from a career. I could be middle class, if I didn't want to rock.

"You don't have to do anything you don't want to do," said Tom. "But I want to extend that opportunity to you."

I thanked him sincerely, and we shook hands like true office-working men, men who believe in the goodness of capitalism. I headed back to my desk to answer the phones and make thousands of tiny changes to websites. After a while, I got up and told Scott about the conversation.

"What are you going to do?" he asked.

"Did you talk to him?" I asked.

"No, not a word. I figured you wanted to stay part-time."

"It would be a real job," I said. "I've never had a real job before."

"Did he say what you'd be doing?"

"Maybe some HTML? Then I might work for you. You could never ask me to take off my pants again."

"No," said Scott. "I couldn't. But he wasn't more specific?"

"He said I had shown myself to be very capable, and that I should consider my options."

"You should," said Scott. "I've been here six years. It's not a bad gig."

"I know," I said. "It's a pretty easy road, actually."

Scott went on to tell me how he'd started at BrandSolve. He'd worked as a programmer for a few years, for Bloomberg, a big finance computer firm. He quit with a few spare dollars, and decided to volunteer to work at a men's health clinic, which was also where his boyfriend at the time worked. He did that for about three months, and saw every single thing that could go wrong with a man's genitals and/or rectum. "This was in the West Village," he said. "With regards to the sad consequences of overeager ass play," said Scott, "I worked at ground zero."

"So you quit and came to work here?" I asked.

"I'm not really the men's health clinic type, it turned out. Also, I broke up with my boyfriend."

"So BrandSolve was better than dealing with grossly infected penises?"

"Yes," said Scott.

"Sounds like a dream job," I said.

But still, Scott had enjoyed six years of pure stability. Did I want that? I didn't know exactly where Tom had gotten the idea that I was a good worker, but if he thought I could add value to the enterprise, why question it? Then again, we had a demo, and a good one. We should be pushing that hard. And if I took a full-time job, I'd be in the same place as my bandmates, trying to balance work and art. I mean, I doubt that I spent more time working on the band than Scott did. But I had more time to think about things, to sing in the shower, to figure my life out.

I also felt a tiny bit hypocritical, because I'd looked down on Scott for the last year, as I worked at BrandSolve, seeing him as complacent, working for the man. Today, the man had asked me to step on board his boat and set sail for the magical country of Careeristan, and I was ready to raise the mast. I'd seen myself as outside of the status quo, following my dream. But, if I admitted the truth, I'd also been *jealous* of people with careers and four-digit bank accounts. I thought of my sprained ankle, about the amazing luxury of visiting the doctor whenever I wanted. Should I sell out so cheaply?

I decided to call Lou Tremolo one last time, and see if he'd heard the copy of the demo I'd sent him, see if there were any possibilities there. I'd kept his card in my wallet, looking at it from time to time to remind myself that people wanted us to succeed, and I pulled it out, the edges softened by wear.

"Oh, hey," he said. "I saw you guys at Brownie's."

"Red Light," I said. "I sent you a demo?"

"Oh," he said. "I moved offices. Send it over."

"Sure," I said. "It's online if you want it."

"No," said Lou. "Mail it."

The next day I dropped it in the mail, priority, in bubble wrap. Scott advised me not to get my hopes up. But within seventy-two hours—well, business hours; there was a weekend in there, too—Lou called back.

"Let's get a burger," he said.

Schizopolis gathered at Mugs, in Williamsburg, on a Wednesday night. Lou was already there, and he squinted when he saw us enter, probably trying to remember what we looked like. We sat down and, at his prompting, ordered hamburgers and beer.

"No vegetarians, huh?" said Lou.

"I used to be a vegetarian," said Jacob. "I gave it up."

"I love meat," said Lou, tearing off a chunk of his hamburger, like a lion digging into a Christian. "All right," he said. "I liked what I heard. I liked 'Hoyt-Schemerhorn.' "

"Those are Gary's lyrics," said Scott.

"And Jacob's," I said.

"It's not an earthshaker, but it's solid. There's some *stuff* in there."

When he spoke, Lou's neck moved faster than his head. I found myself liking him. This was not a random human being, someone off the street, but a representative of that massive glowing orb known as the music industry. Bands were like sperm, trillions of them hurtling toward some half-imagined goal, and the music industry was the egg, refusing access to all but the fewest. And it was also like the vagina, filled with acids that killed the weakest bands. Here we were at Mugs, in Williamsburg, meeting a man with a ponytail who could guide us through the vaginal canal. I looked over at Katherine, who was smiling and nodding.

"So originally you were talking about Parakeet Records," I said. "But then . . ."

"Ha," he said. "They're assholes. Look," he said, chewing, "I just set up a relationship with a guy downtown. I'm advising him. I think he might bite."

"That sounds perfect," I said. What could be more perfect than a manager who was working directly with a label? That was like an EZPass; you didn't stop and pay the toll, but just drove right through.

"What label is it?" asked Scott.

"Original Syn Records," he said, "with a 'Y.' You've heard of Slake?"

"Oh, I know Slake," said Jacob.

"They just signed with him. I helped him bring in Slake. Took some work."

"You're Slake's manager?" Jacob asked.

"I helped him bring Slake in," repeated Lou, whatever that meant. "You know jam bands? OK, so he's got a Christian jam band, the Disciples of Sound. For money. He tells me he wants to get something else in like Slake, round things out."

Lou went on to promise that he'd hand-deliver the demo to Chris Neffly, head of Original Syn, and see what happened.

"Do we need to sign anything with you?" Scott asked Lou.

"Never sign anything," said Lou.

"OK," said Scott. "But—"

"Basically, look, you guys have a good package—"

"I have a fantastic package," I said.

Lou took another bite, ignoring me. "If this works out, we'll talk. I got things up my ass right now. I don't want to screw around with paperwork."

"So we're dating," said Katherine. "We're just out for dinner to see if we like each other."

"Yes," said Lou. "You don't buy a ring just yet."

I admired him for trusting us, for wanting to take a risk on us, when there were so many bands out there. "Sounds fair," I said.

Lou went on to describe his background, which was varied. He'd managed Satisfaction, a group of Rolling Stones impersonators, along with a number of disco and funk groups, the names of which rang no bells. He'd been responsible for the sudden rise of Slicker Than Grace, a techno act that dimly registered in my memory.

"Kind of a big change from the Stones to Slicker Than Grace," said Scott.

In response, Lou told a story about Slicker Than Grace. They had, apparently, fired him when he was only able to get them fifty thousand dollars for a video. "They wanted to be on MTV," said Lou, "and they blamed me for that. And I was, like, stop gashing holes in your face onstage, and fucking thirteen-year-old girls, and then I can help you get a video."

"Well, we've got much more modest goals," I said. "We'd settle for VH1."

"Forget it," said Lou. "Don't even think about videos at this stage. Total waste of money."

I nodded, grateful for the advice, and crossed out the line in my plan that read "Make a video."

Lou paid for the hamburgers and beer, which felt good, and we saw him off in his deep orange 1985 Lincoln Town Car.

"Do you trust him?" asked Jacob. "I mean, managers usually don't work directly with the label."

"But that's always really inefficient," I said. "There's all this waiting."

"I don't know," said Scott. "He seems a little sleazy."

"He's a pig," said Katherine. "He ate the hamburger like a jackal."

"Two hamburgers," said Jacob.

"Well," I said, "we can see where this leads, or we can go looking for another manager. I want to see where it leads."

My bandmates agreed that this was a sensible approach. Katherine descended into the train station, looking back to wave, and we all went our separate ways toward our own apartments.

Back at my place, David was sitting on the couch with a girl on his lap. "This is Lisa," he said, introducing me. She was wearing so much jewelry she looked like a disco ball.

"Hey, Lisa," I said. "How you guys doing?"

"Great," she slurred, "I'm *so* great."

"Glad to hear that," I said, heading into my own room, where I called Para. She was watching *The Daily Show,* and ready for bed.

"I'm so glad to hear your voice," she said. "It always cheers me up."

I told her about Lou. "That is so excellent," she said. "I'm dating a genuine rock star." I remembered all the months when she'd sneered a little at Schizopolis, and felt truly gratified. I'd earned her approval. I lit up a cigarette, and looked through some of the magazines I'd bought the day prior. One was called *Internet Architect* and the other was *Advertising Report.* Granted, the meeting with Lou had gone well, but if I did decide to work for the man, I wanted to understand what he was saying. Except both of the magazines were filled with extraterrestrial marking and language; the advertisers were worried about CPMs and demographic analysis, and the Internet people were on about Java and Web Services. None of it made any sense. Maybe, after all, it would make more sense to stick to the rock.

The Studio

We were supposed to meet Chris Neffly, founder of Original Syn Records, in a bar downtown, but when we arrived, only Lou was there. "Change of plans," said Lou. "Chris wants us to come up to his apartment."

The apartment was in SoHo, a neighborhood I didn't know well. Scott, Jacob, and Katherine were impressed, though.

"Where did he get his money?" Jacob asked Lou.

"Internet," said Lou, with a shrug. Sometimes I feel that I was born too late. Had I come along five years before, I could have started my own Internet company and become a billionaire, or at least a millionaire. Then I could also have my own label.

Chris's building looked sort of tired and rusty, so he couldn't be *that* rich. He buzzed us in. We took the elevator up to his place, and when we got off I looked for a hallway of some kind, until I realized that the entire floor was a single apartment.

"Shoes off!" said a short man with carefully groomed shaggy hair and sideburns, a little on the fat side, calling from many yards away, near the windows. I guessed that this was Chris. "Shoes off!" He had a high, kind of whiny voice.

We removed our shoes. I was conscious of a hole in my right sock revealing an uncut toenail. I checked my bandmates, and Lou, but they had perfect socks. Katherine's were blue with white stripes. We entered the living room—more like an atrium—stepping onto a huge, thick white carpet. It looked like Muppet skin.

"I love this carpet," said Scott.

"That's Donald," said Chris. At first I thought he meant the carpet, and I wondered what that meant. Maybe the very wealthy named their furnishings. But Chris was talking about a tall, thin guy on the couch, about my age. We entered the atrium and went through the regular hand-shaking ritual.

"Busy day," said Chris. He came over to shake our hands. We took seats on the low, angular set of sofas that wrapped around a huge aluminum coffee table. The table was laden with fashion and music magazines with obscure names. Some of them had stickers where the price was in pounds.

"So what do they know?" Chris asked Lou. "Should I give my spiel?"

"Give your spiel," said Lou.

"The most important fact about me," said Chris, "is that I always wanted to play guitar. And if you went back to my bedroom, you'd find that there are six guitars there, many of them vintage, but then you might ask, what does he do with these guitars? And the sad answer is nothing. They remain unplucked and unfingered."

"I know how that feels," said Katherine.

Lou shot her a warning glance, and Chris continued.

"The problem, and this is the second most important fact, is I have absolutely no talent for playing. Actually, I have no talent for practicing. This was a hard lesson to learn, but the world is filled with hard lessons. But I have other talents that are compelling. And earned through experience. One of them is management. And another is brand strategy and marketing. The other is listening."

"I like to listen, too," I said.

"Listening to music, to people, to ideas. And then *acting* on the listening." His voice lowered, and became serious. "Six months ago

I got back from India, where I'd gone to replenish myself. And what I decided, what I realized mattered most, was *music*. It's what people use to identify themselves. It's the most cohesive social force in the world. I'd seen how people reacted to Bollywood movies, how important the songs are. I wanted to bring that here. So I decided to do something I *could* do. Which is create synergy."

"Does this mean you like Indian musicals?" Jacob asked.

"No, what I like is *synergy*. And you know, I'm a big fan of serendipity, and a friend of mine introduced me to Lou." Lou began to say something, and Chris cut him off. "I said, Lou, I want to start a label. And what I want to do is break down the silos in the music industry. I want to work closely with management. I want to work closely with the bands. I want to get rid of the middlemen, and really take everything I learned from the Internet, from the four different companies I founded, from my entire experience, and bring it to bear here, on an independent label. And I want to focus on independent music. Independent rock, electronica. Who cares what kind of music? Those boundaries are artificial. What matters is the word 'independent.' "

"That's the word," I said.

"But you look at independent rock, and there are too many *dependencies*. It's the opposite of independent. The band is dependent on the manager, the manager is dependent on the goodwill of labels and venues, everyone has to deal with booking agents, and so instead of creating something unified, you build something that's shattered, in fragments."

I saw that Donald, who was not a carpet, was moving his hands behind a laptop, probably checking email.

"There are too many layers, too many voices unheard," Chris said. "There are mute inglorious Miltons out there. Mute inglorious Hendrixes, and Lou Reeds. Like a phone. They're out there calling, but we have them on mute." He paused, waiting for the laugh. Scott chuckled in a friendly way. "We have to press that button and get them off mute. So, with help from Lou, and also from Donald, but using my own investment capital, I created Original Syn. Which, you've noticed the spelling? That stands for *syn*ergy. Because that is what I'm looking for. I want to get to the synergy model in a moment, but let me tell you why it's so important. It's because the mute inglorious aspect, which we just discussed, that presents a unique business problem. Because in order to glorify the mute, what do we need to do?"

"Learn sign language?" I said.

"A good guess, and a funny answer, and I appreciate humor. But what we need to do is allow ourselves to understand the marketplace, to see it as a breathing entity, and to leverage the knowledge of other disciplines. We need to get rid of the dependencies. And we need to think seriously about branding. Now, you do not need to think seriously about branding. All right. In truth, I have not heard your demo."

That was a little disappointing.

"But Lou feels that you are a good addition to Original Syn, and that carries *weight* around here, and Donald, you've heard it."

"I've heard it."

"What did you think? And excuse me," he said to us, "but one of the most important variables in the Original Syn equation is openness. Which is why I said that I have not listened to your demo, and why I am asking Donald to present his opinion in front of the group."

Donald, who had been staring into space, shifted in his seat and looked over at us. "It's fine," he said.

"Another opinion that carries weight," said Chris. "You can't run a business like a democracy, but you can run it like a benevolent dictatorship, which is what I am doing, aim to do, once we've gotten the papers back from the lawyers." He laughed to himself and shook his head. "God help you if you want to incorporate a business in New York."

"I've heard it's hard," said Scott. "Actually, regarding branding, I work for a brand consultancy—"

"Hard does not do it justice," said Chris. "But what I do is carefully weigh the analysis of those people who are my partners—not official partners, but this is a partnership organization, and also a learning organization, an organization with a strong knowledge base that comes out of varied experience. So it is a de facto partnership."

"Do you want to listen to the demo?" asked Lou.

"I do," said Chris. "But before we do, I want to tell you about my synergy model. Because when I listen to the demo, that's how I'll be thinking about it."

"Go for it," said Jacob.

"Excellent," said Chris. "So, this is something that I've lost a lot of sleep about. Are you ready?"

"I'm deeply ready," I said.

"There are three kinds of synergy that are relevant to bands today," said Chris, holding up three fingers. "One, there's the synergy between the music and the performers. By which I mean, the way that the performers are able to really represent their music. You have no idea how many demos I get that sound great, but when you see who did it, it's two pasty white guys with laptops."

"We're against that," said Katherine.

"Right. The second form of synergy is what I call pop-culture synergy. That is, when a band is able to really get the zeitgeist, and has a clear weltanschauung that fits in with what's going on out there today."

"We've got weltanschauung," I said. "No doubt."

"The key word is 'gestalt,' " he said. "The gestalt is what matters."

"Gestalt," I said. "Definitely."

Scott looked at me, shaking his head slightly.

"Now the third is what I call media synergy. Which means that,

OK, we're sending things out to radio, but we're also distributing songs on peer-to-peer networks. We've got a website with a message board. We've got the visuals, the clothes, everything, we make that totally consistent. And I think you see that with Slake. Whose new album, by the way, is going to be fantastic."

"I couldn't agree more with that," said Scott. "You need to use every channel."

"So that's what we do," he said. "We make sure that the brand is totally consistent, that there's a real gestalt. The look of the band, and the stage presence, and the website all work together, and people have a complete cognitive portrait of the group. And that cognitive portrait is what sells the music. God, I wish I had this in PowerPoint. Donald, we're going to do a PowerPoint."

"It's done," said Donald.

"Where is it?"

"It's on your computer."

"We'll look at it later. But does the synergy model work? I think when you look at Slake, you can see this working," said Chris. "We took Slake, a band that very few people knew, and we've got them in the studio, we've committed. But we're also looking at how to tell the Slake story. And what is the Slake story? It's about *ecstasy*. Colin is an ecstatic singer. And we're going to manage the Slake tour, and work with partners to distribute the Slake CD. And that means more profits for Slake, and a better bottom line for us. And so we make that the gist of everything related to Slake. We gist-relate."

He looked around, wild-eyed, having lost the thread. I was still trying to figure out what "gist-relate" meant.

"So let's listen to the demo," he said, after an uncomfortable moment. Donald produced the demo from a bag on the floor and handed it to Chris.

"Hot off the presses, right?" said Chris. He padded across the room to a black monolith that I assumed was a stereo. It had about three dials, and a few VU meters. Chris inserted the CD into one of its chambers and returned to the couch.

"Is there anything I should know?" he asked.

"Well, it's still rough around the edges," said Scott.

"Rough is fine," said Chris. He fiddled with a book-sized slab of the same material that comprised the stereo, which appeared to be the remote. The remote cast a weird green glow up onto Chris's face, which made him look like a mad scientist. "Here we go," said Chris.

I'd gone to a party a month earlier, with friends of Para's, and met a transsexual woman, formerly a man, who, from across the room, looked gorgeous. She was wearing a pantsuit. But when I got up close, I could see the stubble on her face, the muscles, the Adam's apple. Listening to ourselves on that stereo was like that; what had sounded great was now naked and exposed. My voice sounded like a chorus of toads.

But Chris was not as horrified. He skipped around the tracks, giving each one ten seconds, then going back to "Hoyt-Schemerhorn." "This one," he said. "What is it? There's something missing."

"No electric," I said.

"Oh, that's amazing," he said. "That's the absence that makes it fascinating." He paused the song. "There's a parable in Daoism, where they point out how a vase is defined by its emptiness."

"That's exactly what we were going for," said Jacob.

"Oh," said Chris. "That's perfect. You don't mind me saying so, but that's the dissonance that makes the cognitive portrait so much more rich."

"We don't mind you saying so," said Katherine.

Chris skipped around some more, nodding. "There's a lot in here," he said. "A lot of thoughts, a lot of work."

"That's very true," said Scott.

Chris pressed a switch and the entire stereo went dim, all the lights shining at half brightness. The silence was as loud as the music. "All right," he said. "Let me think about it."

That was all he had for us, so we said good-bye and left with Lou.

"Chris liked it," Lou said. "He's just totally tied up with Slake right now."

"Who is Donald?" asked Scott. "I wasn't able to get that."

"That guy is interesting," said Lou. "Really skilled keyboard player. He's been gigging since he was maybe thirteen. So the sense I get is, he's dropping out of performing, trying to move over to the label side. But he's totally serious. He's all work."

"He seemed that way," said Scott. "No wasted words."

"Right," said Lou. "He creeps me out, honestly."

"So what happens now?" I asked.

"Just hang out, all right?" said Lou, shrugging. "Whatever you want."

"So you think it went OK?" asked Jacob.

"Yeah," said Lou. He had his cell phone in his hand, and was obviously waiting to use it, so we left him and made our way up to Broadway-Lafayette.

"I have no idea what the synergy model means to Schizopolis," said Katherine.

"I know," said Jacob, "but it seems like he's interested. I talked to my friend Bob, in Toadpond," said Jacob. "They got signed six months ago."

"Oh, I know Toadpond," said Scott.

"Anyway," Jacob said, "he said to go with it, see where it leads."

"Had he heard of Lou?" I asked.

"No," said Jacob. "But there are a million managers. For your first album, you just have to take what you're given. Besides, they're working with Slake. That has to be good."

"We just need to get started," I said. "Then we can worry about the second album."

"Well, we need to finish this one first," said Scott. "It sounded a little raw on that stereo."

I was glad to know that I was not the only one to be mortified when I heard our sound through those trillion-dollar speakers.

"I think Lou is just throwing things at the wall to see what sticks," said Jacob. "He said this thing with Original Syn is really new. So if we're part of that, that's great. We're in on the ground floor."

"God, that name," said Katherine. "Original Synergy. Puke."

"Yeah, but I think the impulse is right," said Scott. "You want to bring all those threads together, and see if you can realize some economy from doing so. It's not stupid."

"Definitely not stupid," I said. "It can only help us."

Two weeks later we went in for another meeting, this time to the offices of Original Syn, in a tiny space on Thirty-third Street.

"The producer I have in mind," said Chris, "is a big deal. I think you guys are worth it. I don't want you to prove me wrong." Donald sat quietly, listening, and Lou was nowhere to be seen. The mention of a producer, of the album actually being made, of Schizopolis getting a deal, was entirely out of the blue. Everyone kept quiet, pretending that we understood.

"Who are you thinking about?" asked Scott.

"Will Parrish," said Chris. "You know him?"

"I don't know," said Scott.

"He sounds familiar," said Jacob.

"He did some work on the last U2 album," said Chris. "He's about huge drum sounds, and I think that is perfect."

"U2?" I said. "We're working with U2's producer?"

"You're not working with anyone just yet," said Chris. "But I think it's possible."

"Remember," said Donald, "there are a lot of people working on a U2 album."

"Sure," I said. "But damn."

There was a stack of six contracts in front of Chris. "The thing is, there's a pretty small window in which he can guarantee his time. Which is three weeks. So you're going to have to move fast in the studio."

"Three weeks full-time?" Scott asked.

"Yes."

"No problem," I said. "That's perfect. For ten songs, that's plenty." We would do the nine songs from our demo plus a new one we hadn't named yet, about the Roosevelt Expressway.

"Great," said Chris, looking around to each of us. "So Lou's been over things with you regarding the contracts?"

"We've talked," I said, not wanting to stop the flow of conversation by revealing the truth, which was that we had never seen contracts, or known we were being signed.

So we were signed. I didn't read my contract very closely; I know I should, but everyone had been pretty decent to us so far, and I trusted them. And it looked pretty standard. The members of the band were going to share publishing and/or royalties—I get them mixed up—equally, which was very fair, as Scott, Jacob, and I had each contributed a lot of music, and we couldn't point to a song and say who wrote it. Even though Katherine didn't write much music, she'd given a lot of feedback, so it made sense to give her 25 percent of the profits, too. We had to give the label part of our tour proceeds, which made sense, because it meant that they were invested in our success as a touring band.

I spent a lonely-guy Christmas in New York. Para had gone up to Vermont for the day, and left me her place to housesit, so that I could keep an eye on Butter. I slept through the baby Jesus's birthday. On New Year's Eve, Para and I ended up at a party at a loft in Williamsburg, near the Metropolitan Avenue stop. A band played, the Rolling Hoopsnakes, and I noticed that I could no longer simply relax and watch another band play; I was constantly analyzing their stage presence, their talents, comparing them to Schizopolis. Thankfully, we were better than them.

The studio in which we were to spend the first three weeks of January was in the Village, on the ninth floor of a blank office building. It was filled with magazines about sound: *MixMaster, Mixing Times, Mix Machine, Sound and Engineering.* There was orange juice and beer in the fridge. I didn't really know how to process all of it. This was where the miracles happened. I felt like a Christian visiting Jerusalem.

A woman named Laura was in charge of the day-to-day at the studio, and she directed us to Studio 2. The door to the studio had a small white plastic light above it that said RECORDING IN PROGRESS. It wasn't lit. We went into a small, warm room filled with instruments. At the center of the room I saw a microphone, with one of those rubber spider things stabilizing it and a wind-screen in front.

I went over and stood in front of the mic, staring through the glass into the mixing booth, where a man with a gray beard was adjusting things. The stand was a little too high for me, so I began to lower it; it was surprisingly heavy and substantive compared to the mic stands I was used to.

The room filled with a huge amplified voice. "Jesus Christ!" it said. "Leave that alone." I looked up to see the engineer yelling at me.

"I'm sorry," I said. "I was just setting it up."

"It *is* set up," he said. He came in and adjusted the stand back to where it was, then looked at me and lowered it fractionally. "Just stand right here," he said.

"I'm Gary," I said.

"I'm Martin," he said. We shook hands. He looked very tired.

"Isn't the producer supposed to be here?" Jacob asked Martin.

"Don't know," said Martin. He moved quickly out of the studio and back into his glass booth. Under his gaze, I felt like a fish in an aquarium. From the other side, his voice came through again: "Put your cans on." I thought this referred to breasts, and maybe it was some sort of studio lingo, like "Get your ass in gear," but then I watched as Scott reached over and put on his headphones, and I aped him. Martin's voice came again, this time through the headphones. "Everyone hear me? I want to check levels."

Each of us played in turn, at his direction; I picked up an acoustic, which someone else had tuned and prepared, and strummed, then I sang a few notes.

"OK," he said. "We're set. Gary, stay a little bit back from the mic. You want to do anything, or should we wait?"

"You got the DVD?" asked Scott. A few days earlier, Scott had dropped off a disc with all of the gigabytes of session files from the demo.

"Yeah, we're ready to go."

"I think we should wait," said Jacob. "We don't want to waste your time."

"Your call," said Martin.

We went back to the lounge and idled for a few moments, feeling guilty. The studio cost a hundred dollars an hour, and it felt strange to sit around, waiting, as the clock ticked. Finally, Katherine picked up a Ping-Pong paddle from the table that was set up there.

"Come on, Benchley," she said. For the next twenty minutes, she roundly kicked my ass, then Scott's. Jacob put up a fight, but ultimately it was on Katherine.

"Church camp champion," she said. "Three years running."

"You went to church camp?" I asked. "Me too."

"What were you?" she asked.

GARY: Presbyterian.
KATHERINE: Lutheran.

GARY: Infidel.

KATHERINE: God, I got laid, though.

We grew bored with Ping-Pong, and found our way into the studio, where Martin was seated before two huge computer screens, clicking on audio waves.

"Is everything OK with the files?" asked Scott.

"It's fine," said Martin. "Maybe you'd want to de-ess the vocals if you did it again, but we've got that in hand."

For the first time I saw Scott mystified.

"What's de-essing?" I asked.

"Don't worry about it," said Scott.

"What'd you record it on?" asked Martin.

"A Shure," said Scott, sheepishly.

"There you go," said Martin. "We'll fix that."

"What kind of mic is that in there?" I asked.

"Neumann M149," said Martin.

"That's a good mic?" I asked.

"Four thousand dollars," said Martin. "It should do the trick."

"So I shouldn't drool on it," I said. Martin looked at me and showed no expression.

Katherine disappeared back to the lounge, and Scott, Jacob, and I sat on the couch in the mixing booth, watching Martin point and click in mysterious ways. "Not very interesting to watch," Martin said. "But it should save us time later."

Will Parrish, our producer, finally showed up at noon, average-height, all in new black clothes, apologizing, shaking our hands. "I *literally* just got in from Minneapolis," he said. "Fucking *United*, right?"

"Yes, we're finally all united," I said.

"He means the airline," said Katherine.

"Anyway, let's hit it," he said. "I want to start with 'Overpass'."

We all nodded and smiled, then someone realized that this

meant we were supposed to go into the other room and start. I stood in front of the microphone, waiting for further instruction. Will's mouth was moving, but nothing was getting through. "Gary, put on your cans," said Jacob. I did so.

"—so just run it through. Let's hear what it sounds like."

OK. This was the defining moment. This was when we made it real. Rock journalists would eventually write about these first, essential recording sessions, the way that we struggled to make real art, the way we worked hard to build Schizopolis into one of the world's largest bands without ever compromising our principles. This was the state of anti-Train, a totally uncreed moment. I opened my mouth, and flubbed the G sharp.

"Shit," I said. "I'm sorry."

"Don't apologize," came Will's voice. "The mistakes are the most interesting part."

I looked around at my bandmates, to see if they agreed. They all were staring forward, into the bright glass box with all the equipment, trying to figure out what was expected of them, and I was glad to see that I wasn't the only one who didn't know what was going on. Schizopolis, which had previously been four people and a dream, was now a machine with many moving parts, a manager, a label, and now a studio and producer. Somewhere along the line I had lost all ability to predict what came next. I decided to follow orders, and hope that Will would be a force for good.

We ran through the song again, then another time. Then once more. Of course, we'd done this same work with the demo, but the sessions had been interrupted by chatter on a wide range of topics: how jobs suck, whether gaydar can be taught, different kinds of snakes owned by Katherine's friends. There was no interval for chitchat here; it was work.

"Now Gary," said Will, "I'm going to have Martin play this back pitch-shifted at half-speed and I want you to sing along with it."

"OK," I said, hoping that whatever happened next would help me understand what that sentence meant. My own voice, sounding slightly robotic and extremely slow, came through the cans. I began to sing "Overpass": "I went under the overpass / Thought about the past / The people walking here / The end of the war."

"Gary," said Will's voice in my ear, "I want you to sing it slower, not down an octave."

"All right, bro," I said.

"Dude, you sound like a monster movie," said Jacob.

I tried it again, and after a few more takes, Will said, "I want to work the bass." He had Jacob play the same three measures over and over. "Syncopate it," he said, "duh-duuh-duh-duh-duuh-duh-duh." Jacob struggled to play Will's rhythm.

"Do you want a click track?" Martin asked Jacob. A click track is a steady clicking noise that helps you keep the beat.

"I guess I do," said Jacob.

It was well past time for lunch. We were handed a book of menus. I ordered a pulled pork sandwich from Bait & Tackle.

"I love this free lunch," I said.

"It's not *free,*" said Scott. "We're paying for it."

"It feels free," I said.

Scott had been back over our contract several times, and raised some concerns about the budget; he seemed to think that it would be hard to record an album in three weeks. And I was like, *Three weeks and nothing else to do! Dude!*

Will made some phone calls, then came in to sit down and eat lunch with us. We were all finished, but stuck around to watch him chew. "I want to take a moment to get to know each of you," he said. "But I wanted to get something down as quickly as I could, get a sense of what we're working with."

"What do you think of the demo?"

"I love it," he said, "There's a lot there to work with." For a moment I had a suspicion that he hadn't heard it. "Overpass" is the first track on the demo. Then again, he'd worked with U2. I decided to be more trusting.

"Originally I was thinking I could produce it myself," said Scott. "Now that I'm here, I'm really glad someone else is involved."

"Absolutely," said Will, drawing back a little from Scott. "Focus on the music, on the performance."

Will went on to tell us about his approach, which was based on something called "oblique strategies." "I'm basing it on Eno," he said, "but a lot of it is mine."

"Brian Eno?" I said.

"Yes, Brian," said Will.

"What's an oblique strategy?" I asked.

"Like this, Gary: sing with your mouth shut."

"You mean, hum."

"Yes, but sing with your mouth shut."

"That *is* humming," said Katherine.

"Maybe not that one," said Will. "Another one of my favorites is, faced with a choice, do both. That's from Arto Lindsay."

Scott nodded, looking thoughtful. Will reminded me of my roommate Charles, talking about Yogic Drumming. Martin came in and sat down, saying nothing.

"What was it like working with U2?" I asked Will.

"Very intense," he said. "They take it seriously."

"You work on the last album?" asked Martin.

"A little bit," said Will, very casual.

"Which part?"

"A lot of the drumming. The interesting drumming."

"Ohhh," said Martin, drawing it out. There was a hint of sneering in his voice. I didn't know if I liked Martin. But he was apparently a really good engineer, and had worked on a lot of albums I'd heard, stuff by the Prison Fires and the Mine Disasters, bands like that.

Lunch ended, and we headed back to duty. I remembered to put on my cans.

"Scott, we're going to focus on you," said Will. "I want you to play the melody like you're jumping off a tall building."

"Would I have a parachute?" asked Scott.

"No parachute. The ground is coming up to meet you."

"Can he land in a swimming pool?" I asked.

"Asphalt," said Will. "I want it to be manic."

"You know, there's a couch in here," said Martin through the cans. "The rest of you don't have to stay in the booth."

So the three of us left Scott, and went in among the mixing boards to watch Martin's back as he worked with his glowing computer screens and mixing board.

Will would say something like, "Give me more tension. Like your fingers are frozen." Martin would tap his console, and Scott would play, trying to make his fingers freeze. Repeat. Repeat.

"Like your fingers are snakes," said Will.

"Like Vladimir Horowitz."

"Like you're singing opera."

"I feel like I'm in some sort of terrible time-travel movie," said Katherine, quietly.

"I know," I said. "Imagine what it would be like if we didn't have the demo."

The day came to an end, finally. The only one of us not to receive much attention that day was Katherine, who would be the focus of attention starting on Tuesday. I took the train home, going over my new vocabulary: cans, mixing booth, studio, M149, oblique strategy. After I got in the door, I called Para. "Did you miss me?"

"It's weird not to see you at your desk," she said. "I was, like, who's going to come to lunch with me?"

I'd asked Tom for three weeks off, explaining the studio time, and Scott had taken three weeks of vacation. Tom had been very understanding, and told me that he'd welcome me back when the recording session was over. Scott had faced a little more pressure, but as he had saved up a great deal of vacation, not much could be said.

"Did people notice we were missing?"

"Oh, yeah. Scott, too. Like, who knew we had rock stars in our midst?"

"Not rock stars yet," I said. "How are you?"

"Well . . .," she said.

Things had been stressed since Bush won the election. Para had gone down into her own deeps, watching too much television, moping. She was back on her meds, but not sure if she wanted to stay in therapy. "I don't know if therapy is helping," she'd said.

And the previous week we'd had a fight, not a huge one. She'd suggested that we go away again, now that my ankle was healed. I told her that I couldn't plan. I had no money, and we were recording the album. Then we'd talked about what it would be like if I went on tour, and I joked about "road rules," and she made a frustrated face and began to berate me for being immature and disloyal.

"I don't know if I can trust you," she said. "I don't know if you're going to be there."

I wanted to say, "You're the one that gets depressed and pulls away for months on end, and hides in her shell like a turtle." And for some reason, I did.

"*Months,*" said Para. "Like a turtle."

"Well, it seems like months."

"Because I get *depressed,*" she said. "That has nothing to do with you."

"You knew you were dating an artist."

"Did I know that? I was dating Gary Benchley," she said. "Not Gary Benchley, Rock Star. I tried to call you today, and there was no answer, for hours. And I was, like, where is Gary?"

"I was in the studio. I have to turn my cell off."

"Well, I wanted to talk to you."

"You're talking to me now."

"I know," she said. "And personally, it's a little disappointing."

The next morning, Will focused on Katherine. He had a hard time with her; oblique strategies didn't work too well. Jacob went out for a walk, and Scott and I sat in the mixing booth, watching from the couch.

"A little less madcap," said Will. "Just tap the cymbals."

Katherine would try, but it was like trying to train a cat. She knew one way of doing things, and that was to make the drums sound like a trash truck driving off a cliff. She'd be mouse-gentle for thirty seconds, then start smashing the toms, and then off she'd go, all over the place.

"Turn up her click track," said Will to Martin. But that didn't help. "Give her playback on those last two takes, let her hear the difference," said Will to Martin. But Katherine found it difficult to react, and she'd look up from the drums, squint at us, furrow her brow, then play her take in exactly the same way.

"I'm not getting through," said Will.

"This hurts to watch," I said.

"She's just got her own way," said Scott, looking up from *Sonic Times* magazine. "It's an asset onstage."

"We'll work it out in the mix," said Will. Whenever he said that—and in the weeks to come he said it often—Martin would shake his head a tiny bit. "The mix" would take place later, probably in Chicago, where Original Syn had developed a partnership with a recording studio.

At the end of the day, Will went home and Katherine said, "I never want to hear that song again. I hate that guy."

"We have to finish it tomorrow morning," said Scott.

"I can't do it," she said. "I'll kill myself."

"It's almost over," said Scott.

"Then we have to do it nine more times," said Katherine. "My God. This is being a rock star?"

"Come on now," I said. "Being a rock star happens on tour." You have to do the hard work to reap the benefits. It's better than building a giant persimmon, isn't it?"

"Not at all," she said. I knew that was just the stress of the day talking. This *was* a dream come true, but that didn't mean you didn't have to work for it.

By day three, we'd moved on to the second song and, sparked by Will, the ideas began to flow. Scott was in heaven; he clearly loved the studio synth, which looked like a compact upright piano and had a computer screen attached to it so that he could tweak every possible aspect of the sound. During a break in the lounge, Will and he communed over the importance of the band Yes and discussed which string settings to use on the synth, trying to decide whether the strings should be obviously synthed or sound real.

"Gary, what about you? Any ideas you want to get out? Nothing is off-limits."

"I definitely have some ideas," I said. "I was thinking, what about some brass? Like a tuba. No one would expect that."

"Excellent," said Will. I felt triumphant, vindicated, and looked at my bandmates, each of whom had a horrified look on his or her face.

"*What, yo?*" I said.

"Tuba?" asked Jacob.

"Gary," said Scott, as lunch was winding down, "can I talk to you for a minute?"

"I believe I have the time," I said.

"Can you let me know before you suggest a brass combo?"

"It was just an idea," I said. "You know. I thought it would sound good."

"But we have a really limited budget, and we need to get these songs right. I don't think we want to add too much at this point."

This hurt my feelings. "Will seemed to like it."

"Will likes a lot of things," said Scott. "We need to just get this thing done."

"And it's not like the budget is that limited. We have thirty thousand dollars."

Scott shook his head. "Not really. Will is costing us thirty-two hundred a week, and you have duplication costs, and it's going to be about five hundred dollars for the brass. And lunch."

"I'll pack my own lunch," I said.

"You don't have to pack your own lunch. I'm just saying, go easy, and talk to me first, OK?"

"It's a deal," I said.

I spent the weekend with Para, walking around Brooklyn. We wanted to get dinner. I had no money. I had sort of thrown myself on fate, planning to stretch my savings for those three weeks without any income. That meant no beer, and that my midday lunch at the studio was my primary meal. My credit card already had started squeaking in my wallet. I suggested we get some hummus and go back to her place. Para, on the other hand, was flush as always, and wanted to go somewhere nice and sit down. "I'll pay," she said. But that made me feel like a no-account boyfriend, and I told her as much.

"I don't care," she said. "It doesn't matter."

"It matters to me. I don't want to be taken care of."

"You never minded when I paid in the past."

"Yeah, but—I'm trying to make things work, and I'm trying to keep on my budget."

"Which is why I'm going to pay."

She didn't understand where I was coming from. I didn't want my girlfriend to have to cover me. I would have rather just not eaten, in fact. In the past, it hadn't been such a big deal, but for some reason now it really bothered me. It was frustrating, in fact, to be working so hard and not have anything real to show for it. The only artifact of our studio time, after the first week, was a lot of files on a hard drive, and my diminishing bank account. I wondered if after things were over at the studio, I shouldn't take a full-time job at BrandSolve.

We ended up apologizing for our mutual bad moods, and Para took me to a French place on Smith Street, but it stung when the waiter delivered the check to me and she put her hand on it and slid it across the table. I know that feminism should make these things irrelevant, but I felt inadequate.

"I owe you dinner," I said.

"You don't owe me anything," she said. "I wanted to come here."

"I'll cook you dinner, then," I said.

"Oh, no," she said. "I'm not letting you in my kitchen." Para was serious about cooking, and watching me arbitrarily throw pepper on something, without consulting a cookbook was, for her, like watching someone staple-gun a baby in the eye. I'd only cooked for her once, and the misery of doing the cooking as she hovered over me was matched only by the misery of watching her wrinkle her nose as she took a bite.

"You're right. I'll stay out of the kitchen," I said.

"When your album sells a million copies, you can take me to Balthazar," she said.

"That's a good plan," I said, thinking of the last discussion, when she'd accused me of abandoning her for the studio. She and I discussed what to do next, because the night was still fairly new, but Para said she was exhausted. I was, too, so we parted ways and went home to our respective neighborhoods.

*　　*　　*

The next morning there was, as I expected, a trombonist, a tuba player, and a trumpet player waiting for us. The first one I saw was the trombonist, warming up alone. The tuba player and trumpet player were off scoring free muffins in the lounge.

"How you doing?" I asked him.

He shook my hand. "Everyone else is in the lounge," he said. Eventually the other brass players filed in, carrying their black instrument cases. Directed by Will, reading off of Scott's sheet music, they played through "August" a few times. As I sang, I looked at the sheet music, amazed to see our musical ideas converted to paper, to something as traditional as bass and treble clefs. If we ever got really big, I reasoned, we could have one of those symphonic albums, like Pink Floyd or Radiohead. *Symphopolis,* it would be called.

Will's voice came through all of the headphones. "I want the brass to play as if they're in the bottom of the Grand Canyon, trying to get the sound up to the top," he said.

"OK," said Otto, the tuba player. "I can do that." And when he played, you could hear that he *did* know what it was like to be on the bottom of the Grand Canyon. Later, I found out he graduated from Eastman and was doing a doctorate at Juilliard, and I felt a hot shame that he would be playing anything we had created. He didn't seem to mind, though.

At lunch, with Scott beside me, I said to Will, "I know I asked for it, but I'm not sure how much the brass adds."

"Oh, we'll work it out in the mix," said Will. "Let's just get everything we can out of them while we've got them."

Donald showed up as the brass band tootled. I watched him enter the studio, sit for a few minutes, and then talk to Will. I wanted to say hello, but by the time I was released from my singing duties, he had left.

*　　*　　*

During the second week in the studio, I realized why rock documentaries have so many jump cuts. To show more than ten seconds of anything that happens in the studio would ruin rock for everyone. It's probably different if you're a solo artist, because then you're doing the work yourself. You end up being a sort of coproducer. But with the band, you just take your turn, wait, and take your turn again. It was as boring as a game of Parcheesi.

Many bands, I knew, went to places like Biscuit Road studios in Fredonia, New York, or One Horse in Kansas City, sequestering themselves while they recorded. They'd leave their lives behind. I was glad we hadn't done that, because I definitely needed New York City right then. Just walking up through the Village toward the L helped me keep my sense of perspective. On the train, I'd think, *I'm probably the only person on this train who has a record deal.*

As Will focused in on specific band members, we each found ways to occupy ourselves. Jacob would fire up his laptop and work on articles, although I spotted many a game of Tetris on his monitor. Katherine would knit. Scott would call in to the office to manage his department.

To occupy myself, I read magazines. Sometimes I would imagine the documentary about our experiences, twenty years later. *Behind the Music: Schizopolis.* We had all the requisite ingredients, although we didn't really fight that much. If one of us had a drug addiction, that might make the story more compelling. Katherine seemed like a good bet. Maybe if we hooked her up with some heroin?

VOICE-OVER: . . . and then, dark days came to Schizopolis.

FORTY-SOMETHING GARY: We tried to keep Katherine from using heroin. We really did.

OLD KATHERINE, IN HEAVY MAKEUP: I was out of control.

OLD SCOTT: She was out of control.

OLD JACOB: There was nothing we could do.

NARRATOR: Yes, there was nothing they could do.

By the middle of the second week, we were working on "Jesus Was a Union Man," about Union Square Park, the third song on the album. My throat felt like I'd swallowed an angry cat, and I was living on lozenges.

I'd become a machine for the generation of music, a sort of Benchley Device that sang and played acoustic when you yelled at it. I learned to love the words "we'll work it out in mix," because they meant I could stop performing whatever repetitive singing task I'd been charged with, safe in the knowledge that the recording would be handed over to some mysterious man in a mysterious studio, someone we might never see, and that person would take all of our effort and transmute it into audio gold.

I tried not to complain, reminding myself that this was a tremendous privilege. The only ugly moment came on Friday when Will insisted that we add electric guitar to two tracks—"August" and "Overpass."

"We don't have an electric guitar," said Scott. "That's one of the things about us."

"See, you're committed to that orthodoxy," said Will. "Orthodoxy is our enemy! I want to break you out!"

"Before, you said that not having a guitar gave us a spiritual center," said Katherine. Which was true. Will had said that a few days before (or maybe a few hours before). In the windowless world of recording, time slips by. "Katherine, that's completely true. But some guitar would make that center all the more apparent, you know?"

"We have seven songs left to record," said Jacob.

"I know that. And I can tell you're worried. But you have to include the relationship we've built, the startup time. I think it's very strong. We're really working now," said Will. "So I think we have good flow. You know about the concept of flow? By Csikszentmihalyi?"

"You really want guitar?" asked Scott, in his tired voice.

"I have a guy who sits in at the Knitting Factory all the time. We can bring him in tomorrow." Will looked each of us directly in the eye, in turn, to gauge our pliability. We were all pretty pliable. "If it doesn't work, it doesn't work."

"It won't work," said Martin.

"Good, I'm glad to hear your opinion," said Will. "I'm just asking you to give me some breathing room, to make this into a truly astounding album."

"Astounding sounds good," said Jacob. "If you think so."

"Excellent," said Will.

On Monday morning a cool-looking man with a pack of cigarettes in his shirt pocket appeared in the studio. I never learned his name. He came in, heard the songs through playback, and, while smoking, improvised over the top of them under Will's direction. He went through five or six takes, then left an hour later without saying anything to any of us.

"That was excellent," said Will. Will then excused himself and left with the guitarist, saying he had to run some errands. In response, Scott became incredibly angry.

"I don't want to do this," he said. "Why bother if we don't control anything?"

Jacob looked at his hands. Katherine looked at me.

"It's not shit," I said. "I mean it, sounds good. We need to have faith. Martin, it sounds good, right?"

"Best album I've ever recorded," said Martin. "Without a doubt."

"Really?" Jacob asked.

Martin shrugged.

"I'm just wondering when it ends," said Scott. "I mean, next thing we'll have to add sitar and bugles."

"I don't think it'll go that far," said Jacob.

"Why? We already had a brass combo," said Scott. "It's like *The Music Man*."

"Look, we already discussed the brass combo," I said. "Have I suggested anything else?"

"No, thank God," said Scott.

Katherine sighed. "Do we have any choice but to go with the flow?" she said.

"With a week," said Scott. "How the hell do we keep this up for another week? Like antelopes?" (This was a reference to the time Will asked Jacob to perform like an antelope being chased by flute-playing lions.) "We're going to be totally humiliated when this album comes out."

"If we get humiliated, who cares?" asked Katherine. "The worst thing that happens is that no one wants to hear the album."

"Donald says not to worry," I said.

"Does Donald *do* anything?" asked Jacob. "I mean, he's like a ghost."

"Where the hell is Lou in all this?" asked Scott. "He's supposed to be our manager."

"He works for the label," said Jacob. "I knew that was a bad idea."

"It's a little too late to work that out," I said.

I walked away from the discussion feeling tired and frustrated. Will returned, and told us that he wanted to start moving on the other songs. "The guitar is great," he said. "They're going to devour that in Chicago."

Later, at lunch, Martin and I sat together in the control room. Everyone else was in the lounge. "What does working it out in mix mean?" I asked him. "I mean, I know what it means. But it seems to bug you."

"It means that Tuxedo Pants is flying blind."

"Tuxedo Pants?"

"You didn't notice Will's tuxedo pants?"

"With the stripe down the side?"

Martin nodded.

"I thought those were cool."

Martin huffed. He was forty-two, divorced, and shook his head constantly.

"So how do you think we're doing?" I asked. "Honestly."

He turned his right hand from side to side—so-so. "Everyone's working hard. That's good."

"We're a little new."

"You're kidding."

"OK, I know," I said. "I mean, how do we make this week work? We've got to get down two songs a day."

"Just keep going," said Martin. "That's the only choice you have. And you have to say no. If he wants a guitar, and you don't want a guitar, fight him on it. You guys roll over too easy."

"I was a little disappointed by the sudden appearance of the guitar," I said. "We're really big on not having guitar."

"You mean Will's cousin?"

"That guy was Will's cousin?" They did look kind of alike, in retrospect.

"He didn't tell you?"

"He might have mentioned it," I said. "It just didn't register." I wanted to defend Will, because Will was the future of Schizopolis. "And he did work for U2," I said. "That counts."

"Do you know what he actually did?" asked Martin.

"He worked on their last album."

"I was curious," said Martin. "I got that out of him. What your boy did, he remixed the drums on a B-side disco version of a track for Chinese markets."

"That's it?"

"That's it. Before that, he was a guitar tech for a bunch of indie bands. I don't think he ever met Bono, if that's what you were thinking."

That was what I'd been thinking.

"Chinese markets?"

"Chinese markets are huge."

"But it's not producing a whole album."

Martin and I had a serious conversation then, sharing information, and Martin told me what he'd learned from listening to Will's cell phone calls. Which was: Will had lined up a producer's role for the next Slake album; he was a friend of Slake's lead singer, and Slake had pushed hard to bring him in. Original Syn wasn't sure, because Will was fresh off the boat and didn't have any albums under his belt. So Chris gave Schizopolis to Will as a test, a way for him to confirm his skills before he worked with Slake. Slake was going to start recording in the same studio after us.

It was all kind of hurtful and confusing. We'd gone to the label with good intentions and put our faith in them, and they'd given us an unproven producer who had never put down an album before. Part of me wanted to cry, but another part realized that we were playing a grown-up game with grown-up money. Schizopolis was both a player in the game and the pieces that people moved around on the board, at once.

Scott walked into the lounge, and I returned to something that had been bugging me. "Right, but Martin—back to my question— what does 'working it out in the mix' actually mean?"

"Get every possible sound you can out of these songs, then ship it out to whoever you've got in the pipeline. And then whoever that person is will figure out what to do with it."

"Is that in our budget?" I asked.

"Not my department," said Martin.

"So we don't control the final sound," I said. "Do we have any control over the album at all?"

"You're recording it now," he said. "That's control."

Maybe this was why bands had managers that *didn't* work with the studio. If Lou had been working for us, we could have complained, gotten more money or time. But that didn't fit in with the three-part synergy model, and here we were, our future handed over to strangers with checkbooks, with five days to get through seven songs.

And then . . . what? We were supposed to go out on tour. That had been the plan, but if the album was crap, would they even bother?

I decided to call Donald, in the hope that he'd have some advice. Martin didn't care if we lived or died, Will was strategizing obliquely, and Chris spent his days contemplating synergy. Of all the people involved besides the band itself, Donald at least seemed to care if the album got done.

"Will keeps saying we'll work it out in the mix," I said into the phone. "But we don't want to lose control of the album."

"I hear you."

"I'm worried about that," I said. "We definitely have a vision for this album, a way it should sound."

"OK," said Donald.

"Is there anything we can do? I thought that three weeks would be enough."

Donald laughed. "Work hard all week."

"Is that even possible?"

"I definitely think so."

"I can't believe we burned through thirty thousand dollars like that."

"It happens," said Donald.

The next day, Donald came down to the studio, making sure to spend some time telling me that Chris was happy, and that no one was worried about anything, and to put our faith in what would happen in Chicago. Besides that visit, it was ten or eleven hours a day, jetting through songs, take after take.

Will became more strategic than oblique, and had less to say about instrumentation or arrangement; he barked commands at each of us: "Katherine! Syncopate your triplets." "Jacob, slow, then fast," "Scott! Think King Crimson, not Rachmaninoff." "Gary, for fuck's sake, it's a chord change, that means you sing different notes. Not the same notes."

"Yes," I said. "OK."

The third week ended not with champagne and celebrations, but with the whir of a computer's hard drive as it burned the files we'd created to a set of seven session-file DVDs, to be handed off to Original Syn, and with a train ride home, to sleep.

One song remained unrecorded, the untitled track about the Roosevelt Expressway, and an executive decision was made by Will, in conference with Chris and Donald, to cut it from the album and replace that with an extra, extended mix of "Hoyt-Schemerhorn," which would be created in Chicago. "Don't worry," Donald said, when I called him to check in. "You guys are doing a fine job."

Para wanted to see me on Friday night, when everything was over. I'd promised her that it would be all over then, that we'd spend some time together. But I canceled; the idea of talking about anything, of trying to be a human after a week of being a music-producing machine, was simply too much to handle.

And so the files were shipped off, delivered to a city I'd never visited, into the hands of mixing elves—yet more strangers who controlled our destiny. It was they who would take the thousand or so takes of our songs and transmute them, through some form of cut-and-paste alchemy, into accessible pop-inflected independent rock. I offered to fly to Chicago, since I had time, to represent the band, but no one thought that was cost-effective.

The word "independent" didn't mean much anymore; Schizopolis was by now entirely dependent on Original Syn. According to Donald, we were in hock for forty-two thousand dollars, when all of the expenses, the sandwiches, cab fare for Will, unnamed session guitarists, and duplication costs were tallied. We'd have to make that up in album sales, and we also owed Original Syn 25 percent of tour profits until we sold enough albums. It seemed extremely unlikely that we'd ever get rich off of our album.

February, we played with four other bands at CBGB. This should have been a profound experience, sharing the stage on which the Talking Heads and the Ramones had performed. But being one of five bands that night, with a few dozen people watching—it didn't quite live up to the fantasy.

I worked my part-time days, and Katherine found a boyfriend. It stung, but I couldn't get angry with her, given that I was also in a committed relationship. He worked with her on movie sets. He seemed kind of slackjawed and dumb, but he came to the show at CBGB, and showed up at practices and listened intently as we played.

"Katherine thinks you're awesome," he told me.

"Dude, we all love Katherine," I said.

"She wears silk pajamas," he said, which stung to hear.

The other gig that month was a party on a boat, off Pier 42 in Manhattan. It was for a friend of a friend of Katherine's, a Vassar girl with a huge amount of money and a penchant for indie rock. We made $250, the most we'd ever been paid for a show. The birthday girl got drunk and showed everyone her breasts while she danced on a table. From the stage, I watched her shimmy and wondered where the Gary Benchley I had once been had gone. In a past life this would have been one of the most profound moments of my life. My ability to rock had turned a snooty rich girl into a topless slut. But I felt absolutely none of the thrill I expected. I just wanted to get home and take off my shoes.

I had thought that we'd be on tour by now, with March rolling around, but there was nothing to do. Jacob wanted to see if we could manage our own tour, get a van and push out into the world, but Scott suggested patience, saying that this would be a bad idea given Original Syn's commitment. Also, he was in hot water for taking three weeks off, and needed to show his dedication to BrandSolve.

Donald and Lou both told us to stay calm. "Let's get the album back," they said. "And we'll see where it goes from there."

It felt odd to return to my half-complete, part-time existence. We'd been through the songs so often that rehearsals were fairly straightforward; all of us were competent now, comfortable enough onstage. Scott would occasionally come up with ideas for using a projection screen, and he added the necessary equipment to his arsenal of gewgaws; Jacob bought a video camera, and the two of them worked to edit impressionistic videos of the songs to go with the music. One featured Jacob wearing a paper bag on his head riding the subway, in slow motion. It was more boring than C-SPAN.

Scott found a boyfriend as well, refusing to provide any details, and for two weeks he was cheerful around the office, constantly trying to hide the chat window on his computer when I came by to talk. Then, one day, the chat window was gone, and he was back to his surly self.

I'd wanted to stay working part-time, so that I could think, and wander New York, and fully explore my options as a lead singer and rhythm guitarist. But with another winter here, and the accompanying wet sludgy streets, having the freedom to go down to a coffee shop, sit with a pad and paper for three hours, and write lyrics, hoping that someone would ask me what I was writing—it didn't seem like such a privilege. I spent too many days mostly alone, with only David for company on some evenings. And he was too tied up in living a completely hedonistic life to be much company.

"Dude, I was raging last night," said David one typical night. *"Raging."*

"That's cool," I said.

"Tranquilizers, man. All around. Then shotgunned beer. Bro, it was insane. I had no idea where I was. Totally pissed myself. Like literally. Also, Sue called. She wants to get back together."

"What are you going to do?"

"I already sold the ring, so I told her no."

"You sold the ring?"

"Yes. I took a five-hundred-dollar loss on it. So, you know, not bad."

I had the suspicion that the money had not gone back into his bank account, but up his nose. And I started avoiding him, creeping home past his door late at night, flopping into bed. Now that the recording was done, I had too much time, too many hours alone, with no reason to wake up in the morning.

So I took a full-time job at BrandSolve, and vowed to make it work in conjunction with the band. Scott was my supervisor. I had plenty of experience taking orders from him with Schizopolis, and knew how to navigate his bad days. For the short term, I would learn how to build websites, and maybe over time I would learn to do some programming.

It sounded fine by me, and it pleased my father to no end.

DAD: Coming up in the world.
GARY: That appears to be the case.
DAD: Very proud. Pat is, too.

After two weeks full-time, paging through HTML guides, wearing some new oxford shirts and slacks, sitting in on meetings where Scott explained system architecture, I began to feel that I was accomplishing something. I went to a client meeting and listened to someone from a bank explain their goals for a credit card services intranet. None of it made sense, or mattered. There was a sense of things *happening*, of things being built and getting shipped. And that was kind of exciting. I could see why Scott liked it.

On the other hand, while work was going well, I found myself getting really sick of Para. I was tired of working near her, tired of dating her, tired of her depressions and the bad sex. Familiarity was breeding contempt. *She has never been behind Schizopolis*, I thought. *She has never really said she loved me. She is a self-absorbed stupid horrible woman who cares only for graphic design and has no sense of true love, of what really matters in this world.* I began to write her an email, telling her this, editing it furiously, when she came over and asked if I wanted to get lunch.

"Sure," I said, "whatever."

We went down to the Chinese place on the corner, and she told me about Butter, who had defecated dramatically outside of his litter box in protest at some unknown slight. She told it with her eyes rolling, her hands moving, and with such a look of disgust on her face that I laughed and made her tell me the entire thing again.

Then she said, "You seem upset."

"Everything is up in the air," I said.

"You got a full-time job. That's not up in the air."

"True," I said. "Are you happy with me? Are we doing OK?" After saying that, all of my anger faded.

"I'm sort of happy," she said. "I think I am. I don't always know."

"I know what you mean."

"But if you mean, am I bothered that we're not really talking much anymore, then yes."

"Well, I guess I've gotten busy." I took a bite of my egg roll. "What do you want to do?"

"I don't know," she said. "I don't want to break up."

"I don't either," I said, even though twenty minutes earlier it was all I'd wanted.

"Winter is hard," she said. "It's really hard."

So we made plans to spend more time together, to take another trip when we could, without any horses.

I bought albums by the dozen, stocking up on everything new and interesting. I could hear the way the studio shaped a song, now, and it was interesting to note who was using which effect, to read liner notes and see which guest musicians had been brought into the studio. I could read liner notes like a short story, imagining the surly engineer, the producers in their designer clothes, the guest musicians who may or may not have been welcome.

And so it went, typing away, learning about source tags and codes. The weeks went by, and mid-March came, and we received word that *Dancing about Architecture,* our first album, was finished. Did we want to hear it on Thursday at lunch?

Yep, I thought, *that would be very nice.*

We went over to Original Syn's new office. "Why is this a drum and bass track?" Scott asked.

"That's the Will Parrish trademark sound," said Donald.

"What about the Schizopolis trademark sound?" asked Jacob.

"It's still there," said Donald. Donald paused the CD. "Will and Chris both wanted to show that you guys could do something different."

"But we didn't actually do that different thing," said Scott.

"It's still your melody," said Donald.

"I can't play drums like that," said Katherine. It was true. The drumming on the track was glitchy, lots of stops and starts. Not like Katherine at all. "How am I supposed to play that way onstage?"

"You'll use a backing track," said Donald. Theoretically, we could burn select tracks to DVD, and then play them back, sort of like indie rock karaoke. We'd have to do that if we were going to use the guitar parts on the album, or the drum sequences of the "Hoyt-Schemerhorn (Baghra Mix)" that had appeared suddenly, with two other remixes, at the end of the album, bringing the total number of songs to twelve.

"I guess so," said Katherine, disappointed. I could tell what she was thinking; she was already the least flexible member of the band, musically, and having to use a backing track felt like a failure.

"Chris loves the mixes," said Donald. "He says they take this album somewhere else. Feels it's money well spent."

We skipped through the entire CD, with Donald explaining the choices that had been made in Chicago. At first it was unsettling, because it was radically different from the demo—whole stretches of vocals had been processed through reverb, and there was a weird droning-flange intro on one song that lasted about twenty seconds. But even with all of that, when we were done listening, I felt a huge relief.

Jacob said what I was thinking: "Taken objectively, it's not an embarrassment at all."

"I kind of agree," I said. "Of course, I wish I could hear the vocals a little more cleanly."

"There are a lot of synth takes on there I wouldn't have kept," said Scott.

"Where are *my* drums?" Katherine asked.

"Just take a step back," said Jacob. "I mean, as a music critic, I kind of like it."

And it was *done*. Where before there was a demo, now there was an album. Something needed to be fixed with the mastering, to repair the levels on two tracks—I couldn't hear it, but Donald seemed to feel that this was an essential step. And then they were going to press four thousand copies.

"This is a lot for a band like Schizopolis," said Donald.

"How many copies would you press for Slake?" asked Jacob.

"Slake is in a very different scenario. They've had a successful first album with college radio play."

"But how many?"

"Twenty-five thousand," said Donald. I quickly worked this out. Slake was 6.25 times bigger than we were.

"Now look, this is the plan," said Donald. "We didn't bring this up because the details are kind of random, but you might want to start thinking about it. Slake is going out in May to promote *The Tomorrow Forgotten,* and Chris thinks you should go out to support them."

"Open for Slake?" asked Scott.

"Yes."

Tour! This was it, finally. The chance to go out, to prove myself, to make an impact, to generate buzz, to gain a following.

"Where would we play?" I asked.

"The goal is fifteen cities," he said. "New York to Seattle. I've got confirmation on all but three of them. Now look—"

"May?" said Scott. "If I take off three weeks in May I'll be killed."

Donald frowned. "It's in your best interest that you go out," he said. "Chris feels that Schizopolis and Slake are a good match."

"I'm just saying, May is tough."

"It's also in your contract that you'll work with us to promote the album."

"I know that," said Scott. It was a little unnerving to have the contract, a barely remembered beast of a document, brought up in conversation. I wondered what else was in there, what sort of evil tasks I'd promised to do. After the weirdness in the studio, I'd been feeling less trusting. I vowed to read the contract, really read it, as soon as possible.

"This is a good opportunity for you," said Donald. "People are very curious about Slake right now, and Chris wants to do as many tours with labelmates as he can, because he wants everyone to start thinking about Original Syn rather than just the individual bands. So you guys are his natural choice."

This meant, I think, that Donald had some other band in mind, and had been shut down by Chris. The synergy model was working in our favor. Promising to send us the details, Donald let us know that he had a busy day, and we showed ourselves out of the Original Syn offices, back to the street.

I played the meeting back in my mind. "Look," Donald had said. "The deal is, you go out, you give a good showing, you sell some albums. Slake gets you a built-in audience, and you get that exposure. A band like this one, there's usually no way you could play these venues."

Slake was in the studio through the end of March, working with Will Parrish. Martin, however, was off the project, and a new, younger, less cranky engineer had been installed. I learned this from Donald, as he explained the issues involving tour support, transportation, and the other miscellany of going on tour.

"But basically, you get in a van and go, right?" I said.

"Yes, basically," he said. "But you want to pay attention to the details. First, we need to talk about costumes."

"Costumes?" Katherine asked.

"Actually, let me get back to costumes. We're still working that out. Let's talk about merch."

Merch(andise) was where tours could make money. Normally, I'd learned, you brought along a merch girl, whose job was to stand fetchingly behind a counter at a venue and shill your crap. I'd seen many merch girls in my life, and bought many things from them, but it had never occurred to me that they were actually with the band. Slake, Donald said, would probably let us share their merch girl if she could have the standard 10 percent cut of the gross.

This was an unusual arrangement, but it might make life easier for us. We were responsible for our own merch, which meant we needed to make T-shirts, and buttons, and blow-up dolls and board games and whatever else we thought someone would pay for. We kept all the profits from the merch. And here we were fortunate:

Katherine could be in charge of merch manufacturing. Monotreme had a silkscreen studio, and Katherine had proficiency.

So we pooled resources and spent over five hundred dollars on two hundred T-shirts. We planned to buy our T-shirts from American Apparel, in order to avoid sweatshop labor, but when we saw the prices, we had to compromise on our principles, and buy shirts made by little slave children with tiny fingers. It was either that or spend well over a grand for the same T-shirts made without torture. We went with torture.

"I don't like sweatshops," said Katherine.

"Sometimes you have to kiss the devil's hoof," I said. "Just a peck."

I thought of asking Para to help us design a logo. She'd offered to help with the album cover, but Original Syn did all of that in-house and refused any input. As a result, we had no idea what the album looked like; we'd simply emailed them our individual liner notes, I'd handed over a compiled version of the lyrics, and that was that. I decided that bringing Para in on the logo would be a mess; I could imagine Scott and Jacob criticizing her work, and Para and Katherine looking at each other suspiciously. In the end we just put the word SCHIZOPOLIS across the shirts, in a random typeface that Katherine liked.

At BrandSolve, Scott went in to tell Tom that he was going on tour in May, as was I, each taking three weeks off. I thanked God that Scott was willing to deliver that news, instead of me.

Tom didn't take it well, calling us in for a meeting.

"Look, first of all, Gary, you *can't* take three weeks off in May. You only get two weeks, and you started under a month ago."

"Then . . . I don't know what I'll do," I said.

"Scott, for you—I mean, I know you have some vacation left over."

"I do, Tom. I didn't think it would be such a problem."

"You're a manager. You know it's a problem."

"Craig can keep an eye on things," said Scott, talking about a senior programmer. "And I'll have my cell phone."

"Shit," said Tom. "I'm *all for* pursuing your rock star dreams, but this is a pain in the ass."

"It's one time," said Scott, although he and I both knew that if things began to work out with Schizopolis, we'd need to tour constantly. "Three weeks, and then I'm back, and I won't go anywhere for a year. I'll work Christmas."

"I'll work Christmas too," I said.

"We just had Christmas," said Tom. He looked over to his yacht picture for a long moment. "All right. I'm going to say yes. But I'm pissed."

"Thank you, man," I said.

"Actually, Gary, let me talk to you alone," said Tom.

Scott left and I sat back down. "Look," said Tom, "I can't hold you back from what you're doing, but it really puts me in a position. I just hired you, and now you're bailing on me. What I'm saying is, I have to put some thought into this."

"What kind of thought?"

"Honestly, OK, total honesty here."

"Lay it down, bro," I said.

"It stings. We're trying to bring you into BrandSolve and you're taking off before you've even started to add value back into the enterprise."

"I'm trying to add value," I said.

"I know, but what I'm saying is that right now, you cost me more than you're worth. To be frank. I'm worried that I'm going to sink a lot of money and time, that Scott is going to sink money and time, into getting you up to speed, and then you'll bail on us."

"I would never do that," I said. "I really appreciate the opportunity I've been given."

"All right, whatever," said Tom. "But seriously, no more vacation for a year. That's it."

"I hear you," I said, genuinely grateful. "I'll be back in here; it'll be like nothing happened. And no more tours after this."

Slake had started recording on February 1 and, according to Donald, had been doing fantastic work.

I'd heard their previous album a few times, and while it was a little too much with the drawn-out guitar solos, they were a solid group with Seattle roots. Kevin, their guitarist, could play like the Byrds one minute, and Kurt Cobain the next. And while their vocals were whiny, the lead singer, Colin, could deliver a line with authentic feeling. They were pop with enough grit to take the guilt away, and Pitchfork had given them a 7.5 for their first album, *And Tomorrow Until the Stars*.

Slake and Schizopolis. We were going to be a merry band of bands, delivering rock across the nation. I fully expected us to bond, to get along. We could teach them what we knew, and they could share their knowledge of the road with us.

As March ended, Slake was finishing up in the studio, and we met up with them for drinks. Along with Colin and Kevin came Brad, who played bass, and Mike, their drummer. We met up at Rowboat, on Smith Street in Brooklyn. Brad and Kevin shook our hands, then immediately headed to the jukebox and began to argue over which songs to play.

"So, I want to know," asked Colin, "did Chris give you guys that shit about synergy?"

"All of it," said Scott.

"A pile of crap," said Colin.

"Chris told me about you guys getting some sweet threads," said Mike the drummer. "That is so excellent. I hear his girlfriend is a genius."

This was a sore spot with the band. Chris had a girlfriend who designed clothing, and one part of the synergy model required us to be dressed in her fashions. "What I do is mix," she said. "You guys mix the sound, and I mix the fabrics."

"The hats are a little big," said Jacob. She'd given us hats that were a full foot tall, with wide brims. They were made of knit fabric—a cross between a sombrero and a skully.

"It's nice to have a look," I said to Mike. "It brings us together."

"So I hear you want to use our merch girl," said Colin. His speaking voice was like his singing voice, loud and gravelly but a little nasal, surprising in a man who couldn't be more than twenty-eight.

"If that's cool," said Scott. "I mean, she'll get the same cut."

"She said she'll do it for fifteen percent instead of ten percent," said Colin.

"Donald told us ten percent," said Scott. "I thought that was already set up."

"Her call. Besides, we're not playing anywhere that takes a cut of merch, unless maybe Austin," said Colin. "So it's not going to hurt too bad."

We ran over the particulars. Jacob was carrying a printout of our itinerary. We were playing Cambridge, Philadelphia, Washington, D.C., Memphis, Norman, Austin, Denton, Albuquerque, Phoenix, San Diego, Los Angeles, Santa Cruz, Eugene, and Seattle, carving a huge "U" across America. As we looked at the printout, Brad came over from the jukebox and sat down quietly, unsteadily. He was clearly already drunk, which was miraculous given that we'd only been there for a half hour. He didn't say anything, until he looked at Katherine.

"You have wonderful breasts," he told her. "I would hump them if you let me."

Katherine picked up her drink and threw it in his face. It dribbled down his shirt, and ice cubes settled on his lap. There was a moment of quiet, and then all of Slake began to laugh, Brad the hardest of all.

"I'm sorry," he said. "Was that out of line?"

"Asshole," she said. "And yes, it was out of line."

Slake, collectively, went "Ooh!" Brad stood and wobbled toward the bathroom to towel himself off.

"I'm sorry for that," said Colin. "Brad likes to do it up. He's all professionalism on tour."

"He's been a little out of sorts," said Mike, the drummer. "His bitch just dumped him." Then, realizing that the word "bitch" could be construed as offensive, he said, "Oh, sorry."

"She was a bitch," said Colin.

"I'm sure he was a perfect boyfriend," Katherine said.

"Yeah, well," said Mike. "You know."

Katherine arched her eyebrows.

"God," Katherine said to me. "That is why I'm single."

"You're single?" asked Scott.

"I dumped Boyfriend last night," she said. "He was clingy."

"Good for you," said Scott.

I didn't say anything; one part of me felt a little thrill that Katherine was back in the running and available, even though I wasn't in the running myself. Another part of me was bothered that Katherine could just shrug someone off like that. And yet another part was jealous that she could now hook up on tour without cheating on anyone. It seemed unfair.

Brad came out of the bathroom and sat down hard, and Mike went over to check on him, to see if he was OK. I admired the way the rest of the band worked around Brad's drinking. They really seemed to have a grip on it, handling it like experienced musicians. Before long, Brad nodded his head forward and began to snore a little.

Slake was renting a van and leaving the sublet they'd been sharing in New York, heading back to Seattle.

"Sorry to leave you guys with the drive home from Seattle," said Colin. "That's Donald's planning. Sort of a rough drive."

"It's OK," I said. "I'm looking forward to it. It's a chance to de-compress." It would be fine, I thought, to just have a few days of mindless driving after all the hard work of the tour.

"You guys got a van?" asked Colin.

"It's my friend Bob's," said Katherine. "He's renting it to us."

"Good deal," said Colin. "Definitely pack light."

The Tour

Before I left the apartment, I brushed my hair in the bathroom mirror.

GARY: Attention!

MIRROR GARY: Yes?

GARY: You're going on tour. You're bringing Schizopolis to the people.

MIRROR GARY: This is exactly as it should be.

GARY: You're going to get in the van and rip America in half. Nothing is going to stand in your way, ever again. Triumph is right around the corner.

MIRROR GARY (*devil sign, slow nod*): Aw yeah.

GARY (*devil sign*): Aw yeah.

I waited outside my apartment in the middle of the day, my life packed tightly into two bags, a guitar by my side. I had a new, hundred-dollar haircut, and in my bag, expensive gels to maintain the tousled look that I thought would serve me well onstage.

A homeless man came by and began to root in the trash to my left. He looked at me for a while. We didn't speak, and eventually he wandered on.

Finally, the van pulled up, Scott driving, Jacob in the passenger seat, and Katherine behind them. It was maroon, and dented, and smelled like fish and air freshener. Apparently Katherine's friend, who owned the van, had taken it on a fishing trip then left the fish in the cooler, and despite repeated attempts, had been unable to get the smell out. Still, it was ours for a hundred bucks a week.

I got into the van and tapped Katherine's knee.

"We're on tour," I said.

"That we are," she said.

I wished there had been some sort of way to mark this event, our real birth as a band, leaving the New York mothership for parts unknown, on a great trek of the world. Someone should have been making a documentary about this. I'd given David and Charles notice that I'd be away from the apartment for three weeks, and then stayed awake all night, too excited to sleep, imagining what it would be like to be out in the world.

We headed for Cambridge, Jacob directing Scott, using directions in a binder. I watched the city go by, bright in the midday. My head nodded forward.

When I woke up it was cloudy. I asked where we were.

"Connecticut," Jacob said. "I've got music. Anyone mind?"

No one did, and Jacob put the new Starfind into the CD player as we drove. And drove. It began to rain. No one had much to say. The excitement would come later, I figured.

Fourteen cities, seventeen days. And tour support—five thousand dollars to spend however we chose. I had never experienced this level of freedom before.

We drove over bridges and looked at yachts in their moorings. Jacob switched the CD to the new Spoon. We stopped at a McDonald's to use the bathroom, and bought soda. Scott drove the whole way. I offered to drive, but Scott said he liked being behind the wheel.

"Do we have a set list for tonight?" I asked. "Any changes?"

"I think we should play 'Hoyt-Schemerhorn (Baghra Mix)' six times in a row," said Katherine.

"Maybe we should open with that," I said. "That's our single."

"Single," said Scott. "Except maybe twenty people have heard it."

Cambridge looked like Brooklyn Heights. The club looked like any club, except it was across the street from Harvard, which felt kind of intimidating. There was no place to park the van, so we unloaded our stuff (this is officially called the "load-in"), and Scott went off to find parking.

The guy at the door motioned us in, nodding at the name "Schizopolis," and in we went, to sit. Slake slouched in an hour later.

"Gary Benchley!" said Colin. He hugged each of us. "So it begins."

"Hey," I said. "How was the drive?"

"Great," he said. "A little dreary. Did you guys have any luck with the CDs?"

This was a sore point. We were supposed to have received two hundred copies of *Dancing about Architecture* three weeks earlier, but there had been some problem with the master, and then with the production schedule, and they hadn't materialized. We'd paid for the two hundred copies ahead of time, putting up one thousand dollars of our own money.

Slake hadn't had any problems with distribution, and had about a thousand discs in cardboard boxes in their trailer, which held their equipment and Katherine's drum kit.

The lack of CDs made Scott insane. "They've got us buying things that don't exist!" he'd yelled when he learned that we'd be going out on tour empty-handed.

"I don't think they mean to screw us," I'd said, but I had to admit that it was frustrating to be going out to promote music that no one could buy. Ideally, the CDs would be in stores, and sent out to radio stations. Still, as Donald had pointed out, the opportunity to tour, to go across the country and share Schizopolis with the masses, was too great to turn down.

And Donald *had* been apologetic, explaining that the mixup was good for no one. The last thing Original Syn wanted to do was to have us go on the road without an album to sell; it cut into their profits. And he promised to FedEx us the CDs wherever we were, the moment they came in. It was simply an unfortunate situation.

"We'll pay for the FedEx too," Scott had said. "I want them to die for this."

"I'm sure it will work out," I'd said.

As we unpacked our equipment, Jacob announced, "Do you think we'll find any Internet? I need to file a story tomorrow afternoon. A review of the new Word Menu CD."

"Do you have wireless?" Scott asked.

"Fah," said Jacob. "What do you think? Am I some sort of savage? Of course I have wireless."

I didn't have wireless, or a laptop. I kept my notes in spiral binders. "How is Word Menu?" I asked.

"They suck," he said. "Like the Decemberists with a robot for a lead singer."

I watched Slake set up. They started their soundcheck, which took a long time, as Colin was very particular about the sound of his voice. He had an effects box with a collection of settings, and he liked to hear how each setting worked, and tweak the effects box while the guy at the mixing board tweaked in response. They took a solid hour, and when they were done, we had about ten minutes for our own soundcheck before the doors opened. We scurried to get onstage and go through a song.

Doors opened. About ten people showed up. We waited a half hour to go on, at which point the audience grew to thirty. A few people waved to Katherine, and she waved back—Boston friends. We took the stage and went through the show, but I couldn't hear myself in the monitors, so my voice went all over the place, and

Scott's projection screen setup simply didn't work for some reason; his fifteen-hundred-dollar projector sat there, its lens like a shut eye. Later we found out that the guy at the mixing board had unplugged it in order to charge his cell phone.

Did we rock? Well, we attempted to rock. I couldn't really hear myself, or the rest of the band, and my hand motions to the mixing guy didn't seem to have much effect. He would nod, move his hand over the board, and the sound remained the same. Katherine's big hat fell off, because she moves wildly when she drums, and she let it lie there. Scott also took his hat off after a few songs and threw it on the ground. Jacob and I stayed behatted. After the show ended we got offstage to a smattering of applause. A Pedro the Lion song came over the sound system to help people through the long moments they'd have to wait before Slake took the stage.

"Well, that's the not-worst show we've ever done," said Katherine.

"I couldn't hear myself," I said.

"I feel like a circus clown," said Scott, pointing to the large, fluffy knit hat in his hand. His was bright green. Mine was orange.

"Gary, you were pretty remarkable," said Jacob.

"That bad? Should I have bought the Auto-Tune?"

"It wasn't that bad," said Scott.

Jacob thought for a moment. "It was pretty bad."

We did load-out, and Scott pulled the van up to the front of the venue. Slake still hadn't taken the stage by the time we were done, so we bought drinks and sat at the bar. I kept looking around, expecting someone to come up to me and say something, like "Can I buy an album? I love your band!" At which point I could lament the sad state of the music industry and our bad luck with getting CDs, and write down the person's name, and we could start a mailing list, which I've read is very important to developing bands. But no one said anything.

But this was, I figured, because if anyone wanted to buy the album, they'd go over to the merch table. So that's where I went, to talk to prospective album buyers, so that I could mitigate their disappointment at not being able to purchase *Dancing about Architecture* and get a mailing list started, and try to sell them on a T-shirt.

Murphy, the Slake merch girl, was selling Slake merchandise before they'd played, pushing the new album. She was Colin's ex-girlfriend, or Brad's, or both—I couldn't tell. She had cool tattoos and punk rock hair. I asked her how things were going.

"Fine," she said.

"Cool," I said.

Looking at Murphy, I found myself thinking about Para. We'd been together for how long? Too long, trying to make it work around her depression, around the age difference. I'd won her over to the idea of Schizopolis, and the fact that she supported my career had made the fact that I was in a mostly sexless, lonely relationship with an isolated, uptight woman unimportant. When I got back to New York, I figured we should have a serious conversation, and then I could have sex with lots of different girls pronto, as befits a lead singer.

Finally, Slake took the stage. The audience greeted them warmly and with great cheer. As they launched into their first song, my cell phone began to vibrate in my pocket, probably Para, and I decided to call back later.

"We need CDs," I said to Scott.

"Don't talk about it," Scott said. "God, is this how it's going to go for the next three weeks?"

It did look a little disappointing; but then, I reasoned, every rockumentary talks about the hard times, the struggle, the strife, the years of trying to build an audience. We were already *way* ahead of the curve; we'd already arrived, if you looked at it in a certain way.

"It's seventeen days," said Jacob. "Don't stretch it out."

"Plus driving back from Seattle," I said. "So three full weeks."

"Great," said Scott, shaking his head.

A few minutes later I checked my phone to see who had called. The number on my display was my mother's, which was unusual; she didn't usually call this late. I rang back and got Jad.

"Hey there, buddy," he said. "You got a moment?"

"What's going on?" I had a sudden fear that he was leaving my mother, and was calling to say that he didn't want there to be any hard feelings between us. "Hold on a second," I said. Slake was a loud band, impossible to yell over. I ran to the exit of the club and outside, and leaned against a wooden railing.

"Your mom is pretty sick," said Jad.

"Sick like how?"

Breast cancer, he told me. She was going under the knife to-morrow. It was operable and everyone was predicting great things, great things in this case meaning *not dying*.

Apparently the operation had been scheduled a week ago, but Mom had told Jad not to call me. He'd been up late thinking about it, and decided that I'd want to know. I told him he'd done the right thing, and thought of a television special I'd seen about breast can-cer. It hadn't ended well.

The right thing to do was to go to Albany, immediately. My brother and sister were on their way. I had no idea how I was going to do that.

"I'm in Cambridge, Massachusetts, and we're driving to Philly tomorrow," I said.

"Well, if you can't make it, you don't worry about it. I'm seri-ous. Your mom didn't even want me to call you."

"Maybe there's some sort of emergency discount on the plane or something."

"I think that's only for funerals," he said.

Inside there was the roar of Slake finishing a song, Colin's voice yelling back to the crowd.

"It's good to be back here!" he yelled.

I told Jad I'd see what I could work out, and hung up. I tried to go back into the club, but the guy at the door wanted to see a hand stamp. I told him I was in Schizopolis, and he looked at me blankly. "The opener for Slake," I said.

"I'm sorry," he said, waving me through. "There are so many acts."

Everyone in Schizopolis was very understanding when I explained what had happened. I would rent a car tonight and drive to Albany, then drive to Philly the next afternoon, and take a cab to the club there. Given the recent expenditures in tour preparation, including a hundred-dollar haircut, and the fact that I was paying rent on an apartment I didn't occupy, while I didn't work for three weeks, this extra five hundred dollars would wipe out my bank account. I thought of all the new CDs I'd bought on my salary, lots of them special imports from Europe and Canada, musicians like Feist, and felt like stabbing myself in the eye for my wasteful ways.

We all drove to the airport together to rent a car. I felt bummed that I wouldn't get the full Schizopolis experience tonight, sleeping together in a motel room to save money, then getting into the van in the morning and heading toward Philadelphia. But I did need to go see my moms; there was no way around that. The man behind the rental car counter was suspicious after I explained my convoluted travel route, and asked for extra identification. It took me awhile to realize that he was looking at our outfits, the silver shirts and tuxedo pants, and probably had decided we were associated with some sort of carnival, and thus not to be trusted with rental vehicles.

"We're in a band," I said. "We wear these onstage. I'm going to see my sick mom."

That seemed to calm him down, and before long the printer rattled and spit out my paperwork.

"You're only three hours away," said Jacob. "It won't be a bad drive."

*   *   *

After the noise of the rattling van, the darkness of the club, the smell of beer, it was strange to be alone in the hushed space of the rental car. Before I left I used the huge road atlas in the van (Scott's purchase) to plan a route, and I found my way to Albany without much confusion.

Jad opened the door for me at 4:30 A.M.

"I got your message," he said. "It's good you came."

"Oh, man, go back to bed," I said.

"I can't sleep," he said. "Just as well. You want to rest, or you want coffee?"

I was going without any sleep, except for a van nap, and I worried that the coffee would make me insane. "I have to sleep a little," I said. We talked for a bit about the surgery, which sounded terrible, about my mother's stubbornness, her desire not to mess up my life by having me leave the tour.

"I always loved her breasts," said Jad. "But I don't care if one of them isn't there. I'll love the one that is there."

"Love the one you're with," I said, trying not to let that conversation go any further. "Absolutely."

I did sleep, for a few hours. The last time I'd been in a hospital, the same hospital where my mother was now sleeping before she went into surgery, I was nine, and my grandfather was dying.

Mom went under the knife at 8:30, and we could visit her in the afternoon. My brother and sister appeared at the house around breakfast; they had coordinated travel, with my brother flying in from the West Coast, renting a car, and picking up my sister at the train station.

"That was good planning," I said.

"It was all Elizabeth," said Bill.

We went through our lives, Bill on leave from the navy, Elizabeth back at school. We left at one, in a small caravan, Bill and I in our rentals, Jad in his pickup. We walked up a long, sloped hallway until we found Mom's wing of the hospital. I looked sideways into the other rooms, television on in each one.

We followed Jad into Mom's room, and there she was, unrecognizable and pale. She was totally out of it, asleep. It felt bizarre that I could just walk in and see her—I wanted some doctor to warn me, to put it all in context.

"Before she went in," said Jad, "she was talking about how all three of you were born in this hospital. She showed me the caesarean scars." That sounded like her.

We stood around my half-alive mother, until Jad said, "It's OK to take her hand and talk to her." I took her hand and felt her palm. It was soft and dry.

"Hey," I said. I couldn't think of anything else. "I came to see you." Elizabeth put her hand on Mom's elbow, and my brother went around and took her other hand.

I looked over at my sister. She wasn't the cheerful, confident woman who'd visited me in New York, or the pain in the ass that Bill and I had tackled on Thanksgiving. She was her eleven-year-old self, biting her lip as she looked down on our mother-ghost. Bill was standing firm, falling back on his military bearing, but you could see that his chest weighed a million pounds. I felt like a little boy in a pullover sweater, walking to the park.

"We came from everywhere to see you," I said. "I'm on tour, it's going great. We're really tearing it up." My mother, of course, said nothing.

"That's true?" asked Bill.

"You should see us," I said. "We're going to play San Diego. You'll have to come see us. I'll get you the dates."

"I will if I can," said Bill.

"Hear that? Your children are traveling all over the world," said Jad.

"We're truly rocking," I said. "We are rocking the United States."

The nurse came in and drew the curtain, and did nursish things. We went out to sit in the waiting room. Jad told us that most of

Mom's right breast was gone, and that she was going to be in the hospital for up to a week. She'd be a little more cogent tomorrow, he said.

I kept checking my watch, worried about getting on the road to Philly. It was four. Doors opened at 9:30, so I needed to leave by five at the absolute latest.

"I'm going to have to leave soon," I said. "It's awful."

"She'll understand," Elizabeth said. "Totally."

"Go in and talk to her for a moment," said Jad. "We'll wait here."

So I went back into the room and stared at my mother for a while, not sure what to say. "Mom," I said, "I made it down here, it was really hard. But I really love you, and I want you to get better. I want you to come see Schizopolis play in Albany, if we ever play."

Suddenly she was half-awake, her eyes opening narrowly. She mumbled something. I tried to think of something to say, something that might sound like a reply. Would she remember this moment? "Mom, seriously, they say you're going to be fine. You can call me and nag me all you want." Then I began crying, suddenly, but I stopped myself. I didn't really want to face Bill with snot running down my nose.

I jumped into the rental car and took off for Philly, feeling bleached and frail. Luckily I had a Polyphonic Spree CD to keep me company. I wasn't going to take any chances on, say, Dead Can Dance, or Coil. I turned on my cell phone; it had been off in accordance with hospital regulations. There was a message from Para. I realized that I hadn't called her in the last day; I'd been on autopilot. "We need to talk," she said, through the voice mail. I needed to talk, too, but about something besides my relationship with Para.

I called her. After a moment of clicking and beeping, I heard her voice.

"Where are you?" she asked.

"Driving to Philly," I said. "You want to talk?"

She sighed. "I do."

"What about?"

"You're gone. I tried to call you last night."

"Last night was a little busy," I said.

"Look, Gary," she said. "I don't know what I'm doing anymore."

"My cell is getting bad reception," I said.

"I don't want to do this over the phone."

"It's over," I said. "That's it, right?"

She said something, but I couldn't hear it through the bad connection. I asked her to repeat herself.

"Yes, it's over," she said.

"OK," I said.

"OK? That's all I get?"

"Yes, that's all I say." What did she want? Months and months of hard relationship work down the drain, of conversations and television watching, of graphic design and horseback riding. None of it, it turned out, meant anything, all of those minutes adding up to zip. These last few months we'd been avoiding this discussion, barely sleeping together, avoiding any topics of substance.

"You want to fool around on tour, and you don't really care about our relationship," she said. "I expected this."

"No, that's not it," I said, although I did feel, a little, that by staying with Para I was being cheated of my groupie destiny on this tour.

"You're probably already sleeping with someone," she said.

"I have been *totally* faithful to you," I said. "I have never screwed up once."

"Well, that's good for you," she said. I sensed something in her voice, a little note of pride and power. My stomach knew what was coming next, because it instantly filled with bricks.

"Have you cheated?" I asked. "Is that something I should know?"

"Does it matter?"

"I guess not anymore," I lied, hoping my nonchalance would sting her. "Given that it's over."

"Good," she said. "Because I have."

That was an unexpected fact after all the other facts that had been delivered to me in the last twenty-four hours. So rather than pursue the conversation, I turned the phone off immediately. It did its little I'm-turning-off song and dance. "Good-bye," said the phone, in a high female voice.

I had no intention of turning it back on. Eventually, I figured, the batteries would run out and no one would ever be able to call me again. Then I could die.

There was only one remedy for this situation, and that was classic rock. I searched around on the car radio until I heard the end of "Eminence Front," by the Who.

There was a little interstitial: *"No ad rock block!"* someone screamed, their voice run through a vocoder. And it was *fucking* Elton. The last thing I needed right then—"Goodbye Yellow Brick Road." What could be more pathetic than an indie rocking twenty-three-year-old in a big gray Chevy rental, hurtling toward Philadelphia, trying to follow directions hand-written on a napkin, and getting emotional while Elton John sang? I tried hard to push the song away, to keep its emotional claws out of my chest. But Elton John and Bernie Taupin were victorious. They penetrated my body with their chords and ambiguous lyrics like vampires, and I wept huge hot tears for my mother, for Para, for the entire world of the dumped and lost and lonely.

Not long after, as darkness came to Philadelphia, I pulled up, red-eyed, to the place I was supposed to turn in the rental car, and before long I was in a cab to the club, a place called the Candy Bar. Schizopolis had spent the morning in Boston, hanging out with Katherine's friends, and had yet to arrive. For something to do, I paced the block, and found a coffee shop. Inside, I drank a huge cup of black coffee, to keep my hands busy, and to push back the exhaustion that was creeping around behind my eyes. This was a terrible idea. By the time the van pulled up across the street, with Jacob, Katherine, and Scott getting out, my heart was racing and my hands were shaking.

Katherine embraced me.

"Do you have your hat?" asked Scott. I did, in my bag. They had been worried that it had been left behind in Cambridge. I told them about my mother, letting them know that she would be OK, leaving out the catastrophe with Para. I sat at the bar and bought a pack of cigarettes from the bartender, smoking three in a row and washing them down with a few beers. I felt like a losing lottery ticket. But I had to go onstage, and give whatever I had left to the audience. It paid less than minimum wage, and had no benefits, but it was my job. The audience had the luxury of staying home if they didn't feel like going to the show, but I had made a deal, and I was going to fulfill my part of the bargain.

Slake only pulled in forty at the Candy Bar, and Schizopolis sold nothing, no T-shirts, no buttons.

"Sell anything?" I asked Murphy, the merch girl.

"Not, uh, yet," she said.

"Thanks," I said. It was as if our merchandise had leprosy.

I'd hoped to turn my pain into art, to show the suffering in my voice. But Schizopolis doesn't write particularly soulful tunes. We write jouncy rock that goes all over the place, and so I doubt I came across as anything except tired. It was the best I could do. The caffeine and cigarettes left my voice thin and nervous-sounding, and I was jerky onstage, tense, tired.

After Slake's set, the manager informed both bands that he couldn't pay us. We hadn't sold out our guarantee, or something like that. I didn't really care.

"Friday nights it's like that," said Colin. "People go home and then don't come out."

"Might as well go out ourselves, then," said Brad, putting his bass into its case. "Philly is a good town."

"What about it?" said Colin. "We hit the town?"

I took this moment to check messages, forgetting my vow to never use my cell phone again. I lit a cigarette and listened.

"I'm sorry," Para said on the first message, "I screwed up. I want to talk to you."

The second and third messages were more of the same, with sobbing, and then there was the fourth, colder, and stern: "We still have to work together at BrandSolve. Please call me immediately. Don't do this." I swore at the phone. Katherine looked over at me, questioning.

The last message was Jad, telling me that my mom was doing OK in the hospital.

I was torn. I wanted to call Para and get every possible detail. Was it some old boyfriend, on some night when I was gigging with Schizopolis? Or someone from work? Could it be Tom? Craig? I needed to know the number of adulterous incidents, the frequency, the name or names of the man or men involved. I needed to gauge my exposure to the venereal diseases.

At the same time, I wanted nothing to do with that whore, and fuck her cat, too. It was a bind. But while I contemplated, a plan was put into place to drive both vans to a cheap hotel that Mike knew about, then pile into the Schizopolis van, which lacked a trailer, and go out drinking.

"Who's designated?" asked Scott.

"Not me," I said.

We ended up at some bar in Philadelphia, a bar that was simply a bar, with tables and chairs. It had a small stage in the back, and Mike had played here in some prior band years ago. It was so strange to be in a bar that wasn't something else, a bar that didn't look like a Zen rock garden, or a French palace. I shotgunned two scotch and sodas, and began smoking.

"Gary, I heard about your mother," said Colin. "I'm sorry."

"She's fine," I said. "At least, she'll be OK."

"I think we'll see a good crowd in Memphis," Colin said. "We had good luck there a year ago."

"I hope so," said Scott.

Colin smiled thinly. "You guys have no idea. I mean, I know it's a pain being the opening act, but having this setup—"

"Oh, God," said Mike. "This is cake."

"I mean, this is heaven," said Colin. "Hotel rooms. Hotel rooms are true luxury. This is the best tour we've ever done."

I was jealous of Slake, jealous of their suffering, their hard work, their headline status. Original Syn had not taken a chance on them, as they had with us; Slake was their sure thing.

In Albany, I'd had the fantasy of doing what Slake had done. But it had come too easily, too quickly. We hadn't worked as hard as they had. Maybe we weren't truly indie; maybe we were cheating. I looked at my bandmates with sudden loathing. They had it so easy, hadn't really worked for it. They were complacent, and soft. They wanted it handed to them. What did Jacob really care about? *His* career. And Katherine was, to be honest, a second-rate drummer. Did it matter that she had a cool look? Scott had talent, but no real drive. He wanted a casual life with good furniture. And they were all so old. Scott was in his thirties.

I looked around the table and felt only betrayal and rejection. But then, this was all I had. There wasn't anything else. I raised my voice. "I would like to let everyone know," I said, "that my mother has cancer, and my girlfriend and I broke up this afternoon after telling me that she cheated on me. So the only thing in my life, from this point until I die, is Schizopolis."

The conversation died down, everyone looking at me.

"Now that," said Brad, the only person drunker than I was, "is a real man."

"Shit," said Jacob.

Katherine looked at me and frowned. "Is that true?" she asked.

"In the car on the way here," I said, "Para and I broke up."

"Gary, I'm so sorry."

Maybe, I thought, looking into her deep green eyes, maybe Katherine would sleep with me tonight. That would be retroactive revenge cheating, since I'd had a crush on her those months ago. Granted, it wouldn't stand up as cheating in relationship court; it would fall instead under emergency sex, but it had its appeal.

"It was a long time coming," I said.

"The cheating is bad," said Colin. "That gets a man angry. You liked her?"

"I loved her. I told her I loved her. I think I loved her."

"Oh, well, fuck that. If she got you to say you loved her she had no business cheating."

"They're all bitches," slurred Brad. "Except for Murphy and Katherine."

"Except for Katherine, she's awesome," I said, eyeing Katherine's full breasts, which were much plumper than Para's. Katherine was wearing a T-shirt with a monkey riding a rocket ship, and the silkscreen was stretched out by her chest. Katherine, I thought, was everything Para was not. Not willowy, but curvy. Easy to talk to. Not uptight. Katherine was beautiful. Also, Murphy was kind of cute. But Katherine was definitely my preference.

"I love you, Katherine," I said.

"That's nice, honey," she said. "Drink your beer."

We went back to the hotel, Scott driving. We had two beds and a cot. Our budget allowed one room per night, which meant that someone slept on the floor, or people shared beds. The most logical arrangement was Scott and Katherine in one bed, and then Jacob and I took turns between the other bed and the cot.

I watched as people took their beds, hoping that Katherine would hop into a bed alone, and then I could sit on the edge of the bed and talk to her, and then pass out right there in her arms. That was my plan, but as the rest of us milled around the room, Scott emerged from the bathroom having just brushed his teeth, wearing honest-to-God pajamas, and got into bed.

At first I was too amazed to remember my cuddling plan. "Those are *jammies*," I said.

"You didn't see those last night," said Katherine. "He broke them out. They're amazing."

"I sleep in pajamas," said Scott. "That is something I do."

"I sleep naked," said Jacob. "But I've decided to go with sweat-pants for the duration of the tour."

"Scott," I asked, "do you want a bedtime story?"

"I want you to drink a lot of water," said Scott, "and then you go to bed."

I went into the bathroom. I had, I realized, gone way past my limit. I wondered if I had a drinking problem. That would be good to add to the relationship problems, the mother problem, the credibility problem, and the fiscal problems. I fell to the floor and found the toilet, vomited loudly, and then lost track of time. I was somewhat aware of Katherine holding my head, saying soothing words.

"I love you," I said. "I really do. I just want to hold you." A small bit of chunky drool fell out of the side of my mouth onto my chin. Katherine wiped my face with some toilet paper.

"OK," she said. "That's OK. Is it all gone?"

"It's all gone," I said, and I began to cry. "Everything is gone." I reached out my arms to hold her. She pushed back from me, and leaned over to flush the toilet.

"You need to wipe your face and drink some water," she said. I did as she said. I filled my hands with water from the sink and lapped it like a dog.

"I wanted to be your friend," I said to her. "That's what I wanted." I considered the situation. "I hope to God I don't remember any of this tomorrow." Then I began to cry.

"There's a good chance you won't," she said. "But now you have to go to bed."

"I'll try again tomorrow," I said.

"That's the plan," she said, and then she led me out, and helped me get out of my jeans, and put the blankets over me.

"I think you are so great," I said.

"Sleep," she said.

I woke up a few hours later, the light coming in. Scott was snoring, and Katherine had a pillow over her head. I realized that we were really, truly on tour! About to get on our way to Washington, D.C., the cradle of our government, and then on to Memphis, birthplace of Elvis. We were heading south, into the pure heart of rock.

Then the events of the last forty-eight hours came back to me, my two days of misery, my attempt to seduce Katherine that ended with her scrubbing my chin of puke, and I leaned back onto the cot and hid myself in sleep.

We were early to Washington, D.C., and did some sightseeing. I'd been there last in high school, getting out of a yellow bus with my friends. It had seemed majestic, then, like an enhanced, expanded version of Albany, but after New York it seemed to have been reduced in scale; the Washington Monument seemed normal-sized. We walked on the mall as the light fell.

"You know, I never thought of it as phallic," I said. "Now I definitely do."

"I always saw it more as a weapon," said Jacob. "When I was a kid, I had this fantasy that it was a kind of missile, and it could launch up and stab aliens when they tried to descend. Or Russians, when they tried to attack."

"Remember *The Day After*?" said Scott. "I swear, my first three words were 'mutually assured destruction.' Nuclear war and the *Challenger* explosion were my entire childhood."

"I remember that day," said Katherine. "I was playing with my friend Nessa and my mother called us in and told us."

"I have the image burned into my brain," said Jacob. He drew a "Y" in the air—the smoke trail.

"I don't have any youthful traumatic events," I said.

"None?" asked Scott. "Didn't anything happen to you?"

"O.J.," I said. "And I sort of remember the first Gulf War. Because my brother was really into military stuff. And the Twin Towers, you know."

"Yeah, well," said Jacob. "That one comes up a lot."

"Fucking day," said Scott.

"Anyone lose anyone?" asked Katherine. I was a little surprised that this question had never come up before, but then, people tended not to talk about the Twin Towers very often in New York. It was odd that the conversation was happening in Washington, D.C., rather than Brooklyn.

"Friends of friends," said Scott.

"Me too," I said. "Well, friends of acquaintances." Actually, a girl I'd sat next to in my sophomore English class lost her boyfriend. "A couple of alumni from my college died, actually."

"My cousin's husband," said Jacob. "Worked for Cantor."

"Shit," said Scott. He looked at Katherine. "You?"

"No," she said. "No one I knew."

"I used to go through those buildings every day when I lived in Jersey City," said Jacob. "Take PATH to the station in the basement. It still freaks me out."

"Fuck yes it freaks me out," said Katherine. "The other day I was down there, and suddenly I caught this whiff of air. And it was the smell. Do you remember it?"

"Oh, God, do I remember that smell," said Jacob.

"My mind just totally popped up with it. Burning whatever."

"Drywall," said Jacob. "And plastic."

"What was it?" Scott asked. "Six months?"

"I think so," said Katherine. "I went down the week after. I tried to volunteer but they didn't need anyone by the time I got there."

"I stayed away," said Scott. "I didn't go down there for a month."

"I went down the next week," said Jacob. "It was so intense."

"What I remember," said Katherine, "was soldiers everywhere. Like a huge base, and all this camouflage and guns. I remember thinking, there it goes. There goes everything I learned in social studies. So long!"

"I don't like the soldiers," said Jacob.

"It's weird having a brother in the navy," I said.

A little while later, we headed to the venue, getting lost on the way, and then I found myself faced with going through the ritual of playing. I felt like a zombie. What I needed was a pep talk. The problem was that I was the best cheerleader Schizopolis had.

"Scott," I said, "cheer me up. Get me ready to go on."

"What do you want me to do?" he asked.

"Tell me I rock," I said.

"You rock, dude," said Scott.

"Dude, what the *fuck* was that?" I asked.

With a little more enthusiasm, Scott said, "You totally rock."

Colin came over. "You guys feeling good tonight?" he asked.

"Scott here is trying to boost my spirits," I said.

"I'm telling Gary he rocks," said Scott.

I looked at Colin. "I need a charge," I said.

"Oh, dude!" said Colin. "You fucking totally rock. You are going to get out there and go insane and bring the Schizopolis vibe to the masses, and everyone is going to be awestruck, like some sort of rock comet smashed into their houses. They're going to be standing there with their jaws on the floor."

"Goddamn right!" I yelled. "I'm going to rock the nation's capital. I'm going to blow up the Capitol—"

"Not so loud," said Colin.

"—with pure rock energy. Spelled N, R"—I paused and looked at Colin—"G."

"That's what I want to hear," Colin said. "Wrap your arms around the devil and pray for salvation."

"When I'm onstage," I said, "I rule the world."

"That's right, motherfucker," said Colin. "Fingers!"

We high-fived, then low-fived. Colin went off. I turned to Scott.

"That is a pep talk," I said.

I knelt down to open my guitar case. It felt like a sacrament, like opening the church doors. The guitar was black and shiny, with pick scars on the soundboard. It was hollow, and my job was to fill it with sound, to fill the room with sound. To complete the ceremony.

There were two things that were totally clear about this moment:

1. No one cared about my troubles.
2. They were here to see Slake, anyway.

So I took to the stage with this in mind.

"We're Schizopolis," I said. "And I've had a really bad couple of days—"

"Who cares?" someone yelled from the audience.

"Exactly," I said. "And thank you. That was going to be my point. I'm going to put all of that aside for a little bit, and we're going to sing you some songs. I hope you like them. This one is called 'Jesus Was a Union Man,' and I'd like to dedicate it to my mom. Also, please excuse our outfits. We have no say in the mater." Then, before anyone could yell, "Fuck your mom!" I turned to Scott, and he started the arpeggiator on his synth, and nodded to Katherine, and there were the drums. It felt very good.

With my mother in the hospital, with my recently ex-girlfriend somewhere having sex with some other man, did I nail the crescendo? I did. Did I get in close to the microphone on the part of "East River" when I start to stutter quietly (an homage to the Talking Heads' "Psycho Killer")? Yes.

I also missed cues, as did Katherine, who came in on the fourth bar of the intro on "August," not the third. It sounded nothing like the album, which was fine, because the album didn't really exist anyway; it was just a story that Original Syn told us to keep us happy. We sounded like what we were: four people trying to find a voice, and sometimes finding it. Scott brought forth huge, artificial-sounding strings from his keyboard, Katherine pounded like a puppet on meth, and Jacob took his bass on a cruise down the Potomac, then up again. I sang and moved my fingers without knowing I was moving them, hammering the guitar. We just kept driving, moving forward.

I knew that I was a minister preaching to a mostly indifferent congregation. These people owned too many albums, and saw too many bands, for us to be more than a passing moment, a diversion from their days of driving and working. If I'd turned my back and fallen into the crowd, I would have broken my tailbone; no audience was going to catch me. Yet my own voice came back through the monitors and assured me that, even though I was singing for silhouettes, I, Gary Benchley, was real.

Another motel. Scott woke me at four in the morning, throwing a pillow at my head because I snored. I stayed awake for a while, listening to the different breathing patterns in the room. Katherine had a nose whistle. Jacob would cough in his sleep. Scott was mostly silent, but he flipped around in the bed and mumbled. It wasn't anything I'd ever mention, but it felt good to be here, with these other creatures, warm and human.

Between D.C. and Memphis was chain-store America. We stopped in a Starbucks and checked email on Scott's computer. Scott opened his browser and looked at the Slake message board, to see if anyone had anything to say about the show.

After a few minutes, he announced: "Here's something about us: 'The surprise of the evening was Schizopolis, a Slake-alike who dress like they're going to the circus in the Bronx.' "

"We don't sound like Slake at all," I said. "We don't have guitar."

"That almost seems racist, that part about the Bronx," said Jacob.

"I'm not wearing those fucking outfits anymore," said Katherine.

"We have to," said Scott. "Chris Neffly orders it."

"So where are our CDs?" asked Katherine. "I've worked at craft fairs that were better organized than this shit. Slake came out of the studio more than two months later and has their CDs, wrapped in plastic."

"Well, Slake," said Jacob. "I mean, we need to be realistic."

"You are so far up their ass you can taste their breakfast," said Katherine.

"I respect them," said Jacob.

"They're not bad guys," I said. "Anyway, the point is we hate wearing those stupid hats. And the stripey pants."

"And the silver shirts with the triangles on them," said Scott. "I feel like Mork."

"So I'd say we could come to a decision, as a band, if asked, that people weren't responding well to the outfits, and while they were a brilliant idea in theory, in execution we just couldn't make them work."

"Will Donald buy that?" asked Jacob.

"Donald doesn't care if we live or die. Scott, do you agree?"

"That Donald doesn't care? No, Donald doesn't care."

"I don't understand this branding and synergy crap," said Katherine. "Isn't this supposed to be a rock tour?"

"Exactly," I said. "Where are the groupies? Maybe the big hats are getting in the way."

"Well," said Jacob, "I've been considering that. I think that groupies are probably between point-one and point-five percent of any audience. And so in order to get groupies we need to get at least two hundred people to show up."

"We're out of luck given those odds," I said. It was disheartening. Now that I was single, and had probably blown my chances with Katherine, I might as well have sex with strangers to validate myself. Which, it turned out, was probably going to happen, because when I asked to use Scott's laptop to check my email, and skipped through the spam, I found this message:

HEY WHAT'S UP. I saw you in Cambridge when I was up there last week but I live in Phoenix. I see from the Slake site that you are going to be coming through. Want to get dinner? I think you are cute :) Here's a picture. Allie

She also included her cell number. I showed the picture around. It was a huge relief, that sense that someone wanted to hook up with me.

"Hit that," said Jacob.

"Those look fake," said Scott.

"They're real," said Katherine, who didn't seem jealous at all. I wrote back with my phone number.

In Memphis we played Oscar's, a bar and barbecue, and we rocked. Perhaps it was the smell of meat, bringing out our animal nature. The crowd cheered and hooted. Colin nodded to me as I came offstage. "Nice work," he said, and it felt great, as if a torch had been passed between indie rockers. Of course, Slake immediately took the torch back and jumped up onstage. As Slake played, at least three people came over to me and asked where they could buy our album.

"We had a little mixup, but it'll be in stores soon," I said, hoping that this was true.

Slake played a mediocre show, for them, but I had to admit that they could handle their instruments. Brad was handy with the bass, plucking and slapping it like it was some sort of unwieldy animal that he had to keep in check, and Mike kept the beat without flaw, occasionally arcing into some nifty drum pyrotechnics.

Three hundred people showed up. Slake said it was the best night they'd ever had, ever, and when it was over, they were nine hundred dollars up, and we were three hundred dollars richer.

"We didn't lose money today," said Scott. "Check that out."

"Let's go crazy," I said. "Let's get premium gas."

"Of course, seventy-five dollars belongs to Original Syn," said Scott.

"Then at least high octane," I said.

Colin was chatting with a good-looking girl in boots, who was waiting for him, and Brad also had a woman in his sights, a pudgy girl in tights and a short skirt. Murphy was looking on from the merch table, shaking her head. Mike and Kevin were packing up Slake's equipment, sending resentful glances in the direction of their two more fortunate bandmates.

"Looks like Mike and Kevin are sharing a room tonight," said Katherine.

There were no groupies for Schizopolis, just my prospective groupie in the wings. So we decided to get a lead on the next day's eternal drive, and bid farewell to Slake.

"We'll catch up," said Colin, smiling.

I offered to drive, and Scott took me up on it. I drove and

thought of Allie, with her possibly fake breasts, in Phoenix. Of course, we had several stops before Phoenix. I didn't have to limit myself to Allie. That would be pretty amazing, I thought, hooking up with a girl in, say, Austin, then another in Denton, and then one in Phoenix. It was almost a *goal*.

"How far is Oklahoma again?" asked Scott.

"Nine million miles of white people," said Jacob. Once you leave the seaboard, *what you are* becomes very important, more important than *who you decide to be*. In New York, you can decide to be a hipster, buy some old T-shirts and big shoes, and you are a hipster. You're what you do—an artist, writer, independent musician. But out here in America (and also, I realized, growing up in Albany), the categories changed. Scott was less of a computer programmer and more gay. Jacob was suddenly not a writer-bassist, but a black guy. Katherine was a large-breasted, round-bottomed woman. Well, she was that in New York, too, but it seemed more pronounced in this part of the world. Only I, being a young white man with middle-class bearings, didn't really stand out in any way. But then, this was the plan in starting the band—to make it diverse, to make it represent more than the sum of its parts, to be a portrait of America. That was probably a more important kind of synergy than the kind we realized by wearing big floppy hats.

That synergy also explained the weird looks we got from the desk clerks when we pulled into random motels and asked for a single room. I'm sure they imagined all manner of perversions and sins, seeing us pile out of our maroon van. Clearly we were not on a business trip.

We arrived at Borderlands, in Norman, Oklahoma, to find Slake standing in a cluster by the door to the club. I'd slept for much of that day's seven-hour drive.

"Thank God you're here," said Colin. "Jacob, there's a kind of emergency."

"I'm good in emergencies," said Jacob. "What is it?"

"Brad," he said. "He's in the back of the van."

We all went over and looked in the back, to see Brad passed out, drooling, with his leg jacked backward in an uncomfortable position. Just looking at him made me want a drink.

"That doesn't look good," said Jacob.

"What happened?" asked Katherine.

"He went on a bender last night, and then had some hair of the dog this morning, then more hair of the dog after that."

"He finished up with some hair of the dog," said Mike, shaking his head.

"You guys need to talk to him," said Murphy.

"We'll talk to him," said Colin. "Usually he's got it in check. But it's taking a pretty serious turn."

"Um, how can I help?" Jacob asked. "I mean, you want me to get him some coffee?"

"No, man. We were wondering if you could help us out tonight."

"Dude," said Jacob, "I don't know your songs."

"I know," he said. "But you know them well enough to fake it, right?"

"Air bass?" Jacob looked confused. "Sure."

"Perfect," said Colin.

"But there'll be no . . . notes," said Jacob.

A low moan came from the van, as Brad's head lolled back, over the edge of the seat. It just hung there. Then he moaned again.

"We've got everything on a backing track," said Colin.

Jacob contemplated this. Looking at him, I wondered what I would have done. Of course, it wasn't really an option for a singer to fake vocals. I would have had to do a lot of humming to get through the songs.

"Isn't it going to look cheesy?" Jacob asked.

"It'll look fine," said Colin. "Just stand behind Kevin if you feel lost."

"Why don't you just play without a bassist?" asked Scott.

"No, man," said Colin. "There needs to be a bass player. You can't cheat."

"But you can cheat," Scott said, "when it comes to him actually playing?"

"That's how I see it," said Colin. Personally, I understood his point. "So, Jacob?"

"OK," he said. "I'll help out."

Slake did their soundcheck. Jacob looked nervous, but obviously was digging the challenge of playing air bass. He and Colin conferred several times during soundcheck, and Jacob pretended to work through the songs as the backing track played. He looked pretty convincing; he was a big Slake fan, so that must have helped. Jacob just stayed onstage when Slake was done with soundcheck.

"How do you feel?" I asked.

"Nervous," Jacob said. "I mean, this is a band I've *reviewed*."

"You'll be fine," I said. "If they ever make it huge, you can say you played with Slake. How cool is that?"

"Pretty cool," Jacob said, nodding.

"Jacob is our karaoke bassmaster," said Scott.

"That's right," said Jacob, smiling thinly at Scott.

For our soundcheck, the tech took his time and helped us get things right. We made it clear that Jacob's bass would be off during Slake's set, and on during Schizopolis's, and he seemed to get that.

Doors opened. Jacob left the stage, then went back on twenty minutes later with Slake, and Colin announced from the stage that Jacob was a special guest.

By Slake's third song, Katherine came over to me and poked my shoulder, pointing out Brad, who'd just stumbled into the club. He was looking pretty dour, and/or hungover. He saw Jacob onstage and nodded his head.

We waited to see what would unfold. After Slake left the stage, we went over to Jacob, and Brad also came up.

"You motherfucker," said Brad. Then he smiled and shook Jacob's hand. "You saved my ass."

"No problem, man," said Jacob. "Anytime."

"I'm grateful. I sort of went off the deep end. Things are a little weird right now."

"I understand," Jacob said. "Don't sweat it."

"Anyway, I appreciate you helping us out," said Brad. "Won't have to do it again."

"Definitely," said Jacob, packing up his bass. "One-time thing."

"Damn right, I'm never letting that happen again," said Brad. He went over to the bar and ordered a beer. Colin came over to Jacob. "I've got someone you should meet," he said, and he pointed back to a girl wearing '50s-style sunglasses and a short skirt that showed her thighs. She had a quirky smile, and hair that touched her shoulders and looked unkempt, but was probably carefully styled to look that way. She looked like a librarian who worked in a porn store, and was the sum total of all indie rock wet dreams. Even Scott looked jealous. Jacob went over, shook hands with the girl, and Colin came back to see us.

"Thanks for letting us poach your bassist," he said.

"It's not a problem," said Scott. "You guys need to think about Brad, though. That guy isn't right."

"We're thinking about him," said Colin. "Trust me. That wasn't cool, last night."

"Jacob seems happy," I said. The girl was touching his side, and laughing.

"She's a big fan of Slake," said Colin. "She volunteered to be our merch girl the last time we came through. She and I became kind of close, you know?"

"That so?" said Katherine.

"Yep," said Colin, pronouncing the "p" in "yep" so that we all knew what "kind of close" meant. "Yep, yep, yep. But this time, she wanted to meet Jacob. And I'm glad to do him the favor. We call that the Slake Effect."

"It doesn't work that well for Brad," said Katherine.

"No, it doesn't," said Colin. "It used to, though, when he could stand up."

A little while later, Jacob came over and said that he'd meet up with us in the morning. The girl stood behind him, giggling.

"Aren't you going to introduce us to your friend?" Katherine asked.

"This is, uh, uh . . ."

The girl laughed and said her name: Devlin. Then she took Jacob's hand and walked out. I looked around for a groupie of my own, but there were none. Someone did come up to me, though, and tell me that our bassist was awesome. "Total variety in styles," he said.

So we headed to the hotel and fell asleep. In the morning, Jacob showed up from wherever and stuck his head in the van. He looked pretty worn out, like he'd just moved a lot of sofas.

"I'm going to ride with Slake," said Jacob. "You guys are sick of me, right?"

No one said anything for a moment. "Sure," said Scott. "That's cool. We'll see you in Austin."

"I'm just going to leave my stuff in the van," said Jacob.

"Of course," said Scott.

Jacob closed the van door, and we watched him wander off to some other part of the motel, where his new friends were.

"Well, I just got dumped," said Katherine.

"We all got dumped," I said.

"It's no big deal," said Scott. "We're all a little sick of each other."

"I love *you*, Scott," said Katherine.

"I love you too, honey."

I imagined the conversations they would have in the other van. They'd make fun of Schizopolis, I knew.

SLAKE: Dude, Jacob, I don't know how you do it. I'd kill myself if I was in that band. Schizopolis is a bag of fuck.

JACOB: No, man. Those are my friends.

SLAKE: We're your friends, too, man.

JACOB: That's cool.

SLAKE: But to prove your allegiance to Slake, you have to kill everyone in Schizopolis.

JACOB: All right. I'm cool.

Maybe that wasn't realistic. But it hurt to see Jacob's big head in the van, nodding and laughing in front of us, and I was relieved when a semi cut us off and Slake vanished from view for the remainder of the drive.

I'd expected true band fellowship on the road, but Slake and Schizopolis barely spent any time together. It was like we both had the same job, but worked different shifts. The only conversations we had were to complain about the label. I'd once tried to talk to Colin about his approach to singing, and he just looked at me, pointed to his heart, and said, "It comes out of here, man. I don't have any technique." Which left me feeling like a total sellout. Murphy the merch girl didn't even speak to us, and answered our repeated inquiries about T-shirt sales with a sad shake of her head.

"Well, now we can talk about how we hate Jacob," said Katherine. "I will go first. I hate the way he name-drops bands."

"I think we should make up a band," I said, "and see if he says he knows it."

"OK," said Katherine. "How about the Green Soldiers?"

"What about the Cotton Mathers?" asked Scott.

"The Red Light Skulls," I said.

We kept coming up with band names: Polenta, Biscuit Mary, the Porn Dogs, Alphabet Sandwich, Juan the Macademic, Survival of the Filthy, Manual of Style, Table Logik, Tina's Odyssey, and Oskar the Blue Bear.

"Let's say Polenta," said Katherine. "I'll ask him if he's ever heard of Polenta."

"Five dollars he's heard of it," said Scott.

"I'll take that bet," I said, "and then I'll never pay you when I lose."

"Cool," said Scott.

Challenging Jacob gave us something to look forward to, because the southern American heartland went by very, very slowly. From the highway, the southern American heartland is made of: cows, flatness, and chain stores. I wondered what it was like when you left the highway. Was it more cows? Or more flatness?

"We're playing Austin," I said. "That's pretty amazing."

"Yep," said Scott, staring down the long, straight road.

"Sure is," said Katherine, falling asleep.

A little while later, my phone began to ring; it was Colin, in the other van. "We've got some news," he said. "We're canceling San Diego."

"OK," I said, not sure what that meant for us. "Why's that?"

"According to Chris, we're supposed to turn around once we get there and fly to New York so that we can play for a taping of—what show is it?" I heard some mumbling in the van. *Good Morning with Yuki.*"

"Oh," I said, *"Good Morning with Yuki."*

"It's some Japanese TV show that's in New York for a week. A talk show? Apparently it's a huge deal in Japan. Chris is very concerned about Japanese exposure."

"Yeah," I said. "You *need* to keep your eye on Japan."

"But what that means is that we're leaving you guys high and dry."

"So do we just go ahead and play the show without you?"

"That's going to be up to you and the venue," said Colin. "You might want to call Donald. Jacob has offered to drive our van to L.A."

"That's nice of him," I said. Katherine asked who it was, and I said it was Colin.

"Ask him if Jacob's behaving."

Colin overheard her through the phone. "Jacob is great," he said. "He's like one of the band."

"All right," I said. "Let me work this out and call you back."

I called Donald. "I can talk to the venue," he said, "and see if they just want to put you on the bill. I don't know. Maybe they could get a local opener."

"That would be great," I said.

"But you'll need to see about getting people in the door."

"Oh, we can do that," I said. "Any progress on the CDs?"

"Apparently they're on their way here now."

"Could we reroute them? Get them sent to San Diego?"

"I don't want to mess with that," said Donald. "Let's just get them here."

"All right," I said. "It's a plan. Maybe you could send them back with Slake?"

"Maybe," said Donald.

We made it to Austin with plenty of spare time. At load-in, while Slake set up for soundcheck, I cornered Jacob. "We were wondering," I asked, "did you ever see Polenta play out?"

"Oh, I know Polenta," he said.

"You like them?"

"I do, yeah. They're a cool band."

I called Katherine and Scott over, and told them that Jacob liked Polenta. They laughed, and Katherine let Jacob in on the joke. But he refused to be finished.

"No, I swear to God, there's a band called Polenta," he said. I spied Brad, looking very nervous and sober, unpacking his bass.

"Maybe they opened for Korn," I said.

Katherine made a moaning noise at that, like a seal with cramps.

"I'm telling you, there's a band called Polenta," said Jacob.

"Bullshit," said Scott. "There is no band called Polenta. Describe to me the exact circumstances under which you saw them or heard of them."

"I never *saw* them. But there are, like, a million CDs floating around the *Matchstick* offices," he said.

"All right," said Scott. He pulled out his cell and dialed a number. "Sam," he said to the person on the other end, "are you in front of a computer? Good. Can you google for the words 'polenta band'?" He waited for a minute. "How about 'polenta rock'? Nothing? Thanks." He hung up. You had to wonder what Sam got out of that conversation.

Scott looked at Jacob. "Polenta was the bread of ancient times," he said. "But it is not a band."

"All right," said Jacob. "So maybe there is no band named Polenta."

"Jacob," said Katherine, "do you like the Blue Dawn Orchestra?"

"I don't know them," said Jacob.

"Is that so? I thought you knew every band."

"Are they real?" asked Jacob.

Katherine smiled. "They're totally real. You're paranoid now, aren't you?"

"Bitches are ganging up on me," he said.

"Maybe there's another band you'd prefer to hang out with," said Scott.

In Austin, we played a solid set to a crowd of 150, earned some applause, and made a hundred dollars. All of that was nice, even if we were slowly sinking into a terrible financial hole. But both the success and my financial worries were secondary to something else:

I earned my first honest-to-God groupie. Her name was Kari. She was pretty cute—maybe a little thick in the middle, and perhaps a B cup, but she had high cheekbones, and I try not to objectify women.

"Hey," she said after we left the stage, "you guys were great."

I shook her hand. "Thank you," I said. "We never played Austin before."

I bought her a beer and sat through her catalog of favorite local bands. I bought her another beer, and she touched my shoulder, and asked where she could buy a CD. I told her about our distribution problems, and she replied by telling me that it didn't matter, because Schizopolis clearly had a great future and were going to be huge.

"That's the plan," I said. "I mean, we're working on it."

"I'll be able to say, 'I saw them when.' "

"That you will," I said.

"Where are you staying tonight?" Kari asked.

The Austin Motel, I told her.

She told me that it was a cool place, the hippest hotel in a very hip city. I told her that we were sharing a room, and that it was getting a little tiresome. "I'm hoping to do laundry," I said. "Although I don't have any detergent. I could probably use some hotel soap, though." All of my underwear had become thick and sticky. Since I'd planned on wearing a costume onstage, I hadn't packed enough clothes.

"You know, I have laundry in my building," she said. "And detergent."

She gave a big smile and made her eyes very large. It took me a moment to catch on, because who picks up a girl by complaining about detergent? But that was definitely what was happening. Someone wanted to go home with me because I was in a band, namely Schizopolis, based on my physical attractiveness and my singing ability. And anyway, any morning where I wouldn't wake up to the sight of Jacob's ass crack, and Scott and Katherine nuzzling each other, sounded like Disney World.

"I could definitely do some laundry," I said.

"We can make that happen," she said.

So I helped with load-out, and then delivered my news.

"You guys," I said, avoiding Katherine's eyes, "I'll meet up with you tomorrow."

"We need to leave by noon," said Scott.

"It's cool, bro," I said. "I'll be, I think, ten minutes from the hotel."

We drove a few minutes to her apartment, somewhere in Austin, Kari told me she was a graduate student in business administration. She wanted to work overseas, maybe in France. Her apartment was large and comfortable, with lots of windows, and comfortably messy—a few dishes in the sink, a bra on the couch. Para would have sneered at the Monet prints on Kari's wall, but to hell with Para.

She brought out a bottle of whisky for the couch, and we drank a bit, and then I put my hand on hers. *Here you go, Para,* I thought. Then I felt guilty for using this woman for revenge against my girlfriend. Then again, Kari was clearly not into me for the long haul. So she was getting something out of it, too. Maybe she'd just been dumped, as well. I almost brought it up, but we made out instead.

I'd never had a random hookup like that before, where I didn't know the girl's email address. And it was strange to be with someone who wasn't Para. Instead of Para's familiar hands and mouth on my zones of pleasure, smooth and comfortable, this stranger didn't know what triggered me, what would make me feel good. We tried a little of everything, all the regular stances, fingers, mouths, etc. Kari wriggled out of her skirt, but kept her big clunky shoes on, which was kind of hot. She pulled out a condom from her dresser, tearing one off from a row of ten. It was a classic AIDS-blocking latex model with nonoxynol-9 and a reservoir tip, the kind that you learn to use during freshman orientation. I rolled it on, and she hopped on top and jumped around for a while, moaning and whistling through her nose. I enjoyed it. Her skin pinked, and she made a sound like a siren winding up. Having fulfilled my role as a sensitive, orgasm-inducing male, I had my big moment, then fell back into the bed exhausted. Kari got up to pee. "Don't want a UTI," she said.

"No, of course not," I said. Ah, romance. I closed my eyes, then felt her get back into bed, and heard her shoes come off, falling to the floor. She put a light blanket over the both of us, and we passed out.

There you go, I thought, and fell asleep.

I woke up a few hours later, a little hungover, and took a moment to get my bearings and remember where I was. I turned over to find Kari naked, and looked her over, enjoying her bareness, the curve of the hips, the slope of the breasts, until I saw that she was missing her right foot.

I looked away, then looked back. It was still missing. I thought about this for a moment, but didn't come to any conclusions. Then I got up, put on boxers, and went to the bathroom. There, on a shelf next to the sink, I saw five Left Behind books, action-adventure books about the return of Jesus. I'd never slept with, or met, anyone who had read them.

When I emerged from the bathroom Kari was up and dressed. For the first time, I noticed her almost imperceptible limp.

"You like coffee, or tea?" she asked, footlessly.

"Coffee would be great," I said, thinking both of the foot and the books I'd seen in the bathrooom. She went into the kitchen to start the percolator, and I sat at a table outside of the kitchen.

"Your apartment is huge," I said.

"Really?" she yelled out to me. "It seems small to me."

"By New York standards," I said.

"I go to New York and I think I'm in a sardine can. I'm like, how can you *live* this way? I hate it."

"You've been to New York a lot?"

"Just once. With the school band. I saw *Cats*." I noticed that she had a drawl. It hadn't been apparent the night before.

In my mind, I exhaled a very long sigh. "You're from Texas?"

"I'm from Bee," she said. I guessed that was in Texas. "Do you live in Manhattan?"

"In Williamsburg."

"Where's that?"

She didn't know. I told her it was in Brooklyn.

"Where are you going next?"

"Denton?" I said. "I don't really know where that is."

"I've got friends in Denton. I wish I didn't have so much work to do, or I'd come up and catch you guys play." Yesterday, that idea might have appealed. But now I was rewriting the story: does a footless groupie still count as a groupie? I mean, if I called Para and said, "I just had sleazy revenge sex with a girl in Austin," she might be really hurt and jealous. But if I called and said, "I just had sleazy revenge sex with an amputee," she'd probably pity me. And then there were the books in the bathroom.

But then, I wasn't going to let some whining inner Para dictate my feelings. By my own measurements, all things considered, Kari *did* count as a groupie. Even if she was Christian and gimpy. It wasn't her fault that she'd lost her foot, whether it had been through car accident, birth defect, or shark attack. And her faith—well, it wasn't any worse than astrology when you think about it. And maybe when you lose a foot and pick up lonely rock hopefuls at clubs in Austin, you need the spiritual fulfillment that serious Christianity offers. I hoped she didn't feel guilty about hooking up with me, given that she was religious. I mean, she should have gotten something out of the situation, too. That seemed only fair.

"It's not a long drive?" I asked.

"It's about four hours. Not bad."

"I forget that four hours of driving is no big deal out here."

"Yeah," she said.

Then she said, "Can I ask you something?"

"Sure," I said, thinking, *Here it comes about the foot, or Jesus,* and vowing to act like I didn't care.

"Did you vote for John Kerry?"

"Yeah," I said. "Of course."

She brought out coffee in a mug with the UT seal printed on the side, and a big ugly ceramic mug for herself. She shook her head. "I *thought* so. You know, I'm, like, the only Republican in Austin," she said.

"Really?" I said. "Huh." Suddenly, the Left Behind books made more sense, and I knew I was in trouble. Deep trouble. "What time is it?" I asked, praying that it was 11:50, that we would have to get into her car and burn rubber to the hotel to get me back to the van on time.

"Eight," she said. "You've got plenty of time. We can talk about everything. You want to do that laundry?"

"So how did that go?" asked Katherine as I opened the door and slid in behind Jacob. Katherine was the absolute last person I wanted to speak to at that point. Unfortunately, being in a band together meant that we'd have to spend the next several days together, sniffing each other.

"Do I have to answer you?" I asked.

"It's a four-hour drive," she said. Scott got on the road, a few quick turns, Jacob telling him where to go. We drove in silence for a few minutes.

"OK, Gary," said Jacob. "Let's hear about it."

"Well," I said, waiting until the moment was right, "she had no foot."

"Who had no foot?"

"That girl," I said. "Kari. Also, she tried to convert me to Christianity. And she wanted me to register as a Republican."

Jacob said, "I'd personally like to back up to the place where she had no foot."

"How did she lose it?" said Katherine.

"I didn't ask," I said. "It didn't come up, actually."

"I would have raised that subject," said Scott.

"There's nothing wrong with not having a foot," said Katherine. "It's not her fault."

"Also, I got you all something," I said. I reached into my bag and pulled out three books, from the stash I'd found in Kari's bathroom that had scared me so badly. I passed them around. "I got you one each."

"What's this?" Katherine asked.

"That's a Left Behind book," I said. "I borrowed them from her."

"She gave these to you?" Jacob said.

I made a shrugging noise.

"You stole them?" asked Scott.

" 'Stealing' is a harsh word," I said.

"Like 'amputee,' " said Jacob.

"Exactly," I said.

"What are these?" asked Katherine.

"They're the most popular book series in America," said Jacob. "They're about Jesus coming back. They're thrillers."

"Oh, no," said Katherine. "I don't want this book."

"I worked hard for it," I said. "Keep it."

"And she was a Republican?" Scott asked.

"She told me that gay marriage was evil. And tried to get me to register. That was after she told me about Jesus in her life."

It had been a very uncomfortable morning. I had no idea where I was in Austin. I was dependent on Kari for getting me back to the Austin Motel, back to the van. Kari had said, "Gary, I'd feel really weird about letting you leave before I told you about someone who's very important in my life." I thought she might have a kid, but the important person turned out to be the *lamb*.

"This is too weird," said Scott.

"Oh, please," said Jacob. "Like you haven't gone to bed with a fundamentalist amputee and not noticed before."

"How could you not *notice*?" Katherine asked.

"I got up in the morning, you know, to brush the hair out of my teeth—"

Katherine made a gagging noise.

"—and when I came back she was wearing jeans and sneakers. So I guess she's good at hiding it."

"But she slept with you despite her love for Jesus," said Jacob.

"I'm still not sure how that works out," I said. "I didn't really ask her to clarify."

We passed the time by having Katherine read out loud from her Left Behind book. The story was about a group of people, called the Tribulation Force, fighting the Antichrist. It was hilarious.

"I can't believe people believe this shit," said Jacob.

"Believe it," said Scott. "I grew up in Pennsyltucky. My mom had an evangelical phase, and we heard all about the Antichrist."

"I hate it," said Katherine. "I hate that people are into this stuff. I don't want this book."

"It's a gift," I said. "Besides, if you give it away, someone will just read it."

"I want to destroy it," she said. "Can we run it over with the van?"

"Sure," said Scott. "We'll pull into a rest stop."

We did so, a few minutes later, and with the rest-stoppers of Texas watching on, we put the books on the ground, opened, and Scott ran them over five or six times with the van, until they were just bits of paper. We drove off, leaving them there.

"Now *this* is being on tour," said Jacob. He put in a CD—Bonnie "Prince" Billie, a classic—and we sang along down the highway. I was in good spirits. I had a terrible story to tell, we'd run over Christian America with our van, and all told, people liked our band, we liked one another, my mom was about to go home from the hospital, and I'd gotten laid, beginning the long process of getting Para out of my head.

But my good spirits faded quickly, because, at around three in the afternoon, my groin became extremely itchy. I shifted around, trying not to scratch, but it soon became pretty bad. Every lesson of high school health class came back to me, every terrible story about warts, herpes, lesions, and death. It was unfair, that my first groupie would give me some dread disease.

I asked for a pit stop. We found a Starbucks. The person at the counter looked up at us suspiciously, the same suspicion I felt when we checked into hotels. What *was* so weird about a mixed-gender-preference, mixed-age, mixed-gender group piling out of a dirty van, looking hungover and sickly? Scott pulled out his laptop and got that email junkie's look in his eyes, waiting for his fix.

In the Starbucks bathroom, I looked down and saw that my nether region was red and inflamed. I began to hyperventilate. I jumped up and down and backed up in order to get a better look in the mirror above the sink. Definitely red and sore. I put some cool water down there, then patted it off with paper towels. Someone was pounding on the door outside, and I quickly put myself together, then opened the door to let in a crabby Texan.

"Sorry," I said.

"Can't wait," he said. "It's pokin'."

Smiling nervously at this totally uncalled-for detail about a stranger's needs, I went over to stand next to Jacob and Katherine at the counter, waiting for their various drinks to be prepared at slow Texas speed; Jacob's leg was twitching as he watched the woman behind the counter decant his drink. I didn't know what to do, and then I remembered—Scott had worked at a men's health clinic. I went up to him, and although I barely had words to describe my worries, I realized that I needed to say something before the rest came back to the table.

"Scott, I have a kind of emergency," I said.

He looked at me and shook his head. "What?"

"I have a rash. I don't know what it is."

"I'm sure it's nothing," he said. "We're in the car all the time."

"No," I hissed, "it's down there."

"Down where?"

I looked at him. He nodded, very slowly, and perhaps sadly. "Benchley, you're shitting me."

"I'm serious. That girl I hooked up with."

"The footless Republican."

"I *got* something. It stings."

He narrowed his eyes. "Did you wear a condom?"

"Of course."

He tapped the space bar on his laptop. "What does it look like?"

"*Red.*"

"Does it hurt?"

"Really bad." Previously it had just itched, but now, my mind had transformed the pain into something epic, as if all the heat of the sun was concentrated below my stomach. Scott put his head in his hands. "Do you know what it is?" I asked. "You worked in a clinic."

Jacob came back to the table with his coffee. "Are we staying or driving?" he asked.

"Driving," said Scott. "We'll be out in a minute."

"Can I have the keys?" asked Jacob. Scott handed them over to him, and he went outside.

I looked at Scott with my worried frown. "I don't know what to do," I said.

"All right," said Scott. "Let's go into the bathroom and take a look." He packed up his laptop, taking his time, sighing a lot. We waited outside the occupied bathroom, and the huge Texan emerged, and saw me again.

"Still got more, huh?" he said to me, and Scott and I slipped in together.

"Oh, God," said Scott, wrinkling his nose, "it's *awful* in here."

"I really appreciate you doing this," I said.

"Let's see it," said Scott.

I dropped my pants and Scott bent over and cocked his head. He looked for a moment. Then he laughed.

"Folliculitis," he said. "It's just an infection. See, it starts where the condom stopped. We'll get you some cream."

"What could do that?" I asked, zipping up. "Could I get it that fast?"

"Dirty woman parts," Scott said. "It's a rash. It doesn't take long to show up."

"But she was a Christian."

There was a knock at the door. "You can't be in there together," came a woman's voice.

"Oh, Jesus," said Scott. He opened the door.

"We're just washing our hands," I said, zipping up my fly.

"There've been complaints." Behind her, the tall Texan was eyeing us.

"Complaints about what?" asked Scott.

"About men being in there together," she said.

"I have a medical condition," I said.

"Shut up, Gary," said Scott. "We're going."

We walked past her, and she pushed against the wall to let us pass.

The tall Texan was standing there, staring. I asked him, "Is there a drugstore nearby?"

"There's an Eckerd about a mile down the road," he said. He frowned. "But you people are sick."

"We're in a band," I said.

Katherine walked out from behind the Texan, her latte in hand, and stared at us both. We all walked outside together. Jacob was asleep in the backseat, headphones on; Katherine stretched out in the second seat.

"What the hell was that?" I asked. "Two men can't go into a bathroom together? What law did we break?"

"Texas," said Scott, shrugging. "We're going to stop by a drugstore," he said to the van. "Anyone need anything?"

"Does someone want to tell me something?" Katherine asked.

"Gary has a problem, and needs an ointment," said Scott.

"Do you want me to drive?" I asked. "I can still drive."

"I've got it," he said. The van started up with a gasp, and we left the parking lot. I felt the eyes of Texas upon us as we left.

"I would like to leave this state right now," I said.

"Tomorrow," said Katherine. "But could you please tell me what happened?"

The balm Scott recommended soothed my pain, and we played a respectable set. We had to tell Slake what had happened, including the footless part and the Starbucks bathroom.

"Now that," said Colin, "is a story."

After our set a young, doe-eyed man came up and spoke with Katherine, obviously hitting on her. I was a little upset to see it, but I realized that there was absolutely no room for me to be jealous given my recent adventure.

Still, I was relieved when I realized that the doe-eyed man wasn't after her, but Scott. Scott and the young man sat at the bar and chatted, and Scott consented to let the young man poke his shoulder several times. We drove to the hotel, and Scott said he wanted his own room, and paid for it himself. Which was fine and not fine, because Jacob and Katherine took one of the hotel beds together. I don't think either one of them wanted to be too close to me given my ointment situation.

We went to bed joking about Scott's conquest.

"God, I hope he gets laid," said Katherine. "He could do with some cheering up."

*   *   *

The morning after, I grabbed a bowl of cereal from the motel's continental breakfast, then went out to the van, where Scott's friend from last night sat behind the driver's seat.

"I'm Steve," he said. "How you doing?"

"I'm cool," I said. "I saw you last night."

"I loved your show."

"Thanks," I said. "What'd you think of Slake?"

He shrugged, indifferent. "I liked you guys better." I felt a great, spontaneous warmth toward him. "I'm coming out to Albuquerque," he said. "If that's cool."

"Sure," I said. "Always room for fans."

Scott got into the van. "Hey," he said. "Gary, this is Steve."

"Yeah, we just met," I said.

"Steve's got a cousin in Albuquerque; I said we'd give him a ride."

"Already established," I said.

Steve smiled. His hair was tousled and he looked sleepy and happy.

"So what'd you get into last night?" I asked Scott.

As we drove from Denton, I made up some facts about New Mexico.

1. The official state color of New Mexico is dusty.
2. The official state tree of New Mexico is the red pepper.
3. The official state bird of New Mexico is whatever bird happens along.

If you want a burrito, a thrift store, or a gun, it's your state. If you want to play a rock show to a club with more than fifteen people in the audience, then it's probably not the right state for you. We drove on.

*　　*　　*

We made it to Phoenix by Sunday. The show was scheduled for Monday night, which left the rest of the band with little to do. I, however, had a phone number for Allie, the girl from the email I'd received outside of Memphis. The ointment had done its trick, and I was ready to try again.

Allie picked me up at the motel. Her photo had been accurate—she was pretty foxy. We went to dinner in downtown Phoenix.

Everything in Phoenix looked clean and white, lots of plastered, adobe-style buildings of one or two stories, and even the chain restaurants seemed to nod to the local styles by including red tile roofs.

Allie told me about her work for a large consulting firm, which required her to fly all over North America. She specialized in analyzing product flow, she said. Her boyfriend had moved out of her place after living with her for six months, and she was always being reviewed at work, where she occupied a cubicle when she was not traveling. It got to her, she said; she felt she could be fired at any moment. I told her about Schizopolis, leaving out the body skank and infections. Doubtless she left things out, as well.

She knew New York well, and we talked about the tree lighting at Rockefeller Center, the *Today* show, and the Empire State Building. "That is one perverted place," she said. "I've gotten into some wild situations in New York."

"It can be pretty wild," I said. Suddenly, I remembered David walking in on me as Charles nursed my broken ankle, and that made me think of Para, a low, pit-of-stomach sensation that I pushed out of my head.

Allie was twenty-four, but seemed older to me—a job, a car, an apartment of her own. We drove back to her apartment building, which was three stories tall and nestled inside of a suburb. I had the strange sensation of knowing what came next: we were going to fool around. We didn't know each other, there wasn't anything like love, and she'd only seen me once, onstage, before that night. But somehow I'd caught her eye, like the cover of a book, and she'd picked me up and decided to buy me. She seemed pretty comfortable with the idea, so I decided to be comfortable as well. This sex was about each of us getting what we wanted, as long as what we wanted was totally without substance, quick, and fleeting. But at the same time, I was in Schizopolis, not Mötley Crüe, so there had to be some conversation, some discussion, a sense that this was in some way special. And private.

"This is it," she announced, turning a key. Her apartment was small and comfortable, and more than anything I wanted to sit on the couch and watch TV. She brought out champagne, for no reason, and sat down next to me on the couch, close enough to touch. Then she put her hand on my knee.

"I can't believe you're here!" she said. "I wrote you an email, and now you're here."

We looked at each other tenderly. It was sort of pleasant, when you thought about it. It was a very adult situation, I realized. You didn't get involved. I revised my earlier thoughts regarding a bookstore: it was more like she was checking me out of the library, because when she was done she'd return me.

"I totally had to have you out to dinner," she said. "I knew it when I saw you onstage. You looked so tired getting up there, and then you just belted things out." She looked directly into my eyes. "I want a copy of your album."

"So do I," I said. "We're having some distribution problems."

"You know, that's my specialty, distribution problems."

"Oh," I said, "maybe you could help." I was willing to discuss that a little more, because we genuinely could have used some advice regarding the issue, but she kissed me. We made out for a while, hands moving around freely, until the requisite amount of mutual stiffening/loosening took place, and then she said, "I really like to be tied up. Do you want to tie me up?"

Less than anything else, I wanted to tie her up. I didn't want to rape, dominate, control, violate, or hurt any woman. But I said, "Whatever you want," and followed her, now in her panties, to her bedroom.

There she produced some silk ropes from a box under the bed, placing a condom on her bedside table. I noticed that the ropes had dirty marks on them from use. She stripped naked and stretched on the bed. "Fuck me, Brian," she said. I sighed, wondering about Brian, and proceeded to snap on a condom, but everything was wilting.

"I'm not really comfortable with this," I said.

"What do you mean? You want me to turn over?"

"I'm just . . . it's not for me. Not right now."

"Are you kidding? This is every man's fantasy."

"Um, not every man, I guess."

She asked me if I was gay, and I told her I wasn't. Then she asked me to untie her.

I did so, and we sat together on the bed. "I'm sorry," I said.

"Don't you want to do this?"

"Kind of not, honestly." That felt good to say. Better than sex, almost.

She sat still for a minute, and then she began to cry. "I want you to go," she said.

"I'm sorry," I said. I put my hand on her knee, and she pulled it away.

"No, I mean it! I want you to go. Get out of my apartment. Now."

"OK, but—"

"Now! Leave now!"

Her face was screwed up, furious, hot tears running down her face. I went out to the living room and retrieved my pants, then sat on the sofa to put on my shoes.

"Where am I?" I said.

"I don't have to take this shit," she said.

I was missing a sock, but rather than look for it I just put my shoes on as quickly as I could and went for the door, then out down the concrete stairwell, in front of the apartment building. I found myself on the street, cursing the woman upstairs, with no idea how I'd gotten here.

Well, here's another story for the van, I thought. I pulled my cell phone from my pocket, bracing myself for Scott's tired voice, but the battery was entirely dead. I resisted the urge to throw the phone on the ground and stomp on it, screaming, and looked around for a pay phone, but of course there were none. This was the suburbs.

However, I'd grown up in the suburbs, and, I reasoned, they all followed the same rough pattern, lots of houses and cul-de-sacs, leading out to highways and main thoroughfares. I began walking, noting that I was on Lark Street, and turned on to Wren. Then I took Baylor. Before long I was back on Lark, but an entirely different section of it. The suburbs were infinite, filled with traps, the houses all built to the same two-story configuration, with two car garages. As I walked, I triggered garage light after garage light.

A few cars passed, but I couldn't find the highway. If I didn't find a way out, I was caught until morning. Finally, I heard a car pull up behind me, slowing, but I didn't turn around. This was it, I thought, young singer–rhythm guitarist raped and beheaded in suburbs. That would sell albums. Chris would be happy, Lou would be happy, and Scott, Jacob, and Katherine would probably not be miserable.

"How you doing," came a man's voice, and I turned around to see a black and white police car, with a man leaning out the window of the driver's side. I walked around to him, making sure to keep my hands loose.

"Hey," I said. "I'm out for a walk."

"What's your name?"

"Gary Benchley, sir."

"Kind of late for a walk, Gary."

"It is that, sir."

"You drunk?"

"No," I said. "I've had a few, but—no, I'm not drunk."

"You sure?"

"I'm sure."

"Something wrong?"

"I'm just trying to get back to the Day's Inn, in Phoenix."

"Long way to walk."

"It is. Especially when you're lost."

The officer shook his head, and looked over at the other policeman to his right, who nodded. "You want a ride?"

"God, yes, I want a ride."

"Get in," he said.

I opened the back door and got in. There wasn't much room for your knees. It's not supposed to be comfortable in the back of a cop car, I guessed.

"I'm Alan," said the policeman. "This is Doug." He pointed to a man with a mustache in the passenger seat, who held a cup of coffee. Alan got on the radio and spoke in police jargon. Doug coughed. "What brings you out tonight, Gary?" he said.

"Well," I said, "you're used to hearing messed-up stories, right?"

"Truly, I am."

So I told them what had happened. I kept talking as we drove. I told them about Schizopolis, our tour, about Slake, about the email, and about the silk rope. The silk rope interested Doug.

"Apartment building on Lark Street?" he asked.

"Yeah," I said.

"She was tied up and naked, and you just said, no, thanks?"

"I guess so," I said.

"Goddamn, son," said Alan, "that's every man's fantasy."

I felt like I did whenever I entered the company of real men, men speaking about football and fishing. In this case, men with guns and in uniform. I'd been given a scene straight out of a porn film, and turned around and walked out. They were mystified.

But then, they were right. A few weeks earlier, when things with Para were collapsing, that night on Lark Street would have seemed like a very specific dream come true. Why hadn't I gone through with it? "Well, my mom just got breast cancer," I said. "And my girlfriend just dumped me."

"I'm sorry to hear all that," said Doug.

"Oh, well, no wonder your dick doesn't work," said Alan. "That would do it to anyone."

"Your mom going to be all right?" asked Doug.

"Touch and go," I said. "But it looks good." It was a huge relief, to have the police understand what was wrong. They asked me about the next night's show, and knew the club where we were playing.

"You know, if you want to come by," I said, "I could put you down as Doug plus one."

"We're probably working," said Doug. "But thanks for the invitation."

"You like indie rock?" I asked.

"Alan likes the Butthole Surfers," said Doug.

"I love Gibby Haynes," said Alan. "He's a lunatic."

"What about you, Doug?" I asked.

Alan replied for him, singing the words "I am beautiful, no matter what they say."

"You like Christina Aguilera?" I said.

"I think she's hot," Doug said.

Alan continued singing the song, making fake sobbing noises and rubbing his eyes.

Music was a good subject, and the longer I could talk about it, the longer I could avoid them asking questions that would show how little I knew about football or guns. "What about U2?" I said. "Do you like the new album?"

"We were talking about that the other day," said Doug. "I'm more of a *Joshua Tree* kind of guy."

"I like the new album," I said.

"Hear that?" said Alan. "I'm telling you, Doug. I'll burn you a copy."

"I don't need any more music," said Doug.

It was only a twenty-minute drive to the hotel, a definitely walkable distance. Alan pulled the police car up in front of the doors, and both he and Doug got out to shake my hand. "Watch out for those girls with silk rope," said Alan.

"That," I said, "is very good advice." I thanked them a dozen times.

"Get some sleep," said Doug.

At the desk, I asked a tired-looking Chinese man to call up to the room in Scott Spark's name, and after a moment he handed me the phone.

"What," Scott said, "in God's name."

"I'm in the lobby," I said. "I need to crash. What room are you in?"

He had to get up to find the folder with his key card. I heard shuffling noises from his room. Finally, he gave me the number, D4.

"I'll be right up," I said.

I took the elevator, and knocked quietly at Scott's door. He let me in, bleary and confused. Jacob and Katherine were sharing a bed, both hard asleep. I took a pillow and a sheet from Scott's bed and crashed on the carpet.

Donald had set things up with the venue in San Diego, which was willing to keep us on the bill. So when we arrived we found a copy shop, where Scott used his laptop to email a copy of our flyer to the tired-looking clerk. It was nothing that Para would have approved of, but she was always too critical of everything. She just didn't get the DIY aesthetic.

We printed up five hundred copies for twenty dollars, and then tried to figure out what to do. "We need to split up," said Katherine. At first, I thought she meant the band, but she meant we should split up and pass out flyers. We asked the copy shop clerk, a skinny bald guy wearing a NO KNIFE T-shirt, where to hand out flyers. "Hill-crest," he said, looking at Scott. "Or Kettner Boulevard."

We triangulated and drove from the copy shop. Scott and Jacob decided to stick together, but Katherine and I went solo. I stood on Kettner Boulevard, handing out pieces of paper with directions to the venue for anyone who would take one. My salesmanship skills are pretty good, but San Diego was hard to crack.

GARY: Hey, there!
PERSON 1: Thanks, but I'm already saved.
GARY: This is for music, not religion.
PERSON 1: Oh, then eat me.

PERSON 2: What is this?
GARY: It's a flyer for our band. We're playing tonight. It would be great if you came.
PERSON 2: Is it free?
GARY: It's five dollars.
PERSON 2: I'll wipe my ass with it.

PERSON 3: I only go to comedy shows.
GARY: You might like this anyway.
PERSON 3: But it's not comedy?
GARY: No.
PERSON 3: Well, give me one anyway.

One guy promised to bring his friends. "We love good music," he said. I told him he'd be sure to hear some that night, and we shook hands. If the other band members had been as successful as I had, we'd have at least fifty people at the show. It would be respectable, and my brother would see that I was on my way to success. I hung flyers on lampposts and telephone polls.

It was pretty luxurious to have soundcheck entirely to ourselves, to get everything just right. The manager was a little anxious about the night's draw, but we told him not to worry, and showed him a flyer. "We've been giving these out all day," I said.

A short while later my brother showed up with his girlfriend, Jen, and there was a middle-aged man with a beard, who kept talking to Katherine during the show. "Hey!" the man with the beard would say, "Drummer girl! Drummer girl!" My brother and his girlfriend were both comped, so the audience had exactly one paying member.

Still, if we could just reach that one paying member, we'd at least have done something. I gave it my best, focusing my energy on the guy with the beard, even as he focused his energy on Katherine, who was ignoring him. The sound was a mess because it was mixed for a crowd, not for a huge empty hollow. In the middle of our fourth song, the man with the beard stood up and left, shaking his head. I didn't look at my bandmates, or at my brother. I sang for the back wall.

When it was over I heard my brother and his girlfriend clapping, and we left the stage.

"I'm a little disappointed with the turnout," said the owner.

"Yeah," I said. "I can see why you might feel that way."

"I'm not giving you guys a cut," he said.

"You know," I said, "I'm just not going to fight you for that dollar. Not even on principle."

"That's good," said the owner, "because you're not getting a penny."

I paid for a beer and sat down. I didn't have the energy to go through load-out. I shook my head to my brother, feeling hopeless.

"It's OK, buddy," said Bill. "You did good."

"I'm glad you could see us play," I said. "There's usually a lot more people."

"You're doing it," he said. "That's what matters."

I looked at him, and he was being serious. He wasn't going to ride me about this, not even a little. I guess a mother with cancer does that to siblings. I felt a huge, overwhelming brother-love. We talked about Mom, about her recent trip home from the hospital. I told my brother that I was going to go back for another visit when this tour ended.

"That's a good plan," he said. "I wish I lived closer to home."

"You know, right after I left Albany I broke up with my girl-friend," I said. "She was cheating on me."

"Holy shit," said Bill. "This happened just after seeing Mom?"

I told Bill about the lack of albums, about how that was driving Scott insane, making him hard to deal with. "He's a good guy," I said about Scott. "But he's starting to hate the entire process. Because we're losing money like this." I made a sound, "whoosh," to illustrate the sound of money being sucked away into a void.

"It'll get better," said my brother.

"Where are you staying tonight?" Jen asked.

"La Quinta, maybe. We have to go to L.A. tomorrow."

"Why don't you all stay with us?" Jen said. "We've got room."

"On the base?" I asked.

My brother looked doubtful, then shrugged. "If someone doesn't mind crashing on the floor. I mean, it's carpeted."

"Oh, no one minds that," I said. "At all."

So we followed them back to the base, Jacob driving Slake's van behind us. With my brother's blessing we raided the fridge. I ate cookies and milk and told them the stories of the road, leaving out the various infections and bodily emissions. The way it came out, it didn't sound that bad, four friends off to conquer the world. Maybe Los Angeles would be better.

After a few minutes, Jen noticed our drooping heads and went off to find blankets enough for the band. The only thing that would have made the evening even more pleasant would have been if she'd tucked me in and sung me a lullaby.

Carrying my blankets to the couch, I heard Katherine laugh. She was looking at a picture of me in high school, a shot of Mom, Elizabeth, Bill, and me from many Christmases ago. I was on my brother's wall. "Look at your short hair," she said. "You look like an upstanding young man."

"Gary was a good boy," said Bill. "Always."

"What went wrong?" said Katherine.

"What did you think of the set?" I asked Jen.

"It was interesting," she said. "Really interesting!"

"That's OK, Jen," said Jacob from his place on the carpet. "You're giving us a place to stay. You don't have to like it."

"No, I really liked it," she said. "Really."

I laughed, and fell asleep on a full stomach, feeling suddenly safe with my brother nearby, and my stomach filled with food.

The California morning sun, coming through the blinds, was extraordinary. As bright as lasers. It called us to get up, to go to Los Angeles, to try again. My brother and I embraced and said good-bye.

"I'm really glad to see you," he said, for the first time in his life.

"Me too," I said, surprised at how true that was.

Jacob continued to drive Slake's van, so it was just Scott, Katherine, and I. For a change, Katherine drove. I stretched out in the back. It was a quiet morning, all of us well fed from Jen and Bill's bacon, eggs, and muffins, until finally Scott began to talk.

"I need to say something," said Scott. "This isn't fun."

"We did not realize the fun potential in San Diego," I said. "But there have been some highlights."

Scott nodded. "Like when you hooked up with that Republican and got a dick infection?"

"Not so much that," I said. "But the van has not crashed, and no one was attacked by koalas."

"My period is over," Katherine said.

"See?" I said. "Katherine sees the bright side. You got laid. Steve was kind of cute."

"Then this is the most expensive date I've ever gone on," said Scott.

"I was nearly arrested," I said, laughing. "That didn't happen to you."

"The day I start to measure how well things are going by comparing myself to you," said Scott, "I'll kill myself."

"Ouch," said Katherine.

I tried a little laugh, to show there were no hurt feelings. Or very few. "I'm sensing some real pain," I said, "some real anger."

Scott was silent.

"Scott, we'll do a few more shows, and then we'll drive across the United States and relax a little. It's not so bad. This isn't suffering. This is a privilege."

"I am *really* looking forward to four days of nonstop driving," Scott said. "What the hell kind of planning is that?"

"Original Syn planning," I said. "It is not the best."

"And where are our CDs?" Scott asked. This was a question for the ages, like, Is there a heaven? or Why did God take John Lennon instead of Paul McCartney? There was no answer. Literally, there was no answer—when I called Donald, to check in, I always got voice mail, and no one ever called back. I guess Original Syn had caller ID.

And I was getting tired of Scott asking his rhetorical question about the CDs; he was acting like he was some sort of Job, the only one who was suffering. The idea of returning to Brand-Solve and working for him, after this, started to look less and less appealing.

I prayed for the creedness to dissipate, for L.A. to give us a sign, besides HOLLYWOOD. The Doors. Guns N' Roses. The Red Hot

Chili Peppers. They had all found fame here. There was always the chance that music industry representatives would appear, and change our lives dramatically.

In your average music documentary, bands often hit this point, where they don't know how to continue. They have to fight the odds and see if they can make it work. Of course, they're usually on their fourth album and breaking out in new artistic directions that the record company executives don't want to support, like Wilco. We were just victims of incompetence.

But lo, in L.A. there was a good crowd. Slake pulled in two hundred, and maybe ninety of them were from the music industry, men and women who took cell-phone calls during the show. After we played our set I waited for someone to come over, to strike up a conversation, to talk about how maybe Schizopolis should sign to a major label. But they were there to see Slake.

Next stop Santa Cruz. We got into the van and drove. A few miles into the ride, Jacob cleared his throat. He looked uncomfortable. "Gentlemen, and lady, I have some odd news." No one said anything. "I guess the easiest thing to do is to say it." He tapped his fingers on the seat. "OK."

"Jacob, you're saying something? I wasn't listening," said Katherine.

"The thing is," he asked, "what do you think the future of Schizopolis is?"

"Limited," said Scott. "With a high chance of failure."

"See, I'm worried about the same thing," said Jacob. "It seems like we're hitting a wall."

"We're just starting," I said. "Our albums haven't been distributed. These are low walls."

"I'm just saying," said Jacob. "I don't know what comes next."

"We go on tour again," I said. "Except we do it right, we do it with, uh, albums. And we don't open for Slake."

"That sounds almost as fun as having sharp needles driven into my urethra," said Scott.

Katherine said nothing. She was staying neutral.

"Jacob, are you done with Schizopolis?" I asked. "Is that what you're saying?"

"I don't know if I'm done," said Jacob. "But after San Diego . . ."

"San Diego was an anomaly," I said. "There will never be another San Diego."

I prayed that I was speaking the truth. Too many San Diegos would be pure Train. I'd rather die.

"Look, thing is, I've got an opportunity, and I want to take it."

"Oh, well, here we go," said Scott. I wondered what had come up. Jacob had probably been offered an editorial job at *Matchstick,* or something. I knew he was pitching a novel to someone, too. Jacob said something, but I was too busy thinking of what he might have in store to actually hear what he said.

Scott said, "You are fucking kidding me," and slumped his shoulders.

"Wait," I said. "Jacob, what did you say?"

"For Slake," he said. "They're firing Brad and asked me to come on as their bassist."

"Oh," I said. I felt like a kid with a balloon, accidentally letting go, watching it fly away. It was shrinking, turning into a dot.

"I know it seems like a betrayal," said Jacob.

"It doesn't just . . . ," I said, trailing off. "It's pretty much a total betrayal of Schizopolis. I mean, we should be clear about that."

"But look at it from my point of view," said Jacob. You could see him forming points in his mind, ready to explain why it was in all of our best interests for him to go have a fantastic career in an up-and-coming band.

I didn't really go in much for yelling, but this seemed like a good time to start. "I deeply, truly, do not give a fuck about your point of view," I screamed. "I truly do not give anywhere near a half a sliver of a penny's worth of fuck." I was suddenly outside of myself, looking down, thinking, *Wow, Gary really is passionate about this band.* Jacob kept trying to say something, and I kept cutting him off:

JACOB: Look—
GARY: Sellout motherfucker!
JACOB: I'm—
GARY: A fucking sellout! That's what you are.
JACOB: Gary, I'm saying—
GARY: A truly self-absorbed shithead.

"*I'm* self-absorbed?" Jacob asked. He wasn't yelling, but it sounded like he had a Doberman in his throat, ready to jump out. "You're in Teen Rock-and-Roll Fantasy Camp. This entire thing is a failure. I'm trying to salvage something from the wreckage."

"Thanks," said Scott from the driver's seat. "That boosts morale."

"We haven't even *started*," I said. "I brought you into this band—"

"Don't *even* go there," said Jacob. "You profiled me—"

Scott shouted us both down. "Shut up! Everyone!"

"I haven't said anything," said Katherine. "I'm just observing."

"Jacob," said Scott, "I assume you'll play the last three shows."

"Of course," said Jacob. "Then I'm going to stay in Seattle for a while to rehearse before we go to Europe. But—"

"Does Donald know about this?" I asked. "Original Syn is going to shit their pants when they find out—"

"Donald and Chris are on board," said Jacob. "Colin had that conversation."

"Well, it's good to know that Donald still takes phone calls from someone," I said.

"The thing is, there's no reason why I couldn't still play with Schizopolis," said Jacob. "I mean, Slake is Seattle-based, but I'm not going to give up on New York. I could still be part of the band, which is what I have been trying to say the entire time."

"You *really* think *I'm* self-absorbed?" I asked.

"Gary," said Scott, "shut up. All right. OK. There we go. We have a piece of information that we didn't have before, and we should be grateful that Jacob made his plans clear."

I tried to say something, but Scott shut me down.

"Later," he said. "Not now."

We drove in silence for a long few minutes. The emotional hurricane was over, but a lot of houses and trees had been washed away. FEMA aid was nowhere in sight.

Katherine was the first to speak. "Look, I have to say, it stings a bit, but it sounds like a good plan for you, Jacob, and I'm glad for you." I looked back at her and realized, suddenly, that she had known about this before all of us, and that was why she'd remained silent. That hurt, that in a group of four people, cliques could form, and lock people out.

"I'm still part of the band," said Jacob. "I don't want you to think of me as disloyal."

"Jacob," said Scott, "you are incredibly disloyal. Don't expect people to love you for it."

"I guess you're right," said Jacob. "Gary?"

"Yes?"

"Are we still friends?"

"I'll let you know when I'm less self-absorbed," I said.

"Gary—" said Jacob, but Katherine cut him off. "Let's just drive for a while," she said.

"Just, could everyone do me a favor," said Jacob, "and not mention this? Brad doesn't know just yet."

*   *   *

We played Santa Cruz, and we were met with great acclaim, if "acclaim" equals a bunch of college students waiting for Slake. We didn't talk much in the van the next day. At our Eugene show I introduced our band for the first time, pointedly leaving out Jacob. Jacob was very understanding. Why not? He had new friends. "You sounded good tonight," he said to me as I came offstage. "Very sharp, very strong."

"You sounded good, too," I said, "Iago."

Jacob sighed. "Look," he said, "what would you do?"

What would I do if a well-funded indie pop band with radio play asked me to be their lead singer, and I was offered a chance to go on a European tour? The answer to that question was one I didn't want to hear. But of course, there it was. I'd dump Schizopolis, the band I'd named, and move on.

So, after all, I was in this for my own glory. I wanted Schizopolis to succeed so that I could succeed. Offered a European tour, I'd dump Scott, Jacob, and Katherine in a minute for the next, better thing.

This was what the music industry was supposed to be like, right? About ego, about self-aggrandizing jerks who backstab? I thought indie was supposed to mean something different, but in the van it didn't. I'd expected to come on this tour and really become a musician, find out what it meant to rock, to own rocking as my own. But this tour hadn't been about the music. It had been about my mother, about breaking up with Para, and about losing our bassist.

All of this self-reflection didn't make me hate Jacob any less. Outside the window it was raining and cold. It was the scenery of betrayal. When we stopped at Starbucks to check email, it was all spam.

"I never want to come into another Starbucks," I said to my bandmates, who were surprised at this outburst. "I hate the frigging logo with that mermaid, I hate the fact that it's called a grande and not a large, I hate the fucking brownies, and I hate the pumpkin-colored walls. I hate that they're identical across the country. There is absolutely nothing unique or individual about them. It just reminds me that I live in a world of unfeeling bullshit. I never want to drink another cup of this coffee in my life."

"I don't know," said Scott. "I kind of like them. They're always there."

By Seattle, we were done. Jacob had Slake in his eyes, and Scott was cursing Original Syn every chance he got.

"You know what I want to do," Scott had said as we drove up the Pacific Coast toward our last show on our first tour, "what I want to do is I want to buy a ticket. And I want to fly home. I want to forget every bit of this shit."

"Then go," I said. "I'll drive the van."

"Hah!" he said. "You're going to drive the van across the country without me?"

"That would be a lot easier than doing it with you."

Scott didn't say anything; he just screwed up his face and drove on, cooking like a kettle. Ten minutes later he began to boil.

"You think you're such incredibly hot shit," he said. "You think you're living some sort of dream."

"You know—" I said, but Scott cut me off. And told me that I was immature, shallow, self-absorbed, and pretentious. He implied that I had sexual hang-ups, was probably a drunk, and just a general, all-around bad person.

As I listened to him, I reminded myself that he had been frustrated by this tour, that he was older than me and less flexible, and that he was probably feeling as betrayed by Jacob as I was. And he had his points. I *was* a flawed person.

But I also remembered driving to see my mother and then, when it was the last thing I wanted to do, driving to Philly to play with-out any sleep, so that I wouldn't let my bandmates down. Maybe I was in this for my own glory, maybe I could be a little bit of a dip-shit, but I hadn't betrayed anyone's trust.

I wanted to say, *Scott, for this I slept on a floor, I learned to be-come a better guitar player, I put up with your moods. I went out and found Katherine and Jacob. I made something. I entered data. I let a man go down on me for rent money. I got onstage in San Diego in front of my brother and humiliated myself. I tried to hook up with groupies and be a big slut. Maybe that kind of success was like winning a gold medal in the Special Olympics. But you know, the guys getting those medals, they have every reason to be pretty proud of themselves. They're working with what they have. I don't have programming skills, I don't write for Matchstick, I'm not in an arts cooperative. I'm just Gary Benchley, who lives in a small room in Williamsburg and works to pay his bills. I'm single, my mother has cancer, and I'm in a band called Schizopolis that prob-ably won't last much longer than today. And you know what, Scott? I set out to rock, and even if I did not rock wholly, I rocked fractionally, and that is better than no rock at all. I had faith, and I acted on that faith. And I'm not going to apologize for that.*

As I thought these words, as Scott scolded me and complained in general, I realized that I had absolutely no desire to continue working for Scott at BrandSolve. I decided that I'd find some other job, try something new that didn't involve branding. If Schizopolis could not be salvaged, I could start a new band. There were always other hopeful musicians. We were the one natural resource that America would never exhaust.

Thinking it through, I realized that it was failure that upset Scott. He had given up his vacation for nothing but regrets and long days of driving. That was what was bothering him. I'd thought of him as a rock, as sensible, but he'd had a rock star fan-tasy of his own, and when it didn't work out he didn't know what to do with that. Somehow the failure didn't hit me in the same way. Oh, it hurt, it hurt bone deep. But I'd always known it could happen. Sometimes the universe gives, sometimes . . .

I said to Scott, quietly, without much anger: "If you want to go home, go home. Take a flight and let me drive. No one will be angry."

"Of course you'll be angry," he said.

"I'll be grateful," I said. "I'll be glad to see you happy."

"You don't mean that."

"You know, I really do mean that," I said. I felt very peaceful, saying it. "I don't want you to suffer."

There really wasn't room for a scene like this in the documentary about Schizopolis. There was no way to turn this into an interview, or a look behind the scenes. It was just the end, and we knew it.

It was a smaller story than I'd hoped, after all: local band tries, falters.

We played the show, at a club called the Mountain. The room was filled with screaming Slake fans out to see another hometown favorite. A few people congratulated me on my set. Jacob looked nervous; apparently Brad was getting the boot after the last show.

And that was it. That was the end of the tour, and of Schizopolis. It ended not with a bang, but with a G chord, the end of "Hoyt-Schemerhorn" trailing out, a little applause, and then the audience cheered as Slake took the stage. I should have felt entirely Train, but I was mostly relieved. That was it. Next chapter.

I looked over at Katherine as I packed up my guitar, and wondered, for a moment, if maybe this wasn't a chance for her and me to finally connect, to realize something from that earlier, embryonic romance. We'd be sharing hotel rooms over the next several days, without Jacob and Scott. We could make love on the ride home, start something new, let our deep affection become the phoenix that rises from the ashes of Schizopolis.

It was a nice idea, but the connection, the sense of electricity from months ago, was gone. She'd seen me in too many compromising positions, heard my stories, watched me buy ointments. All she wanted to do was go home.

After the show we said good-bye to Jacob. I shook his hand, and Katherine embraced him, and he went off to a braver and better life. Back at the motel, Scott got a room of his own.

The next day, I woke up early to get him to the airport, and watched him walk through the revolving doors. He didn't turn around to wave. Katherine and I would split the driving. I turned the van out of the airport and back onto the highway. Three thousand miles away Williamsburg beckoned. Katherine put a blanket over herself and went to sleep. I put on the radio. It wasn't any song I'd ever heard before. But I liked the guitar sound.

Eastward ho.

September

I pushed a demo from a Bushwick, Brooklyn, band across the desk; it was the first one this week worth passing up to Chris. Then I went back to my email, the requests to check out websites, to download MP3s.

There were forty CDs in my in-box, each one begging in its own way. "Dudes," read one cover letter, "we are ready to ROCK THE BROOKLYN HOUSE WITH RAP rock FUSION ALL VOER THE PLASE."

They'd used expensive, opaque paper to print those words. I shook my head. I didn't even play the CD; I'd defer their dream with a form letter. "We wish you the best of luck with all of your future plans," it read. "Sincerely, Gary Benchley, Associate Director, Original Syn Records."

But then one of the emails had a name I hadn't seen in months: Scott Spark. I put the arrow over his name, and then, nervously, with images of the old van in my mind, with thoughts of Katherine and Jacob, I clicked.

We went to lunch in Midtown. Lunch is the Switzerland of meals, perfectly neutral. Scott and I embraced.

"I missed you, you know?" he said. "You look good. You still live in Williamsburg, right?"

"Same place," I said. "Same roommates. Did you see Jacob on *Letterman*?"

"That's why I wrote you," he said. "After I saw that."

"I'm glad for him," I said. "He made it work."

"Every time Slake gets good press it stabs me in the heart," said Scott. "You know I still don't have an official copy of our CD?"

"I'll get you a few," I said. The CDs had come, finally, boxes of them: *Dancing about Architecture*. The cover was a shadowy set of gray angular shapes. I'd pulled it out and listened the other day, and it wasn't that bad an album.

But of course there was no band to promote the songs. At first, when we returned to New York, Original Syn had told us that our breakup was a sign of "bad faith" and threatened to sue us. Given that Jacob was now part of Slake, not Schizopolis, with Original Syn's blessings, this was hard to fathom. Eventually, we figured out that Chris was trying to get out of some random stipulation in his contract. We were glad to let him off the hook, so each of us signed a legal document that stated that Schizopolis had never existed. I felt that it *had* never existed, sometimes.

I never went back to BrandSolve. I was supposed to go back the Monday after I returned from Seattle. But the thought of facing both Para and Scott, and trying to restart my stalled new career, was too much to bear. So I just didn't go. On Thursday, Tom called. And I told him that I wasn't going to be back in the office. He had words to say about that, and I listened to them, and told him that I understood how he felt. Then I hung up the phone.

Then Para called, and she told me that it was ridiculous for me to throw away a career for her, and ordered me to come back in to work.

"There's more to it than that," I said.

She invited me out to lunch. I told her I'd think about it.

"Who was it?" I asked.

"Does it matter?" she said.

"Yes, I think it does."

She sighed. "It was Kenyon."

"Kenyon? From Vermont?"

"He was down in the city, and we went out for drinks. It had been in the works for a while, you know? These things happen."

"Was this before or after the horse riding?"

She sighed. "It was starting before, maybe," she said. "Then it happened after. You and I weren't doing well. I wish it hadn't happened."

"But that guy is a *douchebag*," I said.

"He's my friend," she said. "He's—"

"An annoying douchebag," I said. "I'm sorry, but I've just lost a lot of respect for you." I started laughing.

Para was pissed. She said, "I don't think that you have any right—"

"Oh, shut the fuck up," I said, and hung up. I didn't answer my phone when it rang back, or ever again when I saw her name on the screen of my cell. Of course, we could go out for lunch and talk about old times, and be polite. But why pretend? Why waste another moment?

Unemployed, with few friends or prospects, I considered temping again. I walked around Williamsburg, wondering how I'd make rent. Then I received word that our CDs were in, and I went to pick up a few copies. There, Donald told me he was leaving to go on tour. He'd learned enough about the label side and wanted to get back behind the keyboard.

"Who's going to run the office?" I asked.

"Good question," said Donald.

And so I became the office assistant for Original Syn Records. Lou is gone, fired by Chris for some odd accounting involving Slake. And Chris talks less about synergy and more about money and distribution. Which, I think, is as it should be, even if it means that Original Syn will never sign another act as unpolished and full of hope as Schizopolis.

Scott told me about the office. It sounded about the same: a firing here, a hiring there. I didn't bring Para up, and he didn't mention her. I didn't want to know.

"You hear from Katherine?" I asked.

"I saw her," said Scott. "On Bedford. Two months ago, maybe."

I thought of that endless, grueling ride back from Seattle, the eternal roads, the unknown horizon ahead. I had no band, no girlfriend, no job. Katherine had taken over the wheel when we got close to the city, and dropped me off at my apartment. She got out and embraced me, and told me to keep in touch.

"I will," I said. But I didn't call, and she didn't call me. I wanted some breathing room. I needed to establish a Schizopolis-free zone of being. Except when I walked around Williamsburg I saw her everywhere; every coffee-drinking or burlesque-show-watching or vintage-dress-shopping Williamsburg woman of a certain height looked a little like Katherine to me. Spending that much time in a van with someone, thinking about them, being a little in love with them—they're like a bright light that burns into your eyes, so that when you turn your head they're still there in outline.

A month passed, and I called and left a message. "Hey," I said, "let's hang out. I was thinking about you." She didn't call back, and I'd left it at that.

"She had a boyfriend when I saw her," said Scott. "He's like some sort of punk rocker. Her hair's short. She cut it off and gave it to some organization that makes wigs for kids with cancer."

"Really?"

"Yep."

"You can't really criticize that."

"You can't," said Scott. "So what are you listening to?"

I listed a few bands that he hadn't heard of, people coming up through the ranks, playing at clubs. That was a big part of my job now, going out to different bars, shaking hands, listening as people told me their rock fantasies, hoping that I was a conduit for their own greatness. I kept seeing myself in them, two years ago; they made me feel old at twenty-four.

"I have to keep telling myself that I'm young," I said. "You know? I mean, there are these kids at NYU, in a band called Blender of Hera, they're all nineteen."

"Imagine how I feel," said Scott. "I'm thirty-three. That said, I'm probably going to start another band."

For a moment I thought he might ask me if I would sing, and I was excited, and afraid of that possibility. But he said, "A little more noodly, you know? I got a lot of ideas that I didn't have time to pursue. I'm just thinking about it, honestly. It's not real. You working on anything?"

"Nothing right now," I said.

"Well, you're in the right place if you have any ideas."

"I don't think Chris wants to shell out money for another Gary Benchley project. Things are a little tight as it is."

"Still," said Scott, "you've got experience now. You could do something else."

"Thank you," I said. "That means a lot, coming from you."

After an hour or so, we said good-bye, embracing outside the restaurant and heading in our respective directions. Scott asked about my mother, and I told him that she had recovered well, and now called me every other day. Her illness had made her want to be more involved in her children's lives, even if we didn't want her to be *that* involved. I told Scott about my brother, who was still in the navy but had been reassigned to a desk job on shore, and who was probably going to get married soon.

I walked away from Scott, going in my own direction, and patted my knapsack, feeling the bulk of my hardbound notebook. It was filled with lyrics, with notes, with guitar tabs printed from websites. I decided I'd call Katherine, sometime in the next few weeks. I'd leave a message.

"Hey," I'd say, "this is Gary. I think of you from time to time. Everything is OK here. I've got a job and a good life. I hope everything is OK there. Also, here and there are actually only a few miles away from each other, so there's no reason not to hang out. I hear your hair is short. Be my friend." Who could resist returning that phone call? No one human.

I'm giving Original Syn a year, to learn how labels work, and how they don't. Then, when it feels right, when the pieces seem to fit, I'll start another band, and bring the Benchley message back to the people. I've been saving up to buy a computer and some gear, so that I can record my own songs. I can do it right this time, I'm sure. I've got knowledge, experience, and I've got faith, faith in the rock, faith all the way down to my grace notes.

Acknowledgments

This novel was originally serialized by TheMorningNews.org, as a hoax, under Gary's byline. I would like to thank all who contacted Gary via his email address, whether they wrote to encourage him to follow his dreams, to ask for his demo, or to excoriate him for not being indie enough. Your feedback made this novel far more fun to write.

TheMorningNews.org editors Rosecrans Baldwin and Andrew Womack, along with copy editor Kate Schlegel, kept a careful, nurturing eye on Gary from the moment he left Albany for New York City. Patrick Ambrose, Sara Sarasohn, and Theodore Ross gave detailed editorial advice that made this a much better book. Steve Burns let me tag along on his tour through the Southwest, so that I could get a taste of life in the van, and gave valuable advice on the workings of an indie rock tour. Richard Abate and Kate Lee at ICM helped me navigate the byways of publishing a book, and Jake Klisivitch at Plume brought the book to press, improving it greatly along the way.

Most of all, thanks to Maureen Flaherty, for reasons too numerous to list.

A full glossary of all the pop-culture references
in this book appears at

GaryBenchleyRockStar.com